Adventures Of Little Yaga and Her Friends

To Gene Reams
From
L. B. O'Mills
Enjoy!

Adventures Of Little Yaga and Her Friends

L.B. O'Milla

Illustrations by Petar Denkov

To All Who I Love and Remember

Little Yaga, Big Yaga, and Biggest Yaga

Little Yaga woke up to the smell of breakfast sneaking into her bedroom through the cracks in the door, which was made of logs so roughly hewn that they were still covered with boughs and spurs. Little Yaga used the spurs as hooks for her clothing. Every morning for as long as she could remember, she'd eaten the same food for breakfast. Now she was so tired of it that she would rather have gone hungry, but her grandmother, Big Yaga, insisted she finish every bite. Little Yaga felt like sleeping just a bit longer, but she knew that in less than a minute, she'd hear her grandmother's creaky voice ordering her to get out of bed. She opened her eyes, and sure enough, the banging on the door that almost shook it off its hinges began.

"Hey, you, lazy good-for-nothing," Big Yaga grumbled her customary greeting, "wake up and get out here, or I'll break down the door."

Little Yaga pushed aside the wolf skin she slept under and sat up on the slab of wood that was her bed.

"I'm up, Grandma," she hollered over her grandmother's racket. "I'll be right out!"

"Hurry, hurry!" Big Yaga croaked. "I have to leave soon. And you don't want to be late for school, either, you, lazybones." She punched the door once more before leaving. As soon as the sound of her retreating footsteps faded away, Little Yaga put on her old bathrobe. Lately, she'd been rapidly growing, and now the robe barely reached her knees. Looking down at her fully revealed legs, Little Yaga sighed. Why was her left leg so humanlike? Oh, how she wanted to look like her classmates and most other inhabitants of the Forest! Their left legs had no flesh or skin, only bare bones. Those bony legs could be extended at the knees, allowing the Foresters to take huge steps. When they walked or ran, their joints made squeaking sounds that wild beasts and animals could not tolerate, and they darted away as soon as they heard them. Little Yaga's steps were light and delicate. When she walked, not even a twig snapped under her feet. In the Forest, she was almost as vulnerable as a rabbit.

Little Yaga made her bed and went to the bathroom. A set of her grandmother's dentures hung from a nail near the sink. The false teeth were pinkish in color, except for the four fangs, which were dark brown and sharp as daggers. Little Yaga looked in the cracked mirror at her own pearly-white teeth with no fangs, sighed again, and turned around. There was another set, just like her grandmother's only smaller, on a nail on the opposite wall. Little Yaga took it down, spread a layer of special glue on its inner surface, and pressed it firmly against her teeth. Now, with the fangs sticking out of her mouth, her sad smile looked decent. There was a dentist in the Forest by the name of Dr. Joe who was an old friend of Big Yaga's. Rumor had it he'd been in love with her his entire life. After Little Yaga had been born and it had become clear that her teeth were also human-like, Dr. Joe had offered to secretly make her a set of artificial ones so that she'd look like other Foresters. Big Yaga had agreed. The set Little Yaga had just put on was already her third, and she was due for another update sometime soon.

A sudden bang on the bathroom door made her jump.

"How long does it take you to get your teeth on, you slow-poke?" her grandmother asked and growled.

Little Yaga opened the door. Big Yaga stood waiting outside the bathroom, leaning on her wooden stick that was all bent and twisted. She looked her usual self—a little wild, with her gray hair sticking out in every possible direction. Her crooked nose was set between her beady eyes, and there was an ugly wart covered in thick fuzz on her right cheekbone. Casting an angry glance at her granddaughter's legs, she groaned, "Why am I cursed with a de-formed child? What have I done to deserve this?"

Big Yaga raised her stick over her head as though to break it in two, but she only shook it angrily instead. Once she put it down again, she leaned heavily on its handle and limped away, back into the kitchen. The extendable mechanism on her bony knee had broken years ago. It had gotten stuck in one position, and none of the Forest specialists, from doctors to engineers, could do anything about it.

Little Yaga trailed behind her grandmother, feeling sorry for her. She knew she was the main reason behind Big Yaga's misery, and sometimes she even thought it would've been better for everybody if she'd never been born.

When Little Yaga was only a few months old, something had happened to her mother, Big Yaga's daughter, and nobody seemed to know anything about her father. Stuck with a "little cripple," Big Yaga had tried her best to find a remedy for her granddaughter's condition before everybody in the Forest found out that Little Yaga had no bony leg. In her biggest cauldron, over an open fire in their kitchen, she used to brew potions out of the most powerful herbs and insects. She danced around the cauldron, chanting incantations, while the air in the room filled up with pungent green smog. Then she forced Little Yaga to drink her concoctions. They burned not only the girl's throat but every cell in her body, too, doing nothing to change her left leg that remained humanlike, covered with flesh and skin that was annoyingly warm and soft.

At the weirdest hour of the night, when the darkness and the early-morning light struggled for control over the world, Big Yaga would go down to an old swamp, known for its unique predawn powers, to collect reeds, leeches, and silt, with which to prepare a potent, flesh-eating paste. She would coat every inch of Little Yaga's left leg, from her toes to her groin, with the substance and wrap it in fern leaves. The leg would throb, as though it had been stung by a swarm of ferocious bees, and then it would stay red, swollen, and relentlessly itchy for weeks following the procedure. But alas, there was no sign of the eagerly awaited changes to its appearance. Finally, when the last option—a session of acupuncture using spruce needles dipped in birch tar—also failed, desperate Big Yaga had no choice but to seek out the help of her older sister, Biggest Yaga, who lived on Bold Mountain. The oldest inhabitant of the Forest, Biggest Yaga was so knowledgeable and wise that on several occasions, even Scraggard the Immortal, the Ruler of the Forest himself, had sought her advice.

Holding Little Yaga by the hand, Big Yaga had dragged her up the mountain. The path was treacherous. Thorny bushes scratched their arms and faces, the tall grass entangled their legs, the howling wind tugged at their hair, and the fog blurred their vision. When they finally reached Biggest Yaga's log Hut, it looked deserted. If not for a wisp of smoke escaping through the chimney pipe, they would've thought nobody was home.

The Hut was standing on a chicken leg, as thick and tall as the trunk of an oak tree. The chicken leg had sunk ankle-deep into the ground—a sign that the Hut had not been disturbed for years. It stood with its front to the Forest and its back toward them.

Big Yaga called out:

"Hello, Hut on a chicken leg,

"Turn to us your front,

"And to the Forest your back."

The Hut didn't budge or show any other acknowledgment of Big Yaga's request; apparently, it didn't want to be bothered now, either. Big Yaga repeated:

"Hello, Hut on a chicken leg,

"Turn to us your front,

"And to the Forest your back!"

This time, the Hut made a sound that resembled an exasperated sigh. The chicken leg stretched and shook as it tried to loosen its foot from the ground. A few long minutes later, it finally succeeded and very slowly began turning around. After another half an hour, the front door was finally positioned directly in front of Little Yaga and her grandmother. They climbed up the creaking steps and were about to knock on the door when it swung open. The strong odor of poison ivy filled Little Yaga's nostrils.

Biggest Yaga was sitting on a bench by the hearth, chewing on a poison ivy leaf—her favorite treat. She was huge. Even if she lost half of her weight, she still wouldn't be able to squeeze through her door. She was also very old; there wasn't a single tooth left in her mouth, but she didn't care for dentures. A black raven, almost as old as she, was perched on her shoulder, moving nothing but its eyelids. A shaggy dog, almost as big as she, was sprawled on the floor near her feet, moving nothing but the tip of its tail.

"Hello, big sister," Big Yaga said. "I haven't seen you in ages."

"Hello, baby sister," Biggest Yaga replied. "It's good to see you. Come right in."

Big Yaga and Little Yaga stepped over the threshold, and the door slammed shut behind them.

"I know why you've come," Biggest Yaga said, looking at her great-niece. "Let me see your legs."

Little Yaga lifted her skirt. Biggest Yaga scrutinized the girl's two identical extremities. She pinched them a couple of times, then stood up and went into her bedroom, buckling the floorboards and shaking the Hut with her heavy steps. Soon she returned, carrying a thick, leather-bound book in her hands. Once she'd resumed her position on the bench, she put on her glasses, opened the book to one of its gilded pages, and began reading. Big Yaga and Little Yaga held their breath as they watched her moving lips. They didn't know how much time had passed before Biggest Yaga finally closed the book and placed it on her lap.

"There is no cure for your condition," she said, addressing Little Yaga. "You must learn to live with it."

Big Yaga groaned.

"There is nothing to moan about," Biggest Yaga snapped, turning to her younger sister. "Your granddaughter isn't crippled or deformed. She's just different, and you know why. Accept it."

All the way home, Big Yaga cursed her luck and her life and wondered why she herself had been cursed.

Before long, everyone in the Forest knew Little Yaga was different. There was something wrong with her legs; she couldn't run as fast or jump as high as the others. There was something odd with her voice, too; she couldn't howl or roar like everybody else. While the adults sympathized with her grandmother for having to raise a cripple, the kids made fun of poor Little Yaga, who only had two close friends: Leesho and Kikimra. Leesho was also an object of ridicule; he couldn't howl or roar, either, and he, too, had white, humanlike teeth without fangs. Kikimra lived next door to Little Yaga and had been her friend since they were toddlers. Whenever the other Forest kids asked Kikimra why, she would say, "Little Yaga is like a sister to me. I love her."

On occasions when Kikimra felt like walking slowly, the girls went to school together.

On this particular morning, Little Yaga followed her grand-mother into the kitchen and had her usual breakfast: a bowl of beetles and bugs, mixed with the diced beaks of dinosaur fossils. She hated the mixture, but her grandmother insisted it was the only breakfast that would make her healthy and strengthen her powers. While Little Yaga was finishing her meal with a glass of freshly squeezed poison ivy juice, sprinkled with poplar fuzz,

Big Yaga hurried to dress for work. She put a pair of old hooves on her feet, which were crooked from arthritis. The hooves helped her walk without a limp. A pair of worn clawed gloves went on her big-knuckled hands, and a dome-shaped hat of thin birch bark covered her head.

Leaning on her stick, Big Yaga said, "I am leaving. You must hurry, too. You don't want to be late for school."

She was halfway out the door when she looked back and said, "And make sure to turn the Hut around."

Then she was gone. Little Yaga watched through the kitchen window as her grandmother made her way over to the barrel parked under the sprawling branches of an old spruce tree. Big Yaga jumped into the barrel with such ease, you would've thought she was a teenager, not a centuries-old woman. Leaning over the edge of the barrel, she jammed her walking stick into a special holder on the side, and at once it turned into a broomstick. She blew on it as hard as she could, and the broomstick began to spin—slowly at first, then faster, now looking like the propeller of a helicopter. Soon it was spinning so fast that it couldn't be seen at all. The barrel hopped up and down for a few minutes before taking off. Then it tore upward through the spruce branches and, rapidly picking up speed, disappeared from view.

Ashley

Little Yaga had almost finished her juice when the Cuckoo Bird living in their wall clock stuck her head out of the tiny door of her tiny quarters.

"Little Yaga, it's eight fifteen," the bird announced. "You are running late."

"Why didn't you warn me earlier?" Little Yaga asked.

"I'm sorry. I was sleeping."

"You know you can't do that. You're supposed to call out the time every fifteen minutes. That's what my grandmother's feeding you for."

"I said I was sorry," the Cuckoo Bird repeated, annoyed, and hid behind her door.

Big Yaga forbade Little Yaga to use her powers for the household chores, but now, since she was running so late, she had no choice. She glided her hands over the table, and instantly, all the dishes were sparkling clean. With a snap of her fingers, she placed them in their proper drawers and shelves.

"You know you're not supposed to do that," said the Cuckoo Bird, sticking her head out of her door again.

Little Yaga stopped what she was doing and turned around.

"If you say a word to my grandma," she said, "so help me, I'll…"

"Don't worry, Little Yaga," the Cuckoo Bird replied, having suddenly become overly pleasant. "You know I wouldn't do that." She giggled and went back behind her door.

Little Yaga rushed to get ready for school. Just as her grandmother had only minutes before, she pulled a pair of hooves onto her feet and a pair of clawed gloves onto her hands. Her hat was different, however; instead of birch bark, it was made of vines and lianas woven tightly together. Little Yaga put it on top of her red head, and catching a glimpse of her reflection in the old rusty mirror, she thought she looked pretty good this morning. She gave herself a smile that showed off her pinkish false teeth with the brown fangs and liked what she saw. As always, she hoped today would be the day Damon noticed her. She tilted her head back and tried to howl. Instead of a bloodcurdling shriek, only a pitiful whining sound came out of her throat. That was disappointing. Little Yaga opened her mouth as wide as she could and attempted to roar, hoping to hear a thundering rumble that would shake the walls of her Hut. What she heard instead was a feeble little squeak, followed by the brash laughter of the smart-alecky Cuckoo Bird that was louder than Little Yaga's roar. Angered, Little Yaga looked around for something suitable to throw at the bird, but the nasty creature managed to escape behind her door, still sniggering.

"Just you wait till I come home," Little Yaga threatened, running out the door.

Snapping her fingers, she opened the rickety gate in the wobbly fence separating their property from the rest of the Forest. As she was about to run through it, she heard a screeching voice behind her.

"Where do you think you're going, young lady, without turning me around?"

The voice belonged to the Hut, Little Yaga's friend and confidant. Made of crude logs, it was always there for her, caring and understanding.

"Oh, shoot," Little Yaga said as she looked back. "If I get to school after the head count, I'm in trouble."

"You'll be in more trouble if you don't turn me around. Give me the command and go. I'll do the rest without you staring at me."

"I love you, Hut."

"I love you, too. Don't waste your time; chant the words."

"Good-bye, dear Hut on the chicken leg," Little Yaga sang.

"Turn to the Forest your front,"

"And to me your back."

As the Hut began stretching its chicken leg to turn around, Little Yaga blew it a kiss and ran off.

At this hour of the morning, with the adults having gone to work and the youngsters to school, the Forest looked deserted and uninhabited. Little Yaga sprinted down the narrow, winding path as fast as she could, but she knew it would take her at least fifteen minutes to get to class. If she had a bony extendable leg like everybody else, she would've made it there in no time. Luckily, the playful trees were still asleep and didn't seek to engage her in a game by pulling on her hair or grabbing at her clothes. One old tree trunk that was suffering from insomnia tried to trip her, but she noticed it sticking out its crooked root ahead of time and jumped right over it, without skipping a beat.

Soon, Little Yaga made it to the Rowdy Meadow that was overgrown with luscious grass, twice her height, which always wanted to entangle her legs and tickle her arms and neck. The grass was flapping and swaying every which way in the wind, as though preparing to tease Little Yaga, but Kikimra had taught her how to tame the wayward green blades. Before stepping onto the path that crossed the meadow, Little Yaga raised her arms and clasped her hands over her head. Despite the wind, the grass stopped moving. Instead, it stretched upward and arched over the path, creating a shaded corridor for Little Yaga to run through. She'd almost reached the other side of the meadow when she smelled a weird aroma—foreign but somehow vaguely familiar. It was strong but pleasant rather than repulsive. Little Yaga sniffed the air and, suddenly oblivious to where she was supposed to be going, she followed the smell, which led her to an old stump. It was usually asleep, but today the stump was awake, having been disturbed by the odor coming from the creature sitting on top of it. Little Yaga had heard a lot of stories about such beings, but she'd never met one in real life. Still, she immediately knew she was looking at a human girl who seemed to be about her age. The girl was frightened and on the verge of tears.

"Hello," she whispered, her voice trembling.

Without replying, Little Yaga approached the girl and sniffed her from head to toe. Surprisingly, she liked the smell. By now the girl appeared terrified; she was shaking like a leaf and looked as if she were expecting Little Yaga to bite her. Little Yaga was enjoying her effect on the girl. She regretted not being able to howl or roar, which would've made a much stronger impression.

However, she could show her pinkish false teeth with the brown fangs, and so she did. She stretched her lips into the meanest smile possible and snapped her teeth together right in front of the girl's nose. On seeing that the girl was ready to faint, and Little Yaga, suddenly feeling sorry for her, finally spoke.

"Hello yourself," she said. "Who are you, and what are you doing here?"

"My name's Ashley," the girl replied. "I'm lost. I have no idea where I am."

"You are in the Forest. How'd you get here?"

"I was walking down my street, by the meadow, texting Sonya when my phone lost the signal."

"Your *what* lost *what*?"

"My iPhone—it lost the signal. I guess when I was texting, I didn't look where I was going, and I only saw when the signal was gone that I was in the forest. I never even knew there *was* a forest at the end of my street. I turned around to go back, but I couldn't find the way. I started looking for the road and... I got right here." Ashley's big round eyes welled up with tears, but she managed not to cry.

Little Yaga walked around her. The girl had two legs made of flesh and skin just like hers. She had white teeth with no fangs. Her mouth and nose were small, but her eyes were big. Also, her hair grew only on her head, unlike most of Little Yaga's classmates, who had tufts of hair on their faces, hands, and stomachs. Little Yaga didn't have any on her face or hands, and there were only a few tiny patches on her stomach. Her grandmother said she would grow more when she got older. Snarling like a dog, Little Yaga walked around Ashley once more. Even though, quite surprisingly, the human girl looked a lot like the Forest teens, she was definitely ugly. Still, for some strange reason, Little Yaga liked her.

Right then she thought of the Ruler of the Forest, Scraggard the Immortal, who, according to rumor, wasn't exactly immortal but managed to keep his death out of his body. Her friend, Leesho, who always seemed to know everything, had once secretly told her that Scraggard's death was hidden on the black tip of a needle, buried in an egg lying inside a duck, resting within a goose sleeping inside a rabbit. Leesho added that the rabbit was sitting in a gold chest hanging on an oak tree growing on the edge of a cliff over shark-infested waters. He also said Scraggard the Immortal *could* actually die, but only if the black tip of the needle was broken off.

Little Yaga wasn't sure if that was true, but she knew that Scraggard lived on the energy he drew from other living creatures, mostly animal cubs. Their energy, however, was dull and short-lived. Human energy, on the other hand, lasted for decades, and it was sparkling and vibrant—especially that of human children. Scraggard was prepared to give a huge reward to anyone who would get him a human or, better yet, a human child. The child would be accommodated in the best quarters of Scraggard's palace and given the best food and toys. He or she, however, wouldn't be able to enjoy any of that because every night, one of Scraggard's servants would collect exactly twenty-four hours' worth of energy from the child's windpipe, and not a tenth of an ounce more, so that the energy, and the child, would last the Immortal for as long as possible.

Little Yaga looked at Ashley. As she imagined her lying motionless in bed, being spoon-fed by Scraggard's guards to regain her energy, only to have it taken away the following night, her heart ached. She knew that whoever tried to save a human child from Scraggard would be severely punished, but she came up with an idea for a plan that she thought might work.

"Ashley," she said, "I'll help you get out of here, but you'll have to do everything I say. My name is Little Yaga, by the way."

She extended her gloved hand, and Ashley cautiously extended hers. Little Yaga squeezed it, and the claws on her glove dug deeply into Ashley's skin. The girl flinched and bit her lip but didn't complain.

"Nice to meet you," she whispered, "but I…" Looking down, she didn't finish her sentence.

"Yes?" Little Yaga asked.

"I don't know you at all," Ashley said. "Can I trust you?"

"Do you have a choice?" Little Yaga asked again.

Ashley thought for a moment and shook her head. Little Yaga took off her hooves, gloves, and hat and piled them up on the stump next to Ashley.

"Put these on," she ordered.

"Do I have to?"

"Only if you want to get out of here."

Ashley was reaching for the hooves when something resembling a sharp arrow whizzed by, barely missing her hand and striking the bark-covered side of the stump, which had only just fallen back asleep. The poor old thing cringed and winced, but it didn't wake up. Ashley quickly withdrew her hand.

"It's a leaf," she said, bewildered. "A dry leaf. There's something written on it."

Little Yaga pulled the leaf out of the stump.

"It's a message from Kikimra. She must've sneaked out of the classroom."

"Who's Kikimra?"

"My friend."

Little Yaga read the message.

"She's asking where I am. Our teacher's mad that I'm absent and won't start the lesson."

Little Yaga glided her hand over the leaf, in a single movement erasing Kikimra's message and writing her own.

"Tell Rat to start the lesson without me. I'm stuck in the Funny Marsh. It'll take me half the day to get myself out."

Little Yaga sent the leaf flying back in the direction from which it had come. The leaf zoomed out of sight with lightning speed, then almost instantly returned with a new message: "Are you really?"

"Nope," Little Yaga replied.

"Where are you? What's going on?" Kikimra wrote.

"I'll tell you later."

The leaf zipped back and forth between Kikimra and Little Yaga while Ashley kept turning her head to the left and to the right, following its course until she got dizzy. Finally, the exchange between the two friends ended; the leaf didn't fly back, and Ashley said, "Cool texting, but I like phones better."

Little Yaga pretended to agree, even though she had no idea what Ashley was talking about.

"Now, get dressed," she ordered. "We have to hurry."

Ashley hastily pulled Little Yaga's hooves and gloves onto her feet and hands and put the hat on her head. Little Yaga looked at her and frowned.

"You still look human."

"That's what I am. Aren't you?"

Little Yaga didn't answer. Instead, she shook her head and said, "We have to switch clothes."

"Why?"

"Because you want to get back home, don't you?"

Ashley suppressed a sigh and started taking her T-shirt off.

"Don't bother with that."

Little Yaga came up closer to the stump and ran her hands first along Ashley's body and then along her own. When she stepped back, like an artist, to assess the result of her work, she was satisfied.

"Now you look like one of us," she said.

Ashley gazed down at her long skirt, which was flapping in the wind, then up at Little Yaga, who was now wearing a pair of blue jeans, yellow sneakers, and a pink T-shirt with three spar-kling red letters: *RED*, and she exclaimed, "Wow, you look just like Eric's little sister, Lisa!"

"Who's Eric?"

"My boyfriend," Ashley answered, blushing.

Little Yaga shrugged her shoulders and examined her new outfit.

"Your clothes are crazy," she said, jumping up and down. "They're so uncomfortable. How can you wear them?"

"I wouldn't call *yours* the most comfortable," Ashley coun-tered, tripping over the bottom of her skirt. "Listen, how'd you do that?" she asked, running her hands along her body.

"It's easy. We learned this trick in first grade."

"Oh, I see, it's just a trick."

Little Yaga nodded absentmindedly, but she was getting worried. She looked around and listened intently; everything seemed quiet. If she wanted her plan to work, she knew she couldn't risk running into a Forester. *Otherwise...*

She didn't want to think about what would happen otherwise. "We mustn't waste another second," she said. "Are you a good runner?"

"I'm on the track team at school," Ashley answered looking down at her skirt again. "I may trip on this thing, though."

"Don't worry. Once you start running, the skirt won't be in your way. You'll have to stay right behind me. And don't stop for anything—unless I stop. If you trip and fall, just get up and keep running. If you feel you can't keep up with me, whistle, and I'll slow down. Got it?"

"Yes."

"Are you ready?"

"Yes."

Little Yaga was about to take off with Ashley in tow, but she suddenly remembered something else. "One more thing," she said. "Don't talk. Keep your mouth shut, and don't ask any questions until we're out of the Forest. Got it?"

"Yes."

"Good. Now we can go."

The Stove and the Milkshake River

Little Yaga sprinted off. She was running very fast, but it was still much slower than if she'd had a bony leg. The Forest around her turned into one big colorful blur. From time to time, she looked back to make sure Ashley was still behind her. The human girl, breathing heavily, was managing to keep up. When the gap between them grew wider, Little Yaga slowed down. She wasn't exactly sure how much farther they had to run before they reached the human town.

She, Kikimra, and Leesho had gone on a scouting trip once and reached the edge of the Forest. Kikimra and Leesho were gracious enough to walk at Little Yaga's pace, and even then, it didn't take them very long to get to there. From a distance, the three friends could see human houses, big and weird, standing right on the ground, without any chicken legs underneath, all but one of them turned to the Forest with their backs. There were four-wheeled creatures, big and small, scurrying back and forth along the road behind the houses. They were noisy and stinky. Little Yaga and Kikimra didn't like them. They didn't look like anything the Forest girls had ever seen. Leesho said the things were called *cars*. They were transporting humans around. He confessed he wouldn't mind taking a ride in one of them at least once. Kikimra thought Leesho was only trying to show off, but Little Yaga believed him. She wondered how he always knew everything about everything.

Now Little Yaga was hoping she and Ashley were nearing their destination. So far, they were incredibly lucky not to have met anyone along the way, and if their good fortune continued, they would reach the human town very soon. Little Yaga had never been out of the Forest. She was shivering just from thinking about how it would feel. The girls passed a few clearings, bypassed the Funny Marsh, jumped over the two creeks, and dove into the grass of the Lazy Meadow. Unlike in the Rowdy Meadow, this grass was calm. It didn't want to be bothered or bother anyone back. All it wanted was peace and quiet. Its long blades were bent all the way down to the ground. Even strong winds couldn't disturb them, never mind the two little running creatures. Little Yaga was so happy the grass wasn't after her feet and legs that she didn't notice an almost transparent stream of smoke on the opposite side of the meadow. The girls were halfway across when she smelled something smoldering. The air around them was quickly filling up with the odor, but Little Yaga couldn't pinpoint exactly what was burning. Ashley smelled it, too, and gave Little Yaga a curious look. The latter only shrugged her shoulders.

The closer they got to the other side of the Lazy Meadow, the stronger the odor became. Finally, at the very brink of the field, they saw an ancient-looking wood-burning stove. Little Yaga's heart sank. She immediately remembered everything she'd heard about it. Indeed, how could she have forgotten about *The Famous Stove*? A loyal guard of Scraggard the Immortal, it lived underground, buried deep under the roots of the Lazy Meadow. It rose to the surface only when it smelled the presence of a foreigner, at which point it would bake a loaf of bread until it was burned almost to a crisp and then offer it to the stranger. If the person refused the treat, the Stove would start puffing black smoke out of its rusty pipe and into the sky— a signal for the squad of Swan-Geese, the feathered army of the Immortal, to fly over and seize the visitor. Clutching their booty in their strong beaks, the Swan-Geese would fly him or her to the Immortal's palace, to be used either as a slave or as an invaluable source of energy for Scraggard.

On those rare occasions when a visitor ate the bread, the Stove would instantly shut off, cool down, and, hissing like an angry snake, retreat to its regular position under the ground. Little Yaga's pace began slowing; she knew that if she and Ashley were to reach their destination, they had no choice but to eat the disgusting burned bread, made from skunk flour, no less—the stinkiest flour not only in the Forest but in the entire universe.

The Stove greeted the girls as if they were its most cherished guests, with a smile as broad as its lattice that warmed not only one's heart but literally one's whole body.

"Poor things," it said, emitting puffs of hot, dry air, "you look tired and out of breath. You must be very hungry. Why don't you eat my delicious, nutritious, energizing bread?"

Sliding its lattice to one side, the Stove displayed two blackened, smoking loaves for the girls to see. Then it winked and burst into roaring laughter that was so scorching, the girls had to jump back.

Ashley was a little hungry and wouldn't have minded a bite of bread. When she saw what the Stove had baked, however, her jaw dropped in dismay. She was about to comment, but much to Little Yaga's relief, she remembered that she wasn't to speak until they were out of the Forest. Ashley looked at the Stove and thought to herself about how technologically advanced the things of the Forest were if even such an ancient-looking cooker was programmed to speak.

"Go ahead, darlings," the Stove insisted. "Help yourselves."

"Thank you, dearest Auntie Stove," Little Yaga said, imitating Ashley's voice. "We can't wait to enjoy your delicious, nutritious bread."

She reached into the oven, picked up both loaves, handed one to Ashley, and took the first bite. The bread was so sickening, even the revolting potions her grandmother used to force her to drink tasted better. Little Yaga choked and coughed until her eyes and nose turned red. Watching her, the Stove laughed and laughed until it starting choking, too. When Little Yaga could finally breathe again, she glided her hand over her and Ashley's bread and said, "It's delicious—have a bite!"

Ashley shuddered. Expecting the worst, she closed her eyes and dug her teeth into the burned crust, only to open them again in surprise.

"It *is* good," she whispered.

As the girls munched on their treat, the angry Stove, hissing and puffing out clouds of suddenly icy cold vapor, began sinking back into the ground. By the time the girls had finished the last crumbs, the Stove had fallen through the surface of the meadow and was gone.

With Ashley right behind her, Little Yaga started running again, now knowing there would be more obstacles along the way out of the Forest. And sure enough, the roar that sounded like rushing water soon began filling the girls' ears. A few minutes later, they were standing on the bank of the rapidly flowing Milkshake River, which smelled like Ashley's favorite mixture of strawberry, raspberry, and watermelon. A note posted on the trunk of the weeping willow growing on the river bank said, "If you want to cross it, drink it." Instead of leaves, there were small green cups dangling from its branches. Ashley's eyes lit up, and she reached for a cup, but Little Yaga grabbed her hand and forced it down.

"I don't think you should drink this milkshake," she said, imitating Ashley's voice again.

Ashley opened her mouth to respond, but then remembered she wasn't to speak. Silently, she pointed at the note.

"Don't believe everything you read," Little Yaga whispered.

She turned around at the rustling behind her back. Three lynx cubs, chasing one another, ran out of the Forest and dashed over to the river. They cautiously sniffed the streaming liquid, then dipped their snouts into the milkshake and began lapping it up, all the while purring with delight. Seconds later, their eyes rolled up, their eyelids closed, and like three lifeless logs, they fell into the river. The swift current snatched them up and carried them downstream, toward the Scraggard Canal, which surrounded Scraggard's palace.

Eyes rounded, Ashley gave Little Yaga a terrified look. When the cubs' furry bodies reached the girls, Little Yaga bent down, grabbed their tails, and pulled them out of the river one by one.

"Don't worry," she whispered. "They're not dead—they're only asleep." Turning to look at Ashley, she added, "You see? That could've happened to you."

Just then, the mother Lynx rushed out of the Forest. Frightened, Ashley hid behind Little Yaga, but the mother Lynx paid no attention to the girls. She was relieved to see her little ones saved, but she was angry that they hadn't listened to her and had run away. She bit down hard on their ears waking them up. Still covered in milkshake and looking now more like shabby old cats than lynx cubs, they wagged their tails and hung their heads guiltily. The mother Lynx turned to the girls and bowed, expressing her gratitude. She stretched her front paws forward, lowered her head between them, and arched her back, inviting the girls to hop on. Ashley stepped back, shaking her head, afraid of getting too close to the wildcat, but Little Yaga bravely jumped atop and grabbed the mother Lynx by her ears, as if they were handgrips. The funny tufts of fur on the tips of the ears tickled Little Yaga's hands, and she couldn't help but giggle every time she accidentally touched them.

"Come on," she urged Ashley. "There isn't a minute to lose. Get on behind me—we've got to go."

Cautiously, Ashley climbed onto the Lynx's back. It was warm and furry, and suddenly Ashley wasn't afraid anymore. Feeling snug and cozy she dug her hands into the soft fur and held on to it tightly. The Lynx sprang to her feet and careered along the Milkshake River, with all three cubs running after her. In a few minutes, the group reached a spot where the river wasn't so wide, and although its steep, craggy banks were high, they weren't too far away from each other. The Lynx backed away from the edge as far as she needed to get a running start and then stood there for a moment, rocking back and forth, while the cubs copied her every move. Finally, she tensed her muscles, took a deep breath, briefly exposing her sharp teeth, and charged forward, picking up speed as she ran. When she reached the edge of the bank, she forcefully pushed off with her hind paws and, with astonishing speed, flew over the Milkshake River toward the opposite bank. Terrified, Ashley closed her eyes tight and dug her fingers deeper into the fur. Little Yaga, however, enjoyed the flight and laughed with delight.

Infuriated, the river below splashed its milkshake into the air, but not high enough to reach either the mother Lynx or her riders. When the Lynx landed on the opposite bank, one of her hind paws slipped off the edge, and she almost lost her balance. Luckily, she managed to regain it and dragged herself up to safety on the flat surface of the bank. The very next minute, her three cubs, like three bouncing balls, landed safely beside her one after another.

Little Yaga jumped off the mother Lynx's back and turned to Ashley, who, pale and shivering, was still holding on tight to the wildcat's fur, recovering from the frightening experience. Little Yaga helped her to the ground, and suddenly realizing that she couldn't hear the splashing of the river, she looked down. Where the Milkshake River had been bubbling and gurgling only moments ago, there was now a dry riverbed. She remembered having seen it before, on her scouting expedition with Kikimra and Leesho; at the time, the three friends assumed the river had run dry centuries ago. A sudden commotion behind her interrupted Little Yaga's thoughts. Turning around, she saw the lynx cubs chasing three squirrels, who were scrambling for their lives. The hungry cubs wouldn't let up on them—one more leap, and they'd have their paws around their mouthwatering treats. But just as the cubs sprang up, Little Yaga raised her both arms and snapped her fingers. Instantly, the cubs, paws outstretched and mouths open, froze in midair. Using the same technique, Little Yaga immobilized the mother Lynx and Ashley. When the squirrels were safely out of sight, Little Yaga snapped her fingers again. The three cubs landed softly on the ground and playfully chased one another around, with no recollection of the squirrels. Similarly, the mother Lynx and Ashley started moving again, oblivious to their momentary freeze.

Little Yaga went over to the Lynx and gave her a hug.

"Thank you for your help," she whispered.

Having overcome her fear, Ashley also hugged the wildcat, who gracefully bowed her head. Then, mewing loudly, she called her mischievous little ones. This time, they obeyed at once and trotted away along with their mother, no more straying from her side.

The Oak Tree and the Hedge

Once again, Little Yaga was running through the woods, with Ashley close behind. She knew they must be getting closer to the edge of the Forest, and she hoped that the Milkshake River had been their last obstacle. It seemed she could already smell those weird creatures Leesho called cars. She expected to see them moving up and down the road behind the human houses any minute now.

Suddenly, a blow to her right shoulder almost knocked her off her feet. Right behind her, she heard Ashley groan. Little Yaga turned around; the human girl was holding her left shoulder and biting her lip, trying not to cry. Little Yaga was about to say something when Ashley's eyes widened in horror. She pushed Little Yaga down onto the ground and fell next to her. Before Little Yaga could get angry, she saw a barrage of acorns zipping over their heads, in the very spot where they'd just been standing. If Ashley hadn't reacted so quickly, they would've been badly hurt. Once the whistling of acorn fire ceased, Little Yaga cautiously raised her head and saw the huge Oak Tree in the distance, growing in the middle of the road. Little Yaga didn't remember seeing it during her scouting trip—in fact, she'd never even heard of it before, but she instantly knew that this tree was malicious. Its leaves were drab and wrinkled, as if half-dead. There wasn't a single nest in its branches or a squirrel hollow in its trunk. Not even a small mushroom was growing out of its bark. It was inhospitable and hostile.

Afraid of more acorn attacks, Little Yaga and Ashley stayed on the ground, but things remained quiet and calm. The Oak Tree appeared to have fallen asleep, and the girls ventured to move. The very instant they stood up again, the Oak Tree forcefully shook its branches, releasing swarms of acorns that flew toward them, buzzing like bees. Terrified, the girls threw themselves back down and covered their heads with their hands. Within a few minutes, the buzzing abruptly stopped. Little Yaga opened her eyes and saw an army of squirrels surrounding the Oak Tree. She'd never seen so many at once! Some were hopping up and down, snatching the flying acorns, while others climbed the tree and overpowered its rowdy limbs. Clutching one another's paws, the squirrels formed a ring around the branches and pushed them against the trunk, preventing them from shaking off any more acorns.

Seizing the moment, Little Yaga jumped to her feet, pulling Ashley up with her.

"Run," she whispered and sprinted forward first. As she dashed past the Oak Tree, which now looked as if it were growing squirrels on its branches instead of leaves, she blew their furry rescuers a kiss.

A few minutes later, the girls could see the roofs of the human houses. Excited, they ran even faster until they reached a thick hedge studded with prickly thorns. To avoid crashing into the sharp scrubs the girls had to stop dead in their tracks. The hedge was twice their height and stretched from left to right as far as the eye could see. Little Yaga could've sworn it wasn't there during her scouting trip. Ashley looked at Little Yaga. The question "What do we do now?" was written on her face.

Little Yaga shrugged her shoulders. If the hedge had been placed here by Scraggard the Immortal, she knew she wouldn't be able to do anything about it. Nevertheless, she glided her hand along the bushes to see if they'd vanish, but they didn't. Instead, they burned the palm of her hand, just as though she'd held it over a flame. She quickly withdrew her hand and blew on it. The burn instantly disappeared. Next, Little Yaga extended her arm and snapped her fingers, but not a single thorn on the hedge budged. She glanced around, looking for anything that could help them get over the hedge, but nothing caught her eye. There were no trees close enough to climb up and jump over from, no sticks on the ground strong enough to be used as vaulting poles, and no rocks big enough to stack up like stairs. Once again, Little Yaga wished she had an extendable leg so that she could simply step over the hedge to the human side. She looked at Ashley, then back at the hedge, and sighed. She had no choice but to admit her defeat. It was silly of her to think she could outsmart His Scraggardness and rescue somebody he had lured into the Forest. Just then, Little Yaga heard a croaking sound up above. She lifted her eyes and saw two black ravens flying toward them. They were obviously Scraggard's servants, and now she and Ashley would be captured and severely punished. Little Yaga's shoulders drooped.

"Don't move," she told the human girl because she knew there was no point in trying to run.

Pale and frightened, the girls stood perfectly still, eyes glued to the ravens, who were slowly descending upon them. Suddenly, they heard more squawking from another direction. Shifting their eyes, they noticed a flock of big white birds, either swans or geese, in the distance, swooping toward them with incredible speed.

"Swan-Geese," Little Yaga breathed out, petrified.

The ravens saw them, too. They plunged down, clearly trying to beat the big birds in getting to the girls to prove their loyalty to the Immortal. Grabbing the girls by the scruffs of their necks with their strong beaks, the ravens lifted them off the ground, tore across the sky, and, a minute later, set them back down. The short flight was so abrupt that the girls' heads were spinning. Next instant, the ravens disappeared, leaving Little Yaga and Ashley looking around, a little dazed, trying to figure out where they were.

On the Other Side

"Gosh!" Ashley cried out, laughing. "No way!"

"What?" Little Yaga couldn't understand why this human was suddenly so jolly when any moment now, Scraggard's guards would show up and take them to the Immortal for their punishment.

"I'm home. I don't believe it!" Ashley hugged Little Yaga. "Thank you so much!"

Bewildered, Little Yaga looked around again and realized that she was standing on the other side of the hedge, across the road from a big human house.

"Is this your home?" she asked Ashley.

"Yes."

Little Yaga was confused. She was trying to digest what had just happened. Whose ravens were those? If Scraggard the Immortal didn't send them, then who did, and why? It seemed she suddenly had more questions than answers.

"Would you like to come over?" Ashley asked, distracting Little Yaga from her thoughts.

"Yes, of course. But not now. Now I must go back."

"What about this Saturday?"

"What about it?"

"It's my birthday. I am having a birthday party."

"A birthday party?" Little Yaga was surprised. "Are you turning ten or twenty? You don't look either."

"That's because I'm neither, silly," Ashley said, giggling. "I'm turning thirteen."

"You're celebrating your thirteenth birthday?" Little Yaga asked, even more surprised. "How often do you celebrate birthdays?"

"Every year, of course. Don't you?"

Little Yaga shook her head.

"I've only celebrated mine once—three years ago when I turned ten. In the Forest, we have birthday parties every ten years."

"Wow. You know, you live in a weird place. Don't take it personally, but I am so glad I'm out of there."

"I understand. There's no place like home."

"Tell me about it."

"Now I have to go." Little Yaga smiled, but behind her smile she shuddered at the thought of what awaited her back in the Forest. She shook her head, trying not to dwell on it now. She and Ashley spread their arms and gave each other a hug. That's when they noticed they were still wearing each other's clothes.

"My bad," Little Yaga said and ran her hands along Ashley's body, then along her own. Nothing happened. She was still dressed as Ashley, and Ashley was wearing her outfit.

"Sorry." Little Yaga seemed puzzled. She glided her hands along their bodies again, chanting a special reinforcing charm, but as before, nothing happened.

"Oops." Little Yaga clapped her hands and snapped her fingers. When nothing happened for the third time, she remembered hearing her grandmother say that foresters' powers didn't work out of the Forest.

"If I believed in witches," Ashley said, chuckling, "I'd swear you were one. Let's just change normally, not the weird way you've learned in school."

The girls hid behind one of the benches standing nearby and changed. Ashley, looking like a regular girl again, ran across the road. She stopped by the gate leading to her front lawn and pressed the buttons on the keypad. Slowly, the gate slid open. Ashley crossed the lawn, ran up the brick steps of her porch, and spun around.

"Remember, this Saturday at three," she yelled.

Little Yaga nodded. She watched Ashley ring her doorbell and go inside. Now that she was gone, Little Yaga was ready for her trip back. She turned around and saw no hedge in front of her. In its place, for as far as she could see, there was a luscious meadow, dotted with a few little ponds, nestled at the foot of some weeping willows. The reflection of the setting sun on the ponds turned their glassy surfaces a fiery orange color. Little Yaga began walking along the meadow. Soon she came across a narrow footpath winding through the grass at the end of Ashley's street. Without thinking twice, she stepped onto the path, and the luscious meadow around her instantly transformed into the Forest. Little Yaga sniffed the air and knew she was home.

The Hut

As soon as Little Yaga entered her front yard, the Hut warned her that Big Yaga was beside herself with anger. Very quietly, Little Yaga opened the door; the Hut made sure it didn't creak. She saw her grandmother sitting at the kitchen table with her head down. Her hair was in wilder disarray than its usual mess. Hoping to sneak into her bedroom unnoticed, Little Yaga tiptoed through the kitchen, but the nasty Cuckoo Bird stuck her head out of the clock door and announced, "Little Yaga's home."

Big Yaga raised her head. She had a feral look in her eye.

"Why on earth did you have to help the human?" she asked seething with anger.

Little Yaga raised her brows. "She was running away from me, and I was chasing her, but she was too fast."

Big Yaga wagged her crooked finger in front of Little Yaga's nose.

"Liar," she grumbled.

"She's on the track team at her school!" Little Yaga said. "I couldn't keep up with her—if I had a bony leg, then I would've caught her."

Big Yaga raised her arms toward the ceiling.

"Why am I punished with such an idiot of a granddaughter?" she moaned. "Why didn't you just use your powers, for goodness' sake?"

"Because I am not supposed to unless it's an emergency."

"Well, that *was* an emergency if I ever saw one," Big Yaga replied, lowering her arms. "I'm sure you've heard that His Scraggardness has been looking for a human child as an energy source. You could've delivered him that source today, but you didn't."

"She is not a child; she's a teenager," Little Yaga thought to herself.

"That doesn't matter to him," Big Yaga snapped. The old woman could read minds if she felt like it, although most of the time she preferred not to. She always said most minds were too boring and primitive and not worth her time or effort. "She could've been an adult, for that matter, as long as she was human," Big Yaga continued. "You could've been a hero! You could've gotten a reward—a bony leg, for instance! Scraggard's very powerful; he could've given you anything your ungrateful heart desired. Instead, you've gotten yourself in big trouble."

Big Yaga pushed the bench she was sitting on away from the table and stood up. She had started limping slowly toward her bedroom when suddenly the crystal ball she'd left on the kitchen counter near the sink lit up. It had never dared to act without Big Yaga's orders before.

"What's the matter?" The old woman picked up the ball. Walking much faster now, she disappeared into her bedroom.

"That was His Scraggardness," she said curtly, coming right out. "He wants to see you at once!"

"Now?" Little Yaga asked, feeling every cell in her body began to tremble. "But it's getting late."

Big Yaga only snorted in response.

Little Yaga had never seen Scraggard the Immortal, and she was terrified of meeting him. Still trembling, she reached for her hooves, gloves, and hat, but Big Yaga stopped her. "Don't bother," she said, "there's no time to dress up."

She limped outside. Frightened, Little Yaga staggered after her. On her way out the door, she heard the Cuckoo Bird giggling. Little Yaga wanted to throw something heavy at the bird, but there was nothing within reach. As she and her grandmother were leaving, the Hut heaved a heavy sigh.

"Stop it," Big Yaga barked. "It's her own fault."

"That's debatable," the Hut replied.

"No, it's not," Big Yaga snapped, growing very irritated. "You'd better just turn your front to the Forest and your back to me."

"Say it properly," the Hut requested.

"Oh, come on. Do what I say. I haven't got time for pleasantries."

The Hut didn't budge, its chicken leg stiffening until it was rigid as a steel rod.

Big Yaga grew white with rage.

"I am warning you, my friend," she growled. "Don't mess with me."

Still, the Hut didn't stir. Infuriated, Big Yaga strode over to its chicken leg and kicked it very hard.

A metallic clang sounded in unison with Big Yaga's groan. Limping now on both legs, she backed away.

"Good-bye, Hut on the chicken leg," she said with a grunt. "Turn to the Forest your front and to me your back."

"No problem," said the Hut, turning graciously on the heel of its foot, its leg becoming soft and springy again.

"That's what *you* think," Big Yaga muttered, climbing into her flying barrel. "But I promise you'll have a big problem when I get back. You'll be very sorry."

En Route to The Palace

Big Yaga bent over and, effortlessly, as though her grand-daughter was weightless, pulled Little Yaga inside the barrel. Then she jabbed her cane in the holder, and it instantly turned into a broomstick. Big Yaga blew on the broomstick with all her might, and it began spinning. The barrel hopped up and down for a while, higher and higher each time, until it finally shot up into the sky, above the trees and below the clouds. The night was dark, the wind was strong, and Little Yaga would've enjoyed the flight if they'd been going anywhere but to see Scraggard.

After about an hour, the barrel began descending. Little Yaga looked down to catch a glimpse of Scraggard's mysterious palace, but she saw only pitch-darkness down below.

"Where are we going?" she asked her grandmother. "There's nothing down there."

"Never assume there is nothing only because you can't see it. You better hold on; we're landing."

Little Yaga grabbed the handgrips inside the barrel just seconds before it hit the ground. It was such a rough landing that if she hadn't been holding on, she would've flown right out. After hopping up and down for a while, the barrel finally came to a complete stop.

"Here we are," Big Yaga said, throwing her bony leg over the edge. "Follow me."

Little Yaga heard her grandmother jump down, but it was so dark that she couldn't see her—or anything else, for that matter.

"Give me your hand," Big Yaga demanded.

Little Yaga reached out toward the sound of her voice and felt Big Yaga's cold, bony fingers clutching her wrist. In the utter darkness, her gandmother's smell and voice were comforting. With one strong jerk of her arm, Big Yaga yanked her granddaughter out of the barrel. The minute Little Yaga's feet touched the ground, the moon squeezed through a tear in the clouds and illuminated the Forest. Little Yaga instantly saw a monstrous black structure looming before her. It had a pointed roof that seemed to be trying to pierce the clouds that kept tripping over it.

"Scraggard's palace," Big Yaga whispered.

Instead of windows, the palace had narrow slits protected by thick metal bars. There was a black double door that was three stories high and a hundred feet across in the very middle of the facade. Each of the halves was decorated with a huge carving of a gaunt face, which Little Yaga assumed was a likeness of Scraggard. Six rows of odd-looking trees—all the same height, except for the tall ones at each end of every row, adorned both sides of the broad stone walkway leading to the front entrance. Every tree had two long, thick branches in the middle and a few short, stubby ones at the top of their thickly barked trunks. Their leaves were of such a dark shade of green that they looked black.

Big Yaga was staring around in as much awe as her granddaughter. In all the centuries she'd lived in the Forest, she'd never been summoned to the palace before. Little Yaga was surprised to see her boisterous grandmother so subdued.

"Let's go." Big Yaga sounded more hoarse than usual. She clasped Little Yaga's hand and pulled her toward the walkway. As they neared the pavement, Little Yaga noticed that every stone along the walkway's border bore an image of the same face that was carved on the door. But as soon as the Yagas reached the first row of trees, the tall ones at each end abruptly dropped down their branches, blocking Yagas' way and nearly cutting their faces. The Yagas jumped back in the nick of time.

"Who are you, and what are you doing here?" inquired a choir of hollow voices from both sides of the walkway.

"I am Big Yaga, and this is my granddaughter, Little Yaga," Big Yaga said, turning her head from side to side, unsure of whom, exactly, she should be addressing. "We are here at His Scraggardness's request."

"Step forward and clasp one of our branches," the tall trees demanded.

The branches, dotted with prickles and barbs, looked rough, but the Yagas obeyed. To their surprise, the prickly limbs felt soft and warm.

"Confirmed. You are the Yagas. Take your hands off and proceed."

The trees raised their branches, clearing the way. But no sooner had the Yagas taken two more steps when they had to jump back again because now the tall trees flanking the second row slashed down their limbs, almost knocking both ladies off their feet.

"Who are you, and what are you doing here?"

"We just answered that question," Big Yaga replied, and Little Yaga noticed a hint of annoyance in her voice. She was glad to see her grandmother returning to her crabby old self.

"Who are you, and what are you doing here?" the husky voices repeated flatly.

"I just told your friends who we were. Didn't you hear me?" Big Yaga obviously didn't feel like explaining everything again.

The trees ignored her and merely asked the same question in response: "Who are you, and what are you doing here?"

At the Palace

The Yagas had to answer the same question and hold on to the prickly-looking branches of the tall trees five more times before finally reaching their destination, the giant front door of Scraggard's palace. The door opened slowly, and Little Yaga with her grandmother entered a colossal hall covered in black marble from top to bottom and illuminated by thousands of platinum candles. The flickering flames cast quivering shadows onto the floor, walls, and ceiling. There was only one object in the hall: Scraggard's throne. Made of pure gold and studded with precious stones, it stood gleaming in the very center of the space, emitting sparkling rays of light in every direction. Even Big Yaga had never seen anything so magnificent.

Unable to take their eyes off the throne, the Yagas barely heard the heavy footsteps behind one of the many doors of the hall, turning to the sound only when the door opened. To their surprise, two rows of trees—smaller, with shorter branches and greener leaves than the ones outside—walked in and stood motionless on either side of the doorway. The Yagas finally understood why the branches they had held looked prickly but felt soft and warm. The "trees" were the uniforms of Scraggard's army. The next, and last, to enter the hall was the powerful and almighty, omnipotent and unstoppable Ruler of the Forest, Scraggard the Immortal. He walked slowly, and his every step was accompanied by the jarring creaking of his joints, reminiscent of the squeaky wheels of a rickety old cart. Scraggard was very tall and scrawny, looking as though he had no flesh between his bones and skin. His face was drawn, his mouth was lipless, and his eyes, sunken deeply into their sockets, emitted cold glow. As he passed the "trees," they raised their "branches" and barked out, "Forever live His Scraggardness, Scraggard the Immortal!"

Their proclamation was echoed from every nook and cranny of the great room: "Forever live His Scraggardness, Scraggard the Immortal!"

Scraggard proceeded to his throne, and only once he was seated did the trees lower their branches. Turning to the astounded Yagas, Scraggard stretched his mouth into a smile.

"Thank you for accepting my invitation, my ladies," he said in an unexpectedly gentle voice. Big Yaga smiled back and attempted a curtsy; her unbendable left knee screeched loudly. Scraggard looked at her amicably.

"I haven't seen you in ages, Big Yaga. When was the last time?" He paused, as if trying to remember. "Definitely not in this century. It must've been at least two centuries ago—I think it was in Paris, at a ball. You were dancing with Napoleon. Do you recall?"

Big Yaga nodded and grew pensive.

"Hey, don't be sad. You look great. You haven't changed a bit. Napoleon would still find you attractive."

Big Yaga automatically raised her hands and tried tidying her wild hair. Even in the flickering light, Little Yaga noticed, with surprise, that her grandmother was blushing. She wondered who this "Napoleon" was.

"One of the humans," Big Yaga explained curtly, having read her granddaughter's mind.

"You danced with a human?" Little Yaga asked, astonished. "How did that happen, and where?"

"In one of the human cities called Paris," Big Yaga replied, her eyes sparkling, which was also beyond belief. "I used to love sneaking into the human world when I was young."

"Didn't we all?" Scraggard chuckled, then immediately he grew serious. Moving his eyes to Little Yaga he examined her from head to toe. She shrank under his inquisitive gaze and stared down at the marble floor the whole time he was sizing her up. After what seemed an eternity, Scraggard finally broke the silence.

"Look at me, young lady," he requested. "I'm not going to bite you—yet."

Little Yaga raised her eyes to meet his.

"You are very pretty. You look just like your grandmother did when she was your age."

Little Yaga glanced at her grandmother, failing to imagine her young and pretty. She didn't know if she herself was; Damon obviously didn't think so.

"You have a kind heart, such a rarity these days," Scraggard continued, still smiling, although Little Yaga could see that the look in his eyes was icy cold. She was freezing under his stare. "You felt bad for the human girl and helped her get out of the Forest. It was a very clever idea to trade clothes so that I'd think you were chasing her. I appreciated that. I could've snatched her right away, but I wanted to see how far the two of you would get. Not very many humans make it past the Stove. Even fewer manage to cross the Milkshake River. In all the centuries, I remember only four instances where someone got around the Oak Tree. And only once did a human get beyond the hedge." Scraggard turned to Big Yaga. "Remember?"

Big Yaga heaved a woeful sigh.

"You've outsmarted me, young lady. How could this have happened?"

Scraggard leaned forward and peered into Little Yaga's eyes as if they held the answer. She looked down again, shrugged her shoulders, and whispered, "I don't know."

"I suppose I was too sure of myself. I could never imagine you outfoxing me. By the time I realized I was losing and sent out the squad of my fearless Swan-Geese, it was too late. Your ravens whipped my birds. Look at me, Little Yaga, when I'm talking to you."

Little Yaga lifted her head.

"Who are those ravens? Where did they come from?" Scraggard demanded, his smile gone. His gaunt face was scary without it.

"I don't know," Little Yaga whispered.

"Don't lie to me, Little Yaga. I've never appreciated little Forest girls who lie." Scraggard's voice was no longer gentle.

Big Yaga, quiet until now, put her hands on her granddaughter's shoulders.

"Listen to me, Little Yaga," she said unusually tenderly. "Don't be afraid. Tell His Scraggardness the truth. If you do, he won't hurt you."

"I don't know anything about those ravens," Little Yaga replied, agitated. "I've never seen them in my life! I thought he'd sent them to kill us!"

She was about to say something else, but suddenly, a warm liquid started pouring out of her eyes. She didn't understand what was happening. Was she crying? How was it possible? Unlike humans, Foresters never cried. She must've caught a crying bug from Ashley. Oh, how she wished she'd never met her! Why on earth was she so unlucky?

Shocked to see her granddaughter in tears, Big Yaga covered her wrinkled face with her knuckled hands. The guards in tree uniforms at the door turned around so as not to see Little Yaga weeping. They stuck their fingers in their ears to block out her sobs. Amused, Scraggard leaned back in his throne and waited patiently for Little Yaga to get over her crying jag.

When she didn't, he finally said, "Stop at once, or I'll take you for a human and suck all your energy out." Then, turning to Big Yaga, he muttered, "This is all your daughter's fault."

"I know," she said with a sigh.

"What?" Little Yaga asked, the tears in her eyes instantly drying up. "Are you talking about my mother? What's her fault? What'd she do?"

"Nothing," Big Yaga snapped in irritation. "Please, don't ask any more questions. You know it pains me to talk about your mother."

"He started it," Little Yaga said, pouting.

"His Scraggardness—not *he*," Big Yaga quickly corrected her. "I beg Your Scraggardness to please forgive my granddaughter; she's only a child."

"And a very unruly one at that," Scraggard replied tersely. He stood up and walked so close to the Yagas that they could feel his cold breath and see his sharp fangs.

"Big Yaga," he said, addressing the old woman first, "your granddaughter has broken the law. I'll forgive her, for your sake, but only on one condition: she must return to the human town, bring back the human girl, and deliver her directly to my palace." Then he talked to Little Yaga.

"You, young lady, will go to the girl's birthday party on Saturday—won't that be fun? You'll stay there for as long as you like, but when you're ready to leave, you'll take the girl with you."

"How will I do that?" Little Yaga whispered.

"You'll think of something; you are a smart little Forester."

Scraggard returned to his throne. Right then a piece of the wall in front of him suddenly lit up. Little Yaga turned toward the light and realized she was looking at a large screen embedded in the marble slab.

"Your big sister is trying to get in touch with me," Scraggard told Big Yaga and snapped his fingers. Instantly, Biggest Yaga's huge face was smiling at the three of them from the screen. Her fleshy nose and chin protruded through its flat surface and hung all the way down to the floor. The smell of poison ivy, which she always consumed in huge quantities, filled the entire hall.

"Hi, everyone." Biggest Yaga extended her arm and waved her hand, practically in the Yagas' faces. Dumbfounded, they waved back.

"Hello, my wisest friend," Scraggard greeted Biggest Yaga. "Good to see you. What brings you here today?"

She opened her mouth to respond, but her nose suddenly got itchy, and she sneezed loudly, spraying the floor below with mucus and saliva. Scraggard barely managed to suppress his revulsion.

"Bless you," he said and snapped his fingers, drying the floor.

"Thank you." Biggest Yaga twitched her nose as if trying to fight another sneezing spell and then said. "I've just heard Your Scraggardness is sending my great-niece back to the human town."

"News travel fast in my forest," Scraggard replied.

"I'd like to offer a friendly suggestion, if I may."

"I'm listening." Scraggard's eyes peered into Biggest Yaga's.

"Send Kikimra along with her."

"What for?"

"Just in case. Two forest girls in a strange place are better than one."

Scraggard narrowed his eyes and fell silent, thinking.

"Your suggestion makes sense," he announced at last. "I'll send Kikimra along."

"Yes!" Little Yaga thought to herself, but her face didn't betray her emotions.

"Happy, aren't you?" Big Yaga asked gruffly, and Little Yaga knew her grandmother had read her mind again. Scraggard signaled Little Yaga to approach. She obeyed.

"Before you go, let me give you something." He took her right hand and put a seal ring on her fourth finger. The ring bore the engraved image of his gaunt face, with two big sparkling diamonds in place of his eyes.

"If you need help or find that you must move instantly from one point of the universe to another, simply rub these stones, make your wish, and it will be granted," he explained. Then, towering over Little Yaga's head, Scraggard the Immortal pronounced in a hollow voice, amplified by the echo reverberating throughout the hall, "Remember, never take this ring off. If you lose it and somebody else finds it, an unpredictable disaster may strike." Upon those words, he returned to his throne. "Thank you, ladies, for coming over. Now you may leave."

Both Yagas curtsied. Even Big Yaga could lower herself gracefully before the Ruler of the Forest. When they straightened up again, they found themselves in the kitchen of their Hut, facing the nosy Cuckoo Bird, who was dying to know what had happened at the palace.

Damon

For the first time ever, Little Yaga was popular. As she ran to her homeroom class, down the tapering stone staircase between the two giant rocks, one by one and word by word, the steps under her feet sang out: *She was at Scraggard's palace yesterday! She saw the Great Scraggard the Immortal with her own eyes!*

When she walked into her classroom, Little Yaga didn't recognize her desk. Stuck in the far corner of the room, it was usually short and narrow and the same drab color as the walls. Today, however, it was bright red and almost as tall and wide as the desks of all the popular kids. In addition, one of its corners was decorated with a few dry twigs.

Little Yaga stopped in the doorway and looked around to see if her desk had been moved to another location, wondering if this lovely one belonged to somebody else.

"Looking good, ain't I?" her desk boomed. "I've just had a 'popular desk' makeover." And with that, it burst into resounding laughter.

"Shush." Little Yaga put her finger to her lips walking over to the desk. "Not so loud."

"Hi, Little Yaga," she heard a familiar voice behind her back. When she turned to see whose it was, her heart practically leaped out of her chest. She could hardly believe her eyes!

"Hello, Damon," she whispered.

"I heard you were at Scraggard's palace yesterday."

"Yes," Little Yaga replied, knowing that all the girls in her class were watching her and wishing they could be in her place. She'd been dreaming of this moment for years herself but had never imagined it would ever come.

"How was it?"

"Awesome," Little Yaga said, although she wasn't sure what, exactly, was awesome—her visit with Scraggard or talking to the boy of her dreams.

"I want to know all about it." Damon smiled, revealing his sharp brown fangs. "Scraggard the Immortal has always been my hero."

Only now did Little Yaga notice a strong similarity between Scraggard and Damon. At thirteen, Damon was almost as tall as the Immortal and very thin. His cheeks were drawn, and his black eyes were seated deeply in their sockets. He even shaved his head, revealing a skull that was as bumpy as Scraggard's. Unlike the Immortal, however, Damon didn't look or move like a zombie. He was full of energy and pep.

"We have to meet and talk," Damon said. "When are you free?"

"What?" Little Yaga doubted she heard him right. She thought Damon couldn't possibly mean what he'd said and that he must surely be making fun of her. She looked around, expecting to see her classmates sneering, but they weren't. Her newly colored bright-red desk grew wider still—it was nearly as wide as Damon's now, extending from one side of the room to the other.

"When are you free?" Damon repeated his question.

"I'm free on weekends," Little Yaga said.

"Great! How about Saturday? I'll pick you up at your house, say, at three?"

"Sure," Little Yaga agreed. She was in heaven. That is, until she remembered where she was supposed to be this Saturday at three.

"Sorry, Damon," she stammered. "I completely forgot. I've got plans for Saturday. Would you like to do it another day?"

"You've got plans?" Damon asked, genuinely surprised. "So, cancel them, or reschedule, or—whatever! Explain to whomever you're meeting that I've invited you out—they'll understand." He laughed and winked.

"I only wish I could," Little Yaga replied, knowing she was blowing her only chance with this boy. She'd never been so miserable in her life! "Couldn't we just get together another time?" she asked timidly.

"I'll think about it," Damon said with a smirk. Turning on his hooves, he walked coolly away.

Little Yaga went to her desk, which had returned to its petite, drab self; the dried twigs lay on the floor, broken. Upset, she sat down and instantly got a swift kick in the shin from one of the desk's legs.

"Ouch!" she exclaimed, looking down just as the desk's other leg took aim at her other shin. "What are you doing? Are you crazy?"

"You're the crazy one," the desk retorted. "I was never so insignificant and unnoticeable—not until I was assigned to you, that is. I'm tired of it. I want to be big and brightly colored!"

"I had no idea you were so vain," Little Yaga said.

"I'm not vain, but I need recognition."

"What for?"

"For my own satisfaction," the desk replied. "But you wouldn't understand that. I hate you!"

The desk stomped all its legs so hard that Little Yaga was jolted out of her seat and very nearly fell smack onto the floor.

"You're nuts!" she shouted. "I almost fell down!"

"Too bad you didn't," the desk said obnoxiously. "And if you ever want to sit here again, you'd better do something about getting my favorite size and color back. The sooner, the better."

"Damon!" Little Yaga hollered, trying to get the boy's attention before he reached his own desk. "I didn't tell you what my plans for Saturday were."

"Am I supposed to care?"

"I'm doing Scraggard a favor. That's why he summoned me to his palace last night, and that's why I am not free this Saturday."

"Really?" Damon's eyes sparkled with curiosity. "That's a different story." He walked back to Little Yaga. "Why didn't you say so in the first place?"

"You didn't give me a chance."

"Would you like to meet on Sunday instead?"

"Sure." Little Yaga tried to sound nonchalant, even though her heart was pounding against her rib cage so loudly that she was afraid the whole class could hear it.

"Then I'll pick you up on Sunday at three. Is that OK?"

"Yes."

Little Yaga returned to her desk—once again wide and tall as all the other popular kids' desks and a shimmering red color. Even the broken twigs were whole and lay nicely adorning one of its four corners.

"That's more like it," the desk said. Then it added chivalrously, "Have a seat, please!"

Little Yaga sat down and noticed Leesho staring at her from the opposite corner of the room, where he sat at his narrow desk that was of the same drab color as the walls.

"What?" she mouthed.

"Nothing," he replied, shaking his head.

"You look disappointed."

"Do I? No kidding."

"Let's talk after school."

"You don't want to waste your time on such an insignificant and unpopular person."

"Stop it. I'll meet you after school at our place. Where's Kikimra?"

"No idea."

Kikimra

Kikimra stood before Scraggard the Immortal, who sat staring at her from his sparkling throne.

"Kikimra, I trust you more than I do Little Yaga," he said after a long silence. "She's made a big mistake and deserves to be punished, but I want to forgive her. Would you like to help your friend fix her mistake?"

"Of course, Your Scraggardness. What'd she do, and how can I help?"

"This Saturday, the two of you will go to the human town. You'll help Little Yaga bring a human girl to my palace. That's all."

"What girl?"

"The one Little Yaga foolishly helped escape from the Forest yesterday."

"So that's why she wasn't in school…"

"Precisely." Scraggard smiled, revealing his long, sharp fangs.

"I've never been to a human town before," Kikimra admitted. "Don't we lose our powers when we leave the Forest?"

"I'll give you a special ring. If you need any help, you can rely on it." Scraggard leaned forward and took Kikimra's hand. A ring, identical to the one he'd given Little Yaga the night before, sparkled on the ring finger of her right hand.

"It can also transfer you from one place to another. Simply rub these diamonds and say where you want to go."

Curious, Kikimra examined the ring.

"Is it for me to keep?" she asked.

"When you return with the girl, we'll talk," Scraggard promised. Then he stood up and, towering over Kikimra, pronounced, his hollow voice reverberating throughout the hall, "But remember, never take this ring off. If you lose it and somebody else finds it, an unpredictable disaster may strike."

Just as he was about to dismiss the girl, the monitor embedded in the wall in front of his throne lit up. Scraggard snapped his fingers. Instantly Biggest Yaga's fleshy face appeared on the screen and smiled at Kikimra. As before, the smell of poison ivy filled the great room. It was so strong that Kikimra sneezed. Biggest Yaga sneezed, too, spraying mucus and saliva all over the marble floor once again.

Scraggard's mouth curled down in disgust. He snapped the floor dry and asked, "What has brought you here today, Biggest Yaga?"

"Another friendly piece of advice, if I may."

"I'm listening."

"Remind the girls to hide their fangs when they go to the human town."

"Thank you, ma'am." Scraggard looked down at Kikimra and asked, "Did you hear what the venerable Biggest Yaga just said?"

"Yes, Your Scraggardness." Kikimra smiled, revealing humanlike teeth, straight and white, with no fangs.

"Smart girl," Scraggard praised her. "I can see you'll be a big help to Little Yaga." Then, addressing the screen, he added, "Thank you, Biggest Yaga, for suggesting that Kikimra should go along."

Biggest Yaga bowed her head in response. Then she beckoned Kikimra to approach and whispered something in the girl's ear. After that, her image disappeared; the screen went black, becoming practically indistinguishable from the marble wall behind it.

"You may return to your class now," Scraggard said. Looking at Kikimra he snapped his fingers, and she was gone.

Once he was alone, Scraggard collapsed into his throne. He was gasping for air and feeling weaker than ever. He desperately needed a burst of energy to restore his waning vigor. This morning, his hunters had brought him a newborn bear cub. Scraggard was furious; he hated bear energy. It was sluggish and dull, but it would have to do until he got the human girl back. Scraggard closed his eyes. The hunters deserved to be thrown into the bear's den and torn to shreds by the mother bear, but he didn't have the strength.

Leesho

Little Yaga was sitting next to Leesho on the trunk of a tree that lay across a bubbling brook. The water under their dangling feet was crystal clear; they could see the texture of the smallest pebble on the bottom. There were schools of sparkling fish zooming back and forth in the water beneath the shimmering rays of sunshine on the surface. The friends sat in silence until the sun hit one of the diamonds on Little Yaga's ring, releasing a spray of multicolored sparks of light from the precious stone.

"A ring?" Leesho asked, taking Little Yaga's hand. "Where did you get it? Whose face is on it?"

"Scraggard's," Little Yaga replied.

"Scraggard looks haggard."

"Doesn't he? He gave me this ring to wear to the human town—it's supposed to help me and take me anywhere I want."

"That's interesting. Can I see it?"

"Here." Little Yaga raised her hand to Leesho's face.

"Can I see it closer?"

"Isn't this close enough? I don't want to take it off—Scraggard warned me not to lose it."

"Why would you? I'll give it right back."

Reluctantly, Little Yaga tried to pull the ring off, but it suddenly wasn't so easy. Either her finger had swollen or the ring had shrunk, but it wouldn't come off.

"I can't—you see?" she said.

"Let me try."

Leesho took Little Yaga's finger and blew on the ring. At once it easily slid off into his palm. Little Yaga wondered how he always knew what to do to solve any problem.

Leesho carefully examined the ring. He noticed two tiny mirrors on the inner rim, inlaid opposite the sparkling diamonds. In the minuscule space between the mirrors, he saw an inscription in letters so microscopically small that he was unable to read it. Leesho blew on the ring again, snapped his fingers, and whispered an incantation, but the letters didn't expand.

"What are you doing?" Little Yaga asked.

"I'm trying to see what it says."

"What?"

"There is something written right here." Leesho pointed to the tiny space between the mirrors.

"I don't see anything. Can I have my ring?" Little Yaga reached forward, and Leesho gave it to her.

Either he let go of it a split second too soon or Little Yaga's hand wasn't level enough, but the ring fell through their fingers and into the water. It disturbed the stillness of the brook, and suddenly the water swirled and churned until it formed a vortex, into which the ring was quickly drawn, where it promptly disappeared.

Having swallowed up the ring, the water instantly returned to its tranquil state, although it had grown murky and dark. Shocked, Little Yaga stared at the brook, but neither she nor Leesho could see a thing below its surface. Unable to utter a single word, Little Yaga turned to Leesho, who smiled reassuringly despite the fear that was etched into the girl's face.

"Everything's going to be all right," he promised, trying to pat Little Yaga on the shoulder, but she shrank away from his touch.

"No doubt," she said heatedly feeling very angry. "Scraggard will only suck all my energy out, that's all."

"No, he won't," Leesho objected.

As proving him right, the water under their feet rippled, and the toothy snout of a shark surfaced, holding the ring in its teeth. Little Yaga jumped up to her feet, but Leesho bent down and pulled the ring from the fish's jaws. Instantly, the shark disappeared under the dim surface of the water.

"What was that shark doing in our brook?" Little Yaga asked hoarsely, still somewhat shaken.

"It swam over to give you your ring back."

"It's a silly joke."

"I'm not joking."

"But why?"

"I'm not sure." Leesho admitted. "But I've no doubts one day we'll find out." He smiled and put the ring into his pocket.

"What are you doing?" Little Yaga shouted again. "Give it to me!" She didn't feel like showing her friend she was no longer angry with him.

"Don't worry. I'll give it back to you...soon." Leesho stood up. "Let's get out of here." Balancing on the narrow tree trunk, he crossed the brook. Little Yaga followed, walking more slowly but more steadily.

On the other side of the brook, Leesho found a big rock and hid the ring underneath it. Having been born and raised in the Forest, Little Yaga knew to refrain from asking too many questions. Leesho then returned to the brook, took Little Yaga by the hand, and led her back across the tree trunk to the other side and straight to their hiding place among the piles of dead bushes and trees. There it was safe to talk.

"So?" Little Yaga asked. "What's this all about?"

"Scraggard's ring," Leesho said. "He gave it to you because it may help you and transfer you anywhere you want."

"I know—I'm the one who told you that," Little Yaga snorted.

"But the ring has another power, which Scraggard neglected to mention."

"Like?"

"Like the power of surveillance. Have you noticed those mirrors on the inside?"

"Yes."

"Well, they reflect everything you do, so while you're wearing his ring, Scraggard is able to watch your every move and hear your every word."

"Wow," Little Yaga said. "How do you know all this? From the writing?"

"I couldn't read it," Leesho confessed. "The letters were too small. I have a gut feeling, though, that it holds some important information. We'll get to the bottom of it when you come back from the human town. But while you're there, remember:

whenever you don't want Scraggard watching you, take the ring off and put it as far away from you as you can."

⚔

Leesho walked Little Yaga home. When they got to her gate, he asked, "Why do you like Damon so much?"

"I don't know. He's good-looking and so confident. There's something very attractive about him. Maybe his black lips and black eyes? I'm not sure what it is exactly, but every girl in our school is in love with him."

"That's what I've heard," Leesho said, aware that his blue eyes and pink lips were no match for Damon's—or anybody else's in the Forest, for that matter.

"How about you, Leesho? Do you like anybody?" Little Yaga asked.

"I don't want to talk about it."

"Well, *excuse* me," Little Yaga said, pretending to be insulted. "I answered your question, so you have to answer mine."

"Well, there is one girl I sort of like, but I don't think she likes me back."

Little Yaga seemed genuinely surprised.

"But how could she not? You are so sweet and smart—she must be very silly. Is she from our school? Do I know her?"

"Kind of."

"Who is she?"

"I'm not telling."

"Why not?"

"Just because. Now stop asking." Changing the topic Leesho said, "You better go home and get some rest before tomorrow."

"You're right—I should." And on that note, Little Yaga gave Leesho a hug, snapped her gate open, and ran up the path toward her Hut.

"Be careful with those humans tomorrow," he shouted after her.

Sean

Sean's jaw dropped as he looked out the dining room window, and he called out to his sister, "Ashley! Who are those two scarecrows at the gate?"

Ashley came out of the kitchen and went up to the window to see for herself.

"That's Little Yaga!" she exclaimed. "She's the girl from the forest I keep telling you about."

"There is no forest, Ashley. You made that whole thing up," Sean replied firmly.

"You can say and think whatever you want, but that girl's right here before your very eyes."

"Who's she with?"

"I don't know—a friend, I guess."

"Why are they dressed that way? Didn't you tell them it's your birthday party, not a rehearsal for Halloween?"

"I've told you—that's how they dress in the forest."

Sean squinted and leaned forward for a better look.

"What are they doing out there?"

Little Yaga had forgotten that she had no powers out of the Forest and kept snapping her fingers, trying to open the gate to the yard of the human house.

"Stop it," Kikimra said, grabbing her hand. "You can't do it that way here! Let's ask Scraggard's ring for help."

She was about to rub the diamonds on the ring when Ashley came out through the garage, holding an elongated, rounded stick. She thrust her hand forward, and the gate began sliding open.

"Do you see what she's doing?" Kikimra whispered in Little Yaga's ear. "She's using a magic wand."

"Humans don't have magic wands," Little Yaga whispered back.

"But she's using one to open the gate—look!"

"I see it." Little Yaga frowned. "It makes no sense!"

Ashley was beaming. She walked down the driveway with her arms wide open to greet her guests.

"Hello, Little Yaga! I am so glad you've made it! The party's going to be a smash! You'll love it!"

Ashley gave Little Yaga a hug and kissed her on her cheek. Little Yaga had heard of the weird human habit of kissing one another and thought it was gross, but surprisingly, it didn't feel too disgusting. Kikimra couldn't help but giggle. Beaming, Ashley turned to her and introduced herself.

Kikimra smiled back, feeling weird without her fangs, and repeated what Biggest Yaga had told her to say: "I've heard so much about you. I'm glad Little Yaga's brought me along."

"I'm glad, too," Ashley replied.

"Yes, Ashley, this is my best friend, Kikimra. Is it all right that I've taken her with me?"

"Sure!" Ashley said with a smile. "No problems. The more, the merrier."

On seeing Ashley's bare skin, Kikimra understood why Biggest Yaga had made her blow the clumps of hair off her hands and the rest of her body.

"Little Yaga," Ashley said, "was it Kikimra you were texting with on that leaf?"

"Yup."

"Nice to meet you, Kikimra." Ashley gave her a hug, too.

Involuntarily, Kikimra snapped her teeth together by Ashley's ear, barely resisting the temptation to bite the human girl's earlobe, but Ashley only laughed gleefully.

"You guys have to prove to my brother that you live in the forest because he doesn't believe me. He says there is no forest around."

At first, Ashley wanted to bring the girls in through the garage, but then she changed her mind and took them up to the front entrance. She rang the bell, and Sean opened the door. He was tall and slim, with black hair, brown eyes, and thin lips—he didn't look anything like his sister. Kikimra thought he could easily pass for a Forester. She found him cute.

"Hi, guys," Sean said, flashing a toothy smile. "I'm Ashley's brother, Sean. Welcome to our *casa*. He jokingly bowed down from the waist, and the girls responded with two deep curtsies. Sean chortled, but immediately apologized,

"Sorry," he said. "Come on in!"

He ushered the girls into the family room, which was flooded with sunshine pouring in through the two skylights in the ceiling. Blinded by the glare, Little Yaga and Kikimra covered their eyes with their hands.

"It always gets too bright in here this time of the day." Sean explained. He picked up a stick, similar to the one Ashley had used to open the gate, and aimed it at the ceiling. Instantly, two blue screens moved slowly across the glass, blocking out the glare.

"What is that?" Kikimra asked, staring at the stick. "A magic wand?"

"What else?" Sean grinned, and Kikimra liked his smile.

"I didn't know they existed in your...home," she mumbled, catching herself before she said *world*.

"You seem to know very little about my home," Sean said, now serious. "And I know nothing about yours. Where is it? Ashley says it's in the forest somewhere—is it really?"

"Yes," Kikimra replied warily.

"But there is no forest nearby."

"It's not too close and not too far—it's out there." She waved her hand in no particular direction.

"I'd like to crash your forest one day," Sean said.

"Crash our Forest?" Kikimra was shocked. "What for?"

"You girls from 'out there' are a little out of touch." Sean laughed. "*Crash* means visit."

Kikimra wouldn't have minded a visit from this cute human, but for the sake of his safety, she didn't think it was a good idea.

"Of course," she lied. "One day, when we're having a party, we'll invite you over, right, Little Yaga?" Kikimra moved her ears subtly, for only Little Yaga to see, signaling her to play along. It was a secret code they'd used since they were little, whenever one of them needed the other's backing up.

"Sure, come," Little Yaga said. "You're so full of energy, and I know at least one person who'll love that about you."

Kikimra moved her ears in the opposite direction now to show Little Yaga that she didn't appreciate her sarcasm.

"Great, it's settled then." Sean smiled. "You can expect me at your next party. Ashley's told me so much about your place. I want to see it with my own eyes. Now, girls, why don't you have a seat, and I'll bring you something to drink. We've got water, soda, and juice. What would you like?"

"I'll have water," Little Yaga said.

"I don't know if you have it," Kikimra ventured, "but I could go for some poison ivy juice."

"Poison ivy juice?" Sean stroked his chin as if he were thinking, and then he said, "I believe we're all out of it. Seriously, though, I've heard of poison ivy allergies but not poison ivy *juice*. You're kidding, right?"

"No, it's one of the most popular juices in the Forest."

"Are you serious?"

"Yes. It's odd you've never heard of it."

"The closest thing to poison ivy juice I can think of would be, maybe, rat poison dissolved in water," Sean joked.

"That's a possible alternative," Kikimra said. "I tried it once—it wasn't that bad."

Noticing Sean's bewildered expression, Little Yaga laughed as loud as she could.

"Isn't she funny?" she hooted, bending over with laughter, but Kikimra didn't appreciate being laughed at.

"What's so funny?" she asked gloomily.

"Your story about the rat poison!" Little Yaga smiled stiffly, hoping her friend wouldn't start emitting fumes from her mouth. Now it was her turn to move her ears for Kikimra to see. "It's Kikimra's favorite story," she told Sean. "She loves to shock people just to see their reactions. It's her way of testing a person's sense of humor."

At last Kikimra noticed Little Yaga's ears and started laughing even louder than her friend.

"Gotcha!" she exclaimed. "And don't say you didn't believe me."

"For a minute there I did," Sean admitted. "You sounded very convincing."

"Gullible people!" Kikimra exclaimed, and she burst out laughing, but this time for real.

Ashley's Closet

When Ashley came into the family room, Little Yaga and Kikimra were drinking orange juice. They were taking the smallest sips possible to keep from gagging and showing how disgusted they were by the beverage.

"Sorry, guys, my other guests are running late," Ashley said, "which isn't bad—it'll give us time to do something before everybody gets here."

"Do what?" Sean asked, evidently more curious than the girls were.

"Nothing of your concern, Sean—it's a girl thing." Ashley turned to Little Yaga and Kikimra. "You know, I am so glad you've come. I want to introduce you to all my friends—I know they're going to like you. The thing is, though..." she continued, hesitantly, as if trying to find the right words, "I love your outfits—they're so unique, and I know that's how you dress in your forest. But here, in our town, the style's a little different."

Kikimra looked over at Little Yaga and agreed. "You're right, Ashley. Why didn't we think of that? I mean, really. We want to look just like everybody else. Don't we, Little Yaga?"

"We do."

"I'm glad you feel that way." Ashley smiled. "Let's change your clothes, then."

Kikimra snapped her fingers and moved her hands up and down along her body. When nothing happened, she slapped herself on the forehead, remembering she had no powers in the human town.

"I know you like to change the way they taught you in school," Ashley said, sensing Kikimra's frustration, "but why don't you try on something from my closet? I've got tons of clothes! I am sure you'll find something you like."

A few minutes later, Little Yaga and Kikimra were standing in front of the mirror, both dressed in shorts. Ashley had insisted shorts were the most comfortable clothing for the weather. She'd given the girls a few pairs to try on and stepped out. Little Yaga was staring at Kikimra's bony leg, feeling painfully jealous. Kikimra was also scrutinizing her reflection.

"No," she said after a while, "this isn't for me. To wear clothes like these, I'd need legs like yours."

"What?" Little Yaga asked cautiously, and her heart skipped a beat. She'd suddenly remembered her great-aunt, Biggest Yaga, saying the only way Little Yaga could possibly get a bony leg was if somebody voluntarily agreed to trade one with her. Her grandmother, Big Yaga, had only laughed bitterly in response and asked, "Who in their right mind would do that?"

But on hearing Kikimra say she needed legs like hers, Little Yaga felt a glimmer of hope.

"Do you really mean you'd want legs like mine?" she asked, gingerly.

"No," Kikimra replied, shaking her head. "I never said I *wanted* legs like yours. I said I'd *need* them to wear clothes like these. I mean, I doubt humans would appreciate my bony leg in these shorts."

"So, what are you going to do?" Little Yaga asked, feeling a twinge of disappointment.

"I'll wear pants."

Kikimra quickly changed into a pair of slacks Ashley had laid out for them, and this time she found her reflection in the mirror as decent as it could be, considering she was wearing human clothes. She adjusted the tank top that was barely covering her belly button, feeling relieved, again, that Biggest Yaga had insisted she snap her belly fur away. She gathered her hair into a ponytail like Ashley's, and now not a person in the world would suspect she was anyone but a human teenager.

"Don't these humans dress weird?" she asked, turning to Little Yaga, who'd decided on the shorts.

"Crazy weird," Little Yaga replied. "Can you imagine us showing up at school dressed like this? If Rat saw your belly button and my legs, he'd turn both of us into a two-headed snake."

"Or two All-You-Can-Eat Tablecloths."

"No—two vials of poisonous potion."

The girls snickered and laughed until Kikimra started howling, at which point Little Yaga stopped short and put her hand over Kikimra's mouth.

"Shush. You're not in the Forest!" she whispered loudly.

"Sorry." Kikimra pushed Little Yaga's hand off her mouth and turned back to the mirror to study her reflection.

"Well, what do you think?" she asked.

"About what?"

"Do you think that guy, Sean, will like me when he sees me dressed like a human?"

"What?" Little Yaga exclaimed. "Don't tell me you have a crush on Sean."

"What are you talking about? Of course not. A crush? Not at all. Absolutely not." Kikimra suddenly grew so angry that she could barely contain the growl and fumes seething in her throat and mouth.

"OK, relax," Little Yaga said, taken aback by Kikimra's outburst. "I'm kidding."

"Actually, you're right," Kikimra admitted matter-of-factly, her anger having subsided as quickly as it had arisen. "I do have a crush on Sean."

"What about Damon?"

"Damon who?" Kikimra snickered lightheartedly, but Little Yaga didn't laugh.

"Sean is a human," she said. "We don't mix with humans. Relationships with them always mean trouble."

"Really?" Kikimra asked, with the most innocent expression on her face.

"Oh, come on! Don't act like you've never heard that before."

That very second, Ashley's voice from behind them exclaimed, "Wow, girls, you look great!"

Little Yaga and Kikimra spun around; Ashley was staring at them, truly amazed. "If I met you outside, I'd never recognize you!" she said. "You could pass for any girl from my school. Now, if you're ready, let's go back downstairs. Some guests have already arrived—I'll introduce you to them!"

Sonya

Most of the kids in the family room were Ashley's class-mates; one girl was talking to Sean.

"What an ugly human," Kikimra whispered into Little Yaga's ear.

The girl's blond hair was long and wavy; her almond-shaped green eyes were framed by dark lashes, and every time she smiled, two dimples bejeweled her rosy cheeks. When she spoke, her voice was as gentle as the murmur of a mountain spring. She was sitting on the sofa next to Sean, and Kikimra didn't like the way he was looking at her. She wished she had her powers so that she could turn this green-eyed human into a green toad, covered all over in nasty warts.

"Hey, Sean," Ashley called out, "why don't you introduce Little Yaga and Kikimra to Sonya?"

Sean smiled and waved the girls to come over.

"His smile is killing me," Kikimra whispered.

"Stop it," Little Yaga whispered back. "Remember, he's a human. You don't belong together."

"Sonya," Sean said when Little Yaga and Kikimra approached, "I'd like you to meet Ashley's friends from the forest."

Little Yaga introduced herself and curtsied.

Sonya laughed.

"I've only seen curtsies in movies," she said.

Little Yaga shrugged her shoulders.

"It's simply good manners," she replied.

"Of course," Sonya agreed. "I like it!"

She got up off the sofa and tried to curtsy, but she lost her balance and, laughing, fell over onto Sean.

Kikimra growled, and Little Yaga pinched her on the arm to get her to stop.

Sonya rose back up and asked Kikimra what her name was, but the latter only stood there glumly, so Sean replied for her.

"This is Kikimra. She's a real joker—she told me she'd once drank dissolved rat poison."

"Really?" Sonya chuckled. "Nice to meet you, Kikimra."

She tried another curtsy and managed not to fall over this time.

"What forest are you from?" she asked. "I don't know of any close by."

"You can come over and see it if you like," Kikimra said, cheering up at this idea. "It's a beautiful place—you'd like it so much that it'd be hard for you to leave."

"Kikimra," Little Yaga said in a cautionary tone.

"I'd love to," Sonya said.

"That's great!" Kikimra smiled.

"I've already been invited to the next party there, by the way," Sean said, flashing Kikimra a heart-melting smile.

"Awesome!" Sonya exclaimed. "Can I come, too?"

"You don't have to wait for the next party, Sonya. You can come over anytime, even tonight."

"Kikimra, can I talk to you in private?" Little Yaga squeezed her friend's elbow.

"Later."

"Now."

"Why?"

"Because." Little Yaga turned to Sean and Sonya and said, "Sorry, guys. Kikimra and I have to chat. We'll be right back."

"Sure, go ahead," Sean replied. "We're not going anywhere!"

From the Foyer to the Office

Pulling Kikimra out of the family room and into the empty foyer, Little Yaga confronted her.

"What do you think you're doing? Are you crazy?" she asked heatedly, bringing her face up so close to Kikimra's that she would've burned her friend's nose if she'd released the fumes boiling in her mouth.

"What are you talking about?" Kikimra asked in response, blinking her eyes in fake innocence.

"Why are you trying to talk that girl into going to the Forest?"

"I hate her," Kikimra barked, a tiny puff of smoke escaping through her angrily squeezed lips.

"Keep your fumes to yourself," Little Yaga retorted. "What did she ever do to you? You don't even know her."

"I still hate her," Kikimra insisted.

Little Yaga sighed; at times Kikimra could be so unreasonably stubborn that it was hard to deal with her.

"Did you see how Sean was looking at her?" Kikimra asked. Her eyes had turned red with anger, and Little Yaga was glad her friend had no powers at the moment. Fortunately, Kikimra seemed to have forgotten she could seek the help of Scraggard's ring.

"Wow," Little Yaga said. "I get it now: you're jealous!"

"So what if I am?" Kikimra asked defiantly. "What difference does it make which girl we bring to the Forest as long as Scraggard gets his energy source?"

"Where's Scraggard's ring?" Little Yaga asked, suddenly changing the topic.

"Right here." Kikimra put out her right hand, where Scraggard's ring was gleaming on her ring finger. "Why?"

"Give it to me."

"What for?"

"Just give it to me—I want to see it."

"It's exactly like yours."

"Give it to me!" Little Yaga demanded.

Kikimra looked annoyed, but she tried to take the ring off.

"I can't," she said. "It's stuck to my skin."

Little Yaga attempted to take hers off, and also was unable to do so. She remembered how, back in the Forest, Leesho blew on the ring and it easily slid off her finger. She could've done the same thing now if only at the moment she weren't as powerless as a human.

"Here you are!" Ashley said, walking into the foyer. "I've been looking all over for you! Are you all right?"

"Fine." Little Yaga nodded.

"What are you guys doing?" Ashley saw Kikimra trying to remove her ring and said, "If you wet your finger with soapy water, it'll slide off by itself. When you're done, come back to the party. Most of the guests are here. And pizza's coming!"

Little Yaga and Kikimra soaped their fingers, and the rings slipped off with amazing ease.

"These humans know a few tricks that sure work like magic," Kikimra said.

"I know. Weird, isn't it?" Little Yaga took both rings and looked around the foyer. In the corner near the stairs, she saw a tall plant in an ornate pot. She went over there and stuck the rings deep into the cool soil.

⊰⊱

That very second, the built-in screen before Scraggard the Immortal went pitch-black; a few bits of soil fell onto the marble floor near his throne, and the smell of moist earth filled the hall. Scraggard rose, went up to the screen, and touched it with both hands.

"What's going on there?" he muttered, wiping his muddy palms on his robe.

⊰⊱

"What are you doing?" Kikimra exclaimed. She went to dig her ring out of the pot, but Little Yaga clutched her wrist.

"Don't," she said. "Let me tell you something."

"What?" Kikimra asked, irritated, trying to free her wrist, but Little Yaga squeezed it harder.

"Let's get out of here."

"Ouch!" Kikimra cried. "You're hurting me. Let go!"

Little Yaga loosened her grip. "I'm sorry," she said, seeing the purple indentations her clawlike nails had left on Kikimra's skin. "I didn't mean to."

"You could've fooled me," Kikimra snarled, rubbing her wrist as she followed Little Yaga into a dark room off the foyer. The room looked like a library or an office. The walls were lined with overcrowded bookshelves. A large desk in the corner was strewn with papers. Little Yaga closed the door behind them, and the ceiling lights lit up, momentarily blinding the girls.

"How'd you do that?" Kikimra asked, squinting against the sudden brightness. "Have you got your powers back?"

"I didn't do anything," Little Yaga said, bewildered. "Those candles just lit up on their own."

Looking up at the ceiling, Kikimra said, "Hey, those things aren't candles! How bizarre! I wonder what they are and how they work."

Little Yaga looked up, too, and studied the luminescent bulbs in the recessed lighting.

"I've no idea," she finally said.

Kikimra looked around and whispered, "Listen, I think we're missing something about humans. They aren't as simple as they seem at first. To be honest with you, I think they've got powers that are stronger than ours."

"Then why does Rat at school lies to us about humans having no powers?" Little Yaga asked.

"I don't know." Kikimra shook her head. "But I'll tell you one thing: we ought to be very careful around here, because we don't really know what we're dealing with."

Just then, on the corner of the desk, a screen that the girls hadn't noticed before lit up and started ringing. Two circles, one green and one red, popped up on the background.

Little Yaga panicked and looked at Kikimra, who shook her head.

"Ignore it!" she whispered hoarsely, and the girls tried to, but the screen kept ringing, so Little Yaga leaned over and touched the red circle with her finger. The ringing stopped.

"How did you know to do that?" Kikimra asked.

"Lucky guess."

"Smarty-pants."

The screen turned back to black. The girls did a high five, but only seconds later, the screen lit up again. The ringing sounded three times louder than before. Little Yaga grumbled, leaned over, and touched the green circle. Instantly, a vaguely familiar-looking boy, but whom she could've sworn she'd never seen in her life, popped up on the screen before her.

"Hi there." He smiled. "Where's Ashley?"

"She's with her guests."

"Oh, and who are you?"

"I'm Little Yaga, and this is my friend, Kikimra."

"Hi, Little Yaga. Hi, Kikimra." The boy seemed unfazed by their exotic names. "I'm Eric!"

"Hi, Eric," the girls said as they curtsied. "Nice to meet you."

"Same here. Listen, can you do me a favor and tell Ashley I'm running a few minutes late?"

"Sure," the girls answered in unison.

"Great, thanks—see you in a few!" Eric's face disappeared from the screen, which made a funny sound and turned black again.

Kikimra looked at Little Yaga.

"What was that?" she asked.

"What?"

"The screen! It's almost like Scraggard's—not as big, but still…This is so strange."

Kikimra's eyes were glaring. "These humans have magic objects all over the place!"

"You know," Little Yaga said. "I'm beginning to think Rat is clueless about humans. He says they have no powers, but to be honest, I don't think he's ever been out of the Forest."

"I don't think he's ever been out of that rat hole of his they call our school," Kikimra said, taking Little Yaga's observation a step further.

"I know, right? Anyway, let's get out of here." Little Yaga headed for the door.

Kikimra was about to follow suit, but she suddenly stopped and said, "Wait a second. Weren't you going to tell me something?"

Now Little Yaga halted, too, and swirled around to face Kikimra.

"Yes, of course," she replied. For a moment she hesitated, unsure of how to begin. "Listen," she said at last, "let's not take any of the girls to the Forest with us. I mean, why should we, anyway?" She shrugged her shoulders.

"Because that's what we've been sent here for," Kikimra reminded her. "And if we don't, we'll be in trouble."

"But I feel sorry for those girls. You know what's going to happen to them, right? They'll become living zombies and have to spend the rest of their lives in Scraggard's palace—how dreadful!"

"And if we *don't* bring the girls," Kikimra countered, a thin trickle of smoke coming out of her mouth, "Scraggard will use one of *us* as his energy source."

"No, he won't. Scraggard only feeds off human or animal energy, and we're neither, so we've got nothing to worry about."

"What if you're wrong?" Kikimra leaned toward Little Yaga, her breath now scorching hot. "What if you've got some human makeup in you? The tiniest bit is enough for Scraggard's purposes. How can you be sure you're human-free?"

"How can *you*?" Little Yaga asked, leaning away from Kikimra.

"I can't, and that's why I'd like to bring Sonya back with me."

"What have you got against that girl?"

Kikimra giggled, let out a final puff of smoke, and said, "Everything."

Popcorn

By now, the kitchen and family room were full of teenagers, all talking and shrieking with laughter. They were very loud, but the music was louder still, causing the china in the kitchen cabinets to rattle and jump up and down to the beat. Little Yaga and Kikimra covered their ears with their hands. They hadn't heard that much noise even during the First Forest War against the seven-headed dragons and the Second Forest War against the deep-sea army!

"There you are," Ashley said, stepping out of the crowd on seeing them. "I thought I'd lost you again!" She was hollering, but even so, Little Yaga and Kikimra could barely hear her. "Where have you been?"

"We've got a message for you from Eric."

"Is he running late?"

"How do you know?"

"He's always late. I can't wait till he gets his driver's license, but that's not for another few years."

"What's a driver's license?"

"You don't know?"

The girls shook their heads and Ashley explained, "It's a document that allows people to drive."

"Drive what?"

"A car, of course—what else?"

"Oh yeah, a car—of course!" Little Yaga exclaimed, pretending she'd known all along. She and Kikimra looked at each other and remembered Leesho telling them about those four-wheeled noisy and stinky creatures.

"How does he get around now?" Kikimra asked, genuinely curious.

"His mom drives him," Ashley answered. "She's one of our school counselors. She's a sweetheart. I truly love her, but there's something wrong with her left leg. When she rushes, she walks with a limp. She hates that, so she moves extra slow. I try not to get annoyed when Eric's being late, but sometimes I can't help it."

"Who's Eric, anyway?"

"Oh, he's my boyfriend. He's *so* good. When you meet him in person, you'll like him right away; everybody does."

"Hey, Ashley!" someone called out.

All three girls turned in the direction of the voice and saw Sean waving at his sister from the couch.

"Come over here!" he shouted. "Somebody wants to wish you a happy birthday!"

"Sorry, girls," Ashley said with a smile, "but I've got to go."

"Sure. Go. Do you need any help?"

"Yes, please. Thanks so much!" Ashley opened a kitchen cabinet and took out a flat paper pack that emitted a strange odor. "Could you pop this in the microwave?"

"What is it?" Little Yaga asked, carefully taking the pack with her two fingers and holding it at arm's length like she might a poisonous snake.

"Come on, it's not a bomb—it's only popcorn!" Ashley laughed. "Put it in the microwave and push the popcorn button—that's all."

"What's a microwave?"

"Girls," Ashley exclaimed with a laugh, "you are as unique as your names! A microwave's a speedy oven."

"But how long do we keep this thing in the speedy oven?"

"Until it's done!"

"How do we know when it's done?"

"The microwave knows. It's not as advanced as the stove in your forest—it doesn't talk, but it'll shut off when the popcorn's ready."

"Really?" Little Yaga and Kikimra looked at each other, astonished. "By itself?"

"Yes, really!"

"Your place isn't at all how we'd imagined it," Little Yaga said. "And where's that magic microwave?"

"Over there, above the stove—thanks, girls." Ashley smiled again and rushed away to the other room.

Little Yaga placed the paper pack on the glass tray of the microwave, closed the door, and pushed the popcorn button. Suddenly, a strange popping sound filled the kitchen. It was as loud as the pounding hooves of the Immortal's herd of wild buffalo. She stiffened with terror; Kikimra, white as a sheet, stuck her fingers in her ears. The girls looked frantically around. To their astonishment, everyone else was oblivious to the noise.

"What is it?" Little Yaga whispered.

"I don't know," Kikimra replied hoarsely.

They tried to peer through the opaque window in the microwave door but couldn't see a thing.

A few minutes later, the microwave beeped loudly and then fell silent; the word *End* appeared on the small rectangular display where the clock had been.

"Open the door," Little Yaga asked Kikimra, but the latter shook her head, no.

"Girls," Ashley called as she waved from the family room, "if the popcorn's ready, bring it over."

Little Yaga took a deep breath, cautiously opened the microwave door, and gasped. Kikimra peeked in, and her eyes bulged out; the once-flat pack now looked like an inflated balloon, giving off an odor that was unpleasantly sweet. Turning to Kikimra, Little Yaga said, "I don't wanna touch it."

"I don't, either." Kikimra stepped away and hid her hands behind her back.

Little Yaga tightened her lips, wrinkled her nose, and with the same two fingers as before, she pulled the hot pack out. She carried it over to the family room, holding it as far away from herself as possible. Ashley popped the pack open and held it out to Little Yaga and Kikimra, inviting them to try some of the odd-looking things in it.

Kikimra recoiled—nothing in the world would make her taste *that*. Out of politeness, Little Yaga took one piece and sniffed it.

"Smells OK," she told Kikimra. "Here, see for yourself." When Kikimra stubbornly refused, Little Yaga put it in her mouth and started chewing while Ashley and her guests watched in amusement.

"Not bad," Little Yaga admitted, finally swallowing the piece of popcorn, and everybody laughed.

"Hey, guys," one of the girls said, "you must be from a pretty strange forest if people there don't know what popcorn is!"

"It must be an enchanted forest," another girl joked, and everybody laughed again.

"No!" Kikimra and Little Yaga cried together.

"It's a regular, normal forest," Kikimra said, "like any other."

"Not exactly," Ashley started to say. She wanted to recount what she'd gone through when she was lost there, but a new guest arrived. Little Yaga and Kikimra recognized him at once as Eric from the screen in the office. He wasn't too tall, but he was still lanky. He had a bright smile, a square chin, hazel eyes, and a full head of dark-brown hair.

Once again, Little Yaga thought his face was vaguely familiar, even though she was sure she'd never seen him before.

Mrs. Rosebar

Suddenly, Little Yaga smelled a strange odor and looked at Kikimra. Her nostril was twitching; she must've smelled it, too. It was a very strong human odor. Little Yaga turned in the direction of the smell and saw a slender woman with black hair, black eyes, and a long neck coming through the doorway; her gait was very slow. She entered the room and suddenly stopped as if she'd come up against an invisible barrier. She sharply turned her head and looked at Little Yaga in wide-eyed surprise, but then, quickly regaining her composure, she smiled and approached Ashley.

"Hello, my dear," she said. "Happy birthday!"

Ashley gave her a hug.

"Thank you, Mrs. Rosebar."

"Lisa wishes you a happy birthday, too. She wanted to come, but you know she's away on a school trip."

"Oh, that's sweet," Ashley said. "Please tell her I love her and that we'll get together when she's back."

"I will," Mrs. Rosebar promised, opening her purse. "Sweetheart, let me give you your birthday present."

Ashley blushed. "You don't have to."

"I know I don't," the woman said as she fumbled around in her purse, finally pulling out a neatly wrapped little box, "but I want to." She handed the box to Ashley.

Ashley tore off the wrapping paper, opened the box, and looked inside. There she found a bracelet made of tiny gold acorns strung on a delicate gold chain. Ashley took it out, and Eric helped her fasten it around her wrist; the acorns sparkled liked tiny gold stars under the bright overhead light.

"It's awesome," Ashley exclaimed, extending her arm and admiring the shimmering bangle. "I love it!"

"It's a charm bracelet," Mrs. Rosebar explained. "It'll bring you luck—if you still believe in lucky charms in our sophisticated days," she added with a chuckle. "Anyway, it looks good on your wrist. Enjoy."

"Thank you so much!" Ashley gave Mrs. Rosebar another hug.

"Be ready for a lot of luck," Eric commented sarcastically.

"For that I'm always ready," Ashley told him with a smile.

"Eric, what'd *you* give Ashley for her birthday?" Sonya asked.

"He painted a portrait of me," Ashley replied for Eric. "It's downstairs in my game room—wanna see it?"

"Sure!"

"OK, dear," Mrs. Rosebar said, squeezing Ashley's hand gently. "I'm glad you like the bracelet. I'll get going now, and you enjoy your party." She turned around and slowly walked out the door without giving Little Yaga or Kikimra another glance.

In the Game Room

Ashley's game room wasn't like anything Little Yaga or Kikimra had ever seen. It was huge! There was a sea of lights, blinking and glimmering all over, and three of the walls were painted in all the shades of the rainbow. One of them was hung with the kind of screen Scraggard the Immortal had, only much bigger. There were multicolored sacks strewn all over the floor. Everybody called them "beanbags." Little Yaga thought them hideous, but many of the kids plopped down, sank into them, and looked comfortable and happy. There were a few leather rocking chairs without any legs, rocking back and forth right on the floor. They were outfitted with colored wires, which were connected to what looked like colorful arcs with rounded pads at the base of each side. Everybody called them "head-phones." A few of the kids settled down in those chairs, put the headphones over their heads and ears, and instantly started jerking their arms and legs, as though stricken with some peculiar disease.

A life-size portrait of Ashley adorned the fourth wall. Her eyes gleamed under the flickering lights, and her skin absolutely glowed, while her slightly opened mouth seemed to be moving. The portrait was so lifelike, it looked like her widespread arms were ready to hug everyone in the room. If Ashley herself hadn't been standing right next to the painting, Little Yaga could easily have mistaken it for the real girl.

"It's amazing," she said in astonishment. "Eric, you're very good. I know what I'm talking about. My grandmother owns a few works of art, and your painting is not any worse. You're really very talented!"

"Thank you, Little Yaga," Eric said, trying not to show her how flattered he was. "What sort of artwork does your grandmother have?"

"Mostly paintings that were gifts from her artist friends. She has quite a big collection, but she never shows it to anyone. She keeps it upstairs, in the attic."

"Interesting. Has your grandmother been friends with anybody famous? Is she an artist herself?"

"No, she isn't. To be honest, my grandmother's pretty ugly now, but apparently, she was beautiful when she was young, and a lot of artists wanted to paint her portrait."

"I've been studying art. Do you remember any of their names?"

"Only the ones I like the most," Little Yaga said, thinking, "like Leonardo, Vincent, Pablo, and there's another one...what's his name..."

She looked at Kikimra, hoping she might know, but Kikimra shrugged her shoulders and shook her head.

"Oh yes," Little Yaga remembered, "it's Sandro."

Shocked, Eric stared blankly at Little Yaga.

"You mean, your grandmother received gifts from da Vinci, van Gogh, Picasso, and Botticelli?" he asked once he was able to speak again.

Everybody around them stopped talking and looked at Little Yaga. She stood there, blinking, until she noticed that Kikimra, gloomy as a cloudy sky, was biting her lower lip—always a sign of agitation.

Little Yaga had stuck her foot in her mouth.

"Did I say that?" she asked, thinking feverishly.

"Did you not?" Eric asked back.

"I never said da Vinci, van Gogh, Picasso, and Botticelli. I only said Leonardo, Vincent, Pablo, and Sandro."

"But those are their first names."

"Maybe so," Kikimra intervened, "but not *only* theirs. Leonardo is our art teacher, and Sandro is our school custodian, but they're also artists…"

"Whereas Vincent and Pablo," Little Yaga said, gratefully picking up where Kikimra had left off, "they're our wolves."

"What?" Eric and a few other kids asked.

Little Yaga bristled. She couldn't believe she'd just said that. Pablo and Vincent were indeed wolves, the leaders of the two rival packs. They'd been named after Picasso and van Gogh—Pablo for looking like the wolf in Picasso's etching *The Wolf* and Vincent for his missing ear. However, Little Yaga should've known better than to just blurt it out. She was afraid to look at Kikimra, knowing how furious she must be. She was sure her friend was using all her willpower to keep from letting fumes out of her mouth in front of the humans.

"Little Yaga meant the *Wolfs*," she heard Kikimra say. "Pablo and Vincent Wolf. They're brothers, and both are good artists."

"Are they famous?" somebody asked.

"I wouldn't think so." Kikimra shook her head lightheartedly. "They're not *that* good."

"Let's see," Sean pulled a mysterious-looking little device out of his pocket and touched it with his finger. The device lit up. Kikimra was amazed! She could never light anything up with just a touch of her finger; she would need a snap and an incantation. She was growing convinced that these humans were more powerful than the Foresters. Meanwhile, Sean touched the screen again, summoning a whole fleet of multicolored dancing squares. Then the squares disappeared, and with every touch, the screen would change—from being blank, to being covered with words, then with pictures, and then it was covered with words and pictures combined. Kikimra suddenly realized it was some kind of a magic looking glass. She'd only ever heard of them, and she was stunned to see one in the hands of a human.

After fiddling around with the device for a while, Sean finally said, "Let's see if Siri knows."

Instantly jealous, Kikimra asked, "Who's Siri?"

"My personal secretary," Sean answered with a chortle. Then he spoke loudly to the device, "Hey, Siri, who are the Wolf brothers?"

"I don't know," a mechanical voice replied.

Kikimra wasn't surprised that Sean's magic looking glass could talk; she knew they all did. She was surprised it didn't know the answer. After all, the whole point of having one was to get an answer to any question you could think of.

"Very bad, Siri," Sean scolded his "looking glass".

"I am sorry," the mechanical voice responded.

"It's OK," Sean relented.

"Aren't you going to snap it away?" Kikimra asked.

"What do you mean?"

"Your magic looking glass. It's not doing what it's supposed to, so get rid of it and snap yourself a new one instead." Kikimra tried to snatch Sean's cell phone away from him.

"Hey, wait a minute," he objected and raised his arm high above Kikimra's head.

At that point, Kikimra wished she was able to extend her bony leg and show him how tall she could be if she wanted to.

"Nothing's wrong with my phone. If Siri doesn't know the answer, we'll ask Google."

"Who is this Google?" Kikimra asked. "Is he some kind of a wizard?"

"You've got that right." Sean laughed. He touched the screen a few more times and said, "Here we go—I told you Google would know: the Wolf brothers, Pablo and Vincent, are the owners of the Exotic Meats Shop. Is that them?"

Sean showed Kikimra the screen. She peered at the picture of two smiling men in fur vests, with knives in their hairy hands, standing in front of the hanging carcasses of the slaughtered animals. Kikimra noticed how sharp their teeth were. One of them had a short and spiky haircut, and the other had hair down to his shoulders. Kikimra had a feeling she'd met them before, but she couldn't imagine where or how.

"Exotic Meats Shop?" Eric asked. "That's where my mother buys all her meat. She says they have the best variety and the freshest meat of any store in the area. I had no idea the butchers were also artists. I wonder if my mom knows."

The Dancing Game

"Hey, Ash, what did your parents give you?" one of Ashley's girlfriends asked.

"Gaming Place Action Five, with a lot of dancing games. We should play some—they're fun!"

A few girls sprang to their feet.

"Cool! Let's play one now!" they exclaimed, practically in unison. "Come on, let's dance!"

"Girls," Ashley asked, looking at Little Yaga and Kikimra, "do you like dancing?"

"I don't think so," Little Yaga answered, shaking her head. "I've never tried."

"I haven't either," Kikimra admitted. "We don't dance in the Forest."

"Really?" Ashley felt sorry for her forest guests. "Let me tell you something: you live in the most boring place on earth. Dancing's so much fun! I'll teach you. You'll love it—I promise."

She went over to the cabinet by the huge screen and picked up an elongated stick similar to those she and Sean had used before.

"It's the witchcraft dance series," she said aiming the stick at the box standing on the floor near the cabinet.

"The witchcraft dance?" Little Yaga and Kikimra cried out. "What do you mean?"

"You'll see!"

Ashley pushed one of the buttons on the stick, and instantly, the huge screen lit up displaying a luscious meadow, with a bonfire right in the middle; "Come Closer" blinked in the corner. Ashley, Little Yaga, Kikimra, and a few other girls stepped up closer and saw themselves on the screen, standing around the fire. Now "Start the Game" popped up in place of the first words.

Little Yaga and Kikimra's jaws dropped. They couldn't grasp how it was possible for all of them to be in Ashley's game room and on the screen at the same time. Even Scraggard the Immortal was unable to be in two places at once!

"It's not us up on the screen," Ashley explained. "It's only our images."

"What's *images?*"

Ashley wished she knew a short answer. "An image is like a reflection in the mirror," she said, hoping her explanation wasn't too far from the truth. She pressed on another button, and immediately, a loud croaking sound filled the room. A large black bird appeared above the bonfire. Slowly flapping its wings, the bird began descending. As soon as it touched the ground, it turned into a young woman wearing a black gown and a pointy hat. She turned to the girls and shrieked, "Are you ready?"

"Yes, we are!" shouted the girls in the room and their images on the screen.

Little Yaga and Kikimra remained silent.

"Are you ready?" Ashley asked with a smile.

"Ready for what?" Little Yaga asked.

"To dance!"

The bird-woman on the screen waved her arms, and the images of the girls around her, including Little Yaga's and Kikimra's, were suddenly clad in black gowns and pointy hats, too.

Little Yaga looked down at herself; she was still wearing Ashley's shorts.

"What's going on up there?" she asked, staring at the screen in bewilderment. "Who is this woman?"

"Don't worry," Ashley answered, calming her. "She's just a cartoon character. This is only a game, a dancing game. Watch what she's doing and repeat after her. It'll be fun! Look!"

The bird-woman shook one of her arms, and a tiny flute fell out of her sleeve. She caught it before it hit the ground, brought it up to her lips, and began blowing. The sounds that came out of this miniature instrument were unexpectedly loud. The bird-woman began waving her arms and hopping up and down to the rhythm. The girls in the room and their images on the screen copied everything she did. The louder the music played, the higher the woman and the girls hopped, and the more the gowns on the screen flapped. They now looked rather like fluttering wings than gowns. Suddenly, the image of the girl hopping the highest turned into a bird, and her gown indeed became her wings. The new bird circled above the bonfire and flew away.

One after another, the images hopping the highest turned into birds and flew away until only the motionless figures of Little Yaga and Kikimra remained by the bonfire. The bird-woman stopped playing the flute, pointed it at Little Yaga and Kikimra, and burst into laughter. "LOSERS" appeared in the corner of the screen and floated across, flashing.

Ashley turned to Little Yaga and Kikimra.

"Don't take it personally," she said. "It's only a game. In a minute, there will be another round with real music, and you'll get your chance to win, too."

"Ashley," Sean interrupted his sister, "I get that it's your birthday and everything's about you today, but why don't we play at least one racing game?"

"You're absolutely right," Ashley replied. "It's my birthday, and I hate racing games."

"That's not fair!"

"It wouldn't be fair if it was *your* birthday."

"What's a racing game?" Kikimra asked.

"You don't know?" Sean gave Kikimra a sympathetic look.

"Nope."

"I don't, either," Little Yaga confessed.

"There's nothing to know," Ashley said, pouting and turning both her thumbs down. "Bo-ring."

"Your dancing is what's boring." Imitating the girls, Sean wiggled his hips and shook his shoulders. A few of the kids laughed.

"Not funny," Ashley snapped.

"In your opinion."

Ashley looked at Little Yaga and Kikimra.

"Do you really want to play a racing game?"

"What is it?"

"Nothing special. You just press buttons on the remote, and the cars on the screen race one another and crash. Boring."

"Fun!" Sean exclaimed, smiling from ear to ear.

"Is it like riding in a car?" Kikimra asked.

"Not exactly—why?"

"I know I'd be scared, but I'd like to know what it feels like to ride in a car."

"You mean you've never been in a car?" Sean asked.

"Never."

"Wow," was all he could say at first. Then he added, "Lucky for you, my dad taught me to drive. I'll give you a ride in my mom's car. Only don't ever tell, or else I'll be in big trouble. Let's go!"

"Now?" Kikimra's eyes sparkled. "With you?"

"Why not?"

"Not now, Kikimra, please," Little Yaga begged.

"How is it possible you've never been in a car?" Ashley looked bemused. "I can't imagine that."

"There are no cars in the Forest."

"How do you get around over there, by horse?" asked one of Ashley's friends.

"Mostly on foot."

"Now I get it," Sean declared, beaming as if he'd just had a brilliant idea. "Your forest is like Amish country—all natural, with nothing modern or artificial. Everything's healthy and pure. You know what your forest is?" Sean looked closely at Kikimra.

"What?"

"A magical place."

"Actually, you're right; our Forest really is a magical place."

"I'm dying to see it."

"You're invited to our next party, remember?"

"Sure."

"Am I invited, too?" Sonya asked, putting her arm around Sean's waist.

"Of course, you are," Kikimra replied sweetly. "I told you you don't have to wait for a party; you can come back to the Forest with us even tonight if you'd like."

"Kikimra's joking," Little Yaga said just as sweetly. "Nobody's coming back with us tonight because it'll be very late. I think we can all agree on that." Turning to Sonya, she said, "You'll come to the Forest with Sean, OK?"

"Can't wait!"

"I can't, either!" Kikimra exclaimed. She couldn't help snapping her teeth, but she resisted the impulse to let some fumes out of her nose, just for the heck of it.

The Uninvited Guest

"Ashley!" somebody hollered from upstairs. "Stanley's here. He's outside in the driveway."

"What? No way! He wasn't supposed to come. I asked Casey to tell him not to!"

"Obviously, he ignored the message," Eric said. He got up from the beanbag and came over to Ashley.

"Why is he here?" she asked anxiously. "He's going to ruin my party."

"Don't worry—he won't," Eric promised. "I'll take care of it. You stay here with your guests." He started up the stairs.

"Be careful!" Ashley hollered. "Stanley's crazy."

"Relax," Eric replied and disappeared behind the door.

"Who's Stanley?" Little Yaga asked.

"A real jerk!" Ashley said fervidly. "He's been stalking me for the past few months. He knows I have a boyfriend, but he doesn't care. He wants me to be with *him*. He says he's willing to wait until Eric and I break up. I told him that I'm in love with Eric and that we aren't breaking up. And you know what he said?"

Little Yaga shook her head.

"He said, 'Ashley, you never know what may happen in life. What if there's an accident and Eric is no more? But don't you worry—I'll always be here for you.'" Ashley shivered. "When he said that, he scared me to death."

"He's a jerk, all right," Little Yaga agreed.

Ashley looked anxious.

"I am afraid he'll hurt Eric somehow. I'd better go and see what's going on up there."

She ran upstairs. Little Yaga, Kikimra, and all the other guests followed.

Even before she got to the last step, Little Yaga heard someone cry, "Oh my God!"

When she finally reached the top of the staircase, she saw a trail of red drops on the floor, leading from the front door into the kitchen.

"What is this?" she asked, turning to Kikimra.

"I don't know." Kikimra shrugged as she looked over her shoulder at Ashley's friends, who were filing up the stairs from the basement, one by one.

"What's this on the floor?" she asked one of the girls.

"Oh my God!" The girl gasped. "Blood!"

"But it's red," Little Yaga said.

"What color is it supposed to be?" the girl asked, bewildered.

"I'm not sure," Little Yaga admitted. "I've never seen blood before."

She followed the girl into the kitchen and saw Eric standing at the sink with his head tilted back. A piece of paper towel over his chin and lip was soaked with blood. Ashley stood by his side, on the verge of tears.

"What happened?" someone asked.

"It's all my fault," Ashley said, sobbing. "I should've stopped him—I knew he could get really hurt."

Eric tossed the soaked piece into the garbage and smirked as he said, "I'll live."

"Let's call the police," somebody suggested.

"Come on," Eric said. "It's only a cut—it'll heal."

"Why didn't you duck?" Sean asked.

"It happened too fast. He punched me before I could even see him—he jumped out from behind your dad's car. I guess he was hiding there."

"Was there anybody else outside?"

"Nope."

"He's a disgusting coward!" Ashley exclaimed, making two fists and shaking them in front of her face. "I wish I could get a hold of him."

"What would you do?" Eric inquired.

"Knock him down!"

"He's twice your size."

"It doesn't matter."

"Listen, let me tell you something that'll cheer you up: he won't be able to sit on his behind for the next couple of weeks, OK?" Eric wiped the tears from Ashley's cheeks. "Feeling better?"

"A little." She smiled through her tears.

"Good." Eric smiled back, and everybody laughed.

The Farewell Picture

"It was a nice party," Little Yaga said as she stood with Kikimra in the foyer by the front door.

"Yes, especially the fight." Ashley frowned.

"Forget about it," Eric said. "It was nothing."

"Really, the party wasn't too bad," Kikimra agreed. She turned to look at Sean, and her eyes grew instantly black because she saw his arm resting on Sonya's shoulder.

"Thank you for inviting us," Little Yaga said.

"Thanks for coming."

"Nice meeting you, guys." Sean removed his arm from Sonya's shoulder and came closer to the girls. "Hope to see you again soon—on *your* territory."

"You bet." Kikimra smiled at him, showing her humanlike teeth. Then she grinned at Sonya and wished she had her fangs back. "Remember, Sonya, you are invited, too."

"Thanks, Kikimra." Sonya pulled a "magic looking glass" similar to Sean's, only pink, out of her pocket. "Before you girls go, let me take your picture."

"A picture?" Little Yaga asked.

"I don't think we have time for that," Kikimra objected. She hated posing for pictures. She had only done it twice in her life—once on her first day of school, which had left her with some vague and unpleasant memories, and the second time on the occasion of her parents' wedding anniversary. It was the most boring experience ever. She'd had to sit still for hours while the artist painted her portrait. It was very difficult; her arms and legs—even the bony one—fell asleep, and she kept shaking them and shifting positions in her seat until the artist asked her parents to cut off her oxygen supply for a while to stop her from fidgeting. Her mother didn't want to do that, so she gave Kikimra a final warning, but Kikimra only stayed still for a few minutes. Then, when she started shaking her arms and legs again, her father snapped his fingers in front of her face, and she froze. She could see and hear everything, but she couldn't move or breathe. The artist was happy to be able to finish the portrait on time, and Kikimra promised herself she'd turn him into a paintbrush as soon as she could move again. Unfortunately, by the time her father restored her supply of oxygen, the artist had gone, and there was nothing she could do about it.

Kikimra had shared that horrible experience with Little Yaga, who was thankful that Big Yaga had never made her pose for a picture.

"Everybody say *cheese*," Sonya hollered, raising her "magic looking glass" to the eye level. "Girls, look over here and smile!"

Little Yaga and Kikimra gaped at Sonya, and they were instantly blinded by a flash of bright light.

"What was that?" Little Yaga whispered, clutching Kikimra's elbow.

"I'm turning her into a toad as soon as I get my powers back," Kikimra promised.

When the momentary darkness in their eyes cleared, Little Yaga and Kikimra saw everybody standing beside Sonya, staring at her "looking glass".

"Girls, come over," Ashley called them. "Take a look. You came out great!"

Reluctantly, Little Yaga and Kikimra approached Sonya, and to their astonishment, they saw a shockingly accurate likeness of themselves, looking totally flustered but absolutely precise, right down to the last, most insignificant detail.

"How is it possible to create such a picture in no time at all?" Kikimra asked.

"Magic," Sean said, wiggling his fingers at her as though he were conjuring up a spell.

"But you humans—I mean *we* humans—we don't have magical powers," Kikimra said.

"Apparently, we do," Sean whispered mysteriously.

"Stop it." Ashley slapped her brother on the shoulder. "The girls will be afraid to walk home."

Sean laughed out loud.

"I'm only kidding, girls," he said. "The world is nothing but a dull, predictable place. Go on home, and don't be afraid. Your forest is a safe haven where, as you well know, there's no place for miracles or magic."

Back to the Forest

As the girls strolled toward the winding footpath that was supposed to take them back to the Forest, Kikimra grumbled and complained. "I can understand why we didn't take Ashley with us. She's too sweet, and Scraggard doesn't deserve her energy. But I will never get why we couldn't take Sonya."

Little Yaga didn't respond; she knew it was better to keep quiet when her friend was in such a sulky mood.

"I don't know what's going to happen to us when we get back home," Kikimra continued, growing gloomier with every step. "I only know it's not going to be pretty."

Again, Little Yaga didn't say anything, but she knew Kikimra was right. The girls finally reached the footpath. Just as they were about to step onto it, Kikimra stopped dead in her tracks and looked at Little Yaga in horror.

"The rings!" she exclaimed.

"Oh no," Little Yaga muttered, stiffening with fright and suddenly feeling weak in the knees.

"It's all your fault," Kikimra snarled, letting black fumes out of her mouth—she didn't have to restrain herself any longer. "Why did you make us take them off?"

"To be free of Scraggard's prying eyes," Little Yaga replied, her voice quivering. "I'll go back and get them."

"Run! I'll wait for you here."

"Don't you wanna go with me?"

"No. Hurry! It's getting late."

Little Yaga turned around and ran as fast as she could, regretting, as always, that she didn't have an extendable bony leg so that she could run faster.

While she was gone, Kikimra paced back and forth along the meadow, shivering so violently that her teeth clattered. She was unable to think of anything but Scraggard's icy-cold look and his warning about the rings.

Little Yaga returned, her face beet red and her hair a mess, just as Kikimra, losing patience, was about to go after her.

"I don't know where everybody went, but the house was empty," Little Yaga managed to rasp. She was winded and had to stop for a few seconds to catch her breath. "They left the door unlocked, and I went in."

"Good. Where are the rings? Did you get them?"

"Nope," Little Yaga said, shaking her head. "I didn't. They weren't there. Neither yours nor mine."

Kikimra stared at her friend in silence for a while before shouting so loudly, she scared the birds out of a nearby tree.

"What?" A thick cloud of black smoke gushed out of her mouth.

"I looked everywhere, under the pot, behind it, around it—I even dug up the plant, for goodness' sake. The rings weren't there. Gone!"

"Well," Kikimra said, controlling her emotions and sounding almost calm, although a thin trickle of fumes accompanied her every word, "let's go back together and look again. Two pairs of eyes are better than one."

"It'll be a waste of time," Little Yaga objected. "They aren't there."

Out of fear, Kikimra's eyes turned completely black.

"You know we're in big trouble now, and it's all because of you!" she said.

On those words, she turned around and stepped onto the footpath. Little Yaga followed. The very second their feet were firmly planted on the path—when the meadow around them was supposed to turn into the Forest—they heard the sound of running and Ashley's voice shouting, "Girls! Wait! You forgot your clothes!"

Little Yaga and Kikimra stopped, looked at each other, and realized they were still wearing human outfits.

"I'm so glad you didn't get too far," Ashley said, sounding relieved as she approached the footpath. "We walked Sonya home, and when we got back, I saw all of your stuff still in my closet—here you go." She held out a plastic bag. "I put everything in here. You don't have to change right now. You can return my things the next time I see you—at your party! I've heard there's one coming up soon."

Little Yaga wanted to take a step toward Ashley so that she could reach for the bag of clothes, but she found that her feet had sunk into the ground up to her ankles. She tried to pull them out, but they wouldn't budge. She twisted her body around to ask Kikimra to get the bag, but before she could open her mouth, Ashley rushed forward. As both of her feet stepped onto the footpath, the meadow around the three of them transformed into the Forest, and a flock of Swan-Geese swooped down from the sky. They picked Ashley up with their bills and tore back upward. Honking loudly, they disappeared behind the tallest trees. Everything happened in the blink of an eye. Little Yaga and Kikimra looked at each other, speechless, barely able to grasp what they had just witnessed.

The Pinecone

The wind, calm until now, had picked up and was becoming stronger with every gust. The huge tree trunks swayed from side to side more and more violently, and their trembling branches scratched at the sky, as though to scrape a hole through the low, heavy clouds that were hiding the setting sun. A shower of pinecones poured down out of a pine tree, bowing to the right and left, over the girls' heads. One of the cones landed on Little Yaga's big toe, painfully hitting it. Little Yaga winced and looked down. Unlike the others, this one was completely round. Twirling like a top, it jumped over Little Yaga's foot and rolled away, zigzagging between trees and forming a footpath along the way.

"Do you think we should go after it?" Little Yaga asked.

"Definitely." Kikimra nodded.

The girls ran along the brand-new path as it unfurled right before their eyes. They didn't get very far before the path ended at a thick root protruding from the ground. It belonged to a tall elm tree with a dark hollow at the top of the trunk. The cone bounced off the root, leaped into the air, and dove inside the hollow. Little Yaga and Kikimra followed it with their eyes.

"Well," Kikimra said, "let me see where exactly it went."

She snapped her fingers, and her bony leg began extending, slowly raising Kikimra upward. When she reached the hollow, she stuck her head inside.

"What's in there?" Little Yaga hollered staring up.

Kikimra pulled her head out.

"I can't see much—it's dark in there."

"Can you see anything at all?"

"Very little," Kikimra answered, sticking her head in again. "I see some kind of a slide. It's very long and twisted." Kikimra's voice was muffled, and Little Yaga had to strain her ears to hear what she was saying.

"Where does it lead?" she yelled.

"I don't know—it's too dark. I see something glowing all the way down. I think it's the cone, waiting for us. I think we should go in."

"But how will I get up there?" Little Yaga asked. "It's too high for me."

Kikimra snapped her fingers and was instantly standing on the ground, her bony leg having shrunk back to its normal size.

"Hop up on my shoulders," she ordered, "and deflate."

Little Yaga had participated in a deflating session during their gym class once. She didn't particularly enjoy the experience, but she knew she had to make things easier for Kikimra, who was about to lift her all the way up to the hollow. Little Yaga climbed onto her friend's shoulders, and although she wasn't heavy, she felt Kikimra's muscles strain under her weight. Little Yaga plugged her nose and ears and exhaled. Swirls of moist air streamed out of her mouth. She felt her body turning stiff and flat as a piece of cardboard and saw that her fingers, digging into Kikimra's shoulders, left no marks because they had become paper thin. Her flat body was flapping in the wind, and if Kikimra hadn't been holding on to her feet, she could've been blown away like a piece of scrap paper.

Kikimra's bony leg began extending again. When her head was level with the hollow, she transferred Little Yaga's flat body from her shoulders to the top of the slide.

"Inflate," she said.

Little Yaga opened her rigid mouth as wide as she could and inhaled. Streams of cool, fresh air began filling her up, rushing to her head, face, stomach, arms, and legs. Much to her relief, her body was fully restored to its normal three-dimensional shape in less than a minute.

"That's better," she said, moving her head, arms, and legs and also frowning and smiling to make sure all of her parts were functioning as they should.

"What a disgusting feeling," she said. "I hope I won't have to do this again anytime soon."

"So do I," Kikimra agreed. She was standing beside Little Yaga at the top of the slide, watching her bony leg retract.

The girls looked down and saw that something was still flickering all the way at the bottom of the slide.

"I'm sure that's our little cone," Kikimra said.

Little Yaga asked, "Do you want to go down first?"

"Doesn't matter—you can go if you'd like."

And down the slide Little Yaga went. She was gliding so fast that if not for Kikimra's bony leg banging against the slide right behind her, she could've heard the air whistling in her ears. A split second later, the girls reached the bottom. It was pitch-black all around. They couldn't even see their own hands unless they made them glow, but they didn't want to waste their energy.

The flickering thing they had seen from above was indeed the cone; it was hopping up and down, waiting for them. Little Yaga bent down to pick it up, but the cone dodged her hands and rolled away into the darkness. It was rolling much faster now than it had on the ground outside. The girls ran after it. With her bony leg extended, Kikimra was able to keep up with the cone, but Little Yaga had to push herself not to fall behind and get lost in the darkness. She wasn't sure how long they'd been running, but it felt like forever. She was getting very tired. When her legs had grown heavy as logs and she knew she was about to collapse, the cone, glowing in the distance, bounced up against a double door that had suddenly appeared in its way. Each half of the door bore a carved image of Scraggard's haggard face. One of the halves slightly opened, letting a trickle of quivering light in. The girls, weary of darkness, felt a burst of energy and sped forward. In a few moments, they ran through the door and, at once, found themselves puffing and panting right in front of Scraggard the Immortal, who was sitting on his magnificent throne, smiling down at them.

"Welcome back," he said softly, standing up. He looked different; his eyes glared, and his cheeks were tinged with color. His joints were limber again, and he moved as silently as a cat.

"Thank you, ladies," he said. "Great job. Mission accomplished. You can go home now."

Stupefied, Little Yaga and Kikimra curtsied and turned around. The cone was gone, and the gigantic front door of the palace stood open before them. Just as they were about to leave, they heard the Immortal's voice behind them say, "Oh, by the way…"

The girls turned back. Scraggard was still smiling, baring the sharps fangs on both sides of his mouth.

"Kikimra, when I gave you the ring to take to the human town, you asked me a question, remember?"

"What question, Your Scraggardness?"

"You asked," Scraggard reminded her, "if you could keep the ring."

"Yes," Kikimra whispered. She glanced at Little Yaga in dismay and furtively slid her ringless hand into the pocket of her skirt. Just then, she realized she was back in her Forest outfit. She didn't know how or when the switch had happened, but she was glad to be wearing her own clothes again.

"Well," Scraggard said, giving the girls a devious wink, "the answer is yes. Both of you deserve to keep them. Just remember, the rings are very powerful. Don't mess with them. Even I—" Scraggard started to say something but stopped himself mid-sentence. "Never mind. You've had a long, challenging day. Go home now and rest."

He snapped his fingers, and before she could say good-bye to Kikimra, Little Yaga was home. She walked through the gate and climbed up the rickety porch steps. The Hut flung its door wide open for her.

When she entered the kitchen, the Cuckoo Bird stuck her head through her tiny door so far that she almost fell out. Louder than ever, she hollered, "It's seven forty-seven; Little Yaga's home!"

"It's nine fourteen," Little Yaga corrected her.

"It doesn't matter," the Cuckoo Bird yelled. "You're home!"

Big Yaga came out of her bedroom, looking gloomier than ever.

"How come are you so late? Don't I have enough worries in my life without having to drive myself crazy over your safety?" she asked. "Explain, why are you doing this to me?"

Little Yaga wanted to give her grandmother a hug but was afraid of being bitten on the ear for such a human display of affection. She looked around; it was hard to believe she'd left her home only a few hours ago. It seemed she'd been gone for a very long time. She smiled. To her surprise, it felt good to be back and not to think, at least for now, about Ashley, Scraggard, or even Kikimra. Little Yaga was very tired. She went straight to her bedroom, fell onto her wooden-block bed, and fell fast asleep. A few minutes later, Big Yaga came in and covered her granddaughter with a worn out but cozy blanket she'd knitted centuries ago before her hands became crippled by arthritis.

"I don't need her to catch a cold," she mumbled, tucking Little Yaga in.

Surly as she was, she looked down at her sleeping grand-daughter, then suddenly bent down and kissed the girl on the forehead with her dry, wrinkled lips.

"Sleep tight," she muttered before snapping herself out of the bedroom.

At the Laings'

A shley's mother, Mrs. Laing, was sitting on the couch in the family room. The tissue in her hand was wet with tears, which were still streaming down her cheeks. Mrs. Rosebar sat next to her, looking very pale. Mr. Laing, Sean, and Eric, with a bandage on his chin, were in the kitchen talking to three police officers and a detective. A crowd of people had gathered outside, including all the party guests and many other townspeople who'd heard of Ashley's disappearance and volunteered to look for her. They'd searched until dark, and now the police suggested they stop until morning.

Ashley's father and Detective Snyder stood listening to the officers, who'd come up with absolutely nothing. They hadn't found a single footprint or any other sign of Ashley, Little Yaga, or Kikimra—anywhere. It appeared the three girls had vanished without a trace. What's more, all attempts to track the identities of Little Yaga and Kikimra proved futile; nobody knew where they'd come from, and no one had reported them missing. Their pictures, downloaded from Sonya's cell phone, were broadcast on every television channel, but nobody came forward with any information. Perplexed, Detective Snyder dismissed the officers.

"I know how discouraged you are," he said, turning to Mr. Laing, "but all we can do is be patient and keep looking for clues. I'm staying at the precinct tonight. If you have any questions or get any information, call me at once. If I learn anything, I'll give you a buzz. Tomorrow, we'll resume the search."

"But the night's so long—we'll lose too much time," Mrs. Laing said, sobbing. "Why don't we keep searching with flashlights?"

"That would be a waste of batteries and people's energy," the detective replied. "Let the search party rest, and try to get some rest yourself. We'll resume the search tomorrow morning."

"Early in the morning?"

"Yes."

"How early?"

"At dawn."

Mrs. Laing was visibly disappointed. "Isn't there any way to start earlier?" she asked.

"Yes—if we get a reliable tip."

"There must be somebody who knows something about those two girls—whatever their names are." Mrs. Laing turned to Mrs. Rosebar. "What do you think, Jane?"

"I'm sure of that," Mrs. Rosebar agreed, looking somewhat detached.

Detective Snyder patted Mrs. Laing on the shoulder.

"Let me handle the situation, my dear," he said reassuringly. "By the way," he added, "the information concerning the reward has already been announced."

He shook hands with Mr. Laing, waved good-bye to Mrs. Rosebar, and left. As soon as the door closed behind him, Mrs. Laing buried her face in her hands. Her body shuddered violently, and Mrs. Rosebar gave her a hug.

"Now, now," she said gently, "Ashley will come back."

"How do you know?"

"I have a feeling."

"Really?" Mrs. Laing raised her head. There was a glimmer of hope in her eyes, and her tear-stained face brightened a little. "I'm glad to hear you say that. I've always trusted your feelings, Jane."

Mrs. Rosebar squeezed her shoulder in response and added, "Detective Snyder was right, Betsy, you need to rest now."

<hr />

Meanwhile, in Sean's bedroom Eric was busy scrutinizing the rings.

"Where'd you say you found them?" he asked.

"I told you," Sean replied. "I saw them under the radiator when I was cleaning up the dirt from the flowerpot."

"They look pretty old. Could they have belonged to the previous owners?"

"There weren't any," Sean said. "We bought this house brand-new."

"Are you sure they're not your parents' rings?"

"Why would my parents keep their rings under the radiator?"

"To hide them from burglars. No burglar in the world would look for valuables under there."

"Come on," Sean said. "That's a dumb idea."

Just as Eric was about to hand the rings back to Sean, he noticed the two tiny mirrors and the inscriptions on the inner surface of each ring.

"Look at this," he said.

"I wonder what that is." Sean looked at the rings more closely.

"Good question."

"Decorative details?" Sean half asked, half suggested.

"On the inside, where no one can see them?" Eric said. "I doubt it."

"Got any better ideas?"

"Nope, but I hope the answer is simpler than we think."

"I don't think anything," Sean snapped. "I'm sure one of the girls dropped them, and she'll come looking for them tomorrow."

"What about the inscriptions?"

"What about them?"

"I wonder what they say." Eric peered at one of them. "I have a feeling they're important, but the letters are too small to read."

"I'll tell you," Sean said with a smirk. "They say something *very* important, like 'John + Sue = Love,' or whatever—who cares?"

"I guess you're right—here." Eric returned the rings to Sean, who slid them into the back pocket of his jeans.

At that very second, Scraggard the Immortal's screen went black.

At the Rosebars'

Eric sat looking at the picture of Ashley he'd sketched only a month before, during their school's deep-sea fishing trip. She was laughing. Her windblown hair was messy and wet with the salty mist. Her eyes were sparkling, and the dimples in her cheeks were so cute that he wished he could poke them with his finger like he always did. But she was literally out of touch. Her cell phone was off. She wasn't on Facebook, Skype, or Snapchat, and she hadn't replied to any of his desperate WhatsApps. The very idea of her being so completely unavailable hurt. Eric heard his parents whispering in the kitchen, and he knew they were arguing because they only ever whispered when they argued.

Just like Mrs. Laing, Eric disagreed with the detective's decision to halt the search. He also thought they were wasting too much valuable time. Seeing Ashley's picture made him realize that he couldn't simply sit and wait till dawn, doing nothing. He went to the garage and got a flashlight. As he walked past the kitchen on his way back, he heard his father say, "It was bound to happen."

"Yes, it was," Mrs. Rosebar replied, sadly.

"I can only imagine how you must've felt," Mr. Rosebar said quietly.

"I thought I would faint."

"How are you feeling now?"

"Still shaken."

Eric stopped by the kitchen door. What were his parents talking about? What had happened? Was his mother ill? Alarmed, Eric pushed the kitchen door open and walked in. His parents turned to face him, and Eric saw that his mother was very pale.

"Are you OK, Mom?" he asked. "You aren't sick, are you?"

"Not at all." Mrs. Rosebar stood up and kissed him on his cheek. "I am in perfect health, as usual."

"Why are you so pale? And how come you felt like you would pass out?"

"Because of Ashley. I'm worried about her." Seeing the flashlight in Eric's hand, she asked, "What's that for?"

"I want to go out and get some fresh air," he lied.

"Darling," Mrs. Rosebar said softly squeezing her son's shoulder and looking into his eyes, "you won't find her tonight. The detective was right; it'll just be a waste of batteries and your energy."

"Mom, don't you realize that every minute counts? If we wait till morning, it may be too late."

"It won't be too late," Mrs. Rosebar told him with a sigh. "At this point, it won't make any difference whatsoever."

"How can you say that?"

"Because I know."

Chest heaving and nostrils flaring, Eric stood looking at his mother for a minute.

"No," he finally said, "I won't wait till morning. I'm going out now, and I'll look for her until I find her. She can't be too far away."

"Yes, she can," Mrs. Rosebar said woefully as she sat back down. "She is so far away that you won't be able to find her on your own."

Eric didn't ask his mother how she knew. He'd noticed long ago that she had a unique gift for sensing things. And she'd never been proven wrong. Once, when he was younger, he'd asked her if she was a psychic. She'd laughed and said, "Of course not; I'm just wise," and that was a fact. Over the years, Eric had gotten used to her gift and started taking it for granted.

"Fine," he said. "No big deal. If I need help, I'll take Sean with me."

"You'll need a different kind of help, darling." Mrs. Rosebar looked into her son's eyes again. "But it won't be available until morning."

"What kind of help are you talking about?"

When Mrs. Rosebar didn't answer, Eric turned to his father.

"What kind of help is Mom talking about?"

Mr. Rosebar frowned. "I knew this would happen one day. Listen, son, trust your mother, go to bed, and try to get some rest—tomorrow you may have a very rough day."

Reluctantly, Eric obeyed. As soon as he left the kitchen, Mrs. Rosebar stood up. She looked as if she might cry, but her eyes stayed dry.

"I don't want him to go there," she said firmly.

"Neither do I," Mr. Rosebar agreed, "but I don't think we should stop him."

"It's too dangerous!"

"He can handle it; he's a man."

"No," Mrs. Rosebar protested. "He's still only a boy."

"He's a boy in love with a girl who needs his help, and we can't stand in his way. And that's all there is to it."

⊰⊱

Eric was so distraught that he didn't fall asleep until just before dawn. As the early-morning sun squeezed its way through the partially open blinds and stroked his face, trying to wake him, Mrs. Rosebar walked quietly into his bedroom. Fully dressed, as if she were ready to go out, she drew the blinds tightly shut, blocking out the playful rays. She was moving unusually quickly, revealing her limp, which was barely noticeable when she walked slowly. From Eric's bedroom, she hobbled down the stairs, to the garage, where she climbed into an old Volkswagen. Pulling out, she lingered in the driveway for a second or two, and then drove away. A moment later, a wiry figure jumped out of the tree in the front yard, ran across the street, dragged a motorcycle out of the bushes, and hopped on, as if it were a wild horse. Seconds later, the engine roared. Spitting clouds of black smoke through the exhaust, the motorcycle rushed off after the Volkswagen.

⊰⊱

Eric sat up abruptly. With the blackout blinds fully drawn, the room was dark. The digital clock on the wall read 11:07, but Eric wasn't sure if it was morning or night. Either way, he was angry—at himself for sleeping in and at his parents for not waking him. Jumping out of bed, he pulled on a pair of jeans, grabbed a T-shirt, and ran downstairs.

"Why didn't you wake me up?" he demanded, storming into the kitchen.

"Because you needed to rest," Mrs. Rosebar answered calmly.

"What I need is to find Ashley! Every second counts, and I've wasted too much time sleeping!" Pacing the kitchen like a wild animal, Eric was inconsolable.

"You wasted nothing," his mother said, setting her cup of tea on the table. "You've restored your energy for the journey ahead."

"What journey?"

"A very dangerous one, but your father thinks you should go."

"Go where?"

"To save Ashley, of course—isn't that what you want?"

"Yes, that's exactly what I want."

"Fine. Eat your breakfast and go to the Exotic Meats Shop. The owners, Vincent and Pablo, will help you."

"How? Do they have something to do with Ashley's disappearance?" Eric clenched his fists in anger. "I should've known. They've always seemed suspicious to me."

"Stop it this instant," Mrs. Rosebar ordered him. "They have nothing to do with her disappearance, but they've kindly agreed to help you find her."

"I don't understand," Eric insisted. "How can they possibly help?"

"Go there, tell them you're my son, and you'll find out soon enough."

At the Exotic Meats Shop

The Exotic Meats Shop was located in an old barn that had been restored as a commercial space. It was situated on the other side of the meadow that sprawled along Ashley's street. There was no paved access road to the store, so to get there, customers had to cross the meadow by bike or on foot. Eric was cycling down the same path Ashley had taken right before she disappeared. Even though every inch of it had been inspected, he was still looking around, hoping to find a clue that had somehow been missed. When he reached the shop, Sean was already there, wearing the same clothes he had on last night. Now they were all crumpled; he'd obviously slept in them.

"What's the 'urgent matter' you dragged me here for?" Sean asked jadedly.

"We have to talk to the shop owners."

"About what? The shop's closed."

"There's no way—they're supposed to help us find Ashley."

"Are they detectives?"

"No, they're butchers."

"How can they help then?"

"I don't know. My mom told me they would."

"If she says so, it must be true—your mother's never wrong. So, where are they?"

"I've no idea. Let me call my mom—she may know."

As Eric was reaching into his pocket for his phone, he saw someone on a bike riding up the path to the shop. He recognized the rider's smiling face—it was Vincent.

"Sorry, gentlemen," the butcher apologized, jumping off his bike. "I had to step out for a few minutes."

He was a stocky man of average height, with long hair down to his shoulders; his arms and the backs of his hands, right up to his fingers, were overgrown with thick gray fuzz.

"I'll let you in right away. Pablo's inside, packaging meat in the back, so I'm sure he didn't hear you knock."

After Vincent had parked his bike, he went over to the front door, unlocked it with a long, rusty skeleton key, and entered the shop, followed by Eric and Sean.

"Our products are the best and the freshest around," the butcher boasted. "I can assure you, your purchase will have been worth the wait!"

"We're not here to shop, sir," Eric said. "My mother sent us—Jane Rosebar?"

Vincent halted abruptly, then spun on his heel to face the boys. The smile was gone from his face.

"What did you say?" he asked hoarsely.

"My mother, Jane Rosebar, said to tell you I am her son, Eric. She said you'd help me find my friend, Ashley."

"How many sons does your mother have?" Vincent asked.

"Only one—me. Why do you ask?"

"Because earlier this morning, I took another young man to the Forest. He claimed *he* was Jane Rosebar's son."

"To the forest?" Eric asked. "Is Ashley there?"

Vincent nodded.

"Where exactly is this forest? We have to go there—now!"

"Hold on a minute, fellas. Before anybody goes anywhere, I must know who Jane Rosebar's real son is—you," Vincent pointed a hairy finger at Eric, "or the young man who was here earlier."

"I am, of course," Eric said.

"How can I be sure?" Vincent moved in so close to Eric that they were practically nose to nose, causing Eric to lean backward.

"Do you want to talk to my mom?" he asked.

Vincent sniffed the air around the boy's head and said, "There's no need."

He bit his lower lip, exposing his sharp, uneven teeth.

"I've been duped. And my gullibility may have caused us a lot of trouble."

"What do you mean?" Sean asked.

Vincent shook his head. His hair swung from side to side, and the boys noticed that there was something wrong with his left ear; it was either terribly disfigured or missing altogether.

"Never mind," he finally said. "Let's figure out how to get you to the Forest as soon as possible."

"I wonder who was here posing as Eric this morning," Sean said.

"Yes, so do I." Eric turned to Vincent. "What did he look like?"

Vincent snorted and then said, "He was an attractive fellow about your age, tall and bony, with long brown hair and grey eyes. His nose was a little crooked."

"Stanley!" Eric and Sean cried out.

"I can't believe he's after Ashley again," Eric said clenching his teeth.

"Or after the reward for finding her," Sean guessed.

"I didn't do him enough damage last night," Eric muttered, squeezing his fist. "I'd like to tear him to pieces, the rat!"

"You need to get to the Forest, first," Vincent reminded him.

"So how do I get there?" Eric demanded, sticking *his* nose in Vincent's face this time. "Is Ashley in any danger?"

"Let's just say the Forest isn't exactly a resort, gentlemen, and you'll be in danger there, too. Are you prepared to take inconceivable risks and jeopardize your lives? If not, I suggest you go home, get into bed, and pull the blankets over your heads. But if you're ready, let's talk business."

⚓

Pablo was shorter and stockier than Vincent. His bushy mustache hid his upper lip and top teeth. His enormous hands, as rich with gray hair as Vincent's, were lined with a web of thick veins protruding through the hair like road bumps. He came into the shop from the back room, wiping his hands on the dirty apron he was wearing over his fur vest.

Introducing him to the boys, Vincent said, "This is Pablo, my business partner." Then he pointed at Eric, saying, "This is Jane Rosebar's son."

"I remember you," Pablo said in a deep, muffled voice. "Your mom used to bring you along when you were little." He smiled at Eric, exposing his bottom teeth, sharp like penknives. "I would never have recognized you now that you're grown." He extended his hand to Eric, who thought his own hand would be crushed in Pablo's iron grip. The boy managed to conceal the pain. Not a single muscle in his face so much as twitched. Only the very tip of his nose turned red.

Vincent introduced Sean with a nod of his head. "This is Sean, Eric's friend and the girl's brother."

"Good to meet you, pal," Pablo said, looking Sean square in the eye as he gripped his hand. Sean also managed not to flinch—but only just barely.

"Well, boys, looks like you'll handle the journey all right," Pablo said, letting go of Sean's hand. "But there's one problem. Neither of us can take you to the Forest before tomorrow afternoon."

"Are you serious?" Eric couldn't mask his disappointment.

"It's OK," Sean said, pulling his cell phone out of the back pocket of his jeans. "If you give me the address, my Apple Maps will get us there."

"We don't have an exact address," Vincent replied, scratching his chin.

"My phone has the newest version. Give me the names of the cross streets, and we'll be fine."

"I don't think we've got that, either."

"Well," Eric said. "No problem. We're good with regular directions, too. Tell us how to get there, and we'll find our way."

"The directions are very complicated," Pablo explained, coughing into his fist. "You'll get lost if you go without one of us."

Sean looked at Eric and shrugged his shoulders. As he tried to shove his phone back into his pocket, he felt something else in there. He reached in and pulled out the rings he had found under the radiator the night before. He'd forgotten all about them. They lay in his hand, shimmering like dewdrops in the light.

Vincent and Pablo stared at them, wide-eyed.

"Where'd you get those?" Vincent asked.

"They were in the foyer at my house after the party. One of the guests must've lost them."

"Or maybe two," Pablo muttered.

"Two what?" Sean was confused.

"Two of the guests."

"You mean Little Yaga and Kikimra?" Eric asked.

"Exactly," Pablo confirmed.

"I don't like them anymore!" Eric said, his eyes glaring. "I am pretty sure now they are the ones who've kidnapped Ashley."

"I wouldn't be so sure, pal," Pablo objected patting his shoulder. "You better take it easy and consider yourself lucky; looks like you'll be going to the Forest sooner than we thought."

"How much sooner?"

"When did you have in mind?"

"Right now."

"Suit yourself."

The Next Morning: Home

Little Yaga couldn't believe she didn't mind eating the breakfast she'd always hated so much. The normally disgusting mixture of beetles, bugs, bird beaks, claws, and fossilized bones tasted good today because she was eating it at home, in her kitchen, surrounded by her grandmother, the Cuckoo Bird, and the Hut. All three were stunned by her recounting of her adventures in the human town.

"I visited human towns quite frequently in my day," Big Yaga said, "but I never saw humans using magic wands, magic looking glasses, or magic ovens. And I've never heard of them being in two places at the same time—I doubt that even Scraggard the Immortal can do that," she added, giving Little Yaga a dubious look. "You aren't making any of this up, are you?"

"No, Grandma," Little Yaga replied emphatically. "Ask Kikimra—she was there, too."

"It's very hard to believe," the Hut said, reluctant to question the validity of her favorite girl's stories, but they were simply impossible to imagine.

"Maybe you fell asleep at the party, and all of what you're describing was only a dream," Cuckoo Bird suggested. "I dream tons of unimaginable things."

"We're well aware of that," Big Yaga said crossly. "I wish you'd dream about telling us the right time once in a while. I don't know why I'm still feeding you—I should've turned you into a winding clock centuries ago."

The Cuckoo Bird flapped her wings angrily. She wanted to peck on Big Yaga's mole, which she did whenever she felt offended.

"Stop fighting," Little Yaga begged. "I'm so tired of it. By the way, Cuckoo Bird, Kikimra was there, too—did she fall asleep and have the same dream?"

"That's an idea," Big Yaga said. "Let's see what Kikimra has to say about this." She limped over to the counter and picked up her crystal ball.

The ball lit up in her hands. It was cloudy at first, but the clouds soon thinned out, and Little Yaga distinguished three silhouettes—Kikimra's and her parents'—as if through a fog. She could hear the murmur of their voices, too, but she couldn't make out the words. When the fog finally dissipated, Little Yaga was able to see and hear Kikimra and her parents as distinctly as if they were right there in the room with her.

"If you don't believe me, ask Little Yaga," Kikimra was saying, spewing dark smoke out of her mouth with every word. Clearly, she was very agitated. "I'm telling you, you don't have to sit for hours at a time to get your picture done over there. All you have to do is say *cheese*, and it's ready."

"So, *cheese* is a new magic word?" Kikimra's father, Kikimor, laughed, and a puff of dark smoke came out of his mouth, too.

"All right," said Kikimra's mother, Kikimora, gently, "I believe you."

"Well, I don't." Kikimor blew fiery sparks out of his nose. "Humans can't possibly be more powerful than us—they never have been, and they never will be. They must've learned a few tricks to fool innocents like you and Little Yaga. Well, let them learn thousands more; it won't change anything. They'll still only be humans—ambitious creatures but powerless against our spells and conjuring. If you want to be successful and truly powerful, Kikimra, you must learn to distinguish between cheap tricks and true magic. Understood?"

Kikimra moved her head, but Little Yaga couldn't tell if she nodded in agreement or shook it in defiance.

"And by the way," her father continued, "if I wanted an instant picture of you, I'd just snap one myself, like this." He snapped his fingers and at once had a little picture of Kikimra in his hand. "But I wanted one by a real artist."

Big Yaga set the crystal ball back down on the counter; it dimmed, grew cloudy, and was completely opaque again within seconds.

"Kikimor has matured into a fine Forester," Big Yaga mused. "I remember him at Kikimra's age, if not younger. But now he's all grown up and sharp as a tack—he caught on right away that all of those so-called 'miracles' you girls are raving about are nothing but human trickery. As always."

"It was pretty obvious," muttered the Hut.

"Aren't you the clever one!" Big Yaga snapped. "It wasn't so obvious to me."

"Well, that's no wonder," the Cuckoo Bird said with a snide grin.

Big Yaga, breathing heavily, looked at the bird. The knuckles on the hand gripping her stick turned white. Little Yaga was afraid she'd lunge at the bird and stab it with the stick as if it were a sword. But the obnoxious fowl swiftly disappeared behind the tiny door of her clock. Big Yaga shook her stick over her head.

"That's it!" she exclaimed. "You've brought it upon yourself—I'm turning you into a winding clock!"

Just as Big Yaga extended her arm to carry out Cuckoo Bird's sentence, the Hut let out a raucous sneeze and shook violently from her roof down to the foot of her chicken leg. Big Yaga dropped her stick and grabbed the edge of the table so as not to fall.

"What was that?" she asked, steadying herself.

"Sorry," the Hut replied innocently. "I sneezed."

"Why must you always sneeze at the most inappropriate moments?" Big Yaga asked angrily, snatching her stick away from Little Yaga, who'd picked it up off the floor. "I could've done it myself," she grumbled at her granddaughter.

"I'm really sorry," the Hut said. "I didn't mean to interrupt your spell."

But everybody knew that if Big Yaga didn't complete her spell on the spur of the moment, she wouldn't start over again. The Cuckoo Bird sighed in relief from behind her little door and quietly giggled.

"Liar," was all Big Yaga said in response. "Little Yaga," she said, changing the subject once she'd sat back down at the kitchen table, "were there any adults at the party?"

"None. Why?"

"Just wondering. Humans have changed—in my day, children couldn't have a party without an adult chaperone."

"Actually," Little Yaga recalled, "there was one adult who showed up, but only for a few minutes—a woman. She dropped off her son, wished Ashley a happy birthday, and left."

Suddenly, Big Yaga stiffened a little in her seat.

"What was her name?" she asked, trying to sound nonchalant, but Little Yaga sensed the anxiety in her voice.

"I don't remember. She had a weird name."

"What did she look like?"

"Uh…She looked human, I guess."

"What do you mean, you guess? Aren't you sure?"

"I'm sure, Grandma. She looked human."

"Was there anything unusual about her?"

"Not really—she just looked like a regular human."

"How did she smell?"

"She smelled human, Grandma, although a bit stronger than the others, but still human."

For a little while, Big Yaga sat silently immersed in her thoughts. Little Yaga cleared the table of the breakfast dishes and put them in the sink. She'd much rather have snapped them clean, but she couldn't do it in front of her grandmother. When she turned on the faucet to do the dishes, there wasn't any water. It was her duty to fill the water tank from the well, but she'd forgotten to do it before going to Ashley's party. Little Yaga picked up an empty pail and was halfway out the door when Big Yaga suddenly asked, "Did she have a limp?"

Little Yaga turned around and gave her grandmother a blank stare.

"Who?" she asked.

"The human woman."

"No, but she was walking very slowly—like a turtle."

"Did she see you?"

"I guess she did. I don't think she liked me, though."

"How do you know?"

"She gave me a weird look. Grandma, why do you ask? What's the big deal?"

"Nothing," Big Yaga replied, as though off the cuff. "I'm just curious."

Stanley

Stanley, standing perfectly still, was turning his head from side to side. All he could see were trees, looming over him like giant green towers—so tall and dense, the early-morning light could barely penetrate their canopies of branches and leaves. It was very quiet, but still, he couldn't shake the nasty feeling of being watched. According to the instructions he'd gotten from Vincent, the butcher at the Exotic Meats Shop, he was supposed to find a bubbly brook, which would lead him to where Ashley was being held captive. But the brook was nowhere in sight, and as he stood there all alone in the semidarkness, Stanley started to wonder how on earth he'd gotten himself into this godforsaken forest—and why.

It all had started when Eric Rosebar defeated him during the elections for class president. Stanley had been the front-runner all day long; naturally, he had expected to win. He'd rehearsed his acceptance speech mentally until it was perfect, but when all the votes were in, it turned out he'd lost, by a slim margin, to Eric. How could that have happened? He'd never considered

Eric a serious contender—the dude was a nerd! Before Eric got contact lenses, he had the dorkiest glasses Stanley had ever seen. He was also the teacher's pet, which, to any normal eighth grader, wasn't particularly cool. Even worse, his weird mother happened to be the guidance counselor for their grade. By contrast, Stanley had always been so popular that even the others who sat at his lunch table—which was "reserved" for the popular kids—considered him the coolest. Among his friends at school and online there were a lot of girls who were always texting him and flirting with him. There wasn't a party in town he wasn't invited to.

After the election results had been announced, his friends demanded a recount, but he declined. Instead, he accepted his defeat stoically, gave his concession speech, and shook Eric's hand, wishing him good luck. From that point on, Stanley started hating the nerd. When he lost out to Eric by two and one-quarter seconds at the swim team tryouts a couple of months later, the nerd became his archenemy. Stanley craved revenge, and when Eric started going out with Ashley Laing shortly afterward, he decided it was time to act. In sixth grade, Ashley had had a crush on him, Stanley, for a while, but when she texted him about her feelings, he had rejected her—he thought she wasn't chill enough for his company. Now he was going to use Ashley as an excuse for his righteous retaliation. He'd wait patiently until Eric was head over heels in love with her, and then he'd hit him where it would hurt him most. Stanley believed that old feelings were always stronger than new ones, and he was confident that he could win back Ashley's affections. Not a single girl he'd ever been interested in could resist his overwhelming charm. By stealing Ashley away, Stanley wanted Eric to experience the same pain he'd had to endure after his own two losses. All he wanted was to get even with that nerd and see him suffer defeat and humiliation.

But Stanley's plan backfired, because his belief in the power of old feelings proved wrong. Ashley wasn't interested in him anymore; she was in love with Eric. All of Stanley's attempts to attract her attention had failed. The harder he tried to win her back, the further he pushed her away. He started to feel as though he was truly annoying her. One day during lunch in the school cafeteria, he invited Ashley to sit beside him at the "popular" table, but she refused, joking that she would only sit next to the president. Stanley felt as though the whole school began laughing at him behind his back. What bothered him most of all, though, was the fact that his popularity started to wane, and when Ashley didn't invite him to her birthday party, he became truly enraged. He knew Eric was to blame for all his misfortunes, so he decided to spoil the party and get back at Eric by beating him up at Ashley's house, in front of all her guests. The fight took place in Ashley's driveway; it was short but fierce. Stanley lacerated Eric's lip and chin, but Eric just about broke Stanley's tailbone. Nobody witnessed the fight, and Stanley, overwhelmed by the pain, fled the scene.

When he got home, he lay on his stomach on the living room floor with an ice pack on his aching backside and ended up falling asleep. Later, he woke up feeling a little better. He reached for the remote control and turned on the television, only to see a picture of Ashley on the screen looking back at him. The news reporter was talking about her disappearance immediately after her birthday party, suggesting she may have been kidnapped. Stanley was shocked. He threw off the cold pack, which was now warm anyway, and sat up; either the pain in his rear had subsided, or he simply didn't feel it from the excitement. A vague smile lit up his face. He couldn't believe his luck. This was his chance to redeem himself and restore his reputation! All he had to do now was find Ashley and rescue her from her kidnapper. As far as he was concerned, that reporter was an angel sent from heaven, just for him!

Stanley quickly devised a plan. He ran upstairs to his bedroom and grabbed his binoculars. Then he wheeled his dad's motorcycle out of the garage. He'd just learned to drive it and knew he wasn't allowed to touch it without his dad's permission, but his parents were away for the weekend, and his young aunt, who was staying with him, let him do whatever he wanted. Knowing that Eric would be looking for Ashley, too, Stanley rode over to his house, hid the motorbike in the bushes, and spent the night in the tree on Eric's front lawn, watching the house with his binoculars. When Eric's mom pulled out of the garage very early the next morning, he decided to follow her to see what she was up to. He parked his scrambler by the footpath leading to the Exotic Meats Shop right behind her Volkswagen and watched her walking up the path and then knocking on the front door of the store, illuminated by a blinking sign that said "Open." He saw one of the owners come out, hug Mrs. Rosebar, and walk her around to the back of the shop. Stanley couldn't get over his good fortune! He raced through the meadow and managed to sneak around the back, too. There he stood hidden behind the smelly garbage bin, which was so close to the butcher and Mrs. Rosebar that he could see them and hear every word they said.

"Is this about the girl?" the owner asked. He was a stocky man with remarkably sharp, uneven teeth and shoulder-length gray hair that covered his ears.

"Yes," Mrs. Rosebar replied, looking very worried.

Stanley's ears burned in anticipation of what they'd say next.

"Send Eric here. I'll take him over to the Forest."

"I am very much against it, but Alan insists I let Eric do what he needs to."

"Alan's right. Eric will be fine. He'll know what to do in the Forest—after all, he's your son."

Ten minutes after Mrs. Rosebar had left, Stanley walked into the shop and said he was Eric Rosebar. Vincent shook his hand.

"You smell very human," he said.

"I didn't have time to take a shower," Stanley explained. "I want to find Ashley and bring her back home as soon as possible."

"I know that. Let's go."

Vincent went outside to get his bicycle, and Stanley went after him.

"You'll be sitting behind me," Vincent said. "I'll explain you how to get to Ashley on our way to the Forest, but once you're there, it'll be up to you to figure out how to rescue her." Vincent looked closely at Stanley and said, "I'm sure Jane Rosebar's son will know what to do. I should warn you, though, that many things, and people, look different in the Forest. Don't be surprised by anything, and most of all, believe in yourself."

Stanley got on the bicycle behind Vincent and grabbed hold of his fur vest. It was only a short ride. As soon as both tires of the bike touched down on the path leading from the shop to the town, everything around them suddenly transformed. The meadow became a forest. Stanley looked down and to his dismay, found that he was riding a wolf and holding on to his long gray fur. The animal was missing his left ear. After a short run, the wolf shook Stanley off its back. The boy tumbled onto the ground, and when he got up, the wolf was gone.

All alone, Stanley reached for his cell phone. It was out of service.

"Darn it!" he exclaimed.

He realized then that if he ever wanted to get out of this place, he had no choice but to look for the brook. He started wandering around in search of it, but he found no sign of water anywhere, never mind a brook. A hint of fear crept into his mind and gradually gripped his chest.

How on earth had he gotten himself into this? In all honesty, he'd never liked Ashley; he only wanted to get even with Eric. He wanted to be better than that nerd, but what for? Who cared? He ought to have his head examined. He could be at home right now, flirting with other girls and enjoying life. Instead, he would surely die here, in this forest, and the wolf with the missing ear would sell his remains in the Exotic Meats Shop.

Stanley didn't remember the last time he'd cried, but now he felt a suspicious tickling in his nose and throat.

Stanley and Damon

"Hi there," someone suddenly said, and Stanley jumped, startled.

He turned around and saw a boy of about his age leaning against one of the trees. The boy was tall and very thin. His black eyes sat deep in their sockets. He had sunken cheeks and a shaved, lumpy head.

"Damon," the boy said, extending his hand.

Introducing himself by name as well, Stanley shook the boy's hand and felt his nails, long and sharp, digging into his palm.

"Nice to meet you," Damon said. "Are you lost?"

"Big-time."

"Where are you going?"

"Your guess is as good as mine," Stanley replied with a grunt.

"You mean, you don't know?"

"I know it must sound crazy, but I'm supposed to follow a brook to meet my friend."

"What a shame. All the brooks are dry this time of year. But where, exactly, is your friend?"

"That's just it—I don't know. The brook was supposed to take me there."

"Brooks are very unreliable guides; they can dry out or change beds. They're very moody." Damon shook his head. "I wouldn't ever trust one."

"I see…" Stanley said, nodding his head, but he thought to himself, "What is he talking about? One of us must be crazy. What's going on here? Where am I?"

Suddenly, a different idea occurred to him.

"I am dreaming. Every crazy thing that's happened to me since this morning is just a part of my dream! When I wake up, I'll be at home in bed, safe and sound."

Just then a bumblebee landed on his shoulder. Stanley tried to brush it off, and it stung him on the back of his hand.

"Ouch!" Stanley looked down and saw his hand swelling up right before his eyes. The pain from the bite was radiating all the way up to his shoulder.

"You're not supposed to feel pain in your dreams," Stanley thought. "So, if I'm not dreaming, I must be in hell."

"Listen," Damon said, "I feel bad for you."

"That makes the two of us," Stanley agreed.

"I'll help you. I'll give you a better guide—more reliable, at least. Only make sure you don't let it out of your sight. Stay close behind it, and you'll be fine."

Damon reached into his pocket, pulled out a small piece of charcoal, and threw it on the ground.

"Follow this. It'll lead you to your friend."

Stanley looked down, perplexed.

"It's just a piece of charcoal," he said.

"For your information," Damon noted, "charcoal is the best guide of all because it glows. And this piece is particularly shrewd and speedy. Just be sure not to lose sight of it."

Stanley squatted down to take a better look at the particularly shrewd and speedy piece of charcoal, but he didn't notice anything special about it. It didn't look any different from any other piece of charcoal he'd seen before. When he stood up again, Damon was gone—he'd vanished without a trace, just like the wolf had a few minutes ago.

"I wonder how they do that," Stanley said out loud, although nobody was around. He was all alone again, and the piece of charcoal was almost indistinguishable from the pebbles strewn around it on the ground. Stanley was at a loss, with no idea what to do next.

Suddenly, Damon reappeared from behind one of the trees nearby.

"Sorry," he said. "I forgot to tell you how to operate your new guide."

"I was wondering about that," Stanley said, relieved.

"It's really easy. You say, 'Go, Charcoal' if you want it to go and 'Stop, Charcoal' when you want it to stop."

"OK—so it's a voice-activated device."

"You could say that," Damon agreed. He slapped Stanley on the shoulder, flashed him a broad smile, and vanished into thin air.

Stanley just stood there, unable to decide what had shocked him more—Damon's vanishing act or his reddish teeth with sharp brown fangs.

Watching the Screen

Full of energy and in good spirits, Scraggard the Immortal sat on his throne, watching the big screen in front of him. He saw Eric and Sean, each of whom was wearing one of his rings, standing near the hedge separating the Forest from the human town.

"Welcome," he whispered. "It's been a while since we've had any excitement around here."

"So, what are we doing next?" Sean asked Eric.

"Good question," Scraggard said, settling in to enjoy the upcoming adventures of his guests—live, as they unfolded. Knowing where and how everything would end was a little disappointing, but their journey would still be interesting to watch. Suddenly, there was a little static, and the image on the screen grew fuzzy. The problem resolved itself quickly—even before Scraggard needed to snap his fingers. However, when the screen cleared up, Scraggard could see a lot of hedge but, oddly, no Eric or Sean.

The Visitor

Every weekend while Big Yaga napped after lunch, Little Yaga did the dishes. She, as always, preferred to snap them washed, but with the Cuckoo Bird spying on her from behind the tiny door of her tiny quarters, she couldn't risk it. Just as she finished drying the last plate, she heard a quiet knock on the window. She looked out, and to her surprise, she saw one of Scraggard's soldiers in his tree uniform standing outside, looking in. Little Yaga didn't want to wake up her grandmother because Big Yaga was hard to deal with when she didn't get enough sleep. Prudently, she decided to talk to the soldier first to see if the matter was worth cutting into her grandmother's hour of rest.

She opened the door slightly and, peering at the soldier, said, "Yes, sir?"

"Don't you recognize me, miss?" the soldier questioned. His voice was muffled by the mask over his head, and Little Yaga wasn't sure if she'd ever heard it before.

"Do I know you?" she asked.

"I hope so." The soldier laughed, and Little Yaga thought she recognized his laugh.

"Are you—" she started to say, but before she could finish, the soldier removed his foliage-covered hat, revealing the blue eyes and humanlike teeth of her friend Leesho.

"No way!" Little Yaga exclaimed in disbelief. "What are you doing in this getup?"

"It's not a getup—it's a uniform. I've joined the Great Army of His Scraggardness, Scraggard the Immortal."

"Give me a break," Little Yaga said. "What for?"

"To defend His Scraggardness from his enemies, of course!" As he said that, Leesho subtly wiggled his ears, just like she and Kikimra did to exchange private messages only they would understand. Little Yaga was pretty sure Leesho wasn't aware of their secret code; his ears must've twitched because they were itchy. On the other hand, Leesho, somehow, did always seem to know everything. What if he'd figured out their code and was sending her a message?

"There are too many enemies around," Leesho continued. He moved his ears again, and this time Little Yaga was certain that there was more to what he was saying than just his words.

"Yes, you're right," she said, playing along. "I see your point. Would you like to come in?"

"Sure." Leesho walked in. "Listen, my belt's too tight," he complained. "The buckle's pressing into my gut. Do you mind if I take it off?"

"I don't care," Little Yaga replied, shrugging her shoulders. "If it's that uncomfortable, go ahead, take it off."

Leesho undid the buckle, sniffed the air, and screwed up his face.

"It stinks," he said. "Here, smell it." He put the belt up to Little Yaga's nose.

She coughed and pushed his hand away.

"You don't have to stick it in my face. I could smell it as soon as you came in. It smells of leather. You'd better take it outside before my grandmother wakes up. I know she's not going to like this odor."

Leesho took the belt and went back outside.

"Don't leave it in the yard," Little Yaga said. "My grand-mother has a sensitive nose. Take it into the Forest, as far away from here as possible."

"Yes, ma'am!" Leesho said with a salute as if Little Yaga were his general. "I'll be back soon."

At the Bottom of the Gorge

Eric and Sean were sitting at the bottom of the gorge into which two black ravens had dropped them. The sparkling rings weren't on their fingers anymore—they must've fallen off while the boys were rolling down the hill. Their trip from the Exotic Meats Shop to the forest had taken a mere instant. They'd put the rings on, rubbed the diamonds, and repeated after Pablo: "Please, Ring, take me to the Forest now." In the blink of an eye, they were standing by a tall hedge that extended as far as they could see in either direction. Right in front of them, they saw the tallest trees towering over their heads, almost up to the sky itself. After another blink of an eye, they were airborne, flying above the trees in the beaks of the two black ravens.

"Eric," Sean whispered, "I have to tell you something."

"Go ahead."

"I'm sick."

"What's wrong?" Eric asked, eying his friend. "You look fine to me."

"No, I've lost my mind." Sean's shoulders drooped, and his ever-smiling face transformed into one of despair.

"Where'd you get that idea?"

"Well, I'm convinced we got to this forest with the help of two magic rings, and after that, we were dropped into this gorge by two black birds who were carrying us in their beaks."

"So far, so good," Eric said. "That's what happened."

"So you believe it, too?"

"I do because that's how we got here."

"Have you ever traveled this way before?"

"Nope."

"That's just it, Eric," Sean whispered feverishly. "Nobody has, and if you believe all of this, you're sick, too. Listen to me, my friend, we've gone insane, understand? You and I are mentally ill!"

"I don't think so," Eric said calmly. "People don't become crazy at the same time. Insanity isn't a flu."

"But I'm hearing voices, too," Sean insisted. "When I was rolling down the hill, I heard somebody say, 'Stay there, until…' I didn't catch the rest of it, but I know it wasn't you, and there was nobody else around."

"I also heard that."

"See what I mean? You've just proven my point—we both lost our minds."

"I thought it was one of the birds."

"Eric, birds don't talk in the wild," Sean maintained, hopelessly.

"What if they do, though?" Eric asked, challenging Sean. "There is more to life than even the smartest scientists know! There are many more questions than answers. Look, Ashley has mysteriously disappeared. And we've entered a mysterious world to find her."

"Well, when you put it that way…" Sean mumbled, unconvinced. "I hope you're right." He looked around the clay gully and saw an occasional stubby shrub growing here and there along the lazily moving creek, which seemed endless. He tilted his head back and saw the rugged roots of the tall trees growing along both edges. The rays of the sun were trapped in their dense foliage, and from down below, the trees looked dark and gloomy.

"Eric, I don't like it here."

"Come on. It's just a forest. We'll leave as soon as we find your sister."

"How are we going to find her?"

"We'll think of something."

Eric picked a stick up off the ground and spontaneously sketched something with it on the clay surface of the canyon.

"What's that?" Sean asked, glancing at the sketch. "A burger?"

Eric looked at what he'd drawn.

"I guess so."

"You're good," Sean praised him, swallowing hard. "It's very realistic. It's making me hungry."

"I guess I drew it because I'm hungry, too."

Eric stood up, licked his lips, and said, "I wish it was real."

"So do I," Sean admitted. "By the way," he said looking over at Eric, "what are we gonna do for food here? I don't see any stores or other eateries anywhere around."

"We'll hunt for food," Eric joked. "After all, we're in a forest."

"Not funny." Sean scowled and suddenly sniffed the air. "What's that?"

"What?"

"That smell."

"Yes, what is it?"

Eric and Sean looked down. There, on the ground where the sketch had been, sat a real burger, juicy and steaming hot.

Stunned, the boys gaped at each other in silence. Sean was the first to regain his power of speech.

"Draw another one," he said, in a husky and slightly shaky voice, "and a bottle of ketchup, please."

Without saying a word, Eric drew another very realistic-looking hamburger and a bottle of ketchup.

"What now?" he asked.

"Let's wait and see what happens."

When, after a few minutes of staring intently at the drawing, nothing happened, Sean said, "You must've done or said something when your first burger became real."

Eric shrugged his shoulders. "I've no idea."

"Please, try to remember. It's very important—I'm hungry!"

Eric pursed his lips, wrinkled his brow, squeezed his eyes shut, and puffed out his cheeks. When still nothing happened, he jumped up and down, first with his arms raised, then lowered, and when that didn't work either, he tried breathing in and out as slowly as possible. He even tried holding his breath. Finally, he turned to Sean and said, "Sorry, I can't remember."

"My grandmother's memory's better than yours!" Sean complained disapprovingly.

Suddenly, a voice that came from behind said, "All you have to do is wish it real, and it will be."

Eric and Sean whipped their heads around and saw a boy about their age standing before them, grinning. He was wearing a tree costume and holding a leafy hat in his hand.

"I'm Leesho," the boy said, extending his hand.

Eric and Sean introduced themselves by name as well and shook Leesho's hand.

"Nice to meet you." Leesho smiled, setting his hat on the ground. "As I was saying, Eric, you should just say, 'I wish it was real,' and whatever you're wishing real, will be. Easy, right?"

Eric knelt down and drew one more hamburger. "I wish all this food was real!" he said very loudly.

"You don't have to holler so that the whole Forest knows. You can say it quietly or even just think it, and it'll come true."

Meanwhile, the two hamburgers and the bottle of ketchup pushed through the clay and became real. Eric and Sean stared at the transformation with their mouths open in disbelief.

"Neat!" Sean finally said. He bent down, picked up one of the burgers, and took a bite.

"Help yourselves, guys," he said, chewing with gusto. "It's good!"

Kneeling just like Eric had a few minutes ago, he drew a can of Sprite. His picture didn't come out as realistic as Eric's, but this didn't stop him from quietly saying, "I wish this can was real."

The three boys stared at the picture, waiting for its transformation. When nothing happened after a few minutes had passed, Sean repeated the incantation, this time a little louder: "I wish this can was real."

A few minutes later, the drawing of the can was still only that. Sean and Eric turned to Leesho with inquisitive looks.

"You have to be at least partially a Forester for your wishes to come true," Leesho explained reluctantly.

"I'm not a Forester," Eric said. "But my wishes came true."

He leaned over Sean's picture and whispered, "I wish this can was real."

Instantly, the can jumped out of its outline in the clay, but it was distorted, a little crumpled, and leaking out of a hole in the bottom.

"Not the best work of art," Eric said, holding the can away from his body so that he wouldn't get sprayed by the content.

"You're the artist—not me," Sean snapped. "I'm proud to have drawn something recognizable at all. Trust me, I'm not usually this good."

Eric got back down on his knees, drew three cans of Sprite, and wished them real. They popped out of the hot clay as cold and misty as if they were fresh out of a fridge. Eric took one for himself and gave the others to Sean and Leesho. Curious, Leesho examined the can, shook it next to his ear, and then snapped his fingers right beside it. The very top of the can burst open, and a fountain of sparkling Sprite shot out. Leesho aimed it into his open mouth. Instantly, his eyes bulged out, and his face turned bright red. He dropped the can and started gagging, coughing, sneezing, and spitting until he got every drop of the liquid out of his mouth.

"That was gross!" he said, still coughing. "I'll need a whole bucket of poison ivy juice to wash my mouth out."

"Do you drink poison ivy juice, too?" Sean exclaimed.

"It's my favorite—you too?"

"No way. But one of my sister's kidnappers said she liked it. I thought she was kidding." Sean turned to Eric and asked, "What was her name? She was very weird."

"Which one do you mean?" Eric asked. "Little Yaga or Kikimra?"

Leesho stopped coughing. "You know Little Yaga and Kikimra?" he exclaimed.

"Unfortunately," Sean admitted with a smirk. "They came over to my house for my sister's birthday and kidnapped her."

"No, they didn't," Leesho objected.

"If they hadn't, we wouldn't be here right now, OK?"

"Little Yaga and Kikimra are my best friends," Leesho said. "They had nothing to do with the kidnapping. They were just instruments at the hands of someone else."

"Whatever."

"I knew you'd be coming," Leesho said. Looking around, he lowered his voice so much that he practically mouthed his next words. "That's why I joined the army and temporarily got rid of my belt."

"How could you have known we'd be coming? We've only just met," Sean replied, suddenly feeling very annoyed. "And how could you have joined the army at your age? And who cares about your belt, anyway? And—"

Before he could finish, Leesho snapped his fingers in front of Sean's face, muting him midsentence. Sean kept talking, but there was no sound coming out of his mouth. He tried to shout, but his vocal cords produced not even a rustle. Infuriated, he went at Leesho with his fists. The Forest boy snapped himself gone, and Sean's fists cut through the air. Meeting no resistance, he lost his balance and fell flat on his face. Eric wanted to help him up, but Sean, spitting clay and brandishing his fists, jumped to his feet on his own.

"Sorry, Sean," came Leesho's voice from behind their backs. "I had no choice. You were asking too many questions too loudly. That's not a smart behavior in the Forest. I promise to give your voice back when we get to Little Yaga's."

"We aren't going anywhere." Eric turned around to face Leesho. "We were told to stay right here."

"By whom?"

"I don't know," Eric admitted. "By the birds, I guess." He smiled sheepishly. "I know it sounds sick."

"Nothing sounds sick in the Forest. Do you know those birds?"

"Of course not."

"So how can you trust them? What if they were sent by your enemies?"

"We don't have any enemies. And how can we trust you? You're Little Yaga's friend, and she's a traitor."

"You have more enemies than you can imagine, but Little Yaga is not one of them. Believe me, she isn't a traitor. And if you want to know whether you can trust me or not, you should ask an independent entity."

"Like Little Yaga or Kikimra, for example?" Eric asked sneering.

Leesho ignored his sarcasm.

"There are only three independent entities in the world," he said, "the Sun, the Air, and the Water. We all depend on them, but they belong to no one. They are free and impartial. You can ask any one of them whether I am trustworthy."

"What are you talking about?" Eric asked, blinking at Leesho, afraid that one of them had indeed gone mad.

"You can ask the Sun, but I wouldn't. You may get badly burned. You can ask the Air, but it's very moody. It may blow a few gusts of wind at you and carry you away. The best one to ask is the Water. It's the gentlest entity out of the three."

"What is he talking about?" Eric turned to Sean who, still muted, stood sulking, his arms crossed over his chest.

"Go ahead," Leesho encouraged him, pointing to the creek. "Ask the Water if you can trust me."

"That's crazy," Eric said, looking at Sean again. "Can you believe this nonsense?"

Sean first pointed at his mouth and then at the creek.

"All right," Eric conceded. "I'll give it a try. This place's so wacky—I guess anything's possible here."

"Now you're talking," Leesho said with a grin.

Eric bent over the stream. The water below was as clear as a freshly washed window. Its surface trembled ever so slightly from its lazy flow.

"What do I do next?" Eric looked at Leesho.

"You wanted to ask the Water if you could trust me, didn't you?"

"Is that what I wanted?"

"Yes."

"It's insane, but I'll do it."

Eric bent over again.

"Water, if all of this is just a joke and somebody's recording me now, I'll be the biggest jerk on YouTube." He looked at Leesho, snorted, and continued. "Please, Water, answer one question. This dude, Leesho, standing next to me, is he trustworthy?"

Suddenly, the water started bubbling as though it were boiling in a teakettle. Dense clouds of hot steam rose into the air and formed three letters that spelled *YES*. The word floated before Eric's astonished face for a few seconds before condensing into rounded drops of water that rained back down into the stream. When the last drop touched its surface, the stream grew clear and almost motionless again.

Stanley and the Oak Tree

Stanley had been chasing his glowing charcoal guide for quite a while. He was tired, and the soles of his feet were burning. He started to slow down and look for a spot where he could rest. When he saw a clearing in the distance, he picked up speed again, raising dust, leaves, and sticks from under his sneakers as he ran. A few minutes later, the forest parted, revealing a narrow, unpaved road that stretched ahead for as far as he could see. A few yards down, right in the middle of the road, an Oak Tree suddenly spread its branches, forming a dark, shady area below, and that's where Stanley decided to rest. Only a few more steps and he could lie down for a couple hours of peaceful sleep. His eyelids grew heavy from the mere thought of it. But as soon as he ran out onto the road, a painful blow to his shoulder knocked him off his feet. Unable to grasp what had just happened and dizzy from pain, Stanley clasped his shoulder and, moaning, pulled himself back up. His charcoal guide had kept rolling along and was way ahead of him now.

"Charcoal, stop!" he hollered, and his guide instantly obeyed; its bright glow slowly dimmed. Stanley took a few slow steps forward, but he was knocked down again, this time by a blow to his other shoulder. Flat on his back, he lay perfectly still, unable to move from the excruciating pain. When it somewhat subsided, he raised his head, and to his horror, he saw a huge acorn flying toward him, aiming for his forehead, right above the bridge of his nose.

Terrified, Stanley dropped his head down just in time; the acorn whizzed over his face, fast as a speeding bullet. "It could've crushed my skull," he thought. Afraid to move, he stayed in that position until his back and neck started to ache. He felt a desperate need to turn himself over, so he tensed his muscles and cautiously rolled onto his stomach. Just then, he heard a strange buzzing sound, and seconds later, a battery of blows pounded his body. Howling in pain, Stanley got up on his hands and knees, and at a speed he'd never thought possible in such a position, he crawled back toward the forest. When he reached the first trees, his behind, still sore from his encounter with Eric, was swollen like a balloon. He sprawled out flat on his belly and shut his eyes tight to hold back the hot tears that were suddenly burning his eyelids.

"Are you OK?" he heard a voice from above ask. He looked up and saw Damon resting on an old stump nearby, legs crossed and arms folded. His friendly smile showed his reddish teeth and brown fangs.

"Acorns," Stanley breathed out.

"You've met the Oak Tree, I see. Such a nasty plant, isn't it?"

"I don't think I'll ever be able to sit again."

"Come on—a few drops of Live Water, and your behind will be as good as new."

"A few drops of what?"

"Live Water."

Stanley didn't know what Live Water was, but he was willing to try anything to ease his pain.

"Can I have some?" he begged.

"Sure…in due time, but it's not a priority right now."

"To me it is."

"You're wrong. The priority is to get you past the Oak Tree."

"I don't want to pass the tree; I want to go home. Let Eric Rosebar rescue Ashley."

"Who's Eric Rosebar?"

"A classmate of mine."

"Is he here, too?"

"If he isn't yet, he will be soon—that's for sure."

Damon sighed. "You can't go home."

"Why?"

"You've come here to rescue the girl, right?"

"I wish I hadn't."

"But you have." Damon sighed again. "You can't leave until you find her. It's the rule of the Forest: you must accomplish what you've come here for."

"Let's break the rule."

"Impossible." Damon suddenly grew very serious. "The rules and laws of the Forest are written in stone!" He put his face right up to Stanley's, let out a tiny streak of black smoke, and whispered, "Whoever breaks them dies."

"What?" Stanley's mouth became instantly dry, and he forgot all about his aching behind.

"You heard me." Damon stared grimly at Stanley, and the latter trembled under his morose look.

"Don't worry." A smile returned to Damon's face. "If you live by the rules, you'll be fine."

"How can I get past that tree?" Stanley asked.

Damon turned silent for a little while, then said, "I think I know what your problem is."

"What is it?"

"You smell too human."

"I am human."

"That's the problem."

"Aren't you?"

"We aren't talking about me right now. This is all about you. We have to de-smell you."

"De-what?"

"Strip you of your human smell."

"How?"

"I've heard of a special potion that can do it, but I don't know where to get it."

"Who would?"

"Biggest Yaga, but she won't tell me. Or our principal Rat, but I won't ask him."

"Anybody else?"

"Let me think."

Resting his chin on the back of his hand, with his elbow on his knee, Damon immersed himself in deep thought. A few minutes later, he straightened up and said, "Master Kastor."

"Who is he?"

"An apothecary. He mixes tons of potions all day long. If he doesn't have it, nobody else does."

Damon sprang to his feet and said, "Wait for me. I'll be right back."

Stanley blinked, and Damon was gone. He blinked again, and Damon was back, with a leather pouch hanging over his shoulder.

"You've got the potion?"

"I've got something else. Master Kastor said it's better than a de-smeller."

Damon untied the pouch, releasing a thin cloud of light-brown dust into the air. It tickled his nostrils. He sneezed and said, "This is acorn repellent. I'll sprinkle it on you, and no more acorns will be able to get to you."

"Are you sure?" Stanley scratched his swollen behind.

"We'll test it on you." Damon chuckled, then quickly grew serious again. "Master Kastor's stuff's usually good. It should work."

He poured half of the pouch's contents all over Stanley's body and gently pushed the boy back onto the road. Stanley started out briskly, taking big, confident steps. The closer he got to the Oak Tree, though, the slower he walked, and the shorter his steps became. By the time he reached the point where he'd been attacked by the acorns, he was tiptoeing, moving as carefully and quietly as he possibly could. He tried not to look at the tree, but a loud buzzing sound forced him to. Horrified, he faltered and stopped altogether. A mass of vicious acorns flew toward him, picking up speed as it approached. Stanley was convinced he had only seconds left to live. He closed his eyes. The buzzing got closer and closer, and soon he was completely surrounded by the incessant, earsplitting drone. Every muscle in his body tensed in preparation for the final assault. A few moments later, when he realized he was still alive, he opened one eye. The acorns were revolving around him like satellites around a planet. It seemed they couldn't get any closer than a couple of inches away from his body as if an invisible wall surrounded him at that very distance. The most belligerent acorns that tried to breach the invisible wall fell to the ground, crushed. Stanley opened his other eye and took a small step forward. The acorns moved forward with him. The most aggressive ones kept falling to the ground, like dry November leaves. Stanley took another step, then another. The farther away he got from the Oak Tree, the more acorns dropped to the ground, smashed to pieces. By the time Stanley caught up to his charcoal guide, which patiently waited for him in the middle of the road, there was only one acorn left, following him like a bothersome fly. Somehow, it managed to get to Stanley's ankle and painfully stab it. Stanley wailed. Furious, he crushed the acorn under the heel of his sneaker and dug it deep into the dirt underneath his feet. He looked back and saw the road behind him, covered with the fallen army of acorns. He took a deep breath, turned around, and said, "Charcoal, go!"

The gray piece of charcoal jolted, lit up, and briskly rolled forward as if it had never stopped.

In Front of Little Yaga's Hut

Leesho snapped his fingers. The gate in front of Little Yaga's Hut on the chicken leg swung open, and the boys entered the front yard.

"I think we should invite Kikimra," Leesho said. "She's smart and very powerful."

"Whatever," Eric muttered with a smirk.

Leesho bent down, picked up a dry leaf off the ground, and glided his hand over it. At once, its wrinkled surface became covered in small round letters.

"What is it?" Sean looked at the leaf and smiled, realizing he could talk again.

"It's a message for Kikimra, asking her to come right over," Leesho explained. "Yes, you can talk, but don't abuse your gift of speech, or you'll lose it again."

Leesho folded the leaf in half lengthwise, like a paper plane, and threw it toward the forest. Eric and Sean expected it to nose-dive right behind the fence, but it zoomed forward, zigzagging between trees, and disappeared into the thick of the woods.

"How'd you do that?" Sean asked, impressed.

"Practice," Leesho replied modestly.

"And the letters?"

"Practice."

"Can you teach us to do that?"

"It depends," Leesho replied vaguely.

"Depends on what?

"On your genetic makeup."

Just then, the leaf rocketed back from behind the trees and landed abruptly on Leesho's shoulder. He picked it up and showed it to Sean and Eric. In place of his lengthy message, there was only one word written in bold letters: "COMING." Before he could toss the leaf away, the boys heard a familiar voice from behind.

"Hi, guys."

They turned around to see Kikimra, dressed in her Forester outfit. Her wide, cheery smile exposed her reddish teeth, with four long brown fangs. On meeting Sean's bemused look, she shielded her mouth with her hand, which was covered with tufts of black hair. Sean fixated on them.

"Oops." Kikimra hid her hands in her sleeves and spun around three times. When she'd completed her third spin, her teeth were pure white, there were no more fangs sticking out of her mouth, and the skin on her hands was smooth, silky, and perfectly hairless.

"You guys snatched me out of a dress rehearsal for the school play," she lied. "I couldn't even change out of my costume!"

"Who do you play?" Sean asked.

"A nice girl from an enchanted forest." Kikimra smiled adoringly.

He smiled back, but he couldn't help blurting out, "Sonya sends her regards."

"Why didn't you bring her along?"

"Next time."

"Be sure you do. She'll get so attached to the Forest that she won't be able to leave." Kikimra tilted her head back and laughed. Sean wasn't sure if he only imagined it or actually saw a white stream of smoke trickle out of her mouth.

"Kikimra, enough," Leesho interrupted. "I didn't call you here to go crazy. Eric and Sean think you and Little Yaga kidnapped Ashley."

"Really?" Kikimra stopped laughing. "We wouldn't do that to her; she's too nice."

"Well, there is a way to prove them wrong," Leesho said.

Kikimra gave Leesho an annoyed look.

"How come you're such a know-it-all?" she asked. "What's the way?"

"Let's go inside." Leesho nodded toward the Hut, which was listening to their conversation with great curiosity. "We'll talk there."

As the kids approached the front door, the Hut suddenly sneezed, and a few pieces of straw flew off its thatched roof onto the ground.

"What's that smell?" the Hut asked, then sneezed again, five times in a row. The straw was falling from the roof like a flurry of snowflakes.

"What's going on here?" Sean looked at the Hut as it shook. "Is there an earthquake or something?"

"It's not an earthquake," Leesho said. "It's only Little Yaga's Hut sneezing."

"Huts don't sneeze."

"They do if they have allergies."

"Huts can't have allergies. They don't have immune systems. Any scientist will tell you that. Huts are just...objects."

"Do you believe in scientists more than your own eyes?" Leesho asked. "You can see the Hut's sneezing. If a scientist has a different opinion, send her here."

He knocked on the door, and Little Yaga opened it at once, as if she'd been standing right behind it, just waiting for his knock.

At the Palace

Damon was knelt on one knee before the magnificent throne of Scraggard the Immortal. His eyes, full of love and devotion, were fixed on Scraggard's face, while his body quivered with excitement.

Scraggard liked the boy. Damon reminded him of himself back in the day, eager and passionate. Scraggard also appreciated the boy's zeal and desire to serve him, the Ruler of the Forest, selflessly and unquestioningly.

"Are you aware, young Forester, that no one has ever come here, into this hall, without having been summoned by My Scraggardness?"

Damon nodded.

"Are you aware that if you've bothered me for no serious reason, you won't walk out of here in the same capacity as when you walked in?"

Damon nodded again.

"What has compelled you to request an audience with me?" Scraggard the Immortal was genuinely curious.

"Your Scraggardness, I've learned something that I believe is crucial for you to know. I felt it was so urgent that it couldn't wait until tomorrow."

"All right. What is it?"

Damon looked around to make sure that only the two of them were in the hall and whispered, "It's about Eric Rosebar."

Damon expected Scraggard to shudder on hearing this name, but the Immortal remained calm.

"How do you know about Eric Rosebar?"

"I admire Your Scraggardness so much," Damon revealed, bowing his head, "that I've learned a lot about you. I've read all your biographies, horoscopes, and prophecies. Once, a long time ago, I came across Eric Rosebar's name in one of the prophecies. I'd forgotten all about it until I heard that name earlier today."

"What, exactly, did you hear?"

"That he's coming to the Forest—if he hasn't already."

"Do you remember what, exactly, that prophecy said?"

"All I remember was the warning 'Beware of Eric Rosebar.'"

Scraggard the Immortal twisted his mouth into a wry smile and said, "Thank you, Damon."

"Always at your service," Damon replied, still on one knee, and looked Scraggard in the eye. "I wonder if this Eric is here yet."

"Yes, he is," Scraggard said with a sneer. "I just don't know exactly where. He seems to have slipped out of my sight."

Allergies

Little Yaga opened the door.

"Come on in," she said, and all four teens followed her into the kitchen.

"What's that smell?" came a raspy old voice from the depths of the Hut.

The Cuckoo Bird stuck her head out of her tiny door and sneezed.

"Yes, what is that terrible stench? It's making me choke!" The bird coughed, and the feathers on her back stood up straight. The Hut also coughed, making all the kitchen dishes rattle in the cupboards.

"What's going on in here?" Big Yaga asked, leaning on her stick, grim as ever, as she limped out of her bedroom in her black nightshirt and cap. Her crooked nose was sniffing the air.

"Grandma, I've got guests over," Little Yaga said quietly.

"What's the occasion? It's not your birthday or my funeral yet. Let's see what kind of guests they are." Big Yaga walked over to Sean, smelled him from head to toe, and then turned to her grand-daughter, livid.

"Are you out of your mind?" she exclaimed. "Why have you brought a human home? Do you know what will happen to us if Scraggard finds out? He'll turn us into a couple of toads and gobble us up for dinner!"

Big Yaga shook her walking stick at Eric and Sean, almost hitting them.

"Out! Out of my house!" she shouted.

"Out! Out of our house!" the Cuckoo Bird squealed, too. She and the Hut were taking turns sneezing. The kitchen floor was covered in the bird's feathers. "If they stay here much longer, I'll go completely bald!" the bird shrieked.

"Excuse me," Eric suddenly said, "but this is not the way to treat guests. We're hungry and tired. Go ahead and chase us out, but first, please, feed us, and let us rest."

For a moment, Big Yaga was taken aback by such insolence.

"Who do think you are, talking to me, Big Yaga, this way?" she demanded indignantly, after a prolonged silence.

"My bad." Eric bowed sarcastically. "I apologize for not introducing myself and my friend. This is Sean Laing. His sister, Ashley, was kidnapped by Little Yaga and Kikimra, right after her birthday party."

"Is that what you think happened?" Little Yaga asked in surprise. "For your information, we didn't do it."

"Right," Eric said, shrugging his shoulders to show Little Yaga he didn't believe her. "Anyway, my name is Eric Rosebar. Ashley is my girlfriend. Sean and I came here to find her and take her back home."

"What did you say your name was?" Big Yaga asked, suddenly docile and totally unlike her usual crabby self.

"Eric Rosebar."

She limped up close to him. Instinctively, Eric leaned backward.

"Don't worry—I won't bite you," she grumbled into his face, sniffing the air around his head.

"I'm not worried," Eric said, grinning.

"Well, Eric Rosebar." Big Yaga stepped back. "I'll feed you and your friend. I'll also let you rest, but after that, you both must leave my house and never return. Understood?"

"Yes, ma'am."

"First, though, I must deodorize you; otherwise, my bird really will go completely bald, and my Hut will fall apart."

"What's wrong with the way I smell?" Eric sniffed under his armpit. "I didn't have time to shower this morning, but I don't think I smell that dirty."

"You and your friend here," Big Yaga said grouchy, pinching her nose with her fingers, "smell disgustingly human."

She used her stick to push aside the small, worn-out rug under the kitchen sink; it was hiding a narrow hatch door in the floor. She raised the hatch just enough to squeeze herself through. Grunting, she lowered herself down to the cellar along a rickety staircase; the steps creaked pitifully under her weight. A few minutes later, she climbed back up, carrying a jar of a rust-colored liquid. She poured some of it into two mugs—a half cup for Eric and a full one for Sean.

"Drink up," she ordered, "down to the last drop."

Sean smelled the liquid and coughed. "I can't drink that!" he said.

Big Yaga limped over to him and grabbed him by the ear with her gnarled fingers. "If you don't drink that," she whispered loudly, "I'll turn you into poison ivy juice and swallow you in one gulp."

"What?" Sean rubbed his ear. "Can I drink only half, like Eric?"

"You're trying my patience, human." Big Yaga's face blackened, and the kitchen light started dimming, too.

"Don't ask questions," Eric said as the room grew darker by the second. "Just drink."

Difficult as it was, the boys emptied their mugs, and the kitchen lit up again. The Cuckoo Bird and the Hut stopped sneezing. Half-bald and very weak, the bird crawled back into her tiny quarters; the Hut's logs, having been shaken out of position by all the sneezing, shifted back into place.

"Now you can eat." Big Yaga snapped her fingers, and the top drawer in one of the kitchen cabinets slid open.

The All-You-Can-Eat Tablecloth

Out of the drawer Big Yaga pulled a tablecloth that was all wrinkled and covered with a thick layer of dust.

"We haven't had company in a while," she explained grimly.

"Not in my lifetime, that's for sure," Little Yaga said.

Big Yaga cast her a warning look and shoved the tablecloth into her hands.

"Go outside and shake the dust off, you chatterbox."

Little Yaga stepped outside, and before the door had even closed behind her, she came back in. The tablecloth in her hand was crisp and white, smelling as fresh as if it had just been laundered.

Big Yaga spread it over the table and invited everyone to take a seat.

"What are you waiting for?" she asked. "Sit down and eat whatever you want."

Eric and Sean looked at each other and sat next to Little Yaga and her friends. The table in front of them, spread with the sparkling clean tablecloth, was absolutely empty.

"Go ahead, help yourselves," Big Yaga grumbled. Seeing the bewildered looks on Eric and Sean's faces, she said, "Little Yaga, you start. Those two have no idea how to use an All-You-Can-Eat Tablecloth."

"I'm not hungry," Little Yaga replied. "We just ate."

"Then have something to drink."

"All right." Little Yaga knocked on the table and said, "Tablecloth, can I have a pitcher of pine juice with chopped needles and a little bit of grated birch bark, please? Give us six cups, for everybody to try."

"That's a great idea!" Kikimra exclaimed. "I'm not hungry, too, but I'll have a cup of Gumbo-Limbo resin." She looked over at Sean, and her eyes sparkled. "You must try it," she said. "It's delicious!"

"Thank you, Kikimra. Maybe some other time," Sean replied.

"You should have a sip from my cup," Kikimra insisted. "You'll enjoy it."

"OK," Sean reluctantly agreed, although he couldn't help but add, "if I survive, that is."

"I'm hungry," Leesho said. "I'll have a dinosaur fossil tail stuffed with chamois horns, a few fried toads, and a pear cactus for dessert."

Sean pursed his lips and looked around. "Well," he started, "can I order something normal, or they only serve here stuff that people die from?"

"I wish," Big Yaga muttered. "All-You-Can-Eat Tablecloths serve every imaginable food that exists in the universe. Go ahead—order anything you like."

"Great, I'm really hungry. I'd like a large double-cheese pizza, half-pepperoni and half-mushroom, and two cans of Sprite."

"Why are you ordering pizza?" Kikimra shuddered. "It's awful! I tasted it at Ashley's party—it could give you indigestion. Order something really delicious—we've got such a variety here."

"Kikimra, don't force your own preferences on others. If he wants pi-piz-pizza." Big Yaga stumbled over the unfamiliar word. "Whatever it is, let him have it."

"I agree with Kikimra," Leesho said. "It's always good to try local dishes."

"Not today," Eric objected. "Let us get used to this place first."

Sean turned to him and asked, "How long do you think we're going to be stuck here?"

"Who knows?" Eric replied.

"Not long enough to get used to their food, I hope," Sean said.

"So do I."

"Eric," Big Yaga called him sullenly, "it's your turn to order."

Eric looked around at everybody and said, "I'd like to try something local…"

"Very good." Leesho rubbed his hands in approval, showing his long, curled nails. "Allow me to recommend a few things for—"

"But I don't feel I'm ready yet," Eric interrupted with an apologetic smile. "I am really hungry, though." He knocked on the table and placed an order. "Tablecloth, can I have three hot dogs with ketchup and mustard, a large order of fries, peach iced tea, and a cup of cookie-dough ice cream with chocolate sprinkles for dessert?"

As soon as Eric had placed his order, the tablecloth shook its tassels, and the food started to appear on the table, seemingly out of nowhere. The pitcher of pine juice for Little Yaga, along with the six additional cups she'd requested, was made of tightly interwoven pine needles. The Gumbo-Limbo resin for Kikimra came in a cup made of chipped bark. Leesho's food was served on a lattice of twigs covered with a burdock leaf, and Sean's and Eric's orders came on two water-lily pads, with Sean's Sprite poured into a tulip bud and Eric's iced tea served in a scooped-out peach. The utensils looked as if they were made of frosted glass, but when Sean picked up his fork, it was so cold that his fingers turned blue. He tried to put it back down, but he couldn't, as it was frozen to his skin.

"I like utensils made of ice," Big Yaga explained with a chortle. "The food stays fresh longer. Their only drawback is that they melt quickly, so if you want to finish your food, you'd better gobble it up fast, or you'll have nothing to eat it with. Bon appétit!" Sniggering, she limped away and disappeared into her bedroom.

Little Yaga stood up, quietly blew on all the utensils set on the tablecloth and on the fork in Sean's hand, and sat back down. It seemed nothing had changed. The utensils looked exactly the same, but the fork that was stuck to Sean's fingers warmed up and, with a gentle jingle, fell down, back onto the table.

"You don't have to rush anymore," Little Yaga said quietly. "Your forks, knives, and spoons won't melt now, so relax and enjoy your meal. Bon appétit!"

Stanley and the
Milkshake River

Stanley was barely able to keep up with his charcoal guide because he was very tired. He didn't know how much longer he'd have to run before reaching his destination, but he didn't feel like taking any more breaks. He was also very hungry. He couldn't remember the last time he'd eaten. His stomach was growling, and he had a bitter taste in his mouth. The forest around him seemed barren. He hadn't seen a single bush of berries or a nut tree along the way. He was stumbling and tripping so frequently now that he was afraid he'd fall down any minute. When his energy was almost gone, and he was practically staggering rather than running, he heard a splashing sound. The sweet aroma of his favorite peppermint yogurt tickled his nostrils. The fragrance was coming from the clearing ahead. Feeling a sudden boost of energy, Stanley picked up speed and sprinted forward, even beating his charcoal guide. Now out of the dense woods, he found himself standing on the bank of the rapidly flowing Milkshake River. Stanley closed his eyes and smiled ever so slightly. He couldn't have wished for a better rest area! He saw a weeping willow tree nearby, with green cups growing on its branches instead of leaves. He tore one off but found it too small, so he threw it away, knelt down, and lowered his mouth toward the milkshake. Like a dog, he started lapping it up with his tongue. Never had he tasted anything better! He was so hungry that he felt he could've lapped up the whole river. The longer he drank, the heavier his eyelids grew. Suddenly, he couldn't keep his eyes open any longer. His breathing grew shallow, colorful circles whirled before his eyes, and it seemed his whole head was spinning along with them. He tried to get up, but being half-asleep, he lost his balance and fell into the milkshake with a loud splash. The river picked him up, and the current carried him downstream.

He couldn't see the three white specks way up in the sky. They were steadily approaching the Milkshake River, and before long, the specks turned into three big white birds—the Swan-Geese. Loudly flapping their wings, the birds landed on the riverbank. Damon and his two friends, Don-Key and Canny, jumped off their backs. Honking raucously, the Swan-Geese took flight and soared back up into the sky.

Damon looked at the Milkshake River and saw unconscious Stanley drifting toward him.

"Here comes that jerk," he said with a snigger.

"Where?" asked Don-Key, who was looking in the opposite direction. He had long, pointy ears, a stubby nose with wide nostrils, and long teeth that stuck out from under his short, meaty upper lip.

"Look up the river, smarty, not down. He's right there, floating along like a log—can't you see?"

Don-Key turned his head and asked, "Over there? He does look like a log," and his whole body positively shook with laughter. "What are you going to do with him?"

"Pull him out, of course. We need him. He may help us find that human, Eric Rosebar."

Don-Key looked sheepishly at Damon and said, "Refresh my memory—what do we need that Rosebar kid for?"

"To protect our beloved ruler, Scraggard the Immortal, smarty."

"Scraggard the Immortal is so powerful—he doesn't need any protection."

"It's the most powerful ones who need the most protection."

"What could that human possibly do to His Scraggardness?"

"Nobody knows. All we know is that there's a warning in the prophecies that says, 'Beware of Eric Rosebar.' We also know that he's in the Forest—somewhere. We must find him and get rid of him before he causes any trouble."

"What do you mean, get rid of him? How?"

"We'll figure that out when the time comes." Damon's eyes flickered ominously.

Stanley's body was slowly approaching. Damon took off his hooves, waded into the river, and pulled the human boy out of the milkshake by the scruff of his shirt. Don-Key and Canny leaned over his motionless body. They'd never seen a human before and were curious about how one looked.

"I didn't know humans looked so much like us," Canny said. With his elongated eyes and narrow, snoutlike face, which was covered with reddish fuzz, he looked a bit foxy.

"Only on the outside," Damon said.

"Do humans breathe?" Don-Key asked.

"Yes, they do."

"I don't think this one does," Don-Key brayed.

"What's so funny?" Damon chided him. He examined Stanley's face; the boy's cheeks were rather gray, and it seemed there was no air going in or coming out of his mouth or nose. Damon put his ear against Stanley's chest and said, "Don-Key, stop your braying and fetch me some Live Water. Hurry! I don't think he'll wake up without it. He spent too much time enjoying the milkshake."

Don-Key left and was back within seconds, holding a vial of blue liquid, clear as the morning sky and streaked with gold, shiny as rays of the morning sun. Damon tilted Stanley's head back and poured the liquid through his parted lips. The boy gurgled, coughed, sneezed, and opened his eyes.

"Mom?" he whispered, looking around. "Where am I?"

"Wake up, son," Damon called with a smirk. "You're still in the Forest. It's time to continue your journey."

Shaking and unsteady, Stanley stood up.

"Where's the milkshake?" he asked, his voice husky and weak.

Damon and his friends turned around. The Milkshake River was gone; its bone-dry riverbed showed no trace of the sweet torrent that had flowed so freely only moments before.

"Good for you, Stanley," Damon said. "One less obstacle in your way, right, guys?" He turned to his friends with a grin.

Don-Key shook with laughter, and Canny nodded in agreement.

"Well, we won't keep you here any longer," Damon promised as he patted Stanley's shoulder. "I know you're in a rush to meet your friend."

"I'm in a rush to get out of here."

"I know—but remember, you can't leave yet." Damon put his thin lips up to Stanley's ear and whispered, "If you want to live, of course." Then he snapped his teeth together, barely missing Stanley's earlobe.

Stanley flinched. "I do," he said quickly, to be clear on the last point.

"Great," Damon replied. "So are you ready to get going?"

Stanley glanced around, trying to locate his "guide" when Damon asked, "Looking for this?" Like a circus magician, he twirled his wrist and opened his fist, revealing the familiar piece of charcoal, glowing, in the palm of his hand. He was about to toss it onto the ground, but his arm halted in midair.

"Oh yes," he added. "I almost forgot: another friend of yours is visiting here now."

"Rosebar?" Stanley asked, a sour look on his face.

"How'd you guess?" Damon laughed.

"I hate him."

"I can't blame you."

"Do you know him?"

"Not personally, but what I've heard about him doesn't excite me in the least."

"He's the cause of all my problems," Stanley admitted, gritting his teeth.

"If you want to get even with him," Damon said, his eyes twinkling, "I can help."

"Can you?"

"It would be my pleasure." Damon flashed a smile that revealed all four of his fangs. "Just let me know when you run into him, and I'll come right over."

"I'll text you. What's your cell number?" Stanley reached into his back pocket and pulled out his iPhone; it was dripping with milkshake. He stared at it, completely distraught, until Damon snatched it from his hand and hurled it in the direction of the Forest. Stanley watched in astonishment as his phone, like a little black bird, soared through the air and disappeared somewhere among the trees.

"Forget about it," Damon said and put his arm around the boy's shoulders. "I don't know what that thing's for, but I know it's useless in the Forest. Besides, it's ruined now anyway."

"But without my phone, how will I reach you if I run into Rosebar?"

"You don't need a phone for that. A dry leaf off the ground will do."

"What kind of leaf?"

"Any kind, so long as it's dry. Just breathe on it, say my name, and send it flying."

Stanley, even more baffled than before, was still hoping this was all just a bad dream.

"Have you ever played with paper birds?" Damon inquired.

"I don't think so." Stanley frowned, trying to remember. "With paper planes, yes. With paper birds, not really."

"Well, pretend the leaf is a paper plane or whatever you call it, OK?" Damon sounded somewhat annoyed. "Dart it straight forward anytime you want to reach me. Remember, I'm only a dry leaf away!" Damon tossed the piece of charcoal onto the ground and commanded, "Charcoal, go."

And at once, Stanley's glowing guide began to roll across the dry riverbed.

Big Yaga's Decision

By the time Big Yaga limped out of her bedroom again, the kitchen was perfectly clean, and the All-You-Can-Eat Tablecloth was neatly folded and back in its drawer. Little Yaga and her guests were sitting around the table, talking.

"Are you still hungry?" gloomy Big Yaga asked Eric.

"No, we're OK now." He smiled. "Thank you."

"So what are you still doing here?" she demanded, angrily banging her stick on the floor.

"Ouch, easy does it!" the Hut protested.

"Grandma," Little Yaga whispered, "you're not being polite."

"Who cares?" Big Yaga replied, irritated well beyond politeness. "We had an agreement. They were supposed to eat and leave."

"Not exactly," Sean objected. "If memory serves me, we were supposed to eat and rest, so now we're resting."

Big Yaga was so furious that she could've burned holes right through him with her eyes.

"And who are you, miserable human, to talk back to me, Big Yaga? One more word and I'll turn you into..." She looked around feverishly, trying to think of what she could turn him into.

"Stop it, Grandma." Little Yaga stood up from the table. "Don't turn him into anything—he's my friend."

"A human is your friend?" Big Yaga asked, her lips trembling.

"Mine, too," Kikimra butted in, looking dreamily at Sean. "Instead of turning him into something, esteemed Big Yaga, you should help him."

"Me—help a human? Never." Big Yaga snorted and turned around, ready to retreat to her bedroom. Suddenly she heard Eric's voice and stopped.

"Please, Big Yaga, help us. We'll never be able to save Ashley without you," he pleaded.

"Do I care?"

"Yes, you do," Little Yaga said, giving her grandmother an imploring look.

"No-o-o-o!" Big Yaga howled like a wild animal and shook her stick over her head.

"Grandma," Little Yaga told her, "you can howl, yelp, and shake your stick as much as you want, but you'll never be a wicked witch because you've got a kind heart, and we both know it. Eric and Sean are here to rescue Ashley. Please, help them."

Big Yaga started hissing like a snake and spewing wreaths of smoke that enveloped her body like a thick gray storm cloud. Next, she started spinning around on her bony leg—faster and faster—while the cloud of smoke spun in the opposite direction. Suddenly, the children noticed that instead of the walking stick, she was gripping a broomstick. Before they could say a word, she jumped on the long handle and flew out the window, which the Hut had hurriedly flung open. Speechless, Little Yaga and her guests ran over to the window after the old woman and watched her heading up toward the moon. Midway there, she suddenly turned around and, faster than a speeding train, rocketed back down.

"Move!" she hollered as she flew back in through the window. As soon as her feet touched the floor, her broomstick turned back into her walking stick. She plopped down on one of the kitchen chairs and said, "All right, I'll help you, but I'm warning you, I doubt there's any hope of rescuing your friend. Ashley's at Scraggard the Immortal's right now, and he's watching her like a hawk. He'll use all his powers to defeat you—and he's more powerful than all of us put together."

"Who is this Scraggard the Immortal, anyway?" Eric asked.

"The ruthless Ruler of the Forest. If you lose, which is most likely, you'll be cruelly punished for your efforts. Are you ready to face the consequences, no matter how brutal?"

"Yes," Eric said firmly and looked at Sean.

"Absolutely," Sean said with a nod.

Big Yaga grunted. "You have no idea what you're getting us all into. I don't know why I've agreed to go along with this, but I've given you my word, and I can't go back on it now. We are up for a very difficult task—I'd say next to impossible. Scraggard has chosen Ashley as his energy source, which means she is a part of him now. She can't hide or run away; he'll always know where she is, and he'll snatch her back in a minute. I'll be honest with you—over the course of many centuries, I know of only one of his energy sources who managed to escape." She sighed and stared at the teens with a look of genuine sadness on her face.

"Then Ashley will be the second," Eric said bravely.

"I wish I had your confidence," Big Yaga retorted. "Anyway, you've been warned."

"Thanks, Big Yaga," Eric said, his eyes full of gratitude. "So what's our next step?"

"Let me think." Big Yaga closed her eyes and hung her head almost down to her chest. She stayed in that position for a while, and Eric wasn't sure if she was deep in thought or simply sleeping.

"Big Yaga," he called her cautiously, "what do we do next?"

The old woman opened her eyes. "I don't know," she replied, but on seeing Eric's disappointment, she quickly added, "Cheer up, young human. My older sister, Biggest Yaga, will know what to do. We must talk to her. She lives up on Bold Mountain. I usually walk there, but it's pretty far."

"Could we maybe give her a call?" Eric asked.

"The phones may be tapped," Sean warned him.

"You're right," Eric agreed "I didn't think of that."

"Boys, the phones in the Forest are never tapped," Kikimra said, giving Sean a playful look. "Do you know why?"

"Why?"

"Because there are no phones in the Forest," she cried out and then began howling with laughter. "I don't even know what phones are!"

"The best way to get to my sister's place," Big Yaga said as she stood up, "is by air."

"Meaning…?" Sean stared suspiciously at her cane.

"Don't worry," Big Yaga reassured him, noticing his look. "You won't be flying on a broomstick—humans never do." Her eyes twinkled mischievously, and suddenly she appeared two hundred years younger. "You'll never know what you're missing," she added with a chuckle.

"Is there an airport nearby?" Sean asked doubtfully.

"I don't know what an airport is," Big Yaga replied, "but whatever it is we don't need it because we'll be flying in my barrel."

"A barrel's good," Sean said, finally willing to accept the weird reality of the Forest and stop being surprised by anything he encountered, no matter how wild. "What do you think?" He looked at Eric.

"A barrel's great! I've never flown in one before—must be fun!"

"It is!" Little Yaga exclaimed. "But, Grandma," she said, looking at Big Yaga, "I don't think we'll all fit into yours."

"You'd better," Big Yaga snapped. "I've got only one. Some of us will have to deflate."

"I hate deflating," Little Yaga said and shuddered, remembering her recent experience.

"You won't need to," Leesho told her. "Eric's a great artist. He'll draw a barrel and wish it real. You ladies will fly in Big Yaga's, and we gentlemen will fly in Eric's."

"Can humans wish things real?" Little Yaga asked, surprised.

"Some," Leesho answered vaguely.

A few minutes later, the two identical barrels soared up into the sky and headed for Bold Mountain.

Stanley Meets the Stove

Stanley's nostrils flared as the delicious aroma of freshly baked bread wafted toward his nose. While he was wondering where it was coming from, his charcoal guide rolled out of the forest and almost crashed into an ancient-looking wood-burning stove. It was huffing and puffing at the edge of the vast meadow, overgrown with long grass, resting lazily on the ground.

"Hello, young man," said a husky voice, and Stanley looked around. Except for the grass and the stove, the meadow was deserted. There wasn't a single bug crawling at his feet or a bird flying over his head. A waft of warm air stroked his face.

"You must be hungry," the voice said sympathetically.

"Yes, I am. Who are you?" Stanley turned to the forest, but the hoarse laughter behind his back forced him to spin around.

"Who am I talking to?" he hollered. "Who is it?"

"Hush, or you'll make my dough fall flat," warned the voice, while the stovepipe puffed out light rings of smoke.

Stanley squinted at the rusty pipe, knocked on it a couple of times, and heard the hollow echo of his own knocking in response.

"What are you doing?" the voice asked. It no longer sounded friendly. "That pipe's very old—you'll break it!"

"Sorry, I didn't mean it." Stanley withdrew his hand.

"I wanted to treat you to my delicious, nutritious, energizing bread, but I don't think you deserve it now." The Stove sizzled and spat black soot out of its pipe.

Stanley's stomach was growling.

"I'm sorry," he said again.

"OK. Only because I am very kind, I'll still let you have some." The Stove relented and slid its lattice to the side, revealing a puffy loaf of freshly baked bread that smelled irresistible. Its crust looked crispy and thin, and Stanley just imagined it melting in his mouth. His teeth tingled at the very thought of taking a bite. He pulled the loaf, warm and soft, out of the oven and closed his eyes in anticipation of the delightful experience. He took the biggest bite he could and immediately choked on it. The bread was burned through and through on the inside, and the chunk he'd bitten off had scorched his mouth and lodged itself in his windpipe. Unable to take a breath, he turned blue in the face, and his eyes rolled upward. He stood there with his arms outstretched, hands groping the air as if he were trying to grab on to something for support.

Spewing clouds of smoke, the Stove rumbled with laughter as Stanley's body wavered from side to side. Another minute and he would've collapsed on the ground, but suddenly, a powerful blow to his back dislodged the chunk of bread from his throat. Stanley bent over, coughing and gasping for air.

"Why'd you do that?" Damon demanded of the Stove. "You know Scraggard the Immortal needs him alive."

"I know," said the Stove, not laughing anymore; its stovepipe hung down like the tail of a dog being scolded. "But I couldn't help it." It chortled, and hissing and spraying cold mist, the Stove fell through the ground.

Damon turned to Stanley, who was still trying to catch his breath.

"Listen," he said. "What's wrong with you, dude? Can't you stay out of trouble? I'm tired of saving you."

"Sorry, but it wasn't my fault," Stanley managed to say.

"Whose, then?" Damon asked.

Stanley only shrugged his shoulders in response. He was too tired to argue.

"All right, don't sweat it." Damon slapped him on the back of his head.

"Stop it," Stanley snapped with a groan, rubbing the sore spot. "You're not my father."

"I just wanted you to relax, sissy."

"You relax!" Stanley yelped, suddenly turning very angry. He clenched his hands into fists and threw himself at Damon, shouting, "I'm sick of your Forest! I am sick of you! I don't need you saving me anymore—get lost!"

The second those last words left his lips, Damon was gone.

"OK, Charcoal," Stanley commanded, "go." But when he looked down, the piece of charcoal wasn't on the ground. He looked around; it was nowhere in sight.

"Charcoal, go!" he hollered again, but it seemed his glowing guide had disappeared along with Damon. Stanley looked up and saw only clouds, floating slowly across the sky, high above his head. He looked down, but he saw only the long grass resting under his feet.

"Hey, anybody!" he yelled at the top of his lungs, but he heard only the echo of his own shout resounding through the open space of the meadow.

Once again, Stanley looked around and realized he was all alone. He dropped down to his stomach, and for the second time that day, he felt his eyes grow moist. He tried to hold back his tears, but there were too many this time. They gushed out and ran down his cheeks in rivulets. Unable to stop the uncontrollable flow, Stanley lay down on his stomach and cried until, completely exhausted, he fell asleep.

At Biggest Yaga's

Big Yaga chanted the customary incantation for the fourth time:

"Hello, Hut on a chicken leg,

"Turn to us your front,

"And to the Forest your back."

But the chicken leg, thicker than the trunk of an oak tree, remained stuck in the ground up to its knee. Big Yaga repeated the request for the fifth time, and the chicken leg finally jerked and began, grudgingly, turning around. Half an hour later, the Hut was finally facing the visitors. They climbed up the wobbly steps, and the door in front of them opened on its own. The pungent odor of poison ivy wafted out from inside the Hut. One by one, the guests filed into the small room. Biggest Yaga was sitting on her bench near the hearth. She'd grown larger since the last time Little Yaga had seen her. The massive wooden bench, buckling under her weight, seemed more like a flimsy hammock. The black raven perched on her shoulder, motionless, could've been mistaken for a feathered statue if it hadn't blinked from time to time. The shaggy dog resting at Biggest Yaga's feet had also gotten bigger. It showed no interest in the visitors and only lay there, tapping the floor lazily with the tip of its tail.

"Hello, Biggest Yaga," Big Yaga greeted her older sister. Little Yaga and Kikimra curtsied. Leesho bowed. Eric and Sean waved.

"Good to see you all," Biggest Yaga said. "I know why you've come. You're facing a very difficult task. My little sister, Big Yaga, told you the truth about Ashley. She is now a part of Scraggard the Immortal, and there's no way she can simply escape."

"We've already heard that," Sean butted in, "and we've come here to find out if there's some other way to get her out of there."

"I've told you, Sean, I know the reason for your visit." Biggest Yaga pushed herself off the bench and stood up. "There's no need to be fresh with me." She smiled and walked slowly into her bedroom. The Hut shook, and the floorboards creaked and groaned with every heavy step she took. She came back out, carrying a thick, ancient-looking book, bound in leather. Once she was comfortably seated back on her bench, she flipped through the gilded pages. Soon she found what she was looking for and immersed herself in reading. Big Yaga and the teens stared fixedly at her silently moving lips. When she finally put the book down and looked up, she was met with six pairs of anxious eyes. For some time, she remained silent, as if she were thinking about how to begin.

"Yes, there is a way to free Ashley," she said at last.

The guests breathed a sigh of relief.

"What is it?" Sean asked.

"All you have to do," Biggest Yaga said slowly, "is get rid of Scraggard the Immortal."

"What do you mean, 'get rid of'?" asked Eric. "You don't mean we have to go to his place and…?" Unable to bring himself to finish his own sentence, he looked helplessly around at the others.

"Kill him?" Sean finished it for him.

"Whatever it takes," Biggest Yaga said flatly.

Eric shook his head. "I don't think I could kill anyone."

"No, you can't," Sean seemed to agree, but his face turned a shade of purple. "You are too kind. Scraggard's been sucking up Ashley's energy bit by bit. Let's have mercy on him and let him kill her instead."

"OK," Eric conceded. "Relax, I was wrong—I admit it, but how is it possible to kill an immortal?"

"I've heard," Leesho said, "that Scraggard's not actually immortal."

"You heard right," Biggest Yaga confirmed.

"So is it true what they say about his death?" Leesho asked.

"What do they say?"

"That it's hidden on the black tip of a needle, inside an egg, lying inside a duck, resting inside a goose, sleeping inside a rabbit that's sitting in a gold chest, hanging on an Oak Tree growing on the edge of a cliff over shark-infested waters."

"That's an accurate description." Biggest Yaga nodded.

"You see?" Sean sounded more cheerful. "We don't have to shoot anyone. All we have to do is find that tree, get the needle, and break the tip off—all very simple." Turning to Leesho, he asked, "Where'd you say the tree's growing?"

"On a cliff."

"And where's the cliff?"

"Over the shark-infested waters."

"And where are the waters?"

"Around Scraggard's palace, which is on the cliff," Big Yaga revealed. "The waters are called the Scraggard Canal."

The teens stared at one another.

"That's where we all must go now," Leesho said, then turned around, heading toward the door, ready to leave.

"Not *we*, Leesho," Biggest Yaga told him. "Only you. It was very clever of you to join Scraggard's army. You've gotten yourself unlimited access to his palace, which may be very useful in the future." Biggest Yaga noticed Leesho's hand reaching for the doorknob.

"Wait a second," she said stopping him. "I've got something for you here." She pulled Leesho's belt out of the bottomless pocket of her skirt. "The place you hid it isn't secure anymore— you didn't notice the sprig of willow that just sprouted out of the ground. You're lucky it hasn't told Scraggard on you. You know how zealous those young saplings are."

"Thank you, Biggest Yaga." Leesho put his belt back on. Knowing he was safe from Scraggard's eyes and ears in Biggest Yaga's house, he decided to ask a question that had been bothering him for a while.

"Biggest Yaga, everybody in the Forest knows you've got the answer to almost any question in the world."

"That's an exaggeration," Biggest Yaga demurred modestly.

"Well, I have one I hope you can answer."

"Let's see. What is it?"

"The ring that Scraggard the Immortal gave Little Yaga before she went to the human town had an inscription on the inside. Do you know what it said?"

"Yes," Eric exclaimed. "I saw it, too!"

Out of the same pocket from which Biggest Yaga had just retrieved Leesho's belt, she pulled a ring. The teens recognized it at once. Eric was the last one to have worn it before it got lost during his flight in the raven's beak.

"Biggest Yaga, how'd you get it?" he asked, surprised.

"I don't want to scare you, Eric, but in our Forest, those who ask too many silly questions lose their noses."

Eric automatically touched his.

"Don't worry—you haven't asked that many yet."

Biggest Yaga examined the inscription. The letters were tiny, and she needed to put on her enhanced reading glasses, which had lenses so thick that they magnified her pupils to the size of big cherries.

"The eye's dark blue, and here's the clue: show your prowess without your powers," she read aloud and then removed her glasses.

"What does it mean?" Leesho asked, bewildered.

"I don't know," Biggest Yaga said. "One of you will have to figure it out. Is there anything else you'd like to know?"

"No, thank you."

"You're welcome. Good-bye."

"Good—" Leesho began to reply, but Biggest Yaga snapped him away with his mouth half-open.

"Biggest Yaga, I have a question," Kikimra said when Leesho was gone.

"Go ahead, Kikimra."

"Do you have my ring, too?"

"Yes."

"Can I have it?"

"No."

"How come? It's mine. Scraggard the Immortal let me keep it."

"Do you know why?"

Kikimra made a stubborn face and said, "Because I've accomplished the mission he sent me on."

"Scraggard isn't that generous. He wanted to keep a close eye on you and Little Yaga—that's the main purpose of your rings and Leesho's belt. Leesho figured that out and warned Little Yaga to take hers off while at Ashley's party. For the same reason, he hid his belt when he went to meet Eric and Sean."

"But you gave it back to him."

"He can't return to the army without it. It's a part of his uniform."

Kikimra got into one of her moods and insisted, "I want my ring back, and I want it now."

Little Yaga felt her friend was about to blow a few spurts of smoke out of her mouth when Sean asked, "Kikimra, are you coming with us to rescue Ashley or not?"

Kikimra gave him another dreamy look. "Of course I am, Sean. With you, I'd go anywhere in the world."

Little Yaga couldn't help it and snorted.

"If Biggest Yaga gives you your ring back," Sean cautioned, "you won't be able to. You'll have to go home and wait for us there. Is that what you want?"

"Of course not, you human cutie."

"Then stop whining, and let's go. You'll get your ring back after we defeat Scraggard the Immortal and free my sister."

"If you defeat him," Big Yaga corrected the boy.

"I know we will."

Big Yaga only grunted in response.

Kikimra turned to Biggest Yaga. "Can I at least look at my ring, or will Scraggard spy on me?" she asked.

"Not on my territory," Biggest Yaga assured her and retrieved Kikimra's ring from her pocket. "Here you are safe."

Kikimra put the ring on her finger and extended her arm. The stones on the top didn't sparkle. She rubbed them on her sleeve, but they remained dull. She took the ring off and brought it up to her eyes.

"Look!" she cried. "There is an inscription on this one, too!"

She returned the ring to Biggest Yaga, who once again put on her enhanced reading glasses.

"*Of all of them by far, beware of the one named Eric Rosebar,*" she read aloud.

"What?" Eric asked, clearly taken by surprise. "What's going on here? Why on earth is my name engraved on Scraggard's ring?"

"Another silly question," Biggest Yaga cautioned.

Alarmed, Eric grasped his nose again. It was still where it belonged, in the middle of his face.

"Make sure you don't lose my ring," Kikimra warned Biggest Yaga as she watched the old woman slip it back into her pocket. "I want it back as soon as I return."

At Nightfall

Stanley was awakened by the wind whistling in his ears and chilling his body. He opened his eyes. The sky was still light, but the sun had disappeared behind the trees. Pink clouds, chased by the wind, were crashing into one another, like bumper cars at an amusement park. The evening mist dampened the air and soaked the long blades of lazy grass and the unruly locks of Stanley's hair. He didn't know how long he'd been sleeping, but he didn't feel rested. Getting up, he heard his joints creaking as if he were hundred years old. As before, the meadow around him was deserted. Looking down at his sneakers, he saw a narrow footpath he had not seen before falling asleep, or perhaps he had been too tired to notice it. It ended only a few feet behind him but stretched out ahead for as far as he could see. Having no other choice, he set out along the footpath toward the unknown.

The daylight faded long before the moon was ready to take over as the primary illuminator of the night. It was pitch-black all around. Before his eyes adjusted to the darkness, he could barely

make out his own hands. Odd sounds kept breaking the stillness
of the night. He walked gingerly until he heard footsteps behind
him and stopped abruptly. His heart raced. Whoever was following him was bound to bump right into his back. Expecting
an imminent impact, Stanley turned around and saw no one.
No sooner did he resume walking when, suddenly, his right ear
was tickled by heavy breathing, and there was a cough at his
left one. Stanley thrust out his arms, ready to grab whoever was
fooling with him, and touched nothing but emptiness. The loud
flapping of wings ruffled his hair as if a large bird were about to
land on top of his head. He looked up. The stars began popping
out here and there across the dark sky, but there wasn't a single
bird in sight. The only normal sound he heard was the screeching of an owl from the trees up ahead. Stanley kept walking, too
terrified to stop.

When the moon finally reported for duty and projected its
beam of light onto the meadow, Stanley saw that he'd come to a
three-pronged fork in the footpath: one led to the right, another
to the left, and the third led straight ahead. A short pole in the
very middle bore three wooden boards, each pointing in the
direction of the corresponding path. The moonlight was bright
enough for Stanley to be able to read the words engraved on
each of the boards:

"Go right, and you'll die of fright," the board pointing to the
right warned.

"Go left, and there will be nothing of you left," the board
pointing to the left cautioned.

"Go straight, and you'll meet your deadly fate," the board
pointing straight ahead informed him.

Stanley's hair stood up on end. He turned around, but the footpath he'd just been walking along was gone—completely overgrown with impassable thorny bushes, tall and wide. Cold fear gripped his young heart. Trembling, Stanley squatted down, looking for something on the ground, and there it was, a single dry leaf, apparently blown here by the wind. He picked it up. Following Damon's instructions, he blew on its surface, whispered Damon's name, and tossed it forward, like a paper airplane.

"No hard feelings," he heard even before the leaf had disappeared from his view. Grinning from ear to ear, Damon and his friends emerged before him, their fangs sparkling in the moonlight.

"Scared you to death, didn't we?" Don-Key asked, beaming brighter than the moon.

"What do you mean?" Stanley asked hoarsely.

"It was my idea to post these signs here." Don-Key pointed to the pole with the wooden boards bearing the bloodcurdling messages. "Canny came up with the words. Witty, aren't they?" he brayed rowdily, waking up the whole Forest.

"Stop it," Canny said, smiling modestly.

"OK, gentlemen," Damon said, "although he's a human, I think Stanley has proven himself to be as determined and fearless as a Forester. I feel he deserves to be introduced to our beloved Ruler of the Forest, His Scraggardness, Scraggard the Immortal. What do you think?"

"I think whatever you think," Don-Key said.

"How about you, Canny?"

"If you both think so, I'm with you."

Damon put the tips of his thumb and index finger together, stuck them between his teeth, and pierced the night with an earsplitting whistle that made Stanley jump and cover his ears with his hands so that his eardrums wouldn't burst. Before the deafening echo faded away, a raucous cackle sounded from above. Stanley looked up and saw four big white birds slowly descending toward them. He'd never seen such creatures—necks long as a swan's, but beaks and legs stubby as a goose's. As soon as the birds touched down, Damon ordered Stanley and his friends to climb onto their backs. Stanley thought it would be easy, but the birds' fluffy-looking feathers were greasy to the touch. Unable to get a good grip on them, he kept slipping off onto the ground, to the indescribable delight of Don-Key, who was falling down with laughter.

"Shut up!" Damon yelped, slapping his friend on the back of his head. That, however, only made Don-Key laugh harder. When Stanley landed on his still-aching behind yet again, Don-Key collapsed right next to him, hiccupping from all the laughter. Angered, Damon snapped his fingers and sent his friend somersaulting to the top of one of the birds.

Meanwhile, Stanley finally managed to climb up on the back of his. Seconds later, clutching its stiff feathers as tightly as he could, he was airborne! Flapping their wings, the four Swan-Geese had taken flight, and with the acceleration of a spaceship, they tore up into the night sky. They rose so high above the earth that Stanley thought he could surely touch one of the countless twinkling stars spattered across the cupola of darkness. Without thinking twice, he let go of the bird's feathers, reached up, and immediately slipped off its back. As he fell, he managed to grab hold of the bird's foot, but the Swan-Goose didn't like that and started shaking its leg, trying to break free of Stanley's grip. Don-Key watched, choking with laughter, as Stanley struggled to hang on for dear life. At last, he lost hold of the Swan-Goose's foot and plummeted downward like a stone.

A Message from Leesho

Biggest Yaga's guests were just about to leave when they heard a faint knock on the door, gentle as a scratch. Little Yaga looked out, but she didn't see a soul. All the more curious, she stepped out onto the porch, and there, behind the door, she noticed a dry leaf stuck in one of the logs. She pulled it out and brought it inside.

"It's a message from Leesho," she said, and she read the words that were pulsating on the leaf: "Hurry! Ashley's suffering."

"What?" Eric stood up abruptly and clenched his fists. "I hate that Scraggard, the monster. Let's go after him!"

"Wait," Little Yaga said as she looked at her grandmother and great-aunt. "Is there any way we can help Ashley now? We don't know how long it'll take us to get to her."

"As far as I remember," Big Yaga recalled, "Scraggard is gravely afraid of any illness. If his energy source falls ill, he stops using it, at least temporarily. Am I right, Big Sister?"

"You are," Biggest Yaga confirmed. "Sorry, I should've thought of that. I must be getting old." She glanced at her wrinkled reflection in the cracked mirror hanging over the fireplace. "Scraggard is extremely afraid of getting sick. Even a minor cold causes him to lose some of his energy, which can never be restored. If he knows someone's ill, he stays as far away from that creature as possible."

"Ashley must pretend she's ill!" Sean exclaimed.

"Exactly."

"Let's send Leesho a message to go talk to her."

"Not a good idea, honey," Kikimra objected.

"Why not?"

"Because Leesho's in the army. First of all, a message to him will be caught. And second, even if he gets it and goes to Ashley, she wouldn't trust him. She has no clue who Leesho is. Most likely, she'll think he's one of Scraggard's agents spying on her."

"You are absolutely right, Kikimra," Biggest Yaga agreed.

"How can we get to her, then?" Eric asked anxiously. "Biggest Yaga, why don't you look it up in your magic book?"

"That kind of information won't be in there," she answered, shaking her head.

"I have an idea," Little Yaga said, and everybody turned to her. "Sean, I saw a lot of magic objects in your house. You were constantly using one of them."

"Yes, a magic looking glass!" Kikimra cried. "I saw it, too!"

"Exactly, that's what I am talking about." Little Yaga nodded.

"What do you mean, magic looking glass?" Sean asked, confused.

"You had it in your hand all night long, remember? You used it to talk to that wizard, Google, or whatever his name, and then to Ashley when she stepped outside with some friends."

"Are you talking about my iPhone?"

"If that's how you call it, then, yes."

Sean scowled.

"It doesn't work in your forest—no reception."

"No what?" Kikimra asked.

"Never mind."

"Listen," Eric said his eyes brightening. "Little Yaga's idea isn't so bad. Instead of an iPhone, we can use a walkie-talkie. What do you think?"

"How?" Sean asked.

"It's pretty much just a radio. It should work even here."

"Yes, it should," Sean agreed, "but I don't know where we're going to find a walkie-talkie set in this forest."

"No need to look for one," Little Yaga said. "Eric will draw it."

"I keep forgetting about that," Sean admitted.

"I'll draw a really small one," Eric promised, "Ashley will be able to hide it in her clothes."

"Draw one with a separate headset," Sean suggested.

"Will do. I'll draw a headset made of clear plastic. It'll be invisible!"

"Great!" Sean smiled excitedly, but in less than a minute, his smile waned. "How will we get it to Ashley?" he asked and puckered his brow.

"Good question." Eric frowned, too.

"I don't know what you're talking about," Biggest Yaga said, "but if you think it'll work, then go for it. My bird, Clair, will fly it over to your friend." She looked at Eric and asked, "Is there anything you need from me?"

"Only two pieces of paper and a pencil."

Stanley Meets Scraggard the Immortal

Stanley opened his eyes and, terrified, closed them again. "I must've died and gone to hell," he thought.

"How are you feeling?" said a voice that was unexpectedly gentle.

Stanley opened his eyes again. Looming over him, he saw a thin face with no lips and no flesh between the skin and bones. Its eyes emitted a cold glow from the very depths of their sockets. The face belonged to an extraordinarily tall, scrawny man dressed in black garments, embroidered with gold bones that corresponded with the skeleton underneath his skin. The flickering light, casting ever-changing shadows, transformed the man's face from simply scary to downright terrifying.

"If Damon had caught you a split second later, you wouldn't be here right now," the lipless mouth whispered.

"If Don-Key hadn't been laughing like a maniac, I wouldn't have noticed him falling," said another, somewhat familiar voice.

"You see? And you always get angry with me and my laughter."

Stanley turned his head and saw Damon and his friends standing nearby.

"The last thing I remember is reaching for a star," Stanley whispered.

"You must've passed out," the tall man said with a smile, revealing his sharp fangs. "The youngsters of the Forest all know not to reach for stars while flying atop Swan-Geese." He turned around and walked slowly away. The back of his clothing was also decorated with golden bones that shimmered in the flickering candlelight. A short cape he'd thrown over his shoulders fluttered as he moved, giving the impression of black outspread wings.

Damon bent over Stanley.

"Do you think you can get up?"

"I hope so," Stanley answered, his back aching from lying on the cold marble floor. Damon gave him his hand and pulled him up to standing. Stanley looked around and saw that he was in a grand hall, more enormous than anything he'd ever seen. The walls were dressed in black marble, and lined with a multitude of doors, all of which had strange trees, with short branches and wrinkled leaves, growing on either side. There was no furniture in the hall, other than a colossal throne made of gold and studded with multicolored stones. The tall man was now sitting on the throne, erect and motionless as a statue.

"Approach," he bade the boys. Damon and his friends moved forward, with Stanley trailing right behind. When they reached the throne, the young Foresters knelt and bowed their heads.

"Enough formalities," the man said dismissively. "Stand up now."

Then he looked at Stanley and announced, "I am the Ruler of the Forest, Scraggard the Immortal."

"Pleased to meet you, sir," Stanley responded, not sure of what else he was supposed to do. He'd never met any rulers before and wasn't familiar with their etiquette.

Scraggard stretched his mouth into a smile.

"Stanley. I've heard a lot about you from Damon. He says you are a brave and determined young man."

Stanley blushed.

"He's exaggerating."

"I tend to believe his judgment, but you'll have plenty of opportunities to demonstrate your qualities—take my word for it. Damon told me you've come here, to the Forest, for your friend, Ashley. Is this correct?"

"Yes."

"It's very noble of you to go to a place you know nothing about, one that may be dangerous, if not life-threatening, for the sake of a friend."

"I had no idea where I was going," Stanley admitted.

"That's precisely my point." Scraggard smiled again. "I think you should be rewarded for your devotion to your friend. Do you agree?"

"I guess so," Stanley replied tensely.

"Ashley will be your reward. You'll be able to take her back home very soon." Scraggard leaned forward and lowered his voice to a very quiet whisper as he added, "But I need a favor from you in return."

Stanley stared at Scraggard apprehensively.

"What kind of favor?" he asked.

Scraggard straightened up again.

"Eric Rosebar," he proclaimed gravely.

Stanley thought he saw a tree by one of the doors behind the throne wince. Neither Scraggard nor Damon and his friends seemed to notice anything.

"What about him?" Stanley asked.

"Is he your friend?"

"He's my worst enemy."

Scraggard nodded in satisfaction.

"Mine, too."

"Really?" Stanley asked, surprised. "Do you know him?"

Scraggard gave the boy an icy stare. "Stanley," he said, "for future reference, *I'm* the one who asks the questions in my palace. Understood?"

Stanley bobbed his head silently in response.

"Good. Did you know that Eric Rosebar is also here, in the Forest?"

"Damon told me. And I know why—he wants to get to Ashley before I do."

"We must make sure that doesn't happen." Scraggard's eyes gleamed ominously. "Most likely, he's already on his way here. I am afraid his visit to my palace will prove destructive. I am not looking forward to it. I'd rather have him captured before he causes any harm." Once again, Scraggard pierced Stanley with his cold stare. "How do you feel about that?"

"I want him out of my way," Stanley affirmed. "I need to get to Ashley first."

"Very good," Scraggard said, contented. "Can I count on you to help me catch our mutual enemy?"

"Yes, you can," Stanley answered after a moment of hesitation. "I just don't understand how I can help."

"When the time comes, I'll let you know." Scraggard's voice was gentle, but his eyes remained cold as two frozen ponds. "It's a great deal, isn't it? I'll get Eric, and you'll get to leave the Forest with Ashley. We'll both win!"

"What do you need Eric for?" Stanley asked.

"Didn't I just tell you who asks questions in my palace?"

Ashley Meets Clair

The sun was gone. It had disappeared behind the tops of the tallest trees. Mortified, Ashley was staring at the darkening sky from her confinement in a drafty yard, high up on a cliff, jutting out over the shark-infested waters below. She felt very weak. The night before, when the last ray of the setting sun had vanished, the doors of the chambers where she was held captive opened, and two soldiers in treelike uniforms came out. They silently unlocked the gold wheelchair Ashley had been forced into, and wheeled it into a crystal room located behind her bedroom. A dreary creature that looked like an oversized mole, with a furry head, thin whiskers, and long, sharp teeth, pushed a button on the back of her wheelchair, converting it to a stretcher. The bright candlelight, reflected in every inch of the crystal room, dazzled her, and a sudden stabbing blow just below her left collarbone momentarily cut off her breathing. Then, a few seconds later, she found herself sitting upright in her wheelchair, shattered and gasping for air. The mole-like creature was gone, and

Ashley, foggy and lightheaded, was all alone, with a piercing pain that seemed to grip her racing heart. Her sense of time suddenly shifted, and she wasn't sure if she'd been at this horrific place for a day, a month, or a year. The only thing she was sure of that she wouldn't survive it here much longer.

When the first pale stars began popping out here and there above her head, a black raven appeared in the sky and flew toward her. Afraid it would attack her and poke out her eyes, Ashley squeezed them tightly shut until she felt something fall into her lap. She opened her eyes and saw a tiny object resting in the folds of her skirt. Ashley reached for it, but before she could touch it, the raven perched on the handle of her wheelchair and pecked at her right ear. Ashley winced from the unexpected tweak and suddenly heard Eric's voice.

"Don't say anything," he said. "Just listen."

"I don't believe it," was all she could think, and her eyes welled with tears.

"The raven's name is Clair—she's our friend. She's brought you a walkie-talkie and put a tiny headset in your ear. The walkie-talkie's very small, so hide it somewhere safe. Don't reach out to me unless it's an absolute emergency, but keep your earpiece in so that I can get in touch with you. What you have to do now is pretend you're very ill. Tell everyone that your throat hurts and that you can barely talk. Cough and sneeze as often as you can. You must look sick and weak, but stay strong. We'll get you out of there soon." A clicking sound cut Eric's voice off.

Ashley turned to Clair and mouthed the words, "Thank you."

The raven slowly closed and opened its eyes in response.

That very instant, the doors behind Ashley opened, and two soldiers ran into the yard. They dashed after the raven, but it bolted upward into the sky, where it turned into a black dot and disappeared from view.

"What did it want from you?" one of the soldiers asked Ashley.

She clasped her throat and coughed a few times before answering him.

"It wanted to kill me, the stupid bird," she complained. "It pecked at my temple and bit my ear." Putting her hand over her mouth, she pretended to sneeze.

"I wonder why." the second soldier said. "What if somebody sent it here?"

"Most likely it was attracted by the gold wheelchair," the first soldier countered with a smirk. "You know what those crows, jackdaws, and ravens are like. They're drawn to anything shiny." Turning to Ashley, he told her, "If it ever comes back, just holler. We won't let it attack you again."

"Thank you," she said hoarsely.

"What's wrong with your voice?" the first soldier asked. "Are you all right?"

"I don't think so. My throat's sore, and my body aches." Grasping her throat with one hand and covering her mouth with another, Ashley sneezed three times in a row and coughed for a while.

The soldiers looked at each other.

"This ain't good," the first one said. "We must inform His Scraggardness immediately."

"It's very drafty out here," the second one noted. "Let's get her inside first."

"I'll do that, and you go report to our beloved ruler."

"I can't. I'm your subordinate. The law does not allow me to report anything to His Scraggardness unless you're wounded or killed."

The first soldier glared at the second and gnashed his fangs.

"Well, there's a good chance I will be wounded or killed after I deliver the news." He growled, more despondently than threateningly. "You know His Scraggardness does not take negative reports lightly," he added before snapping his fingers and disappearing.

The Night at Big Yaga's

Both flying barrels landed in Big Yaga's front yard at the same time. Big Yaga hopped out of hers first. Staring at the back of her Hut, she demanded:

"Hello, Hut on a chicken leg,

"Turn to us your front,

"And to the Forest your back!"

The Hut whirled around and swung the front door open. Everybody walked into the kitchen, where Big Yaga said, "You must all go to sleep at once. The journey ahead of you will be long and dangerous. You better be well rested."

"You sound like my mother," Eric said. Then, realizing that Big Yaga seemed to have excluded herself from the journey, he asked, "Aren't you coming with us?"

"No," she replied. "I've grown too old for such an adventure. I'll wait for you here, in my Hut, with my Cuckoo Bird and my crystal ball—to check on you from time to time."

"How long's the flight to Scraggard's?" Sean asked.

"About an hour at super-speed and three hours at regular wind speed. Why?"

"I just wanted to know how soon we'd get there."

"Well, it'll take you much longer than that."

"Why?"

"Because you're not flying to Scraggard's," Big Yaga answered crossly.

"Why not?"

"None of you has a flyer's license."

Sean gave Big Yaga a surprised look.

"Didn't Little Yaga just fly a barrel back here from Bold Mountain?" he asked.

"Yes, but she was following a licensed flyer, which is allowed in an emergency."

"Then come with us, Grandma," Little Yaga begged.

"I said *no*," Big Yaga repeated. A cloud of gray smoke came out of her mouth, and this time, everybody believed she meant it.

"OK," Eric said. "How long will it take us to get there by car?"

"By what?" Big Yaga didn't understand.

"There are no cars in the Forest," Kikimra answered for her.

"Oh, you're talking about those stinky human things that make a lot of noise and spit out more smoke than all of us Foresters together?" Big Yaga asked. "Kikimra's right; haven't got any of those here."

"I can draw one," Eric suggested.

"That'd be cool," Kikimra said. "I'm dying for a car ride, but there aren't any roads for cars in the Forest."

"I can draw a truck with thick tires."

"It'll get stuck between the trees before it even gets going."

"True again," Big Yaga agreed. "You, darlings, have no choice but to use the oldest means of transportation."

"Which is?" Sean asked.

"Your own two feet," Big Yaga replied sharply. Turning to Kikimra, she asked, "Are you sleeping over here or going home?"

"Here, of course."

"Do your parents know?"

"They do."

"Good. You'll sleep with Little Yaga in her bedroom, and you boys will stay here, in the kitchen."

"What if they snore?" the Cuckoo Bird asked, sticking her head out of her door. "They'll wake me up."

Big Yaga stared silently at the insolent fowl for a moment and then said, "You'd better wake yourself up precisely every fifteen minutes, my feathery friend."

"There you go again," replied the bird. Ruffling her feathers, she twirled around and proudly disappeared into her quarters.

"Are you guys OK with sleeping in the kitchen?" Little Yaga asked, hoping her guests wouldn't think her grandmother inhospitable.

"No problem," Eric assured her. "I'll draw two sleeping bags for us, and we'll be just fine, right, Sean?"

"Yup." Sean yawned, ready to fall sleep anywhere.

"No need for sleeping bags," Big Yaga said. She snapped her fingers, and the kitchen table turned into two wooden cots covered with two soft mattresses stuffed with quail feathers. Bearskin sheets, pillows, and blankets were thrown on the top of each mattress. "You'll sleep like two winter bears," she promised. "Good night!" She snapped her fingers again, and instantly, Eric and Sean, wearing their new furry pajamas, were in beds sound asleep.

In the bedroom next door, Little Yaga and Kikimra were snoozing on the wooden block, which had doubled in width for the occasion.

Antibiotics?

Stanley's terrified gaze was fixed on Scraggard's bony hand, which was slowly squeezing the throat of a soldier in a tree uniform.

"If what you're telling me is true and the human girl's sick," Scraggard whispered, "you are going to die."

The soldier was one of Ashley's guards. He was wheezing, struggling to breathe. When the soldier's face turned blue and his eyes started rolling up in his head, Stanley shouted, "Antibiotics!"

Scraggard eased his grip, and the soldier fell to the floor, gasping for air.

"What did you say?" Scraggard turned to Stanley.

"Antibiotics."

"What is this, some new incantation?"

"It's medicine," Stanley explained. "It treats sore throats and many other things. When people get sick, they take antibiotics, and in twenty-four hours, they're not contagious. I know that for a fact because my little brother had strep throat a few times in a row."

"Where do you get this magic medicine?" Scraggard asked.

"At any pharmacy. All you need is a prescription from the doctor."

Scraggard motioned for a soldier who was guarding one of the doors to approach.

"Get me a doctor in here, now," he commanded quietly.

Everybody in the Forest knew the quieter Scraggard spoke, the angrier he was.

"Yes, Your Scraggardness." The soldier saluted, and Stanley thought he was the same one who'd winced when Scraggard had mentioned Eric's name earlier that day.

The soldier snapped himself gone. Another one appeared out of nowhere and replaced him by the door.

⚌

Eric was awakened by a light knock on the front door. Feeling too tired to get up, he wished he could just snap it open, like a Forester. Automatically, he pulled his hand out from under the blanket, aimed it at the lock, and snapped. To his astonishment, the door noiselessly opened, and Leesho, in his tree-like military uniform, walked in. Eric sat upright on his cot.

"What are you doing here?" he asked.

"I must speak to Big Yaga right away,"

Leesho whispered.

"She's sleeping."

"Let's wake her up."

Big Yaga never appreciated having her sleep interrupted. Eyes closed, she roared like a wounded animal. Clouds of black fumes streamed out of her mouth and nose, and her hair shook wildly with every move of her head.

"What do you want from me, you spoiled youngsters?" she demanded when her eyes finally opened, one at a time.

"Scraggard the Immortal sent Leesho to bring a doctor to his palace to examine Ashley," Eric explained.

"Fine, but what is he doing here? There are no doctors on my premises."

"If you remember, Ashley's not ill—she's only pretending. Any real doctor will figure that out right away," Eric said.

"Well, what do you want me to do about it?" Big Yaga growled.

"Your friend, Dr. Joe," Leesho said, "he can help us."

Big Yaga shook her head.

"I don't think so. He is not a medical doctor—he's a dentist."

"Scraggard didn't specify what kind of a doctor he wanted, just someone who could prescribe abracadabrics."

"What?" Big Yaga and Eric asked together.

Leesho knew he'd mispronounced the name of the medication, but he'd forgotten what it was called.

"Abracadabrics or something," he repeated. "The medicine that treats sore throats and other things."

"You mean antibiotics?" Eric asked.

"Yes, that's it." Leesho nodded.

"Dentists can prescribe them," Eric confirmed.

"Perfect!" Leesho turned to Big Yaga. "You know how impatient Scraggard is. Please, reach out to Dr. Joe and have him come over. He'd never say no to you. I'll take him to the palace with me and explain everything on the way there."

"Are you wearing your belt?" Big Yaga asked warily.

"Don't worry." Leesho lifted his shirt up. "I took it off before leaving the palace."

Dr. Joe

Scraggard the Immortal, seated on his throne and surrounded by Damon, Don-Key, Canny, and Stanley, was watching the screen in front of him. He knew the faces of most of his subjects, but he'd never seen Dr. Joe—most likely because the latter was very old and rarely left his home. His hair was white, his legs were thin, and his rounded shoulders were pulled forward. It seemed as though he had no neck, and his head was sitting atop his shoulders. Leaning on his wooden stick, he looked like a walking question mark. When he entered Ashley's bedroom, he found her in bed, coughing and sneezing. A few drops of her saliva fell through the screen and onto the marble floor before Scraggard's throne. Scraggard frowned in disgust, stuck his feet under the throne, and snapped the floor dry.

"Hello, young lady," Dr. Joe's greeted the girl in his croaky voice.

Ashley turned her head toward him and coughed until she almost choked.

"Well, well," the doctor said, putting his eyeglasses on. "I have not seen a human child in years. Oh my, you look quite miserable. Not feeling well, eh?"

Ashley ardently shook her head. The old question mark of a man smiled. His blackish fangs seemed not as sharp or intimidating as everybody else's.

"His Scraggardness summoned me here to help you," he said, "and I promised him I would."

He put his satchel on the edge of Ashley's bed, unbuckled it at the top, and took out a mouth mirror and a dental probe.

"Open your mouth, human girl. Let me look at your teeth first."

"My teeth don't hurt."

"Why on earth does he want to see her teeth?" Scraggard asked gruffly.

"The infection sometimes hides in the tiny crevices of your teeth, and from there, it slowly crawls down your throat and into your heart," the doctor explained.

"Really?" Ashley asked, eyes rounded.

"Yes, and that could be very contagious!"

Scraggard frowned, and one of his cheeks twitched. Once again, he put his feet under his throne.

Ashley opened her mouth, and Dr. Joe carefully examined her teeth. First, he looked at them with his mirror and then lightly tapped each one with the sharp probe. When he was through, he set his tools aside and asked, "How often do you brush your teeth?"

"Twice a day," Ashley replied.

"Good. Do you floss?"

"At home, yes—but here, no. I didn't know there was floss in this forest."

"We use spider silk for floss."

"Spider silk?" Ashley wrinkled her nose, displeased.

"It's good for your gums. I have a pack with me." Dr. Joe rummaged through his satchel, took out a small, worn-out case, and handed it to Ashley. She pinched a piece of the fine gossamer string between her fingers.

"It's so flimsy," she thought.

"No, it's not," Dr. Joe replied, having read Ashley's mind. He knew it was wrong to read his patients' minds, but he could not get rid of this habit. "It seems delicate, but it's very strong." He put the dental tools back into his satchel and took out a tongue depressor made of pure gold.

"Your teeth are in perfect shape. Now, let me see your throat. Say *ah-ah-ah*."

"Ah-ah-ah," Ashley said weakly. She hardly opened her mouth, afraid the doctor would figure out she wasn't sick. He squeezed the depressor between her teeth and pressed down firmly on the back of her tongue. Instantly, Ashley's mouth popped open, as if she had springs between the joints of her jaws.

"Terrible!" Dr. Joe exclaimed. "Horrible! You've got the worst strep throat I've ever seen! It's a highly contagious strain."

Scraggard paled and snapped the screen off. When, a few minutes later, Dr. Joe walked into the Throne Hall, Scraggard, white as fresh snow, said very quietly, "Give it to me."

"Give you what?"

Scraggard's nostrils flared.

"The prescription, Doctor," he demanded, more quietly still.

"Oh yes, I'm sorry." Dr. Joe reached into his satchel and pulled out a thick prescription pad, which had turned yellow over time. On the top sheet, he scribbled "Antibiotics." Just as he was about to hand it to the Immortal, Damon snatched it out of his hand.

"I'll take care of it," he said. Bowing to Scraggard, he added, "That is, with your permission, Your Scraggardness. I'll be right back."

"Go."

Extending his bony leg for longer strides, Damon left the Throne Hall. As soon as the door closed silently behind him, Scraggard turned to Dr. Joe and said, a trifle louder than before, "Thank you, Doctor. Your loyal service is appreciated."

Dr. Joe opened his mouth to respond, but before he could say anything, he found himself no longer at the palace but at home, talking to his own reflection in the rusty mirror on the cracked living-room wall.

A Slide Show around the Forest

Scraggard snapped the screen back on, and Stanley thought the image it displayed looked just like one from Google Earth.

"Mr. Scraggard, you've got Internet?" he asked, surprised.

"*Your Scraggardness*," Scraggard corrected the boy without taking his eyes off the screen.

"Your Scraggardness, have you got the Internet?" Stanley repeated his question.

"What kind of net?"

"The Internet. Isn't that Google Earth up there?"

"Who's Google? Never heard of him." Scraggard looked at Stanley in annoyance. "This is not Google's Earth; this is Scraggard's Forest."

He moved his eyes back to the screen, which now displayed a different image. A slide show had begun. One after another, the images changed so rapidly that the screen seemed to become one large green blur. The smell of fresh air tickled Stanley's nostrils, and a light breeze ruffled his hair. The loud chirping of birds filled the Throne Hall as if a whole flock had just flown in—a few colorful feathers fluttered down onto the marble floor. Stanley felt like he was back in the forest. A few seconds later, the original image returned and stayed, frozen, on the screen. The wind, the fresh aroma, and the chirping instantly ended; only the handful of feathers on the floor remained.

"Did I miss anything?" Scraggard asked, turning to Don-Key and Canny.

"I don't think so, Your Scraggardness," Canny said as he bowed and peered at the screen. "I think you've checked out every crack and crevice in the Forest."

"Did you notice any non-Foresters?"

"Nope," Don-Key answered this time. "There's none around, except for our buddy, Stanley, here." He slapped the boy on the shoulder. Wearing gloves that looked more like hooves, he couldn't control his strength, and Stanley flew clear across the Throne Hall, crashed into one of the closed doors on the other side, and slid down onto the floor. Don-Key choked with laughter.

"Are you crazy?" Stanley hollered, getting up. "You could've killed me!"

"Come on," Don-Key said, walking toward the angered boy with a friendly smile "That's what Live Water's for. Even if I accidentally harmed you, a few drops of Live Water in your mouth, and you'd be better than new." As he reached Stanley, Don-Key raised his arm to give him another slap, but the boy's half-terrified, half-infuriated look stopped him. Reluctantly, Don-Key lowered his arm.

"I know he's still in the Forest," Scraggard said, standing up.

"Who?" Don-Key asked sheepishly.

"Your Scraggardness, are you talking about Eric Rosebar?" Canny asked.

"Yes, Eric Rosebar. I'll bet you my head on a platter that he's hiding at Big Yaga's."

Breakfast with the Soldiers

The All-You-Can-Eat Tablecloth was covered with food, right down to its tassels. Big Yaga was eating a combination of spiders, leeches, bumblebees, and ticks sprinkled with grated charcoal and generously dressed with cockroach oil. She claimed such a breakfast was good for the damaged joint in her bony leg, and she was convinced one day her knee would be healed. Kikimra was munching on a rattlesnake sandwich on a bed of fried fly agarics, covered in a whipped alabaster spread, and snorting with enjoyment; she believed alabaster spread strengthened her powers. A pitcher of poison ivy juice sat on the table in front of her. She and Big Yaga kept refilling their cups, which were made of poison ivy leaves.

The rest of the table accommodated every imaginable human breakfast food: pancakes, crepes, sour cream, honey, and an assortment of fruit jams. Toasted breads, bagels, doughnuts, and muffins were piled up on exquisite porcelain platters, next to a variety of cream cheeses. Cold cuts, smoked fish, and hard cheeses were set on trays made of fish scales and goatskin. There were hot dogs adorned with mounds of hash browns, sitting on salvers made of straw. Fountains of cereals and melted chocolate flowed freely out of wooden containers into seashell bowls. Fruits from every corner of the world, smelling as fresh as if they'd just been picked, were arranged in ice vases that wouldn't melt. Little Yaga decided to join Eric and Sean and eat human food. To her surprise, she didn't find it repulsive.

The teens were talking about Leesho's late-night visit when, suddenly, in the middle of a sentence, Kikimra snapped her fingers and turned Sean into an old wooden stool. When Eric looked at her in astonishment, he was instantly turned into a rickety wooden bench. That very second, there began banging on the front door that was so strong it shook the Hut. Little Yaga went to see who it was, but before she could make it to the door, it flew open toward the outside by itself. At once, Little Yaga heard heavy thuds, followed by angry growls. Together with Kikimra, she ran out onto the porch and saw four soldiers, hands over their foreheads, getting up off the ground.

The tallest, wearing a wider belt and a hat with more branches on it than the others, climbed the steps and angrily declared, "If your Hut ever decides to play a joke like this on His Scraggardness's soldiers again, I'll snap and burn it to the ground!"

He kicked the door, and his foot got stuck between the logs it was made of. With all his strength he yanked to pull it out, but suddenly meeting no resistance, he flew backward, somersaulted over the railing and fell flat onto the ground. Enraged, he jumped to his feet, ready to make good on his threat to burn down the Hut, when Big Yaga appeared in the doorway.

"Hello, Bravest One," she greeted the soldiers. "What has brought all of you here to my modest abode?"

"We are looking for a human by the name of Eric Rosebar who is visiting our Forest," the tall soldier reported, his anger suddenly subdued. He had never met Big Yaga in person but had heard that she, although not as mighty as Scraggard or Biggest Yaga, was powerful enough to snap her fingers and have *him* burned to the ground. "His Scraggardness is eager to meet this human," he continued. "The ruler knows he's been on the grounds of the Forest for some time now but has not yet made it to the palace. His Scraggardness is worried that his guest has gotten lost. Has he stumbled upon your Hut, by any chance?"

"The only persons who've stumbled upon my Hut," Big Yaga answered, her voice a bit annoyed, "are you and your troops. At present, you are interrupting my breakfast, and I must warn you, Bravest One, that nobody likes me when I'm hungry—not even me," she growled and burst into menacing laughter.

"I am sorry. We didn't mean to disturb your meal, but His Scraggardness has sent us here to speak with you, and—ouch!" the tall soldier exclaimed and grabbed the tip of his nose, which had been scorched by Big Yaga's angry glare. "Why don't you go back inside and finish your breakfast, venerable Big Yaga?" he suggested sonorously. "We'll wait out here and speak with you when you're done."

"I wouldn't dream of making Scraggard the Immortal's soldiers wait outside," Big Yaga said with a sneer. "Come on in and join me and the girls at the table."

The tall soldier followed Big Yaga into the Hut. Little Yaga watched from the porch, through a small round window in the wall, as he stepped over the threshold. As soon as he was inside, the door slammed shut behind him so hard that it smashed against his rear. He went flying into the air and landed, flabbergasted, on one of the chairs at the table. The door opened again to let the next soldier walk through, then sent him flying, too. It performed the same stunt on each of the two remaining soldiers, until all four of them, with bumps on their foreheads and aching behinds, were seated around the table, side by side, facing Big Yaga.

Little Yaga and Kikimra were the last to walk back into the Hut. The door waited until they'd cleared the doorway before gently closing behind them.

"Welcome," Big Yaga greeted her guests again. "Help yourselves, loyal soldiers. Place your orders and our All-You-Can-Eat Tablecloth will serve you whatever you wish."

"What's this?" the tall soldier asked, looking at the human food.

"Human food," Big Yaga replied matter-of-factly.

"Looks disgusting."

He leaned forward, sniffed it, and gagged. "And it smells even worse. Who's eating this? Do you have humans over?" He suspiciously stared around to see who else was in the Hut.

"I ordered it," Little Yaga said. "It tastes better than it looks and smells. When I went to the human town the other day, I tried some there, and I liked it. Why don't you taste it, Bravest One? You aren't afraid to try it, are you?"

"I'm not," said the shortest of the four, and he reached for a muffin.

"Hold it!" Big Yaga snapped her fingers, and his hand froze in midair.

Little Yaga looked at her grandmother.

"Little Yaga forgot to tell you," Big Yaga continued, "that if you want to taste human food, you must take off your belt."

"How come?" the tall soldier asked suspiciously.

"Those are the rules."

"I've never heard of these rules before."

"You've never tried human food before, either." Big Yaga looked at the troops. "Whoever wants to taste human food—pass me your belts."

Three of the soldiers unbuckled their belts and handed them over to the old woman, but the tall soldier shook his head.

"I am fine. This food's not appealing to me."

"You still must give me your belt."

"Why?"

"The rule says that whenever you are next to human food, you must have your belt off."

"That's a strange rule. It doesn't make sense."

"Some rules don't. Give me your belt—now," Big Yaga demanded threateningly, and a trickle of smoke came out of her mouth.

"What if I choose not to?"

"At this point, it's not a matter of choice."

She snapped her fingers, and the fourth belt, the widest, joined the three others in her wrinkled hand. Another snap transported her into the basement, where she shoved the belts into the darkest closet under the staircase.

Master Kastor at the Palace

Once again, Scraggard's screen went black. A strong smell of mothballs mixed with the stale air of the closet filled the Throne Hall.

"Old witch," Scraggard muttered, switching the screen off, "your nasty tricks won't fool me. I know he's hiding in your wicked Hut." He stood up. The creaking sound of his joints reverberated throughout the Throne Hall. "And where is that demon, Damon, with the antibiotics?"

"I am here, Your Scraggardness," said Damon as he appeared from behind the throne, looking pale and tense.

"Well?" Scraggard gave him an icy look. "Have you got them?"

"I have not, Your Scraggardness," Damon admitted with a bow turning even paler.

"Why not?" Scraggard's voice was so quiet now that Damon had to read his lips to understand what he was saying.

"Master Kastor has never heard of them. He has no clue what they are or what they're for. He thinks the human boy has made them up."

Scraggard turned to Stanley. Under his chilling gaze, the boy's body stiffened, his lips turned blue, and his teeth chattered.

"I have n-n-not m-m-made them up," Stanley stuttered, his vocal cords quivering from cold and fear. "Any pharmacist kn-n-n-nows what antibiotics are and what they are for. Your M-Master Kastor must be a phony, not a real pharmacist."

Scraggard looked back at Damon.

"Bring that swindler here now."

Within seconds, Damon had disappeared and reappeared, holding a hunched little man by the scruff of his neck. He was the apothecary, Master Kastor. Scared to death, he was staring at the floor. His small bloodshot eyes were blinking rapidly behind his thick glasses. The apothecary had never been to Scraggard's palace, and apparently, his only wish now was to get out of here alive. When he lifted his eyes and met Scraggard's aloof gaze, he trembled, fell to his knees, and raised both arms up.

"Oh, Mightiest of the Powerful! Oh, Greatest of the Great! Oh, Immortalest of Immortals! Have pity on your humble servant. Don't execute me mercilessly. I've been practicing apothecary for as many centuries as I can remember, but I've never heard of those wretched—antibiotics." He faltered on the last word. "My teachers were the most prominent genies, the wisest wizards, and the smartest alchemists, but none of them ever mentioned such a remedy."

Scraggard's cold look fell back upon Stanley, who was covered in goose bumps that revealed his fear.

"Did you hear what Master Kastor just said?" he asked.

"If Master Kastor had taken lessons from scientists, pharmacologists, and chemists instead of genies, alchemists, and other bogus magicians, antibiotics would've been at your disposal now, sir."

Scraggard shifted his eyes back to the apothecary.

"Did you hear what the human boy just said?"

"He called my renowned and celebrated teachers bogus magicians," Master Kastor proclaimed, straightening up. "I don't think he respects wizardry. I find it insulting." Out of indignation, he stopped trembling.

"Why do you insult our venerated apothecary?" Scraggard asked Stanley.

"I am not trying to be insulting, but I do think your venerated apothecary's confusing pharmacology with wizardry."

Master Kastor removed his glasses, wiped them with the hem of his frayed jacket, and put them back on the bridge of his nose.

"For your information, you brazen human," he noted calmly, "pharmacology and wizardry are twin sisters. I learned this fact centuries ago when, as a young boy, younger than you are now, I was taking my first apothecary lessons."

"Centuries ago, you said?" Stanley smirked. "Have you ever taken a refresher course?"

Master Kastor snorted scornfully.

"With my invaluable experience, why would I need to?"

"To learn about antibiotics, for example, and tons of other medications that have been discovered over the past hundred years."

"Why would I have to learn about those? I don't treat humans, and they would be useless on Foresters." Master Kastor shrugged his shoulders and looked at Scraggard. "Your Scraggardness, I dare say that I find this human urchin unreasonable."

"I don't," Scraggard responded coldly. "We get human visitors to our Forest from time to time, and I hope to have more in the future. A good apothecary must know how to treat them if necessary."

Master Kastor immediately hunched over again and broke into cold sweat.

"If you th-think s-so, I p-p-promise to—"

"Dismissed." Scraggard interrupted the mumbling apothecary and snapped his fingers.

As Master Kastor tumbled onto the floor of his small, dusty lab in the back of his Hut, his hair was standing on end, but he was insanely happy to be alive.

Meanwhile, back at the palace, Scraggard returned to his throne.

"Damon," he said quietly, "I want to see every one of the Forest's apothecaries—now."

"Always at your service," Damon replied, eyes full of dog-like devotion. He bowed and clicked the backs of his hooves together, like an officer. "Your Scraggardness, may I take Don-Key and Canny with me?"

"Whatever," Scraggard said as he leaned on the back of his throne. "Hurry!"

"Always at your service," Damon, Don-Key, and Canny said in unison. Together, the three of them snapped themselves gone.

The New Wall Clock

The Cuckoo Bird opened her eyes and realized she'd been sleeping for at least an hour without having cuckooed the time. Knowing Big Yaga was busy with her guests, she hoped to be spared her wrath. Her usual tactic to avoid punishment was to act as if she'd done nothing wrong and be outraged when scolded. She smoothed her feathers, cleared her throat, and stuck her tiny head out of her tiny door. She saw Big Yaga fussing around the kitchen and Little Yaga and Kikimra sitting at the table across from four soldiers. Eric and Sean were nowhere in sight. Without thinking, Cuckoo Bird asked, "Where are the human boys?"

"Who?" the tallest soldier asked, turning sharply around and fixing her with a stare.

"Eric and Sean."

The tall soldier stood up from the table. A gloomy silence, interrupted only by the ticking of the clock, hung in the air. With an ominous look at Big Yaga, he demanded, "Where are Eric and Sean?"

Instead of a reply, Big Yaga glared angrily at her bird.

"Who are Eric and Sean, you sleepyhead? As if it's not enough that you've overslept, as usual, now you're talking complete nonsense. I am fed up with you." Big Yaga extended her arm, ready to finally make good on her threat and turn the clock into a regular mechanical one.

The Cuckoo Bird realized her mistake and knew she was in real danger this time. She quickly started blinking her eyes and turning her head from side to side, as if she were trying to figure out where she was.

"Wait a second," she said nervously. "It was all so real. I don't believe it was only a dream!"

"Come on, now, birdie," the tall soldier said as he began slowly advancing toward the clock. "Don't play games with me," he snarled warningly. His eyes had turned dark, and black smoke streamed out of his mouth. "You either tell me the truth or I'll wring your neck."

He reached forward and tried grabbing the bird by her feathers, but she dodged his hand, shot a panicked look at Big Yaga, and disappeared behind her door. The soldier clutched the tiny door handle and violently shook it. When, to his surprise, it didn't budge, he raised his massive fist in the air.

"What are you doing, Bravest One?" he heard Big Yaga's voice from behind him.

"I am smashing this clock to pieces," he replied brashly, "a lot of very small pieces, to be precise." He stretched his narrow lips into a wry smile.

"I wouldn't if I were you."

"Why not?"

"Because it's not nice to come to somebody's house and start smashing things, don't you think?"

"I do—unless somebody is harboring enemies of His Scraggardness, Scraggard the Immortal."

"You have no proof of that."

"My proof is my gut feeling. I trust it completely. It has never let me down."

"It's letting you down now."

The tall soldier's face became gray with fury.

"Let me tell you something, you ugly old witch," he said through his clenched teeth. "You are a liar." The swirls of black smoke from his mouth rose to the wooden ceiling. The Hut sneezed, and the floor under his feet shook so violently that he barely managed to keep from falling over.

Little Yaga jumped to her feet. The smoke coming out of her mouth was white. No matter how angry she was, her fumes were never any other color, but she was happy she could produce any at all.

"How dare you call my grandmother a liar?" she asked indignantly.

"Old and ugly, too," Big Yaga added as she walked up close to the tall soldier. The top of her head reached only halfway up his chest, but as she leaned on her cane, she suddenly began rising upward, and so did her cane. Little Yaga could hardly believe her eyes. She'd always known that her grandmother's damaged knee prevented her bony leg from extending. Big Yaga herself was a bit surprised—she'd been unable to extend her left leg for decades; the healing powers of her breakfast mixture must've begun working at last.

When her eyes reached the level of the tall soldier's, she spoke directly to his face and said, "I am tired of you, Bravest One. You came to my house uninvited, you tried to destroy my belongings, and just now, you've insulted me. I don't appreciate your behavior."

The tall soldier attempted to raise himself higher than Big Yaga, but, suddenly, he was unable to move.

"Is that how you feel?" he asked crossly.

"Yes." Big Yaga nodded. "But to be fair, I have also noticed a few of your good qualities."

"Oh, really?" the tall soldier jeered. "Which ones?"

Big Yaga ignored his sarcasm and unexpectedly changed the topic.

"You've met my Cuckoo Bird, that unreliable feathery creature I feed for nothing in return, haven't you?"

"I've had the pleasure," the tall soldier replied, looking gloomily at Big Yaga.

"She always oversleeps and never cuckoos at the right time. It is useless asking her to give us a wake-up chirp. She also talks too much, as you've heard, and she talks back, too. I've known her for ages, and there's no hope she'll ever change. I can get rid of her, of course, but I've kind of gotten attached to the insolent little thing, and she's well aware of that. You, on the other hand, strike me as a trustworthy and reliable serviceman. You take your duties seriously and perform them diligently. You are also presentable. I feel you'd be a valuable addition to my household and a dependable supplement to my capricious and inaccurate bird."

"What do you mean?" the tall soldier asked guardedly, unsure of where Big Yaga was going with this little speech.

Big Yaga smiled, and her wrinkled face crumpled up even more.

"I mean," she replied, "that I am turning you into a military wall clock, and your three companions will be the clock's hands."

On hearing her pronouncement, the three soldiers tried jumping to their feet, but Big Yaga had already snapped her fingers.

Instantly, a new pendulum clock was ticking up on the wall alongside the old one. As promised, the grimacing faces of the three soldiers adorned the tips of each of the hands. The short and stocky soldier glowered from the tip of the hour hand. The steadily moving second hand was tipped with the sulky mug of the long and lanky trooper, and the minute hand was outfitted with the scowling kisser of the third. The tall soldier's gloomy puss sat on the bob of the pendulum, swinging rhythmically from side to side. His nose was flattened, his lips squeezed tightly together, and his eyes glared furiously.

"What time is it, my bravest clock?" Big Yaga barked out, like a general during a military parade.

"Ten o'clock," the face atop the hour hand replied.

"Twelve minutes," the mouth above the minute hand followed.

"And eighteen seconds," the lips over the second hand finished.

"Precisely!" the voice of the tall soldier stated, loud and clear as though reporting on the readiness of his troops.

Kikimra giggled, but Little Yaga frowned.

"Good job," Big Yaga said approvingly, "and now allow me to introduce the human boys to you, my military clock. If I remember correctly, that's who you've come here to meet."

She snapped her fingers, and the wooden stool and the rickety bench by the table instantly turned back into Eric and Sean.

The Apothecaries

Damon, Don-Key, Canny, and Stanley were standing behind Scraggard the Immortal, who sat perfectly erect on the throne—pale and motionless. The Throne Hall was filled with the smell of potions and other concoctions, emanating from the hundreds of apothecaries from all over the Forest who had gathered there at Scraggard's request. They were young, middle-aged, and old; some had beards, while others were clean-shaven. Their fangs were either short and sharp as penknives or long and pointy as spears. Most of the apothecaries were wearing goggles, long rubber gloves, and dusty aprons. They all stared at Scraggard apprehensively, unsure of why they'd been summoned to the palace.

Scraggard stared back at them. His cold eyes moved slowly from one apothecary to the next, making them feel even more ill at ease. Full as it was with Foresters, the magnificent hall was noiseless, as if it were empty. When the silence had become almost unbearable, Scraggard suddenly smiled and said, "Welcome."

His soft voice and a smile calmed the apothecaries. Relieved, they grinned back.

"I don't know if my young disciples told you why you've all been invited here," Scraggard whispered.

The apothecaries shook their heads. Scraggard gave the boys a reproachful look.

Damon walked out from behind the throne and knelt before the ruler.

"Your Scraggardness, we didn't realize we were supposed to," he said.

Scraggard motioned for him to return to his friends and looked at his guests again.

"I need your help, masters. I have a very important visitor staying at the palace. She's fallen ill, and the doctor has prescribed antibiotics to treat her condition. Tell me, who among you can fill that prescription?"

The rumble of a murmur suddenly filled the Throne Hall. Loud at first, it soon began to grow weaker until, a few minutes later, it died down altogether, and the gloomy silence returned to the Throne Hall. Scraggard the Immortal stood up. Once again, his eyes, now darkened, were moving from one apothecary to the next, each of them shrinking beneath his morose gaze.

"I don't hear any answers," Scraggard said, his voice so quiet that if it hadn't been for the absolute silence in the hall, no one could've made out his words. "You leave me no choice but to warn you that if I do not have the antibiotics in my hand by next dawn, each and every one of you will be turned into a test tube and, regretfully, donated to the Forest School for use in the Principal Rat's alchemy lab."

"Your Scraggardness," called out one of the oldest apothecaries with a long white beard and short, obtuse fangs, as he
came forward, "each and every one of us is ready to give our
lives for you, but we've never heard of *antibiotics*. What are they
for?"

"They fight infections," Stanley volunteered from behind
the throne.

"Human infections," Scraggard clarified.

"Human infections?" repeated the old apothecary, spreading
his arms. "None of us has ever treated human infections—or
any other human diseases, for that matter. That's why we have
not heard of antibiotics." He then stepped back into the crowd.

"That's too bad," Scraggard replied coldly. "You have until
next dawn to fill the prescription."

He sat down again, ready to dismiss the apothecaries, when
a young druggist strode forward from the very back of the hall
and knelt before the throne.

"Your Scraggardness, I think I heard of antibiotics when I
was a student. My professor, Master Tabulet, mentioned them
once."

Scraggard the Immortal stood up abruptly.

"Your teacher was Master Tabulet?"

"Yes. She was great."

"Where is she now?"

"I don't know. Nobody knows. One day, she just disappeared."

Scraggard sat back down on his throne.

"Your great professor almost killed me once."

"There's no way, Your Scraggardness. Master Tabulet
couldn't kill anyone; she was too kind. She never experimented
her potions on any living creature, not even a mouse or a fly."

"I broke my wrist once a couple years ago, and she gave me her medicine. It burned my throat like a blazing fire. I couldn't talk or even breathe for fifteen minutes. I swore to turn her into a test tube as soon as I got my voice back and was able to utter an incantation. She read my mind and took advantage of my temporary powerlessness to escape."

"Did your wrist heal?"

"Yes, in fifteen minutes. When my throat stopped burning and I got my breath back, my wrist was fully healed, but by that time, she was gone. To this day, I've no idea how she did it. It is next to impossible for anyone to escape my Forest on their own."

"I am sure she didn't do it on her own, Your Scraggardness," the young apothecary said. "She saved so many creatures of the Forest that many of them, I imagine, were happy to return the favor when she needed help."

"I'd like to find out who assisted her, so I know how many traitors live in my Forest," Scraggard thought to himself, forgetting for a moment that most apothecaries could read minds. "Now," he said out loud as he stuck the prescription in the pocket of the young apothecary's coat, "let me remind you, masters, that if I don't have the medicine in my hand at next dawn, the first rays of the sun will strip you of your Forester forms and turn you into a bunch of very fragile test tubes."

The Broken Screen, or Stanley's Revelation

One by one, four soldiers walked out of Big Yaga's hut, marched through the gate, and disappeared into the Forest.

"There they are," Scraggard the Immortal said, pointing at the screen. "What a surprise! I didn't think I'd ever see their faces again. I was sure the old witch had turned them into fried cockroaches and eaten them for breakfast. If she let my soldiers out, there must be no humans in her wretched hut." Scraggard the Immortal turned to the boys, who were still standing behind his throne, and muttered more to himself than to them, "Where can they be hiding, I wonder?"

"What if the old witch sneaked them out of the Forest?" Damon suggested.

"I don't think so," Scraggard replied. "Humans are very persistent creatures. They've come here on a mission, and they won't leave until it's accomplished. They are also unpredictable and full of surprises which I doubt I'll appreciate. I don't trust them roaming all over my Forest. I'd rather have them right here, in my palace, under my direct supervision…, forever." Turning back to the screen, he continued, "If my soldiers move fast enough, they'll be back here no later than tomorrow afternoon. I can't wait to listen to their stories. They might shed light on the humans' whereabouts."

He snapped the display larger for better viewing. The soldiers were marching directly toward him. Their feet, in hoof-like boots, and their hands, in gloves adorned with jagged claws, periodically pierced the screen, letting the smell of the Forest into the Throne Hall. It seemed that with one more step, they'd jump through the screen and onto the marble floor, right in front of Scraggard. At one point, all four of their faces jutted out into the hall.

A moment later, the road took a turn, and the soldiers disappeared behind the thick, knotty trees, whose long, contorted branches spread out and reached into the Throne Hall, blocking Scraggard's view. Annoyed, he snapped them away, and instantly the screen in front of him was filled with static. A raw, earthy smell oozed in. Strong wind howled behind the darkened display and blew its surface out like a sail on a pirate ship. Chilling draft swooshed through the hall, fluttering the candlelight and ruffling Scraggard's clothing and boys' hair.

The Immortal snapped his fingers, but the monitor remained fuzzy. Scraggard snapped his fingers again and muttered an incantation. Still, the image on the screen wasn't restored. At this point, Scraggard stood up, raised his arms over his head, and chanted something incomprehensible while illuminating the screen with the blue glare of his eyes. When the display showed no sign of improvement, Scraggard hissed with rage, walked over to the screen, and smashed it with his fist. At once, the static disappeared, and the monitor went black.

"Beastly device," Scraggard whispered. "I wish I hadn't turned the human who set it up for me into a shark and thrown him into the ocean when I did."

"Yes," Damon agreed, "Your Scraggardness, if you hadn't, he could've fixed it for you."

"No," the Immortal snarled, "if I hadn't, I would've enjoyed doing it now!"

"Your Scraggardness," Damon said as he knelt down once again, "with all due respect, I implore you to turn that shark back into a human. You may need his expertise to defeat your enemies."

Scraggard's face turned white.

"I have never taken advice from anyone," he whispered, "especially not from a cheeky eighth grader." He raised his arm over Damon's head. "You've overstepped the boundaries and will be punished. I am turning you into a kneeling statue. You'll be placed in one of my sculpture collections, next to the statues of other unruly subjects of mine."

Awaiting his doom, Damon impulsively pulled his head down to his shoulders. When, a few minutes later, he realized that he was still alive, he cautiously looked up and met Scraggard's contemplative gaze.

"Get up," the Immortal ordered him, "and consider yourself lucky. I don't want to waste my energy on you; I've got too little left. And also…" Scraggard trailed off and hesitated for a second. "For some inexplicable reason, I've taken a liking to you."

Damon got up, feeling a little dizzy.

"Regarding that human," Scraggard continued matter-of-factly, "I turned him into a shark so that nobody else in the Forest could have a screen like mine. But even if I wanted to turn him back, I've no idea where he's swimming at the moment."

Damon returned to his friends. Don-Key brayed with laughter.

"What's so funny?" Damon asked gloomily.

"You should've seen your face when Scraggard said he wanted to turn you into a statue. Your eyes popped out of your head and turned red as a couple of tomatoes."

"Yes, it was funny," Canny said, grinning.

"I'd like to see what you'd look like in my place," Damon said gruffly, still feeling rather shaky.

"I wouldn't," Don-Key yapped as he stomped the marble floor with one of his hooves.

Suddenly, Stanley, who had kept very quiet all this time, coughed into his fist and said somewhat undecidedly, "I think—to be precise, I am sure—that two of the four soldiers on the screen looked exactly like Sean Laing and Eric Rosebar."

The Meeting of the Apothecaries

Having been snapped out of the Throne Hall, the apothecaries gathered on the high cliff behind the palace. From down below, they heard the water in the Scraggard Canal surrounding the palace splashing against the rocks. The yellow rim of the sun was already peeking out from behind the trees.

The old apothecary who had spoken to Scraggard climbed atop the Big Rock. His long white beard, the bottom of his silvery gown, and the tassels on the silk scarf wrapped around his thin neck were waving in the gentle breeze. He howled loudly to attract the attention of the crowd below. When all the eyes fixed on him, he calmly said, "Dear colleagues, I hope you realize the degree of danger we're all in. Scraggard the Immortal is very good at keeping his promises. If he does not have that human medicine in his hand in about twenty hours, we won't be able to practice our craft ever again. Instead, we'll be gathering dust on a rack in the Forest School alchemy lab, until we're shattered by the hand of a clumsy student during an experiment. Would any of you like for this to happen?"

"No!" the apothecaries shouted all at once and in perfect unison.

"Then we must all go home and look through the notes we've collected since ancient times. Hopefully, one of us will come across the formula for antibiotics. Whoever does should whistle the Mighty Whistle of the Forest, and we'll meet back here, at this exact spot, and let Scraggard know that his order has been carried out."

"And if there is no Mighty Whistle by next dawn?" somebody from the crowd inquired.

"Oh, we'll still meet up, except it'll be on a rack in the lab at the Forest School."

The young druggist, Master Tabulet's former pupil, approached the Big Rock and tilted his head back to be able to see the old apothecary's face.

"If there was a way to contact Master Tabulet," he called out shielding his eyes from the glare of the sun, "we could get the formula."

The old apothecary grabbed his bearded chin and stayed in that position for a while, thinking.

"I believe," he said at last, "that the only person able to contact Foresters who live outside the Forest is Biggest Yaga. Have you heard of her?"

"I have, but I've never met her."

"She lives on Bold Mountain on the other side of the Forest, far away from here. You may go there if you like, but it's a long walk." The old apothecary scrutinized his young colleague's face. "You're still too young to have compiled very much valuable information in your treasure chest," he continued. "Why don't you go see Biggest Yaga? It may be the best thing for you to do, under the circumstances."

The young druggist contemplated the old apothecary's suggestion for some time before finally responding.

"How do I get there?" he asked.

The old apothecary looked around. "Do you see that cloud right above the bridge?" He pointed to the one slowly floating over the Scraggard Canal towards the Forest.

Young apothecary nodded.

"It seems to be on its way to Bold Mountain. Just follow it, and it'll bring you directly to the steps of Biggest Yaga's Hut."

Moving Forward

After taking their belts off and burying them deep in the ground, Little Yaga, Eric, Sean, and Kikimra sprinted through the woods at speeds that Eric and Sean, both on the track team, had never thought possible. Sharp branches scratched their faces and pulled at their hair. Old stumps and knotty roots tried tripping them over, and swift bats zipped right above their heads, threatening to jab their claws into the teens' scalps. After a few hours of running, Eric and Sean began slowing down, and Little Yaga's pace was no longer as brisk, either. Only Kikimra, with her bony leg extended, was every bit as energetic and fast as before.

"Hey, you guys," she warned, "if you don't pick up speed again, it'll take us a week to get to Scraggard's palace. I don't think Ashley will be thrilled with the idea of staying there for seven more days."

Just then, Sean tripped over a knoll and went flying to the ground. The hoof boots slid off his feet and went flying up, getting wedged between the branches of a tree nearby. Sprawled on his stomach, Sean groaned.

"Are you OK?" Kikimra asked, tapping him on the shoulder.

Sean rolled over onto his back and moaned. "I'm sore all over."

"I'll fetch you some Live Water," Kikimra said, "and you'll feel good again. Now get up and put your hooves back on."

Sean looked at his feet, which were blue and misshapen from the hours of running in the hooves. He tried to wiggle his toes but could hardly move them.

"No more hooves for me," he said, shaking his head "I am not a horse, you know."

Kikimra stared into his face, which was distorted with pain and fatigue, and didn't think it very cute anymore.

"Hey, what do you mean, no more hooves? Without them, you'll be running ten times slower!"

"Listen, I love my sister, and I'm here to rescue her. But she'll just have to wait for a week, OK?"

"Without the hooves, it'll be three weeks."

"Whatever," Sean replied. Turning to Eric, he said, "Why don't you go without me? I'll wait for you right here and join you on your way back."

"You obviously don't know our Forest," Little Yaga said. "In three weeks, you'll either have been picked up by slave hunters and sold into slavery or eaten by wild beasts."

"Or," Kikimra added, "turned into a wood block by one of our classmates, just for fun."

Staggering, Sean got up on his feet.

"I have an idea," he said weakly. "Eric, draw me a horse. I'll ride to the palace."

"That's a great idea!" Eric picked up a twig off the ground. "Why didn't you think of it sooner? I can hardly move anymore myself! I'll draw four horses, one for each of us."

Eric was about to take his backpack off and start drawing when Kikimra burst out laughing.

"Horses!" she exclaimed. "You'll make our jackals very happy. They love horses, but there isn't any left in the Forest—all eaten up. Whenever jackals smell a horse, they come to it one by one, tear it apart, and gobble it up, along with the horseman. If you're interested in meeting our jackals, go ahead, draw yourselves a couple of horses, but let me get out of here first!"

"You girls live in a really sick place," Sean said. Picking up a long stick off the ground, he jabbed at his hooves, which were stuck on the branch above him.

"I hate the thought of putting these back on," he added.

"Wait a second," Eric said, snatching the stick out of Sean's hands. "I know what I can draw."

"What?"

"Wait till you see it; you'll love it."

"What is it?"

Eric knelt down, flattened the rough soil with his hand, and started drawing, while Sean walked around, trying to guess what it could possibly be. Suddenly, he hollered, "Eric, you're a genius!"

Little Yaga and Kikimra bent down to look at the sketch, too.

"What is it?" Little Yaga asked, puzzled, then turned to Kikimra. "Do you know?"

"Nope." Kikimra shook her head.

Eric kept drawing. When he'd finished three more sketches of the same object, he tossed the stick and whispered, "I wish them all real."

Instantly, four identical monstrous contraptions, as weird as anything Little Yaga or Kikimra had ever seen, sprang out of the ground. Each had two thick wheels attached to a low, horizontal platform that was connected to a long vertical rod with two handles on top. The "monsters" were quietly rumbling.

"What are these beasts?" Kikimra shrank back, keeping her distance from the growling creatures.

"These 'beasts' are called Segways," Eric said. "Don't be afraid—they don't bite. They're not your hungry jackals; trust me. We'll use them to get to Scraggard's palace."

"How?" Little Yaga asked nervously. "Do they fly?"

"No, you ride them," Sean explained as he hopped up on the horizontal platform of one of the Segways and circled around for a few minutes. "It's fun!" he exclaimed with a grin, hopping off.

Little Yaga looked hesitant.

"You wanna try?" she asked Kikimra.

"Sure, I'll give it a try!"

Determined, Kikimra walked over to another Segway and hopped on. Confident as if she'd done it many times before, she started riding around. Her hair blew in the wind, her eyes sparkled, and her cheeks flushed from delight.

"It's fun!" she yelled. Overcome with excitement, she threw her head back and howled. Sprays of smoke, colorful as fireworks, gushed out of her mouth and rose up against the darkening sky.

"I'm glad you like it," Sean said with a smile, and Kikimra found him cute again.

Eric turned to Little Yaga, who stood looking on, still apprehensive.

"Cheer up." He nodded toward the rumbling machines and said, "Just pick one and hop on. You'll like it—I promise."

Reluctantly, Little Yaga stepped on the platform of one of the Segways and grabbed the handles. The two-wheeled vehicle tilted forward, almost tossing her over, but she managed to regain her balance. Her knees were shaking.

"Are you OK?" Eric asked.

"Yes," she replied curtly, "but I'd prefer a broomstick."

"How do you know?" Kikimra asked. "You've never even flown one."

"I just have a feeling I would."

"Come on, broomsticks are *so* last millennium. Your grandmother flies one. I'd much rather fly a Segway."

"Segways don't fly," Sean said, smiling.

"You wanna bet they do?" Kikimra's eyes gleamed mischievously. She was tempted to snap her Segway airborne, but the legal flying age in the Forest was twenty-one, which neither she nor any of her classmates thought fair. Kikimra felt she was already mature enough to be allowed to fly, but she knew that if she was caught in the air without an adult, she'd be stripped of her flying privileges for another fifteen years.

"What's your legal flying age?" she asked Sean.

"I think you can start taking flying lessons when you're eleven or twelve, and you are allowed to fly on your own around the age of sixteen."

"You humans are lucky," Kikimra said feeling jealous.

"I didn't know humans could fly," Little Yaga noted incredulously. "What do you fly—barrels or broomsticks?"

"Planes and rockets," Sean answered, laughing. "And we can fly very high."

"How high?" Kikimra asked, unsure whether she should believe Sean's words.

"As high as the moon, for example. Did you know that humans have walked on the surface of the moon?"

"What?" Little Yaga and Kikimra shouted together and stared at the sky.

"No way." Kikimra shook her head, and looking at Sean again, she said, "I don't believe you. Nobody can fly high enough to reach the moon, not even Scraggard the Immortal."

"Humans can."

"Are you trying to tell me that you, humans, are more powerful than Scraggard?"

"Apparently, we are," Sean said.

"Apparently, you're the biggest liar I've ever met," Kikimra retorted. "If you weren't so cute, I'd snap you all the way to your moon."

"The moon isn't mine; it's everybody's."

Kikimra wanted to come back at Sean with something sarcastic, but Eric interrupted.

"Please, stop arguing," he asked. "I can't concentrate." He was looking at the compass on his wrist, which he'd sketched and wished real before leaving Big Yaga's hut.

"Well," he said after a while, "it looks like we have to go in that direction." He pointed toward a narrow, winding path that disappeared behind the trees.

"How does that thing know which way to go?" Kikimra wondered aloud, staring at the compass's quivering needle.

"Human powers!" Sean answered with a smirk and waved his hand in front of Kikimra's face like a magician.

She pushed his hand away. A trickle of smoke came out of her mouth.

"You'd better not mess with me, human," she said crossly. "When I get upset, I can't always control my own powers. You don't want to suddenly find yourself lost in the middle of the Forest in the company of a hungry grizzly bear, do you?"

"Not at all."

"Then don't annoy me."

"OK," Sean promised, making a mockingly fearful face. "I won't."

"Good," Eric said. "If everybody's ready, please start your vehicles and follow me. We don't want to lose any more time."

The Young Apothecary
at Biggest Yaga's

The young apothecary was out of breath by the time he reached Biggest Yaga's Hut, perched on top of Bold Mountain. Surprisingly, its back was already turned to the Forest and its front to him.

"Hello," the apothecary said with a bow.

If the Hut heard him, it showed no noticeable sign of acknowledgment.

"Hello," the apothecary repeated, bowing again.

The Hut remained still and silent, appearing fully oblivious to his presence.

"Hello," the apothecary said once more, bowing for the third time and raising his voice no more than a fraction.

"Why are you shouting like a maniac?" came the Hut's booming response. "I heard you quite well the first two times."

"You didn't say anything," the apothecary replied apologetically, "so I wasn't sure."

"I didn't say anything because I didn't feel like it. Why do I have to answer every stranger who decides to talk to me? I am tired of speaking to you all. I've stood here for centuries without being bothered by anyone. Now, all of a sudden, everybody wants to talk to me. 'Turn to the back, turn to the front; turn to the left, turn to the right.' What do you think I am—a ballerina? Look at me—my poor thatched roof is lopsided, and my poor little leg hurts from all that pirouetting."

The young apothecary moved his eyes from the thatched roof to the massive chicken leg and said, "To be honest with you, venerable Hut, your roof and leg look fine to me."

As soon as those words left his mouth, the Hut's roof slid over to one side, and its chicken leg came out of its socket, tilting the whole house.

"Do they still look fine to you?" the Hut demanded. "Be honest."

"Now they don't."

"That's what I'm talking about, so stop bothering me and go away."

"I don't think so," a calm voice objected from behind the door. "Straighten yourself up and let my visitor in."

"Oh, I'm sorry," the Hut murmured, suddenly pleasant and sweet, hurriedly restoring its roof and leg to their original positions. "Biggest Yaga, I thought you were asleep, and I didn't want anyone to bother you."

"Thank you," came a dry reply from inside.

The Hut flung its door open and squatted down to make it easier for the young apothecary to enter. He walked through the doorway and stopped in front of an old woman who was so big that the hefty bench she was sitting on sagged under her weight.

The ruffled black raven nestled on her shoulder kept turning its head from side to side like it was looking for something.

"Stop that," snapped the old woman, who the young apothecary figured was Biggest Yaga. "If you don't, one of us will get vertigo. Look carefully, you, feathery worrywart. Borzy's under the table."

Biggest Yaga turned to the young apothecary and said, "They can't live without each other—I mean, my dog and my bird. When the Hut decided to play the Leaning Tower of Pisa just now, Borzy slid all the way over there." She pointed to the cluttered table in the corner. The tassels of the tablecloth covering it were practically touching the floor. The young apothecary bent down and saw a dirty-white heap of a shaggy dog peacefully snoozing underneath.

"Sleeping, I bet?" Biggest Yaga half asked, half stated.

"I think so," the young apothecary answered as he peered into the darkness.

"Believe it or not," the old woman told him with a snort, "he was once the fastest hunting dog around. Now he's growing lazier by the minute. You see, even all the commotion hasn't woken him."

"No, it hasn't." The young apothecary straightened up.

"See, you worrywart?" Biggest Yaga squinted at her bird. "You've gotten upset over nothing."

The raven croaked, flapped its wings, and suddenly took off. It swooshed past the young apothecary's nose and dove under the tablecloth. A minute later, it showed up, pulling the sleeping dog by its ear. Gliding across the floor, the dog lazily opened one eye and closed it again. As soon as they reached Biggest

Yaga's feet, the raven let go of the dog's ear, flew up, and resumed its position on the old woman's shoulder.

"Wow, that's one strong bird," the young apothecary commented.

"You better believe it. Clair's so strong that she can raise you into the air." Biggest Yaga patted the bird's beak. "This thing's as hard as a rock."

The young apothecary reached out to touch the beak, too, but the bird made a strange gurgling sound and bit his finger. The young apothecary quickly withdrew his hand, wincing from the pain and barely able to suppress a groan.

"What do you think you're doing, bullying our guest? Don't you know he's come here for help?" Indignant, Biggest Yaga jolted her shoulder. The bird began rapidly beating her wings so as not to tumble over.

"May I ask," the young apothecary said quietly, "how do you know what I've come here for?"

Biggest Yaga chuckled in response.

"I'm sorry—I know you are very powerful," the young apothecary quickly added, looking at Biggest Yaga intently. "Speaking for all the druggist of the Forest, I must say, you are our only hope. If you can't help us, nobody can." The young apothecary grew somber.

"I can't promise you anything." Biggest Yaga stood up, and the floor groaned under her feet. She disappeared into her bedroom and returned a few minutes later with the thick leatherbound book. Back on the bench, she put her glasses on and began reading. Holding his breath, the young apothecary watched her silently moving lips.

"Well," she finally said, looking up from the gilded pages, "the good news is, I've got the formula you need right here in this book."

The young apothecary's eyes shone as he breathed a sigh of relief.

"But the bad news is," Biggest Yaga said as she closed the book, "you haven't got enough time to concoct the medicine. As far as I know, you only have until dawn. Am I right?"

The young apothecary nodded.

"I wish I was wrong." She put the book down on the bench. "Unfortunately, it takes from two to five days before the antibiotics are effective."

On hearing these words, the glow in the young apothecary's eyes died out.

Scraggard Summons the Leader of His Swan-Goose Squad

Gray with fury, Scraggard the Immortal was spinning around like a whirlwind and howling like a wolf. His gaunt face and fiery eyes appeared and disappeared before the awestruck boys. Flickering from the flow of air raised by Scraggard's flailing garments, the candlelight cast bizarre shadows on the ceiling, walls, and floor. It seemed as if the Throne Hall itself was quivering and swaying. Suddenly giddy, Stanley wanted to hold on to something so as not to fall. If he'd known Scraggard would take it so hard, he would never have mentioned Eric and Sean's names. The Immortal spun faster and faster until it grew impossible to discern his face at all. It looked as if a raging tornado had burst into the Throne Hall. When the candles started going out one by one, Stanley finally hollered, "Your Scraggardness, what if I was wrong and those two soldiers only looked like Eric and Sean?"

Scraggard stopped spinning at once. He approached Stanley and whispered into his face, "No, human boy, you were right." The tip of Stanley's nose froze from Scraggard's icy breath. "I've been duped. That old witch, Big Yaga, will pay for her dirty trick."

He clenched his bony fists and brandished them in front of Stanley's face. The bones in his hands rattled, echoing loudly throughout the hall.

"Your Scraggardness," Damon said as he stepped forward, "would you like me to go and drag her here?"

"Yes, but not now." Scraggard walked over to his throne, and the boys followed. "We'll deal with that witch later," he said angrily as he sat down. "Right now, I must see the leader of my Swan-Goose squad." He snapped his fingers, and instantly, a big white bird, with a long swan's neck but the short legs of a goose, appeared, beating its wings over the boys' heads. The image of Scraggard the Immortal was imprinted on its left wing. A tiny red military hat, with a gilded top and a visor, crowned its head. The bird slowly descended and perched on a gold bar that had materialized out of thin air before the throne.

Approaching the Apple Orchard

K ikimra was the first to see the Orchard in the far distance. She shot Little Yaga an annoyed look and muttered, "I forgot all about it."

"So did I," Little Yaga admitted.

Turning to the boys, Kikimra said, "Hey, guys, those apple trees ahead are the most irritating creatures on earth. When we get to them, they'll start begging us to eat their apples."

"I wouldn't mind an apple or two," Sean said. "I'm kind of hungry."

"You don't want *those* apples," Kikimra told him, grinning.

"Why not?"

"They're so sour that they'll burn a hole in your tongue."

"OK, we won't eat them," Eric said.

"But then the trees will get angry, beat us up with their branches, and not let us through."

"Can we take a detour?"

"No." Little Yaga shook her head. "We'll lose tons of time. This Orchard's the largest in the Forest. It stretches for miles in both directions."

"Can you snap it gone?" Sean wondered. "I would if I could." He snapped his fingers in the direction of the Orchard.

"Don't bother," Little Yaga said. "Even if you had powers, you wouldn't be able to snap those plants out. In the Orchard, as soon as one tree disappears, for whatever reason, another one pops right out in its place."

"So what do you guys do? How do you get past them?"

"We pretty much just cover our heads with our hands and run."

"We can't ride the Segways and cover our heads at the same time," Sean said.

"We'll have to leave them behind," Kikimra told him, jumping off hers. "Eric will draw us four new ones on the other side of the Orchard."

"I don't think our hands are a good enough defense against branches and apples," Eric said.

"You're right," Kikimra agreed. "But that's all we've got."

"Can you think of anything else?" Little Yaga looked at Eric.

"Let me see…" Eric paused for a moment, thinking. "I'll draw us some helmets and branch-proof vests," he said. Then he hopped off his Segway and bent down to look for a stick.

"What?" Kikimra didn't understand.

"Helmets and vests," he repeated.

"What are they?"

"You'll see." Eric cleared the ground of any grass, leaves, and pebbles and started sketching lines and circles as fast as he could. Before long, the four friends were wearing their new protective gear: khaki-colored helmets and brown vests, speck-led with green blotches.

Kikimra and Little Yaga eyed each other up and down.

"We look like apple saplings," Little Yaga said, laughing.

"That's the idea." Eric smiled. "Reasonable camouflage never hurts."

Kikimra knocked on her helmet; a hollow sound responded. She and Little Yaga guffawed. They were about to hop back on their Segways when Little Yaga noticed a cluster of tiny white dots, which trembled in the distance against the dark-blue sky. They could've been mistaken for stars if they weren't moving toward the Orchard and growing larger by the second. Little Yaga's lips tightened. She tapped Kikimra on the shoulder and silently pointed at the dots, now resembling tiny white birds.

"Swan-Geese!" Kikimra gasped. A look of panic distorted the normally smug expression on her face. "What do we do?" she whispered.

"The apple trees can hide us," Little Yaga whispered back.

"But we'll have to eat their apples."

"I know." Little Yaga's mouth puckered as if she'd already taken a bite of one. She and Kikimra looked up. The birds were practically over their heads now. Little Yaga clutched Kikimra's wrist and muttered, her voice hoarse with fear, "At this point, I don't think we have a choice."

The Young Apothecary
Meets Vincent

Clair zoomed out the door, holding the astonished young apothecary by the scruff of his neck. She tore up high into the sky, carrying him with ease, as if he were a paper cutout. Now he understood what Biggest Yaga meant about her bird's strong beak! Dazed by Clair's breathtaking speed, he was shocked to find himself standing—in what seemed like a minute later—in front of an odd structure with tinted windows adorned with the brightly blinking words, "Exotic Meats Shop." The building was larger than any hut in the Forest. It stood at the edge of a meadow, directly on the ground, with no chicken leg underneath! The young apothecary wanted to ask the bird where'd she brought him, but the raven was nowhere in sight.

"Clair?" he called out and got no answer.

"Clair!" he shouted again, hearing in response only chirping of crickets in the grass. He looked around and realized he'd been left all alone in this strange place in the middle of nowhere.

"Where am I?" he muttered under his breath, feeling uneasy.

"You are in the human town," a deep voice behind him replied. Startled, the young apothecary spun around, his heart pounding wildly in his chest. Before him he saw a smiling man with a gray mustache curled up at both ends, big hairy hands, and long, sharp teeth. The man was leaning against an odd type of an apparatus that had two wheels and what looked like a saddle.

"You're kidding," the young apothecary said.

"Not really."

"What am I doing here?"

"You're the one who should be telling me."

"And who are you?"

"I'm sorry—I haven't introduced myself. My name is Vincent." The man extended his hand, and the young apothecary automatically shook it. The man's long nails cut deeply into the apothecary's furry palm, but with all the excitement, he didn't notice the pain. "I'm the co-owner of this meat shop."

"Nice to meet you," the young apothecary said as he bowed down. He couldn't think of anything else to say.

"Would you like to go in with me?" Vincent pointed to the store.

"I'd like to go back to the Forest."

"But you must've come here for a reason."

"A raven named Clair brought me here and left."

"She couldn't stay. If she had, in exactly three minutes, she would've turned into a regular crow, unable to ever return to the Forest."

"How do you know?"

"I know lots of things." Vincent laughed. "Let's go inside and chat."

In the Apple Orchard

Little Yaga, Kikimra, Eric, and Sean jumped off their Segways and dashed toward the apple trees. The gnarled branches, heavily laden with small green fruit, hung nearly to the ground. Up in the sky, the Swan-Geese were getting dangerously close. The teens could almost hear their wings rhythmically slashing through the air. Panicking, they ran faster until they finally reached the Orchard. When they tried to dive in for shelter, the branches barred their way.

As quickly as they could utter the words, Little Yaga and Kikimra called out:

"Dear, luscious apple trees,

"Hide us from the Swan-Geese, please!"

The apple trees swayed from side to side, and their branches shook with effort as they tried to lift themselves up, without success. The Orchard responded to the girls' request with a choir of drawling, discordant voices:

"See the heaviness of our limbs?

"We can't raise them to let you in!"

As the Swan-Geese began their descent, trembling Little Yaga and Kikimra repeated their plea—so rapidly this time that it was difficult to distinguish one word from another:

"Dear, luscious apple trees,

"Hide us from the Swan-Geese please!"

In response, the Orchard drawled out a different chant:

"Our apples are tangy and green,

"Feast on them, kids, and we will let you in!"

By now, the Swan-Geese were so low that their wings blocked out the light of the moon. Eric and Sean looked at Little Yaga and Kikimra, wondering what they should do.

Staring at the approaching birds, Little Yaga yelped, "Eat them!"

She picked a few apples from the branch she was closest to. Kikimra, Eric, and Sean followed her example. When their hands were full of the small green fruit, Little Yaga discreetly glided her palm over them. Eric was the first to dig his teeth into one of his apples as the others stood and watched.

"It's burning a hole in his tongue before our very eyes," Kikimra said flatly. "He'll need more than one drop of Live Water if he ever wants to speak normally again."

"Actually," Eric said, licking his lips, "it's really good. My tongue wants more!" Smiling with delight, he chomped into his second apple.

The four friends had eaten all the fruit they'd picked so quickly that they almost choked on them, and at once the apple trees raised their lightened branches, letting them in. One after another, the teens disappeared in the darkness of the Orchard just as the Swan-Geese, loudly cackling, touched down near the trees. The birds tried to rush in after the teens, but the branches, once again heavily laden with the small green apples, drooped down, barring their way.

The birds stretched their long necks, struggling to stick their heads between the branches, only to have their beaks scratched and their eyes poked. One of the Swan-Geese pecked at an apple. Instantly, the piece it had bitten off burned a hole in its beak and fell out through the opening. The birds backed away from the trees and bolted up into the sky all at once. For a while, they circled above the Orchard, peering down, but unable to discern anyone through the thick branches, they turned around and left in the same direction from which they'd come.

"They'll be back," Kikimra muttered, watching them fly away.

"Yes," Little Yaga agreed. "We'd better get out of here before they return."

"They'll be after us wherever we go," Kikimra said gloomily. "Scraggard the Immortal won't get off their backs until they have us in their nasty beaks right in front of him."

"If you're so sure they'll be back," Eric said, "let's get ready to give them a proper greeting."

"What do you mean?" Little Yaga asked.

"You'll see."

Eric knelt down and began drawing. Soon, each of the four teens was equipped with a slingshot and a backpack.

"What is it?" Little Yaga asked, studying the slingshot Eric had handed her.

"It's an ancient weapon for fighting off annoying birds," Sean explained, laughing.

"Really?" Little Yaga looked at Eric. "What is it called?"

"A slingshot."

"Never heard of it." Little Yaga pulled on the rubber band attached to the Y-shaped frame. When she let go, it painfully slapped her fingers. "Ouch!" she cried. "That hurts!" A curl of white smoke came out of her mouth.

"It hurts because you don't know how to use it," Eric said.

"How, then?"

"First of all, it needs the proper ammunition."

"Proper what?" Kikimra asked.

Eric only waved his hand. "Let's just fill our backpacks with as many apples as we can carry," he said. "After that, Sean and I will teach you both how to use your slingshots."

Inside the Exotic Meats Shop with Vincent

The young apothecary finished his story, and Vincent looked at his watch.

"There's very little time left before Scraggard's deadline," he said.

The young apothecary noticed Vincent's watch and was impressed with the design.

"What a great idea," he said, "to make a clock so small, you can wear it on your wrist! When I get back to the Forest, I'll snap one of mine into a wrist-clock. Then I'll always know what time it is!"

"If we don't hurry, young man, you may never need to know the time again," Vincent reminded him as he got up from the flimsy metal chair, which gave off a steely sigh of relief.

"You're right," the young apothecary mournfully agreed. "Soon I won't need to know anything."

"I didn't say that," Vincent objected with a chuckle. "I only said we had to hurry."

"Hurry? Where to? I've told you—Master Tabulet is the only person who can help me, but I have no idea how to find her."

"Lucky for you I know where to find her." Vincent gave the young apothecary a slap on the shoulder that almost knocked him off his chair. "Master Tabulet happens to be a customer of mine and a good friend."

The young apothecary jumped up to his feet and grabbed the lapels of Vincent's fur vest.

"You know Master Tabulet?" he exclaimed.

"For years," Vincent said, carefully taking the young man's hands off his lapels.

"You couldn't have known her that long—she only moved to the human town a few months ago."

"That's right." Vincent smiled, once again showing his sharp, pointy teeth. "But you don't really think this is the first time she's escaping Scraggard's wrath, do you?"

The young apothecary shrugged his shoulders.

"Trust me, she's done it before," Vincent said with a wink. To avoid having to answer any more questions, he asked, "Do you have the prescription on you?"

The young apothecary pulled a wrinkled slip of paper out of his pocket.

"Good." Vincent snatched it from his hand. "I'll fax it over to Master Tabulet and give her a call to make sure she got it."

"What?" The young apothecary had no idea what on earth Vincent was talking about.

"I'll explain later. Right now, we haven't got a minute to lose."

Vincent ran over to a monstrous-looking creature, quietly humming in the corner. He placed the prescription onto a slanted tray and pushed a few buttons; buzzing softly, the creature swallowed the paper.

"What have you done?" the young apothecary fretted looking distraught. "Why'd you feed the prescription to this beast?"

"Don't worry—nobody's eaten anything." Vincent calmly pulled the prescription out of another tray and returned it to the apothecary. "Now, let's see if Master Tabulet received it."

Out of his pocket, the butcher pulled a flat, narrow device the young apothecary had never seen before. He touched the top of it with his crooked finger, and the device lit up, displaying a set of numbers from zero to nine. Vincent quickly pressed some of them, and suddenly, the familiar face of Master Tabulet appeared where the numbers had been.

Amazed, the young apothecary bowed and said, "Hello, Master Tabulet, I was one of your pupils a few years back. I don't think you remember me—you've taught so many of us—but I am in desperate need of your help. I've got here—"

"Buddy," Vincent interrupted him, "this is only Master Tabulet's picture. Wait till she answers; I'll put her on speaker."

The very next second, the young apothecary heard a click and then Master Tabulet's voice.

"Hello, Vince, I got it."

Vincent turned to the young apothecary and said, "She's got the prescription."

The young apothecary looked at the piece of paper in his hand and blinked in confusion. He couldn't understand what was happening. If this was the human town, how come there were mysterious objects performing magic all around him? And if it wasn't, then where the heck had that bird brought him?

"Vince," Master Tabulet said, "I understand the prescription came from…" For a moment, her voice wavered. "The Forest?"

"Yes," Vincent confirmed curtly.

The young apothecary heard a very light sigh.

"Who delivered it?"

"One of your former pupils."

"I see," Master Tabulet said softly. "When does he need it filled?"

"How 'bout two hours ago?"

"Got it. Bring him right over."

"I am kind of busy, but Pablo will do."

"Great! When they get here, the medication will be ready."

Scraggard Talks to the Leader of His Swan–Goose Squad

Scraggard the Immortal was so pale that his skin looked transparent. The bulging veins on his forehead and neck were rapidly pulsating. He was silently staring at the leader of the Swan-Goose squad perched on the golden bar before him. The bird's head was hanging low. Stanley, Damon, and his friends stood behind the throne very quietly. The only sound disturbing the otherwise complete stillness of the Throne Hall was the soft crackling of the burning candles.

At last, Scraggard the Immortal whispered, "You've let me down twice in one month, my trusted bird. Last week, you let the ravens beat your flock and help the human girl escape. Today, you've returned to the palace without the human boys. Nothing like this has ever happened before. What's going on with you and your fleet?"

The bird's head hung even lower. Its military hat dropped off and rolled across the marble floor.

"You know I am a forgiving person," Scraggard the Immortal continued, "but even my patience has its limits. If you let me down once more, I don't think I'll be able to forgive you again."

The bird raised its head upright. Its eyes were glowing with devotion. Scraggard the Immortal snapped the military hat back where it belonged.

"I am giving you one last chance," he whispered. "Do whatever it takes, but bring those kids here, to my Throne Hall. And hurry. Don't make me wait too long. I am running out of patience," he said, then paused for a moment before adding, "and energy."

At Master Tabulet's

Master Tabulet opened the front door just as Pablo's hairy finger was about to ring the doorbell.

"What happened?" she exclaimed, seeing the lifeless body of the young apothecary slung over Pablo's shoulder.

"May I come in?" Pablo asked glumly.

Master Tabulet moved to the side, and Pablo walked directly into her living room. There he dropped the young apothecary's body on the couch and snarled contemptuously, "Sissy."

"Is he alive?" Master Tabulet asked the butcher.

"I don't know," he growled, "and I don't care."

Master Tabulet knelt down near the couch and put her ear against the young apothecary's chest.

"He is, thank goodness!" she exclaimed and stood up. "All he needs is a whiff of ammonia." She took a small vial of clear liquid out of the pocket of her white coat, uncorked it, and stuck it under the young apothecary's nose. He sneezed loudly, coughed, and opened his eyes. Feeling somewhat foggy, the apothecary recognized both faces looming over him. One, scornful, belonged to the butcher Pablo; the other, smiling, to his favorite teacher, Master Tabulet.

"Am I alive?" he whispered.

"Yes," Master Tabulet answered as she put her hand on his forehead.

"I am glad."

"So am I." She smiled, helping him sit up. "How are you feeling?"

"Better." The young apothecary rubbed his temples.

"What happened? Why'd you pass out?"

Master Tabulet's pupil looked at Pablo, who snorted scornfully.

"Vincent asked me to bring this 'chicken'," he pointed his finger at the young apothecary, "to you, Master, to pick up the medication. Is it ready, by the way?" he asked turning to Master Tabulet.

"Yes, it is."

"Good. Well, Vincent and I warned him," Pablo continued, nodding at the young apothecary, "that human towns had things he'd never seen or heard of before. We explained that no matter how terrifying those things might look, they weren't dangerous. We told him to think of everything around him as if it were a dream. We asked him to stay calm, and he promised he would, didn't you, young druggist?" Pablo sneered as he looked grimly at the young apothecary sitting on the edge of the couch, shrinking away from his words.

"It's *apothecary*," young apothecary corrected quietly.

"Same thing," the butcher growled again, brushing him off. "Didn't you promise?"

"Yes, I did."

"What was the matter with you, then? Why on earth did you pass out on me, fall off my bike, and make me carry you uphill for twenty-five minutes? I almost broke my back!"

"I'm sorry, Pablo, but it wasn't my fault."

"Really? I'd like to know whose?"

The young apothecary didn't answer, and Master Tabulet asked gently, "Please, tell me what happened."

"I don't remember," the young apothecary confessed, staring down at his feet.

"OK, I'll tell you," Pablo said reluctantly. "As I rode down Main Street, the druggist here was fine, sitting behind me. He paid no attention to the passing cars, and even when a whole gang of bikers rocketed by us, he only squeezed my shoulders a little harder. He got a bit shaky when a landing plane flew over our heads, but he was still all right. But when an ambulance and three fire trucks rushed by, he lost it. As soon as he saw them, he shuddered, toppled over, and fell to the ground like a dead wolf."

"I don't know what happened," the young apothecary admitted. "The last thing I remember is seeing those hideous monsters appear out of nowhere. They were wailing like sea sirens and hurling bolts of lightning at me! They were approaching with cutting speed. I was sure they wanted to capture me, and then…" The young apothecary fell silent.

"Then what?" Master Tabulet asked.

"Then there was a nasty smell, and the two of you staring at me through a fog."

"All I remember," Pablo said as he plopped down in the armchair by the door rubbing right below his shoulder blades, "is my aching back."

"When you return from the Forest," Master Tabulet told the butcher, "I'll give you a special ointment, and your back will be fine."

"Is Pablo going back to the Forest with me?" the young apothecary asked, surprised.

"Well, rather, I'd say that you're going there with him."

The young apothecary noticed Master Tabulet looking at her wrist. She was also wearing a tiny clock similar to Vincent's.

"You'd better hurry," she said. "Time's running out. Get up. I'll bring you what you've come here for."

"You mean the an-ti-biotics?" The young apothecary stumbled on the word.

"Yes." Master Tabulet left the room and returned with a small zip-top bag.

"The patient has to take it twice a day," she instructed, handing the bag to the apothecary, "one pill in the morning, after breakfast, and one at night, before bed."

The young apothecary squeezed the bag in his hand and looked at Pablo.

"I guess we're good to go," he said.

"Your guess is right." Pablo pushed on the armrests to stand up. "But first, we have to head back downtown and pick up my bike." He turned to the front door, preparing to leave when Master Tabulet stopped him.

"I don't think you've got time for that," she said. "You'd better take mine."

Pablo looked at her doubtfully.

"Is it adapted for the Forest conditions?" he asked. "If you know what I mean."

"Pablo," Master Tabulet replied, "what kind of a question is that? Just tell me where you left yours. I'll pick it up and store it in my basement until you get back."

Stanley and Scraggard's Screen

Sitting high on his throne, Scraggard the Immortal kept snapping his fingers and muttering incantations, but nothing was happening to his screen; it remained dark, as before. He stood up, walked toward it, and snapped his fingers once again. Still nothing changed. Infuriated, Scraggard raised his right arm over his head and wailed, "Dagger! I'll cut this useless miscreation to pieces."

Instantly, a sharp blade glistened in his hand. He was about to hurl it at the stubborn monitor when a voice behind him pleaded, "Your Scraggardness, don't do it."

Scraggard the Immortal whirled around.

"Who dared say that?" he demanded, eyes flashing coldly.

"I did." Stanley stepped out from behind the throne.

"Nobody ever interferes with my actions without punishment," Scraggard whispered.

"Your Scraggardness," Stanley said, his voice quivering, "I only wanted to ask for your permission to try to fix this." He pointed to the screen.

"Are you implying, you brazen human, that you are more powerful than I?"

"No way, Your Scraggardness. I only happened to overhear that your screen was installed by a human…"

"Yes, but I enhanced it with special powers."

"If the problem's related to the special powers, I won't be able to do anything about it, of course. But if it's a technical glitch, I may be able to fix it for you."

Scraggard's face clouded over, so that none of his features could be distinguished, except for his steely eyes.

"OK," he said at last, after a long pause. "I'll let you try to fix my screen, human boy, but if you fail, I'll suck all of your energy out of you in one breath."

"Your S-Scraggardness," Stanley stuttered nervously, "I th-think the sound-activated sensors on your screen got disabled."

"I don't understand what you're talking about, but whatever it is—fix it."

"Sir…. I mean, Your Scraggardness, may I ask you one question?"

"Too many questions, human boy, don't you think?"

Stanley cast his eyes down.

"What is it?"

"When the human installed the screen for you, did he, by any chance, give you a long rectangular kind of a stick with buttons on it?"

"A stick with buttons?" Scraggard frowned, trying to remember. "Oh yes." His face cleared. "You're right, human boy, he did give me something and said to use it if the screen stopped responding to my snaps. I forgot all about it."

"May I look at it?"

Scraggard slowly walked back to his throne and raised one of its armrests, exposing a hidden compartment. From there, he pulled a remote control made of pure gold. It shimmered in the flickering candlelight. In place of the buttons, there were precious stones. The Power key was a diamond as big as the iris of an eye and as clear as a drop of mountain dew.

"Is this the thing?" Scraggard asked.

"I think so," Stanley said, blinking from the glare. "It's a lot brighter than I expected, though."

"I like it bright. The one the human gave me was black and dull. Its buttons were made of rubber." Scraggard snorted arrogantly. "Not up to my standards. I turned it into an object suitable for my palace—a piece of the purest gold, studded with precious stones." A proud smile appeared on Scraggard's lipless mouth.

"I apologize a trillion times for my next question," Stanley began cautiously, "but is it possible to turn this gold beauty back into its original form—a black device with rubber buttons?"

"Nothing is impossible for me, you brash human, but why would I do that?"

"Your Scraggardness, I've never seen a more magnificent remote control in my life. The richest people on earth couldn't own such a beauty, I'm sure."

"Agreed." Scraggard snorted conceitedly.

"But I doubt it will activate your screen. What you're holding in your hand is an invaluable piece of art. What you need for the screen to work is a simple piece of technology."

Scraggard extended his arm, admiring the gleaming splendor on his palm.

"You humans are boring," he whispered, eyes fixed on the gold wonder. "I hope you realize, human boy, that now you're jeopardizing not only your energy, but your life. If what you're saying is wrong, you'll die."

Scraggard snapped his fingers, and the layers of gold melted off the black remote control. The exquisite precious stones became rubber buttons with numbers and arrows. Scraggard lowered his hand. The light in his eyes died out.

"May I?" Stanley took the remote from Scraggard's hand, aimed it at the screen, and pushed the Power button. The smell of apples instantly filled the Throne Hall, and a few of the green fruits fell off the trembling branches and rolled along the floor toward the throne.

The Binoculars

Eric had just finished drawing the binoculars, and then he wished them real. One pair he hung around his neck and gave the other three to Sean, Little Yaga, and Kikimra, telling them to do the same.

"What's this?" Kikimra stared at her pair.

"Binoculars."

"What are they for?"

"To see faraway objects as if they were closer and to make small things look bigger."

"What for?"

"For lots of reasons. Right now, for instance, to be sure there are no surprises waiting for us beyond the Orchard, so we can get out of here safely."

"We're lucky the moon's bright tonight," Sean noted.

"Yep," Eric agreed and looked at his watch. "But sun will be rising very soon."

Kikimra put the binoculars up to her eyes and hollered, "Eric, you're a liar! Nothing's close and big. Everything's far away and tiny."

"You're looking through them backward."

"What?"

"The large lenses shrink things. Turn your binoculars the other way around."

Kikimra obeyed.

"Are you sure?" she asked, confused. "These lenses, or whatever you call them, are so small."

"That's OK—just look through them."

Kikimra grunted and put the binoculars up to her eyes again.

"Goodness!" she exclaimed. "Everything's in my face now. Look, I can touch that tree!"

She extended her arm and poked the air with her fingers.

"Do you see my hand?" She laughed. "It's huge!" Turning to Eric, she said, "Human powers are very strange. Why do you have large lenses to make the world look small, and small ones to make it big? To confuse everyone?"

"Kikimra," Eric said, "haven't you ever heard of physics?"

"Of who?"

"Never mind."

"You humans are very weird," she said again.

"Well," Sean couldn't help but comment, "it's arguable who's weirder, us, humans, or you, Foresters."

"You've got that right," Eric said. "But let's argue that later." He put his binoculars down and looked at his friends. "I don't see anything suspicious out there, so if you all agree, we can get out of here now."

Who Blew The Mighty Wistle?

From far away, the young apothecary noticed the Big Rock looming over the clearing behind Scraggard's palace. When he'd seen it last, the clearing was crowded with his colleagues. Now it was deserted; all the apothecaries were gone, frantically ransacking their shops and labs in search of their ticket to survival: a formula for antibiotics. Clutching the plastic bag containing the precious medicine, the young apothecary was elated. He couldn't wait to tell all the apothecaries of the Forest that they were saved!

"Pablo, if it hadn't been for you and Vincent, the two best humans I've ever met," he started, bursting with excitement, "I would've—"

Just then, a sudden jolt almost knocked him off the bike. When he regained his balance, he was very surprised to see that instead of sitting on the bike holding on to Pablo's shoulders, he was riding a wolf and squeezing its thick gray fur!

The wolf dropped him off at the bottom of the Big Rock and disappeared before the young apothecary could even thank him.

Left on his own, the apothecary looked around and noticed that the seam binding the sky to the earth had turned pale blue. Not wasting another second, he whistled the Mighty Whistle of the Forest. The echo of the whistle had barely faded away when the clearing around the Big Rock was again crowded with his colleagues.

The old apothecary, looking tired after the sleepless night, snapped himself back atop the Big Rock.

"Whose whistle has summoned us all here?" he asked. "Who's holding the formula for the antibiotics?"

The crowd of apothecaries began buzzing with agitation. By this time, right before dawn, everybody's hopes of survival had waned, almost to the point of being extinguished. Now, looking around, they were eager to find out who their savior was. Clutching the plastic bag with his right hand, the young apothecary stepped out of the crowd.

"I knew it," the old apothecary said with a chuckle, and the rest of his colleagues roared with excitement.

The young apothecary raised his left arm and said, "I don't have the recipe on me."

The assembly before him fell silent.

"But I know who does: Biggest Yaga, who lives on Bold Mountain."

"How come you didn't get it?" somebody hollered from the crowd.

"Because we wouldn't have had enough time to concoct the antibiotics before Scraggard's deadline."

"Then why have you summoned us here?" the old apothecary asked, disappointed.

"As I said, I don't have the formula," the young apothecary repeated. Then, raising his right arm, he announced, "But I've got the medicine! The antibiotics are right here, in this plastic bag, ready for an ailing human to use!" And he shook the plastic bag in the air for everyone to see.

An exhilarated roar shook not only the ground beneath the apothecaries' feet but also the Big Rock, so that the old apothecary tumbled over. He wasn't hurt, though, because his colleagues caught him before he hit the ground and, in their excitement, threw him back up into the air several times before lowering him safely to his feet.

The End of the Swan–
Goose Squad

"I don't see anything suspicious out there, either," Kikimra said, her binoculars dangling on a thin string around her neck. "I agree with Eric—I think it's safe to leave the Orchard. We've spent enough time here; the sun is already rising."

"I agree, too," Little Yaga said as she put her binoculars down and rubbed her eyes.

"How about you, Sean?" Eric asked.

"I don't see a soul. The world's still asleep. I think now's the best time to go."

"OK then." Eric looked at his friends. "Let's get out of here. It doesn't seem like we'll have to carry out our plan after all, but just in case, hold on to your slingshots, and make sure you've got enough apples in your pockets and backpacks."

"We've got more than enough," Kikimra retorted, suddenly annoyed. Black smoke streamed out of her mouth. "And stop bossing everyone around. The fact that you can turn pictures into objects does not make you any more powerful than us, true Foresters, OK?"

Irritated, she stepped out of the Orchard.

"What's up with her?" Eric gave Little Yaga a baffled look.

"She's in one of her moods. She gets like that sometimes, especially when she's hungry."

"She just ate a whole tree full of apples," Sean noted, sniggering.

"Apples are not her kind of food. If it had been a bucket of spiders mixed with roaches and mice teeth, she'd be much happier now."

"If I'd known, I would've drawn her three buckets of such a delicious treat," Eric said with a chortle. "Little Yaga, it's your turn—go. Sean, you're next, and I'll go after you."

As soon as Eric came out of the Orchard to join his friends, the light clouds floating across the pale-blue sky turned into big white birds: the Swan-Geese. With blistering speed, they swooped down upon the teens.

A grimace, apparently intended to be a smile, contorted Scraggard's mouth.

"Not bad," he mumbled, his eyes glued to the screen.

The birds had barely lifted their loot off the ground when a loud command—"Shoot!"—reverberated throughout the Throne Hall. Unsure of where the order had come from, Scraggard looked around. A moment later, when he turned his eyes back to the screen, he was stunned by what he saw; all of the Swan-Geese were hopping up and down on the ground, trying to dodge the hail of apples hitting their wings and legs.

Suddenly, an apple became lodged in the leader's throat. Immediately, its eyes rolled up, and its neck stiffened for a second before going limp and hanging down to its chest. The bird fell onto its back and just lay there, its short legs sticking up in the air. Wounded and exhausted, the other birds stopped hopping and stared with unblinking eyes at their fallen leader.

"It looks like this hen is history," Sean said flatly.

Eric walked over to the bird, opened its beak, and pulled the apple out. Not a single feather fluttered on its motionless body.

"I think you're right."

"What do you mean, history?" Little Yaga asked cautiously. "You don't mean it's dead, do you?"

"I do," Sean confirmed, as flatly as before.

"No way—that's impossible!" Kikimra shouted. She squatted down by the bird and put her ear against its feathery body. When she stood up again, her green eyes turned black, and clouds of murky smoke billowed out of her mouth, which was twisted in anger.

"How on earth could this happen?" she shrieked. "This bird's thousands of years old! It's been serving Scraggard for at least three millennia, until you humans came here and killed it—just like that—with an apple!"

"Three and a half millennia, to be precise," Scraggard whispered.

"These apples are famous for their destructive abilities," Eric muttered avoiding Kikimra's outraged glare. "You said so yourself."

"Now I see why Foresters aren't so fond of you humans!" Kikimra kept yelling. "What if I killed you with an apple?" She bent down and picked one up off the ground. "You wanna see how easy it is?" Kikimra flung her arm up into the air, as though she were about to hurl the hard green fruit at Eric.

Before she could do it, Little Yaga grabbed her by the sleeve and said, "Wait." Reaching into her skirt pocket, Little Yaga fished out a tiny bottle with a few drops of a sparkling, golden-blue liquid in it. "Live Water," she said. "My grandmother doesn't let me leave home without this vial."

"But it's almost empty," Kikimra noted grouchily.

"There's enough for the bird."

It took less than two drops of the Live Water for the Swan-Goose to blink its eyes and start breathing again. With Little Yaga's help, the bird stood up, but it fell back onto its behind as soon as she let go.

"I think its legs are broken," Eric said, looking at the bird's crooked limbs.

"It needs Dead Water now to heal the breaks," Kikimra told Little Yaga. "Do you have some on you?"

"Nope." Little Yaga shook her head. "But my grandmother took me to the Dead Water Well once. I think I remember how to get there."

"How far is it?" Eric asked.

"Pretty far. It's on the other side of the Forest."

"Listen," Kikimra said sharply. "We aren't going all the way to the other side of the Forest to treat Scraggard's servants. We've saved the bird's life. The rest is up to him. Let the Immortal take care of his own flock."

She turned to the flustered Swan-Geese and snapped her fingers. The very next instant, the birds, noisily honking and flailing their damaged wings, plopped down onto the marble floor in front of Scraggard's throne.

"You've let me down for the third time, my feathered army," Scraggard whispered sadly rather than angrily. Staring intently at his mouth, the birds quieted down. "That nasty girl, Kikimra, was right; you've served me for a long time." Scraggard stood up. Some of the birds lowered their heads; others stuck theirs under their wings. The tiny military hats slid off their topknots and rolled all over the Throne Hall floor. "That's why, instead of turning you into dust and scattering it all over the Forest," Scraggard said woefully, "I'm going to make you my new gargoyles. You'll decorate the roof of my palace and spit the rainwater away from the walls when there's a downpour."

Leesho's Assignment

ead up, chin forward, shoulders back, taut as a guitar string,
Leesho stood before Scraggard the Immortal, who sat on
his throne.

"I've summoned you here, my soldier, because you've proven
yourself brave and faithful. I need more trustworthy Foresters
like you whom I can rely on."

Leesho clicked his hooves and bowed his head.

"Always at your service, Your Scraggardness," he barked.

A faint smile, as fleeting as a sunray on a cloudy day, momentarily lit up Scraggard's face.

"What's your name, my soldier?"

"Leesho."

"When we defeat this intruder, Eric Rosebar, and his brazen
friends, I'll promote you, Leesho, to the rank of lieutenant."

Leesho bowed his head again. "Always at your service, Your
Scraggardness."

"Now, I'll give you three of my four best regiments. You'll
take them with you to find Eric, capture him and his gang, and
bring them all over here—*alive*."

Scraggard's normally cold blue eyes suddenly grew as fiery as a couple of red-hot burners on a stove.

"I'll enslave the girls," he hissed, "and they'll work for me for the rest of their miserable lives." Clouds of thick black smoke billowed out of his mouth and rose to the ceiling.

"What's the life expectancy of a Forester?" Stanley whispered into Damon's ear.

"Scraggard's immortal," Damon answered, without turning his head.

"What about the others?"

"It depends on the Forester's level of power. A regular working Forester, if nobody turns him into dust or eats him alive, can live for about five hundred years. The more powerful you are, the longer you live. The most powerful stay around for thousands of years."

"Wow." Stanley looked impressed. "That's a lot of miserable days for the girls."

"It's their own fault," Damon said sneering. "But don't you worry, they aren't that powerful."

"The boys," Scraggard the Immortal continued, "I'll keep in the special Chilly Chambers I'll build exclusively for them. There, they'll stay warm enough not to die but cold enough to refrain from any unnecessary body movements, to keep their energy levels as high as possible for as long as possible," Scraggard finished, and his eyes were restored to their usual cold blue color.

⇥⇤

As he stood in the back of Scraggard's palace near the Big Rock that was crowded with apothecaries only minutes ago,

Leesho was silent. He was looking at the perfectly aligned rows of "trees" in front of him. The straight and tall "trees" were twice Leesho's height. The strong wind was unable to bend their crowns or stir their leaves, but as soon as Leesho raised his arm, the "trees" bowed their tops and quietly rustled their leaves.

"Hello, intrepid army of His Scraggardness, Scraggard the Immortal," Leesho greeted the soldiers. He shouted every word louder than the previous one, so the last word was as deafening as a thunderbolt.

"Always honored to serve His Scraggardness, Scraggard the Immortal," the soldiers barked in one booming voice.

"Great!" Leesho slowly walked along the rows, and each "tree" he passed bowed its top for a second, then raised it again.

"I've been appointed by His Scraggardness, Scraggard the Immortal, to be your new commander," Leesho announced, back in front of the troops.

"Always honored to serve His Scraggardness, Scraggard the Immortal," the soldiers barked again.

"Great! The mission we are set to accomplish is very important. With my leadership and your valor, I have no doubt that we will succeed."

"Always honored to serve His Scraggardness, Scraggard the Immortal," the soldiers barked for the third time.

As Scraggard watched his regiments marching off the palace grounds across the drawbridge, his mouth stretched into a wry smile. As soon as the last soldier cleared the bridge, it slowly raised itself again. The first rays of the morning sun shot out from behind the real trees, bidding the army farewell.

Eric's Advice

Lying flat on her back in her quarters, Ashley kept sneezing and coughing. Her eyes had become watery, and her nose was as swollen and red as a ripe tomato. Nobody would've doubted now that she was truly sick. To Ashley's relief, not only Scraggard but all his guards and servants were trying to stay as far away from her as possible. She always had the tiny earpiece in place, hoping to hear from Eric over the walkie-talkie. He hadn't reached out to her since their very first communication, and she couldn't understand why. She was afraid that something terrible had happened and that she'd never hear from him again. Just the thought of it brought tears to her eyes, gave her the sniffles, and made her blow her nose for real.

Suddenly, she heard a soft click and then Eric's muffled whisper. Ashley could hardly believe her ears!

"Be patient," Eric told her. "We're getting closer."

Tears of joy streamed down her cheeks. She was about to say how happy she was to hear his voice when someone unexpectedly opened her bedroom door. Taken by surprise, she jumped up on her bed. A gloomy-looking soldier walked in, holding a small plastic bottle similar to those her mother used to bring home from their pharmacy when Ashley was sick for real. Her heart racing, she discreetly turned up the volume on the walkie-talkie hidden in her pocket.

"Your medication has arrived," the soldier announced solemnly. "You must take it at once."

"What kind of medication is it?" Ashley asked with a cough, and the soldier backed away from her.

"I don't know," he replied, keeping his distance.

"Tell him you're allergic to it," Eric's voice instructed.

"I'm asking because I'm most likely allergic to it." Ashley coughed again. The soldier stepped farther away until he was backed up against the door.

"You are what?" He didn't understand.

"Allergic."

"What's *allergic*?"

"Tell him it's when you take the medication, your blood becomes poisonous with antibodies," Eric coached.

"It's when I take the medication, my blood becomes poisonous with antibodies," Ashley repeated.

"Is it contagious?" the soldier asked, his body flattened against the door.

"Very." Ashley widened her eyes and blew out her cheeks for a stronger impression. Her tactics worked. The soldier groped madly for the doorknob behind his back. When he found it at last, he pulled the door open and bolted out.

Scraggard's Wrath

The last thing Stanley remembered before his eyes rolled up and his head dropped down was the suffocating pain around his neck. Scraggard loosened his grip, and Stanley's limp body fell to the marble floor.

"Your Scraggardness," came Damon's voice from behind the throne.

"What?" the Ruler of the Forest asked, utterly agitated. "Come here—talk to my face."

Damon obeyed and knelt before him.

"Do you really want this human dead?" the Forest boy asked cautiously.

"I am so sick of your foolish questions. I can hardly resist the temptation to turn you into another decoration on the roof of my palace." Scraggard raised his arm; ready to snap, his fingers almost touched Damon's nose. Instinctively, the boy leaned back, tightening his jaws.

Scraggard lowered his arm. "Relax," he said. "I won't do it. For some strange reason, I still like you, you lucky little rascal."

Just then, lying at Scraggard's feet, Stanley groaned. Damon looked at him and saw the human boy's eyelids quivering.

"I think he's coming back to life." Damon stared at Scraggard in surprise. "How is it possible without the Live Water?"

"It's possible because he never died. He simply passed out. It happens to humans. They look dead, but they're actually alive."

"Humans are weird creatures."

"And dangerous. I've told you I don't want them meandering around my Forest unattended."

Stanley groaned again and opened his eyes.

"You see, my pupil, he's fine." Scraggard bent over Stanley's face and smiled menacingly. "I wouldn't kill him," he said, "not yet, that is. That was just a gentle reprimand for neglecting to mention the possibility of an allergic reaction in the human girl."

"What's an allergic reaction?"

"Another one of the million bizarre human conditions."

"Is it contagious?" Canny asked from behind the throne.

"Sometimes," Scraggard replied, turning to Canny. "There have been instances of Forest inhabitants developing allergies after being in contact with humans."

"How about passing out?" Damon pointed at Stanley, who was still on the floor, looking around in a fog. "Can that happen to a Forester?"

"After being exposed to humans, yes."

"Those humans bring too much trouble to the Forest."

"That's why we must get them contained as soon as possible."

Scraggard blew into Stanley's dazed eyes, and the boy's wandering look became focused.

"This nightmare is so realistic," he mumbled, touching his neck, still red and sore from Scraggard's grip. "I can actually feel the pain."

"Listen, human boy, you're going to feel more pain if the human girl doesn't get better by tomorrow."

"She won't get better by tomorrow," Stanley said in a raspy voice, staring up at Scraggard. "Without antibiotics she'll be fighting her strep for at least five more days."

"Well," Scraggard said, lowering his face so close to Stanley's that the pointy tip of his nose cut into the boy's skin, "I'll be extraordinarily patient; I'll give you five more days. And if the girl isn't cured by then, I'll start tapping into your energy."

Leesho's Regiments and the Rowdy Meadow

After leading his army for hours, Leesho finally reached the Rowdy Meadow. It was overgrown with tall grass, blowing and whipping fiercely with every gust of the wind.

"Army, stand still!" Leesho shouted, stopping abruptly at the foot of the path that wound, in and out of sight, across the meadow. Instantly and in perfect unison, all three regiments came to a full stop. Leesho raised his arms and interlocked his fingers over his head. The grass, dancing wildly only a second ago, lay quietly on the ground. Its tall, thick tufts, growing along both sides of the path, stretched up, bent over, and intertwined, creating a green canopied corridor.

Keeping his arms elevated, Leesho commanded his troops, "Army! Cross the Rowdy Meadow!"

One by one, the soldiers entered the welcoming corridor. When the last of them stepped onto the narrow path, Leesho unlocked his fingers and crossed his arms over his chest. Instantly, as if electrified, the grass sprang back up, the canopy fell apart, and the tufts along both sides of the path began fiercely whipping the soldiers while winding around their bodies. Before any of the troops could grasp what had happened, they were tied up from head to toe, looking like giant green cocoons ready to turn into monstrous butterflies. Gobs of grass gagged their mouths.

"Thank you for your service!" Leesho saluted his immobilized squadrons.

Then he quickly unbuckled his belt and threw it far away into the grass. As soon as it disappeared from view, Leesho snapped his fingers and was gone, too.

Don-Key's Mission

Don-Key's braying reverberated throughout the Throne Hall. He was laughing so hard that he fell down to the floor.

"Is he insane?" Scraggard asked Damon.

"Not exactly. Only a little crazy."

"Look at them!" Don-Key shouted, pointing at the soldiers on the screen. Tied from head to toe, the soldiers kept trying to free themselves from the grass's stronghold, but the more they wiggled, the tighter they became entangled.

Scraggard clenched his fists.

"The Rowdy Meadow will pay for this joke," he said. "When I capture the humans, I'll get even with that nasty heap of hay." He bent over Don-Key, who was hiccupping loudly on the floor, and picked him up with one finger.

"You, the closest relative to a four-legged animal," the Immortal said, pointing at the screen, "will go there and free my army. Then you'll find the traitor, Leesho, and bring him to me for the punishment he deserves—understood?"

Don-Key nodded; he'd stopped laughing but continued to hiccup.

"I have a feeling that Leesho's energy will suit my system perfectly," Scraggard said with a sneer. "When he was standing here before me, I sensed a certain smell. I assumed it was coming from our human guest." Scraggard gave Stanley a bloodcurdling grin. "But I'm not so sure anymore." Having plotted his revenge, the Immortal returned to his throne.

"Your Scraggardness," Damon said, bowing down, "I am sure my friend Don-Key will have no problem saving your army from the Rowdy Meadow's grip. But finding Leesho and bringing him here may be a little too challenging for him. My other friend, Canny, would be a better choice for that task."

"I'm not good at finding things." Don-Key snickered. "I am much better at losing them."

"By the way," Damon said, suddenly struck by a memory, "I've always wondered about the smell coming from Leesho at school. Your Scraggardness, you don't mean he's—"

"You're asking too many questions, as always," Scraggard interrupted Damon and peered into his eyes. "I want you to finally get it: in my palace, I ask the questions." His voice suddenly grew eerily quiet. "And everybody else answers them—not the other way around."

Canny on the Prowl

Canny had a gut feeling that the path snaking under his feet would bring him to Eric Rosebar and his gang. He trusted his gut because it had never let him down. Slinking along, he kept sniffing the path, but he detected no human scent. Canny knew something wasn't right. In the distance, he spotted a tree so tall that clouds used it as a rest stop before continuing their journey elsewhere. He rushed ahead, and when he reached the tall tree, he snapped himself up, onto the very spot where clouds loved to hang around, but he was too heavy. Loudly creaking under his weight, the tree bent down, so Canny, not to plummet to the ground, swiftly deflated himself until he was weightless. At once, the tree sprang up again. Canny wrapped his feet around the branch he was sitting on so that he wouldn't fly away with the wind. Now he could see practically all of the Forest—its every path, meadow, creek, and marsh.

At first, he didn't notice anything unusual. But suddenly, way in the distance near the Funny Marsh, he saw Don-Key leaping up and down at the front of the line of the battered and tattered soldiers he had managed to untangle and save from the clutches of the Rowdy Meadow. Even across the distance between them, Canny could hear his friend's jolly braying. He lowered the left corner of his mouth—a sign of his irritation.

"Doesn't this donkey in Forester form realize he's scaring everybody away?" Canny mumbled. Frustrated, he tore a dry leaf off the branch he was sitting on, glided his flat hand over it, and sent it flying toward the Funny Marsh. A split second later, the leaf's sharp stem painfully jabbed the braying commander's behind. Don-Key stopped abruptly in his tracks, and the first row of soldiers, following directly behind him, crashed into his back, knocking him off his feet on their way down. Unable to resist the momentum pulling them forward, the second row fell on top of the first, and, in a domino effect, the third on top of the second, until all three regiments were piled up one row on top of another, like a pile of uprooted trees.

"Jerk," Canny mumbled, and both corners of his mouth curved down.

Don-Key crept out from beneath the pile of soldiers, gingerly pulled the leaf out of his backside, and brought it up to his eyes. It read, "Shut up." He repeated the two words scribbled on the leaf out loud, and a resounding bray of laughter burst out of his mouth. He put his hand over it to muffle the gleeful neighing, but his lips continued to sputter. Finally, Don-Key pinched his fingers together and moved them across his lips, as if zipping them up; at once the sound of his laughter ceased.

Still on top of the tree, Canny forced his eyeballs out of their sockets until they dangled down over his flattened cheeks on long, fleshy, springlike coils. His was the only family in the Forest able to perform such a trick without any incantations or snapping. Protruded in such a way, his eyes became as powerful as a telescope. Now Canny could discern every little detail for miles around. He noticed Don-Key's mouth tightly fastened by a lip-colored zipper. He saw his friend glide his hand over a dry leaf and send it (naturally) in the wrong direction. He watched the soldiers slowly getting up. He spotted many other insignificant things…but no humans.

Aggravated, Canny snapped himself back down onto the ground. By the time he landed softly on his stomach, he'd expanded back to his normal, three-dimensional shape. Without changing his position, Canny turned his head to the side and dug his ear into the dirt of the road. Initially, he heard nothing, except for the rhythmical thuds of the marching soldiers' hooves. Canny dug his ear a little deeper into the ground, and suddenly, he heard a sound so light that at first he thought it was only the wind rustling old leaves. A few minutes later, he realized that what he had taken for rustling was very quiet conversation. Excited, Canny strained all the muscles around his ear and popped it out, just like he'd popped out his eyes a few minutes before. The distant voices grew louder but still not clear enough to make out the words. Without moving his head, Canny stretched his arms and groped the ground until his hand got hold of a long stick. He wedged the stick behind his ear, turning it into a mighty antenna. Instantly, he could hear every sound, distinctly and unobstructed.

"Do you think we can ask Clair for help?" a vaguely familiar voice asked.

"Who's Clair?" Canny wondered. He was thrilled and ready to hear more when a sharp, stinging pain pierced his ear. He wailed and jumped up to his feet. His ear was burning. He grabbed it with his hand and felt it ballooning under his palm. Canny tilted his head to the side and jumped up and down on one foot, like a swimmer after a dive. A fat earthworm fell out of his ear. Enraged, Canny raised his foot, eager to smash the squirming creature to pieces, but the worm swiftly wriggled itself into the ground and was gone before Canny's foot came down.

The Crystal Ball

"Hopefully, Clair will agree to deliver it to Ashley," Kikimra said. "But I still don't understand what Eric's talking about." She turned to Leesho. "Do you?"

"I'm not sure."

"It's OK." Eric sighed. "Even if I drew a webcam and Clair flew it over to Ashley, we wouldn't be able to use it because there is no Internet in the forest."

"No what?"

"Have you ever heard of the World Wide Web?" Sean asked.

"The what?"

"The World Wide Web."

Kikimra looked at Little Yaga, and Little Yaga turned to Sean.

"Have you ever heard of Spiderland?" she asked.

Sean shook his head.

"If you're looking for worldwide webs, Spiderland is the place to go. You've never seen so many webs, trust me. All sizes: short, long, narrow, wide—any size you want."

"The World Wide Web that Sean's talking about," Eric said, "is different. It has nothing to do with spiders or their lands."

"What is it, then?" Little Yaga asked again.

"It's hard to explain in simple terms," Eric answered.

"Try us," Kikimra dared him.

"It's complicated. All I can say is that if your forest had the human World Wide Web, also known as the Internet, Ashley and I could've Skyped."

"Ashley and you could do what?" Kikimra asked. "Please, use normal language, OK?"

"Skype," Sean said. "It's like video chatting."

"Oh, I see," Kikimra purred. "You should've said so in the first place. Now it's all perfectly clear." She smiled sweetly at Sean, who grinned back at her, until she suddenly barked right into his ear, "And what's video chatting, for goodness' sake?"

"Are you nuts?" Sean shrank back, covering his ear with his hand. "You could've ruptured my eardrum!"

"Video chatting is when you can see the person you are talking to, no matter how far away the person is," Eric explained, paying no attention to Sean's groans.

"Is that all?" Leesho asked. "Then why all the fancy words, like *video chatting* and *Skype*, when it sounds like all you need is a plain old crystal ball?"

"Leesho, we aren't allowed to use crystal balls until our graduation," Little Yaga reminded him.

"That law only applies to Foresters," Leesho said.

"You see," Little Yaga explained, turning to Eric and Sean, "we, Foresters, all get our own crystal balls at our high school graduation. Anyone who starts using one before then loses his or her crystal ball privileges forever. That's the law of the Forest."

"Sounds like a pretty strict law," Sean commented with a smirk.

Kikimra responded to his snide remark with a grim look.

"All the laws of the Forest are strict," she said, as if in warning.

⊟⊟

Ashley thought she heard a light knock. She opened her eyes and looked at the double door to her bedroom, expecting it to open. When it didn't, she got out of bed and quietly tiptoed toward it. The door was massive; the image of Scraggard the Immortal was carved in each half, and the two doorknobs glared like Scraggard's eyes. Ashley was suddenly afraid they were camouflaged surveillance cameras.

"Who's there?" she asked, leaning her ear against the crack between the two halves. Nobody responded. "Who's there?" she asked again. Hearing no reply, she pulled on the doorknob. Surprisingly, the door opened quietly and easily. Ashley stuck her head out into a long corridor. It was lit with flickering candlelight and decorated with floating images, like holographs, of the Ruler of the Forest. On her right, she saw a tree-uniformed guard standing still and staring at the images. Apparently, he was oblivious to anything else. Cautiously, Ashley squinted to her left and saw another guard; he was as mesmerized by the images as the first. Right then, she heard another light knock. It came from behind. Holding her breath, she pulled her head back into the bedroom and pushed on the door. It closed as easily and noiselessly as it had opened.

Ashley turned around and saw a bird sitting on the ledge outside her window. She recognized it at once: it was the same raven that had brought her the walkie-talkie. Ashley's heart galloped. Excited, she rushed to the window, squeezed her hands through the solid-gold bars on the inside, and tried to push the window up. The massive frame wouldn't budge. She looked around, hoping to find something she could use to pry the frames open, but except for her bed and the nightstand, the room was empty. Feeling miserable, Ashley returned to her bed, sat down on the edge, and buried her face in her hands. Fighting back tears, she sat still until she heard a screeching sound coming from the window. She raised her head and saw that the bird was carving a small circle in the windowpane with the sharp tip of its beak. When the circle was big enough, the bird pushed an opaque glass ball through to the inside. If Ashley hadn't dashed over to the window and caught it just in time, it would've fallen onto the tiled floor and shattered to pieces.

The very second the ball landed in the palm of her hand, the raven tore up into the sky and vanished from sight in midair, leaving Ashley staring into the blue emptiness up above. When she looked down again, there was no trace of the hole in the windowpane. Clutching the ball in her hand, Ashley returned to her bed. She was about to lie down when she felt a light vibration in her palm. She held the ball up to her eyes, and it suddenly became transparent. She peered inside, and her heart nearly jumped out of her chest.

The Wicked Marsh

Canny spotted a small puddle near the kinky root of the tall tree. Most likely, it was made of the tears shed by one of the clouds resting on the treetop. He rushed over to the puddle and plunged his burning ear into the cold water. Instantly, it began bubbling as if it were boiling in a teakettle. In a few minutes, his ear felt better, but Canny stayed in that position until all the water had turned into steam and evaporated, sucking his pain and swelling away. Again, he was able to hear for miles around. He pressed his ear deeper into the ground, hoping to catch voices he was now certain belonged to the humans. Instead, he heard the distressed braying of Don-Key.

"Stop! Stand still," Don-Key hollered at the top of his lungs. Canny winced and immersed his ear as deep into the soil as he could. For the first time ever, his friend wasn't laughing, and that was disturbing. There were other troubling noises—a lot of plopping and splattering, heavy breathing, and coughing. Soon he began to hear cries for help, and Canny realized that Don-Key and his army had gotten bogged down in the Wicked Marsh.

Unlike the Funny Marsh, the Wicked was evil. It thrived on young Foresters. It liked to disguise itself as a flowery field, attracting the innocent and naïve. As soon as youngsters stepped onto its soggy surface, the Wicked Marsh would clutch their feet, rid them of all their powers, and begin slowly sucking them in. If no one was around to snap the youngsters out, they would perish, as many had, because help was nowhere in sight or came too late. Amid all the clamor, Canny's ear caught a familiar rustle of hushed voices. He needed only a few seconds to locate where they were coming from, when suddenly, Don-Key's bloodcurdling wail shook the earth. Canny wanted to jump up, but his ear, immersed too deep in the soil, anchored him to the ground. His head pounded uncontrollably against the vibrating surface. In a short while, when the earth became calm again, Canny's ears were still ringing and the world around him spinning. Motionless, he waited until he was sure he'd be able to get up without falling right over.

⚏

Scraggard stared at the screen so quietly that Stanley forgot for a moment that he was immortal and thought the Ruler of the Forest had stopped breathing. He cast an alarmed look at Damon, but the latter was too absorbed with what was happening on the screen. Stanley looked up and saw heaps of muddy soldiers, trapped to their waists in mushy soil. Struggling to get out, they were pulling and pushing, but instead of getting themselves free, they were being sucked in deeper with their every move. Don-Key was already in up to his chest. He tried to swim out and raised a storm of slushy blobs. A few landed in the

Throne Hall next to Scraggard's feet, nearly splashing his long, narrow shoes. Disgusted, Scraggard twisted his mouth, moved his feet under the throne, and snapped the mud gone.

Right then, Canny appeared on the screen. He was moving gingerly. He knew that in order to snap Scraggard's army and Don-Key out of the Wicked Marsh, he had to get very close to it, no more than five inches away. One inch more and his powers wouldn't be strong enough to overcome the Wicked Marsh's grip and yank the army and his friend free. But the trick was not to get too close to it, either. The touch of a single toe on its spongy surface would be sufficient for the Wicked Marsh to seize him and never let go. Canny was walking very cautiously.

Scraggard, Damon, and Stanley were fixedly watching his steps becoming shorter and slower the closer he got to the boggy surface. Another half an inch and he would be within the right distance to snap everybody out. Getting ready, Canny extended his arm. Suddenly, a black raven zoomed in front of his face, practically touching his nose with its wings. Startled, Canny lost his balance and leaned forward a bit too far. Trying to regain his equilibrium, he waved his arms, but unable to resist its powerful magnetic force, he was pulled straight down into the Wicked Marsh.

Ashley, Eric, and the Crystal Ball

As she looked at Eric's transparent face beaming at her from inside the crystal ball, Ashley smiled for the first time since her capture.

"We're almost there," Eric's hushed voice said into her walkie-talkie earpiece. "How's your energy?"

"I think I've got it all back," Ashley answered as she flexed her elbows and tightened her biceps.

"Great, but keep coughing and sneezing so you don't lose any of it again."

Ashley sneezed and coughed very loud for the guards outside to hear.

"Once again, don't reach out to me unless there is an emergency," Eric said. "But if you absolutely must get in touch with me, just shake the ball three times."

"That's all?"

"Yup, it's easier than Skyping. Now, I've got to go, but I'll talk to you soon." Eric's face faded away. Ashley gripped the crystal ball, and before she knew what she was doing, she shook it three times. Instantly, Eric's face reappeared.

"Sorry," she apologized with a coy smile. "I just wanted to see how well the ball works. I promise not to do it again unless there is an emergency."

"I hope it'll never get to that." Eric snorted.

"Me too."

"By the way, I forgot to ask you one thing. Have you seen an Oak Tree growing around there anywhere?"

Ashley shook her head.

"Nope. There's nothing growing around here, not even grass. Only guards and soldiers are walking back and forth, looking like half-dead trees. Why?"

"Just wondering."

Three Bats and the Black Powder

"**Y**our Scraggardness," Damon said as he bowed his head before the Immortal, "let me go to the Wicked Marsh to save your army and my friends."

"Your idiotic friends don't deserve to be saved," Scraggard whispered, letting clouds of icy air out of his mouth into the Forest boy's face.

Damon scowled. Even if he wanted to say something in his friends' defense, he couldn't have because his lips had frozen shut.

"However, I won't let my army perish," Scraggard continued, still exhaling the frosty mist. "Unfortunately, we don't have time to go after them right now. I have a strong feeling the humans are coming closer." He leaned against the back of his throne.

Damon's lips thawed out, and he quickly asked, "But what if the Wicked Marsh swallows everybody before we get there?"

"I don't usually explain my actions, insolent youth." Scraggard gave Damon an exasperated look. "But I'll tell you, I'll paralyze it until we're ready to go and rescue everybody. In the meantime, it won't be able to harm anyone."

Scraggard clapped his hands, and three bats whooshed into the Throne Hall through a small round window under the roof. They swooped swiftly to the Immortal and hung upside down on his shoulders. The ruler quietly spoke to them in their tongue before handing each a small black pouch. Grasping the pouches in their teeth, the bats shot up to the ceiling and flew out through the same window.

The very next instant, they appeared on the screen, zipping back and forth over the Wicked Marsh, which was studded with the struggling soldiers. Using their clawed feet, the bats tore the pouches open and showered the marsh's surface with glittering black powder. In no time, it looked as if it were covered with a thick layer of sparkling black snow. A sprinkling of the black dust fell onto the marble floor in front of the throne. Damon bent over to blow it away, but Scraggard snapped it out before the Forest boy could get enough air into his lungs.

"Don't let even a grain of it onto your body, or you'll stay paralyzed for as long as the Wicked Marsh. I don't want that. I've got bigger plans for you, so I need you here at your full capacity."

Damon straightened up, bowed his head, clicked his hooves, and humbly said, "Always at your service, Your Scraggardness."

Danger!

Leesho opened his eyes and remembered that he was sleeping in the tent that Eric had drawn and wished real right before the nightfall—along with five sleeping bags and self-inflatable mattresses. Leesho didn't like the complete darkness of the tent. He snapped a few stars here and there across the black fabric, then looked around and saw his friends quietly snoozing. Kikimra had crawled into her sleeping bag head first. Now only her mossy feet were sticking out. Leesho rolled onto his stomach, trying to fall back asleep, which had never been a problem. Tonight, however, for some peculiar reason, he couldn't. He kept turning and tossing until his whole body ached, so he decided to go out for a stretch.

Outside, it was even darker than inside the tent. There wasn't a single star flickering in the night sky. Leesho brought his hands all the way up to his face and was still barely able to see his fingers. The air was nippy, and he didn't feel like staying outside much longer. Just as he was about to crawl back into the tent, he felt a subtle, barely discernible vibration of the ground under his feet. It was so slight that he hoped he'd simply imagined it. He'd never particularly liked using his night vision, but he knew he'd better do it now. He lowered his eyelids and rolled his eyeballs around their axes three times in one direction and three times in the other. When he raised his eyelids again, the world before him appeared as bright blue and clear as on a sunny day. He looked down. The bugs at his feet were scurrying away in every possible direction. He looked up. The birds above his head were leaving their nests and flying elsewhere.

On seeing this, Leesho rapidly dove inside the tent and hollered, "Danger!"

⚙

Little Yaga, Leesho, Kikimra, and Sean lined up in front of the tent, each holding on to his or her Segway. They weren't aware that Scraggard's screen had located them at last. The Immortal was curiously watching Eric quickly drawing laser pointers on the ground. As soon as the last one was finished, Eric wished them real. He put one in his pocket and handed the others to his friends.

"What do we need these for?" Sean asked. "Whom are we teaching a lesson?"

"Guess."

"The Foresters?"

"Getting warm."

"Scraggard?"

On hearing his name, Scraggard smirked on his throne.

"Getting warmer."

"Scraggard's soldiers!" Kikimra cried out.

"Bingo. Right in their eyes."

"Why their eyes?"

"Because the laser beams will temporarily blind them, and we'll be able to escape. But you have to be very precise."

"What's a laser beam?" Little Yaga asked.

"A very strong and focused light."

"It'll blind them only briefly, right?" Little Yaga looked concerned. "I mean, it's hard to survive in the Forest without sight."

"Yes, so briefly that we'll have to rush to get away before they can see again."

"Why didn't you draw laser guns?" Sean asked. "That'd be cool."

"Do you feel like killing anyone?" Eric asked.

Sean scratched the back of his head.

"I don't think so," he admitted. "Not really."

"I don't, either."

Kikimra directed her pointer at her own face and was about to press the small button on its side, but Eric snatched it out of her hand.

"Are you nuts? What do you think you're doing?"

"Testing it—what's the big deal?" Kikimra reached out to get her pointer back.

"Did you hear what I just said?"

"You talk too much." Kikimra snorted. "What exactly did you just say?" She puffed a couple of light clouds of smoke out of her mouth into Eric's face.

He waved them away and asked, "Would you like to go blind for a few days?"

"I thought you said for a few minutes," Little Yaga mentioned quietly.

"Yes, when you're shooting from a distance. If you're practically touching your eyes with it, you'll be lucky if you go blind for a few days and not a few months!"

Right then, Leesho suddenly dropped down onto the ground and leaned his ear against the grass, which was sprinkled with drops of the early-morning dew. When he sprang back to his feet, he didn't have to explain anything. Everybody could feel the earth quaking beneath them.

Blindness

Scraggard the Immortal saw Eric give Kikimra her pointer back.

"How far can this laser beam reach?" she asked and extended her arm, holding the pointer like a spear, this time directed away from her face.

"Quite far."

"Let me see." She pushed the button, and instantly, a red ray pierced the screen and shot straight into Scraggard's left eye. He uttered a curt groan and covered the eye with his hand. Another narrow stream of red light jetted through the screen. Scraggard flinched and grabbed his right eye. For some time, he rubbed his eyes, as if he were trying to ease the pain. When, at last, he stopped and put his hands down, his eyes were wide open but missing their usual glare.

"Your Scraggardness," Stanley called from behind the throne, "are you OK?"

Sitting still as if made of stone, Scraggard didn't respond.

"Your Scraggardness," Stanley called again, this time a bit louder, "sorry to bother you…"

"If you were sorry, you wouldn't bother me," Scraggard interrupted him.

"I just wanted to know if you were OK."

"No, I am not. I am blind as a mole. To deprive me of my sight, this Kikimra girl used a human device I've never seen before. This is the first time a human tool has affected me."

Scraggard snapped his fingers and blinked his eyes. Stanley waited for the cold glow to return, but it didn't. The Immortal's look remained dull and empty. He snapped his fingers again, recited a long incantation, and opened and shut his eyes a few times, but the glow was still missing.

"That's strange. I can't get my sight back."

Scraggard grew silent, as though he were deep in thought.

"Human boy, are you still here?" he asked in a while, extending his arm.

"Yes, Your Scraggardness." Stanley touched Scraggard's fingers. They were icy cold.

"Do you know I've gotten rid of my Swan-Geese?"

"Yes, Your Scraggardness."

"That was a rushed decision, but I won't be able to bring them back to life."

"Why not?"

"Don't ask foolish questions." Scraggard scowled, but then he explained, "I was too angry and used an irreversible incantation." He squeezed Stanley's hand. A freezing chill pierced through the boy's body. "Human boy," the Immortal said, "I need your help."

"At your s-s-s-service, Your Scraggardness," Stanley replied. He was stuttering from the cold, and Scraggard let go of his hand.

"Good, I need your service now—more than ever." A usual wry smile stretched across Immortal's mouth. "Have you ever dreamed of flying like a bird?"

Stanley couldn't remember if he had. "I don't think so," he said.

"I am surprised. I've heard most humans would like to try flying like a bird at least once in their lives."

"That might've been the case in the old days when there were no planes. Now anybody can get on a plane and fly comfortably, eating lunch and watching movies. I think it's much better than flying like a bird."

"OK, you stubborn urchin. I admit, your human world has changed, but whether you've dreamed of it or not, you are going to fly like a bird now."

"Your Scraggardness," Stanley asked cautiously, "what do you mean?"

"I need you to fly over to the Live Water Spring and fill me a vial. Nothing else will restore my vision."

Scraggard snapped his fingers, and instantly, Stanley's legs shortened and turned into uncomfortable birdlike extremities. His feet got covered in scaly-looking skin and now had only three toes, spread widely apart. Feeling unbalanced, Stanley faltered, nearly falling over. His arms elongated, and within seconds, they grew rough feathers. His neck became lithe, able to rotate almost all the way around. His nose bent down, merged with his upper lip, and hardened into a strong beak. His head shrank to the size of a bird's, and his hair turned into short, soft tufts. The only features left untransformed were Stanley's eyes and eyebrows. Feeling cramped, as if he were wearing a straitjacket, he shook his new body, trying to get rid of all the plumage he was suddenly wrapped in.

Hearing the rustling sound the human boy was making, Scraggard simply said, "Don't bother. You'll stay a vulture until you bring me the vial with Live Water."

"A vulture?" Stanley croaked, shocked. He didn't recognize his own voice, which sounded throaty and crackly.

"For your information, vultures are my favorite birds." The corners of Scraggard's mouth momentarily stretched into a fond grin. "Well, enough talking. I need my vision back, so go ahead, start flying."

"How do I get there? I've no idea where this Live Water Spring is."

"Don't worry—your wings know. They'll fly you right there and back."

Damon Meets Eric and Sean

Damon's army consisted of Scraggard's last remaining regiment and all of his palace guards, except for the two watching Ashley's bedroom. The army shot out from under the surface of the earth, only a hundred feet away from Little Yaga and her friends. Damon, who was leading the soldiers, waved at his classmates standing next to the human boys.

"Hello, Little Yaga!" he shouted.

"Hello, Damon."

"Do you remember we were supposed to have a date?"

"Barely."

"I thought you were all excited about it."

"Not anymore."

"Never trust a girl's heart," Damon said, pressing his hands against his chest and pretending to be inconsolable. Then he turned to Kikimra.

"Hi there."

"Morning." Kikimra raised her hand that was holding the pointer. She was tempted to send red light straight into

Damon's conceited eyes, but she remembered Eric's strict order not to fire without his command and reluctantly put her hand down.

"Hello, Leesho."

"Hi, Damon, how are you?"

Damon smiled.

"Not too bad. I see you've got some new friends."

"And you've got sharp eyes," Leesho responded.

"Don't you want to introduce me to them?"

"In due time."

"What's wrong with right now?" Damon insisted.

"The environment's not cozy enough. Your company's far too big."

"The bigger, the better," Damon said with a sneer, but then he immediately grew serious.

"I want you to introduce me to your friends right now."

"Really?"

"If you don't, I'll do it myself."

"Is that a threat?" Leesho's jaws tightened.

"It's OK, Leesho," Eric said, stepping forward. "Hello, Damon, I am Eric Rosebar, and this is my friend, Sean Laing."

"Nice to meet you at last," Damon replied, oozing delight. "Why don't you come over here and shake my hand?"

"Why don't you?" Eric chuckled.

"Is that what you want?" Damon asked. "Not a problem." Turning to his army, he roared, "Fearless army of His Scraggardness, Scraggard the Immortal, after me!"

He spun back around and charged forward.

"Shoot!" Eric shouted, raising his pointer and firing the rays of red light into the soldiers' eyes.

Little Yaga, Kikimra, Leesho, and Sean did the same. A net of red rays pierced the air. The first row of soldiers shielded their eyes with their hands. Some wavered, but they managed not to fall.

Damon stopped abruptly. Without looking back, he raised his right arm and bellowed, "Army, stand still!"

All the soldiers came to an instant halt.

"What are you doing, Eric Rosebar?" Damon asked. "We were all so eager to meet you. We wanted to give you guys big hugs, and this is how you humans greet new friends?"

"That would be a few too many hugs for us to handle, don't you think, Damon?" Eric chuckled again.

"He never thinks," Kikimra barked angrily.

"Kikimra, I thought you liked me." Damon gave her a charming smile that revealed his sharp fangs.

"In your dreams!" Kikimra growled.

"So, you don't like me, too." Damon's look turned mockingly sad. "Girls, you are breaking my heart." He took a step forward.

"Stop right there!" Kikimra hollered and directed her pointer straight at his eyes. She was about to push the button when a strong force yanked the pointer out of her hand and carried it through the air into Damon's. The same thing happened to her friends' pointers, and in the blink of an eye, all five laser sticks were in Damon's possession.

The Losses

Stanley, in vulture form, flew into the Throne Hall carrying a vial of Live Water in his beak. As soon as his bird feet touched the marble floor before Scraggard's throne, his feathers fell off, like autumn leaves, and he turned back into a human.

"Your Scraggardness," he said, exhaling, "here's your water."

"It took you too long, human boy." Scraggard's eyes glinted with their customary cold glow. "My vision has returned."

"How?" Stanley cried out.

"I wonder, do all humans ask foolish questions all the time, or is it just you?" Scraggard motioned for the boy to move away. "Don't block my view."

Stanley walked around the throne to his spot behind it. On the screen, Damon threw the pointers onto the ground, and they gradually faded away, as if they'd never existed.

"Good job." Scraggard nodded with approval. He extended his arm and snapped his fingers four times. Each snap was as loud as a shot. On the screen, Damon was smiling. His eyes, gleaming with a cold glow similar to Scraggard's, moved from face to face of the small, disarmed group of friends staring back at him from a mere hundred feet away.

"Guys," Damon said in an unexpectedly friendly tone, "you must admit that you've lost."

"I don't think so," Kikimra said. "And by the way, nobody snatches my things away from me. I want my laser thing back." She reached forward and snapped her fingers. When the pointer didn't reappear in her hand, she snapped her fingers again.

"I want my stick back," she repeated, very loudly.

When nothing happened, Damon made a sympathetic face.

"How disappointing," he said. "Your powers are gone."

"That's impossible." Kikimra turned to Leesho and Little Yaga with a bewildered look. "Whoever's born with powers never loses them, right?"

"Unless whoever's born with powers starts helping humans," Damon said, his face still mockingly despondent. "Then they turn into powerless, humanlike creatures."

"Is that true?" Kikimra asked Leesho.

"I don't think so," Leesho replied doubtfully. "I've never heard of that. Whoever's born with powers has them forever, unless they're outside the Forest."

Kikimra snapped her fingers. Once again nothing happened.

"You see?" she said. "They're gone. Try yours."

Leesho snapped his fingers and mumbled something under his breath. Everybody was watching him closely, but he admitted that Kikimra was right—he had no powers.

After a few unsuccessful snaps, Little Yaga found that hers were gone, too.

"Damon must be right." Kikimra looked crossly at Sean and Eric. "All of our troubles are because of those humans."

"Are you ready to surrender?" Damon took another step forward. This time his army moved a step forward after him.

"I don't believe you," Leesho said, studying Damon's face as if he were seeing it for the first time. "Something's not right. A Forester born with powers never loses them. It's a known fact."

"It's a fact of the past," Damon retorted. "Things change."

"But I read somewhere," Leesho continued without acknowledging Damon's words, "that the powers could be temporarily disabled by an ill-meaning third party."

Kikimra's face turned purple with anger. Brandishing her fists at Damon, she shouted, "Have you disabled my powers, you stupid jerk?" The thin trickle of gray smoke writhing out of her mouth was the only remaining trace of them.

"Do you remember reading how long it would take us to get our powers back?" Little Yaga asked.

"Long enough for me to seize you all and deliver you directly to the Throne Hall of the Ruler of the Forest, His Scraggardness, Scraggard the Immortal," Damon replied for Leesho.

He moved forward a bit more, and his army did, too.

"We have no powers," Little Yaga whispered, her voice trembling. "What do we do?"

"Run," Eric and Leesho said quietly together.

"On the count of three," Eric whispered, "we all scatter in five different directions. Ready? One! Two! Three!"

He pushed his right foot forward and almost fell because his left foot wouldn't move. It seemed that his sneaker was nailed to the ground. He bent down, swiftly untied the shoelace, and tried to yank his foot out. It wouldn't budge. He turned to his friends. They looked like a bunch of clumsy ballerinas, each dancing on one foot that was stuck to the ground.

Damon and his army kept slowly advancing.

"Hey, Eric, now you can't deny your defeat," Damon said, grinning.

"You're right," Eric admitted. "Now I can't." He, Little Yaga, Leesho, Kikimra, and Sean stopped their gawky dance and watched silently as Damon's troops were approaching. Their capture was now only minutes away. Kikimra suddenly tried to howl, but without her powers, only a pitiful whine came out of her throat.

Damon and his soldiers were getting closer. A few more steps, and Little Yaga and her friends would be in the hands of Scraggard's army, on their way to his gloomy palace.

The Wolves

"I am proud of that boy," Scraggard said, turning to Stanley. The Immortal didn't look his usual sullen self. His eyes shimmered, and his face blushed with color. "I knew he wouldn't let me down. I had no doubt he'd defeat those traitors and their human buddies. Even if I hadn't disabled their powers, Damon would've won."

"Yes, sir." Stanley nodded and looked back at the screen. What he saw there made his jaw drop; a dense fog of wolf fur was floating in the air, slowly descending to the floor of the Throne Hall. On the screen, wolves from two rival packs were fiercely fighting one another. The pack leaders were especially savage, pounding everything and everybody in their way. From time to time, their huge paws pierced the screen, and Stanley could see their sharp, dirty claws. At one point, one leader's head came through, growling ferociously, exposing its sharp fangs, and dripping saliva all over the floor. Stanley noticed it was missing its left ear.

"I've met that wolf before!" he thought to himself, but re-membering Scraggard's reaction when he'd recognized Eric and Sean, he chose not to say a word.

⚌

"Get out of here, you nasty beasts," Damon hollered. He extended his arm to snap the wolves out but was knocked down by the paws of one of the leaders. He jumped back up and was thrown to the ground once again, where he banged his head on an old stump and passed out. As he lay there, one of the younger wolves latched on to his military uniform with its sharp teeth and dragged his limp body out of view, into the depths of the Forest.

The soldiers, infuriated by the disappearance of their commander, went after the wolves, but within seconds, they were tossed, like paper dolls, in every possible direction by the powerful paws of the raging animals. When the battle-field was cleared of Scraggard's army, the two leaders of the packs dashed toward each other. Their snarling and growling were heard throughout the Forest. It seemed they would tear each other apart! But when they collided, they sniffed the air, howled at the sky, and (unless Stanley just imagined it) gave each other a high five. Incredulous, Stanley closed his eyes. When he opened them again a minute later, the screen before him was blank.

⚌

The wolves had departed as abruptly as they had arrived. Little Yaga, Eric, Leesho, Kikimra, and Sean were staring at one another, barely able to believe they'd been spared. In her excitement, Kikimra let out a strong, booming roar.

"Our powers are back," Leesho noted calmly.

"How do you know?" Little Yaga asked.

"Kikimra's howling again." Leesho snapped his fingers, and the laser pointers, which had been destroyed by Damon, reappeared in everyone's hands.

Out of Energy

Stanley walked out from behind the throne and saw Scraggard the Immortal slumped in his royal seat, staring unblinkingly at the pile of wolf fur on the floor beneath the screen. His skin wasn't pale; it was gray. His eyes were closed, and his head hung down on his chest.

"Your Scraggardness," Stanley called, and Scraggard's body jolted. He raised his eyelids with such effort that they could've been made of lead. Beneath his heavy lids, his eyes had lost all their glow. If not for the narrow black dots of his pupils, his eye sockets would've looked completely empty.

"Are you OK, sir?" Stanley asked.

"No," Scraggard creaked.

"Your Scraggardness, what can I do to make you feel better?"

"Give me your energy," Scraggard whispered with a sneer. "I've got none left—I can't even snap this fur out of here. Those beasts have destroyed my army. When my energy's replenished, they'll pay for it."

"Your Scraggardness, I'd give you anything except my energy. I need it for myself."

"Just one sip, and I'll be OK." Scraggard's voice was raspy and barely audible.

Stanley hesitated, then asked, "Why don't you use Ashley's?"

Scraggard slowly moved his pupils in Stanley's direction.

"She's sick," he said. "I won't use hers until she's fully recovered."

"Ashley's a strong and healthy girl," Stanley said. "I don't remember her ever being ill. What if she's making it up?"

"A Forest doctor examined her. He said she was sick."

"What if the Forest doctor doesn't know the tricks humans play?"

Scraggard moved his pupils away from Stanley again.

"If you wish, you can go and check her out. If she's making it up, bring her here, and I'll suck her energy out, down to the very last drop. But if she really is sick, I'll have no choice but to use yours."

Getting across Scraggard's Canal

Little Yaga, Eric, Leesho, Kikimra, and Sean jumped off their Segways and put them down.

"I don't think we'll be using them again anytime soon," Eric said, and the Segways slowly faded back into flat pictures on the ground.

The teens walked to the edge of the ravine and looked down. Far below, Scraggard's Canal, separating the palace from the rest of the Forest, was teeming with sharks. Sensing the visitors' presence, they stuck their obtuse snouts out of the water, hoping for a delectable dinner. High above, the palace, dark and sinister, loomed on the craggy hilltop. Heavy clouds hung over it, while hawks and vultures circled around the roof, which was adorned with gargoyles in the shape of Swan-Geese.

"How on earth are we going to get all the way up there?" Sean pointed at the palace.

"Good question," Kikimra said.

"Can you snap us over there or something?" Sean asked.

"Even if they were combined," Leesho responded, "our snaps wouldn't be powerful enough to get us all up that high."

"Could you snap only me then?" Eric asked.

"Most likely," Leesho replied. "But I wouldn't."

"Why not?"

"You don't want to be on Scraggard's territory alone. We must think of how to get there all together."

The friends fell silent for a while.

"I know!" Sean exclaimed. "Eric will draw a helicopter big enough for all of us to fit in."

"What's a helicopter?" Kikimra asked.

"A flying machine," Leesho explained. "That's not a bad idea." He turned to Eric. "What do you think?"

"It won't work," Eric said, shaking his head.

"Why not?" Kikimra's eyes brightened. "I don't know what a flying machine is, but it sounds like fun. You humans have got a lot of fun stuff," she added looking a bit surprised.

"A helicopter isn't Big Yaga's barrel," Eric objected. "It needs at least one thing I can't draw."

"What thing?"

"A pilot."

"Why can't you draw one?"

"Because a pilot isn't drawable."

"Come on, Eric," Sean insisted. "You can do it. I am sure you've drawn pilots before."

"Yes, I have. I've sketched people in pilot uniforms many times, but a uniform doesn't make a person a pilot, OK? After all, we don't want to risk our own lives, do we?"

"Nope," Sean reluctantly agreed with Eric.

"Let's keep thinking then," Eric said.

"What about Gorinich?" Little Yaga suggested, looking at Kikimra. "We'll all fit on his tail."

"Don't you see those vultures and hawks up there?" Kikimra pointed at the sky. "Gorinich is terrified of them."

"Who's Gorinich?" Eric and Sean asked together.

"Our friend, a two-headed flying snake," Little Yaga answered. "He would've helped us for sure, but Kikimra's right—flying snakes are vultures' and hawks' favorite treats."

"Yep," Kikimra confirmed as she looked up again. "Those birds would tear poor Gorinich to pieces, and we'd all go plummeting down, right into the sharks' jaws."

"A flying snake could actually work," Eric said.

"Unfortunately, it's not an option, Eric," Little Yaga objected with a sigh. "I mentioned Gorinich without thinking."

"What if I draw protective gear for your snake?"

"Something like we had in the Orchard?"

"Not at all. This one will be made of steel. A full-body suit, from both heads to tail. Any vulture or hawk will break its beak and claws before harming whoever's inside."

"It might be a little too much for Gorinich," Leesho said, doubtful, "all that armor plus us sitting on top."

"I'll draw the lightest steel possible. It won't be heavy—I promise."

"Leesho, we can deflate ourselves and weigh next to nothing," Little Yaga suggested bravely, even though the mere thought of it made her shudder.

"I don't think there will be any need for that," Kikimra objected. "We aren't that heavy. Gorinich has carried heavier stuff on his tail."

The Crystal Ball—Again

From time to time, Ashley took the crystal ball out of her pocket and stared at its opaque surface. She was tempted to shake it and talk to Eric, but she knew she wasn't supposed to unless there was an emergency. Sitting on the edge of her bed, she was counting in her head, trying to keep track of time. Eric said he would be coming soon, but it felt as if it had been an eternity since their last talk. She shivered from all the scary thoughts running through her mind: he'd been captured by some evil creature in this creepy forest; he was eaten by a wild animal; he fell off a cliff and broke every bone in his body...

The longer Ashley thought about it, the more she believed something terrible had happened. Sharp pain squeezed her heart.

"Life isn't worth living without him," she thought.

Once again, she pulled the ball out of her pocket determined to shake it, and suddenly it vibrated in her hand. Before her eyes, its opaque surface cleared, and Eric's smiling face looked at her from inside.

"You're alive," Ashley whispered, and tears glistened in her eyes, magnifying the alarm hidden in their corners. "Where are you?"

"Don't cry, Ashley dear." Eric's voice was so warm that her tears dried up instantly. "We're almost there. Listen, is there any way you can leave your bedroom and get outside, into the yard?"

"Are you talking about the courtyard?"

"I guess so."

"I can't." Ashley looked around as if she were hoping to find an exit she had somehow missed before. "All the windows are locked, and Scraggard's soldiers are guarding my doors."

"Too bad," she heard someone's voice say in Eric's background.

"Is it—will the plan still work?" she asked, alarmed.

Eric laughed. "Don't worry about a thing. As soon as we land in the courtyard, we'll get you out."

"I can't wait." Ashley wanted to ask him what he meant by "land in the courtyard." He wasn't flying here on a plane, was he? She brought the ball closer to her mouth, but the light inside it dimmed, and the sphere in her hand turned opaque and lifeless again.

⚓

Meanwhile, Stanley was on his way to Ashley's bedroom. Following Scraggard's instructions, he blew on the images of the Immortal's face floating around the corridor, and they burst like soap bubbles. He approached the soldiers guarding the double door leading to the bedroom. The guards crossed the thick branches of their uniforms in front of him, barring his way. Stanley whispered the word Scraggard had told him to, and the guards immediately removed their branches and let him through.

The Sharks

Gorinich, ready to take off, was spewing jets of fire out of his two mouths.

"Is everybody ready?" Eric hollered without turning his head. He was sitting at the very front, holding on to both necks, which were clad in steel helmets.

"Yes," replied Sean, who was sitting right behind him.

"No," Kikimra and Leesho hollered from the back.

"What do you mean, no?" Eric turned his head toward them.

"Little Yaga's missing."

"Gorinich, wait!" Eric shouted and jumped off to the ground. "Where is she?"

"She was just here," Leesho said, bewildered, "right behind me."

"Where could she have gone?"

"I don't know. It's not like her to simply disappear."

"Scraggard's kidnapped her," Kikimra wailed, distraught.

"I hope not," Eric reassured her, looking around.

"Wait a minute." Sean pointed to the distant edge of the ravine, where a small figure was bent over, looking down. "Isn't that Little Yaga right there?"

"Yes, that's her," Leesho replied, relieved.

"What's she doing?"

"No idea, but I am going to find out." Leesho dashed toward Little Yaga. Kikimra, Eric, and Sean sprinted after him.

"Sorry, guys," Little Yaga said, blushing. "I couldn't help it. They looked so hungry."

"Who?" Kikimra didn't understand.

"Those sharks."

Everybody peered down to see scores of the toothy predators feasting on chunks of red meat that were floating in the water.

"Why didn't you tell us?" Eric asked. "We almost left without you."

"I thought I'd do it fast, and you wouldn't notice." Little Yaga stared down again. "See that poor little one?" she asked, pointing at the smallest shark. It was swimming by the rocky shore, trying to get a bite of food, but the big fish wouldn't let it. They kept blocking the little fish's way and shoving it back to the rocks.

"Sharks are sharks," Little Yaga sighed. She snapped her fingers, and chunks of meat rained down into the water in front of the lonely little fish. The big sharks tried to get to them first, but a sudden strong current flipped them over and hurled them too far away to return. With the big sharks gone, the little one stuck its tail out of the water and flapped it back and forth, raising a storm of splashes. Little Yaga waved back at it.

A few minutes later, Gorinich, with five passengers on his tail, was airborne, heading toward the courtyard of Scraggard's palace.

Ashley and Stanley

"No way!" Ashley exclaimed, hardly able to believe her eyes. "Stanley, is that you, or am I seeing things?"

"It's me, all right, your loyal Stanley." He bowed low before her, like an actor from the old *Three Musketeers* movie he'd once seen.

"I don't believe it!" Ashley's eyes were shining with excitement. "What are you doing here?"

"I've come to rescue you, what else?"

Incredulous, Ashley shook her head.

"Eric's on his way here, too."

"I know. He'll be coming over very soon."

"How do you know?"

"Because all this time we were in the Forest together," Stanley lied. "Just now, we decided to split up. I went ahead to get you ready. We don't want to lose any time."

"Oh yes," Ashley said. "Eric asked me if I could meet him in the courtyard."

"Exactly. That's where I am taking you."

"Wow!" Ashley's heart jumped in her chest with happiness. "For some reason, he never mentioned you. I had no idea there were two of you in this terrible Forest."

"We wanted it to be a surprise."

"It is!" Ashley admitted.

"How are you feeling now?" Stanley gave her a concerned look.

"Can't be better! Eric's plan worked. Everybody believed I was sick, and I've got all my energy back!" Ashley giggled cheerfully for the first time since her capture. Stanley's face brightened.

"Hush," he said. Putting his finger to his lips, he motioned toward the door with his head. "The guards."

"I forgot all about them," Ashley whispered excitedly. "How'd you manage to get through?"

"It wasn't easy. I'll tell you later."

Stanley tiptoed toward the double door, and Ashley quietly followed. When they reached the door, Stanley turned around and whispered into her ear, "Wait for me here. I'll be right back."

Anxious, Ashley clutched at his sleeve.

"No, don't leave me," she begged.

Stanley gently removed her hand.

"Don't worry—I'm not leaving you," he said quietly. "I just have to get rid of the guards, that's all. I won't be long." He opened one half of the door ready to exit.

"Be careful," Ashley whispered, shivering nervously. "It's very dangerous out there."

⊷⊶

Back in the Throne Hall, Scraggard sat slumping in his throne, withered and barely breathing. His eyes were practically closed. When Stanley and Ashley walked in through one of the side doors, he didn't have the energy to turn his head toward them.

Smiling and holding on to Stanley's hand, Ashley gazed around.

"Where are we?" she asked, and the echo in the hall repeated her question.

"This is the Throne Hall," Stanley replied, solemnly. "I've brought you here to meet someone who's in desperate need of your help."

The smile instantly disappeared from Ashley's face. She let go of Stanley's hand.

"What are you talking about?" she asked, and the echo amplified the quivering in her voice.

"Stop blabbering and bring her here," Scraggard whispered from his throne.

Stanley looked Ashley in the eye. "Sorry," he said. "I must obey." He reached for her arm, but she quickly jumped back.

"Don't touch me!" she shrieked, and the echo of her voice shrieked back at her from every corner of the ceiling.

"Calm down," Stanley said quietly. "Everything's going to be all right."

Ashley was shaking from head to toe like a newborn puppy.

"Stay away from me, you traitor."

"Relax," Stanley said with a smile. "Nobody's going to hurt you."

But Ashley was too upset. "Get lost!" she yelled.

"Ashley." Stanley seemed surprised. "I didn't know you could be so rude. My mother always said you were the most proper girl at our school. I'd hate to tell her she was wrong." He let out a woeful sigh. "What a disappointment."

He sighed again, then suddenly lunged forward and scooped Ashley into his arms. Maddened, she wailed as loud as she could, and this time the echo responded with such a deafening yowl that it caused all the glass candleholders to rattle. Stanley's ears were ringing from the reverberation of Ashley's scream. He wished he could squeeze them shut, but his hands were busy holding on to Ashley, who kept trying to wiggle free. She flailed her arms and kicked her legs with a force that was astonishing for someone so petite. When Stanley finally delivered her to Scraggard, he had a pounding headache, and his whole body was battered and bruised.

Gorinich

Gorinich landed so softly as if the courtyard were paved with feathers. Little Yaga, Eric, Kikimra, Leesho, and Sean jumped off, and Little Yaga ran over to the two heads crowning the snake's long body. She removed the steel helmets and fondly kissed each head on its forehead. The right one smiled from ear to ear, but the left frowned and stuck out its forked tongue.

"What's the matter?" Little Yaga asked, pretending not to understand. "It's not polite to stick out your tongue. Please, put it back where it belongs."

Reluctantly, Gorinich's left head sucked its tongue back into its mouth.

"Why'd you kiss the right head first?" the left head asked, and the rings of fiery smoke from its mouth wrapped around Little Yaga, all the way from her neck down. She blew them away. "You know why," she said.

The left head stubbornly turned from side to side.

"Because last time," Little Yaga reminded him, "I kissed you first, remember?"

"I want you to always kiss me first."

"Believe me, I love you very much, but it wouldn't be fair."

Eyes sparkling, the left head asked, "Do you love me more than you do the right one?"

"I love you both absolutely the same." Little Yaga patted the backs of both heads. "Thank you so much for your help, Gorinich. Without you, getting up here would've been next to impossible."

"Little Yaga," Gorinich replied, "you know that for you, I am always only a whistle away. Remember that if you need me for your flight back." On those words, Gorinich spat a beautiful display of colorful flames out of both mouths and disappeared.

Corridors

Scraggard drew his ashen face so close to Ashley's that the tip of her nose turned blue from his icy breath. The pupils of his eyes were feverishly scanning her throat for the best spot to dig his teeth into to get straight into her windpipe. Ashley tried to wriggle out of his hands, but although he was weakened, he still had an iron grip. Knowing it was only a matter of seconds before she would be depleted of all her energy, Ashley bent backward, stretching away from him. Scraggard bared his long, sharp teeth. Ashley pushed herself back a little farther, and suddenly, with as much strength as she could gather, she jabbed her fists into his ribs, knocking the wind right out of him.

Scraggard began to cough. Eyes bulging as he gasped for air, he momentarily loosened his grip on Ashley. Not wasting a second, she bolted away, dashed over to one of the side doors, pulled it open, and disappeared behind it, leaving the astonished Scraggard fighting to catch his breath.

"She broke my ribs," he rasped when he was finally able to speak.

"I'll go after her," Stanley volunteered, ready to sprint out. Scraggard shook his head and motioned him to stay.

"Don't bother," he whispered, and Stanley didn't like the tone of his voice. "Come here."

Stanley didn't obey. Scraggard beckoned him with his finger, crowned with a jagged yellow claw. To Stanley's surprise, and completely against his will, he found himself gliding toward the throne as if he were being tugged by a strong, tight rope.

Meanwhile, Ashley ran down the narrow, dimly lit corridor until she reached the door decorated with Scraggard's face. She looked around. The only other door she could see was the one she had just escaped through. She had no choice but to push on the handle of the door in front of her. It opened into a corridor, even narrower and darker than the one she was about to leave. Her heart racing, she stepped over the threshold, and the door slammed shut behind her. She turned around and instinctively tried to pull it open again, but it would not budge.

Ashley was trembling so hard that her teeth were chattering. Quiet as a mouse, she tiptoed forward, barely able to see where she was going. She tried to hold on to the walls on either side of her, but they were disgustingly wet and sticky. Ashley didn't know how long it had taken her to reach the next door, illuminated by the weak glow of Scraggard's eyes that gleamed from the carving of his face on the door's surface. She pushed it open. The corridor in front of her was narrower still.

As before, the second she stepped over the threshold, the door behind her slammed shut, and she was suddenly immersed in complete darkness. A raw, moldy smell filled her lungs, and she gagged. Holding on to the walls, which were wetter and stickier than the ones she wouldn't touch before, she staggered forward. Tired and frightened, she expected another long walk, but to her relief, she soon reached the next door. She tried to open it, but it was very heavy. She finally managed to push it ajar and was instantly blinded by the quivering light. As soon as her eyes adjusted to the brightness, she realized she was looking at the back of Scraggard's throne. Hastily, she closed the door, slid down onto the floor, and covered her face with her hands.

Where Is Ashley?

Eric whispered Ashley's name into the microphone of his walkie-talkie, but he heard nothing in response. He shook his crystal ball, tapped on it, tossed it up and down, and spun it around like a child's top. Nothing happened. The ball remained opaque and silent.

"What's wrong with it?" he asked Leesho. "Why can't I get through to Ashley?"

"I guess she's unavailable," Leesho replied vaguely.

"How come?"

"She must've lost her ball or misplaced it," Leesho guessed, avoiding looking at Eric.

"The ball's her only connection to the outside world. I can bet my life she wouldn't misplace it. Something's happened to her, and I know it."

"What if she's out of the reception zone?" Sean wondered aloud.

"Sean," Eric said, putting his hand on his friend's shoulder, "I don't know if you've noticed, but we're in a kind of different world right now. I don't think the notion of *reception* means anything here."

Sean shook Eric's hand off his shoulder.

"I'm just trying to help," he said crossly. "I care as much as you do. Ashley's my sister, remember?"

"Stop fighting, you humans," Kikimra demanded.

"We aren't fighting," Eric said. "Are we, Sean?"

"I don't know, Eric, are we?"

"Please, shut up." Kikimra put her finger to her lips. "I think I hear something." She lay down on her stomach and leaned her ear against the bricks of the courtyard.

⊰⊱

Ashley sat sobbing on the dank floor behind the door to the Throne Hall. She never knew her eyes stored so many tears. They were gushing down her cheeks so abundantly that both of her sleeves were soaking wet, but she couldn't stop crying. She only had two options now: to either die from cold and starvation here, in this dreadful corridor, or go back to the Throne Hall and surrender. Out of the two, she chose the former. As soon as she'd made up her mind, she felt no longer frightened. Even though the air around her was damp and chilly, she stopped shivering. Exhausted, she leaned against the clammy wall. Her puffy eyelids closed, and her breathing grew shallow. The bouts of prolonged sobbing gradually diminished, and within a few minutes, she drifted off into a deep sleep.

Is This a Dream?

She thought she'd been awakened by a bright light penetrating her closed eyes. When she opened them, she realized she was still sleeping and having a wonderful dream. In that dream, Eric was smiling at her and holding her hand.

"Good morning, Sleeping Beauty. I couldn't wake you up."

"I don't want to wake up," she said drowsily with a pensive smile.

"Why not?"

"Because while I'm sleeping, you're here with me. When I wake up, you'll be gone."

Eric stared at Ashley, puzzled, but in a moment, he understood.

"I get it. You think you're dreaming of me, right?"

"I don't think it, I know, and I love this dream. I want it to last until I die."

"Until you what?"

"Until I die—because I'm not going back to Scraggard."

"No, you aren't." Eric grasped Ashley by the shoulders and shook her gently. "Ashley, you aren't dreaming; you're awake. I'm here with you for real."

Ashley smiled again.

"It's such a happy dream."

"Ashley, don't get angry with me, but I have no choice. I've got to do it."

"Do what?"

Eric reached forward and painfully pinched her cheek.

"Ouch!" Ashley jumped to her feet and slapped his hand. "What are you doing? Why are you hurting me?"

"To prove you're awake."

"Am I? Are you sure?"

"Do you want another pinch?"

Ashley shook her head.

"I don't believe it." She stretched her arm and stroked Eric's face. "It *is* you. You *are* real. How'd you find me?"

"It was a long journey."

"How'd you get down here into this horrible corridor? I was sure I'd never see your or any other human face again."

"It was Kikimra. She heard you crying."

"Kikimra?" Ashley's lips trembled, and her eyes glared with anguish and indignation. "I hate her and that Little Yaga, too. I thought they were nice. I believed they were my friends, but they tricked me into coming to this forest and handed me over to Scraggard." Once again, tears filled her eyes. "You don't know what I've gone through."

"Ashley," Eric said hugging her. "It's over. You are with me now. Don't be angry with Little Yaga and Kikimra. They're your friends. They helped me find you. They would never trick you. It was Scraggard. He used them to lure you here."

"How did Kikimra hear me crying? Where were you?"

"Up in the courtyard. I was trying to get in touch with you, but you wouldn't respond. Where are your walkie-talkie and the crystal ball?"

"I must've lost them when I was running away from Scraggard."

"I put my ear against the bricks, like Kikimra. I couldn't hear a thing, but she was sure it was you. Leesho also heard someone crying."

"Who's Leesho?"

"Little Yaga and Kikimra's friend. Then the crying stopped."

"I fell asleep. I was very tired."

"We started banging on the bricks. We hoped you'd hear us. Some of the bricks sounded funny, kind of hollow. Leesho believed there could be a trapdoor underneath. He snapped the bricks away, and there was the hatch. I pulled it open, but I couldn't see a thing down there. It was too dark, so I drew this flashlight." Eric showed her the one in his hand. "When I turned it on, I saw a ladder built along the wall. I climbed down and found you here, sleeping."

Ashley leaned her forehead against Eric's shoulder.

"If it wasn't for you," she whispered, "I would've died down here." She looked at the flashlight and asked, "I don't get it—what do you mean, you drew it?"

"It's too crazy to explain. I'll tell you later. Now, let's get out of here."

Eric took Ashley's hand and pulled her away from the door leading into the Throne Hall. Halfway down the corridor, they reached the ladder. Ashley looked up and saw the sky peeking in through the opening high above. She turned to Eric with alarm.

"I am afraid of heights," she confessed.

"Ashley," Eric said very seriously, "you aren't afraid of anything. You are very brave. Climb up first, and don't look down. I'll be right behind you." He gave her a slight push forward. She drew in a deep breath and put her hands on the first rung. "That's a start." Eric's voice was soothing and encouraging at the same time. "Keep going. You'll be fine—I promise."

I Know That Bird!

Dizzy with happiness, Ashley was moving her eyes from Eric to Little Yaga, from Little Yaga to Sean, from Sean to Kikimra, from Kikimra to Leesho, and from Leesho back to Eric.

"I d-d-don't believe I'm n-n-not dreaming." She stuttered with excitement. "Thank you, guys, so much. Honestly, I didn't think I would ever get away from Scraggard."

"I hate to disappoint you," Leesho said, "but technically speaking, you still haven't, and neither have we. Scraggard can show up here any minute and capture us all. We must find the Oak Tree before Scraggard finds us."

"What tree?" Ashley asked.

"The Oak Tree," Kikimra answered, and then she looked at Leesho. "Where do you think it could be?"

"I have a feeling it's somewhere nearby," Leesho replied, looking around the barren courtyard. "Scraggard would never keep such an important object far from his reach."

"Nothing in the Forest is far from his reach," Kikimra said gloomily.

"That's true," Leesho agreed.

"So what do we do now?" Sean asked.

"I think we should consult my great-aunt, Biggest Yaga," Little Yaga said. "She'll know."

"You're right." Leesho nodded. "We must go back to Biggest Yaga."

"That's going to take us a long time." Kikimra was unable to hide her frustration.

"Do we have any other choice?" Eric asked.

"I can't think of any," Kikimra admitted reluctantly.

"Then we have to go."

"Look!" Ashley suddenly cried, pointing up at the sky. "I know that bird. It brought me my walkie-talkie and the crystal ball."

Everybody looked up and saw a black raven slowly flying toward them. A few moments later, she perched on Ashley's shoulder.

"Hi, birdie," Ashley greeted the raven, looking apprehensively at her beak.

"Don't worry," Leesho said. "Clair's not going to hurt you. She's our friend."

"I know," Ashley replied.

The raven was staring at Ashley. Her eyes wouldn't blink. It seemed she wanted to ask the human girl a question. Ashley bent her elbow, and Clair hopped off her shoulder and onto her forearm. There she noticed the bracelet Mrs. Rosebar had given Ashley on her birthday. Gingerly moving her feet, the bird began sidestepping toward the sparkling bangle. Her claws tickled Ashley's arm, and the girl giggled. When Clair reached the bracelet, she suddenly gave it a quick, forceful peck. The chain holding the set of tiny gold acorns broke. The acorns plummeted down to the ground and, bouncing against one another, rolled across the yard toward the edge of the cliff.

Mesmerized, Ashley and her friends watched the acorns stop right before the precipitous drop. There, they began spinning around a narrow gap between the bricks. At first, they were moving slowly, then faster and faster, until suddenly, one by one, they fell into the crevice. As soon as all the acorns were gone, the raven flapped her wings and flew away.

The Oak Tree and the Gold Chest

"What was that about?" Ashley asked, gazing down at the broken chain lying at her feet.

Even if any of her friends had wanted to answer, they didn't have the time. A crushing sound came from the side of the courtyard where the gold acorns had just disappeared. The earth there began to rise, shattering the heavy stone blocks as if they were made of flimsy plastic. The leafy crown of a tree broke through the earth's surface between the fragments of crushed brick. Within seconds, right in front of the astonished teens, an Oak Tree hatched out of the ground, rose into the air, and stood tall and wide on the very edge of the cliff over the shark-infested waters. An army of ferocious acorns, buzzing like a thousand bees, was ready to attack the petrified youngsters.

"Get down!" Little Yaga hollered and threw herself onto the ground. Her friends dropped down beside her. They all covered their heads with their hands, waiting for the acorns' assault.

A few minutes later, when nothing had happened and the buzzing abruptly ceased, Kikimra, her face against the bricks, asked, "What's going on up there? Can I look?"

"Don't raise your head," Leesho cautioned. "I think they're waiting for us to move before they launch their attack."

"I am very uncomfortable," Kikimra complained. "These bricks are too hard on my body."

"A smash by one of those acorns will be harder."

Just then, Little Yaga heard a strange sound coming from the tree. She turned her head sideways, without raising it, hoping to get a glimpse of what was going on up there.

"Wow!" she whispered to herself in disbelief. Then she shouted, "Guys, get up! We're saved!"

She and her friends jumped to their feet and froze, speechless, astounded by the spectacle before them. There were hundreds of squirrels hanging from the branches of the tree, and hundreds more clung to its trunk. With lightning speed, they were picking the acorns, cracking them open, eating the seeds, and tossing the empty shells onto the ground. Not a single acorn was able to escape, and soon there was none left. Satiated, the squirrels hopped off the branches and the trunk and scurried out of the courtyard.

Silently, Little Yaga and her friends approached the Oak Tree and looked up. There it was—the gold chest hanging from the highest branch of the tree, shining in the sun, and swinging slightly in the wind.

"How will we get it down?" Sean wondered, squinting from the blinding sunlight reflected in the gold of the chest.

"What do we need it for?" Ashley asked.

"Somewhere, inside this trunk, there is an egg with a needle that holds Scraggard's death on its very tip," Kikimra explained raising her arm. "I'll get it down." She snapped her fingers at the chest. It budged the tiniest bit but remained on the branch.

"Be careful," Little Yaga warned. "Go easy—you don't want it to break."

"I am being careful," Kikimra said and snapped her fingers again. This time, the chest didn't move at all.

"You don't have enough power to bring it down alone," Leesho said. "You need help."

"I'll help her." Little Yaga offered, raising her arm. "On the count of three. Are you ready?"

Kikimra nodded.

"One, two, three." Little Yaga and Kikimra both snapped at exactly the same time. The two snaps sounded like one, only louder. The chest jolted and tilted down for a moment, but then it recovered its position and stayed on the top branch of the tree.

"I'll help you," Leesho said and raised his arm, too. "One, two, three." Their three simultaneous snaps were as loud as a shot. The chest tilted down and stayed that way, but it still didn't fall.

"This is harder than I thought," Kikimra admitted, and then looking at Eric she said, "Every little bit counts. We need your snap, too."

"How about mine and Sean's?" Ashley asked.

"Yours won't work."

"Why?"

"You are humans."

"Eric's human, too."

"I know, but oddly, his snaps work."

"Why?"

"How should I know?"

Little Yaga, Kikimra, Leesho, and Eric extended their arms toward the chest. Leesho counted to three. Together, all four of them snapped their fingers. The snap, deafening as an explosion, shook the Oak Tree from its roots to its crown. The chest slid off its branch and, slowly rotating in the air, came down. It landed as softly as if it were made of rubber and rolled onto its side. Its lid flung open. A gray rabbit tumbled out and scampered quickly away.

Suddenly, a huge shaggy dog appeared out of nowhere and tore after it. In two gigantic leaps, it reached the rabbit and pawed its trembling ears. Scared to death, the rabbit opened its mouth. A white goose flew out of it and into the sky. Immediately, a hawk soared after the goose and clutched it in its beak. Out of the goose's mouth came a duck, holding an egg between its legs. The duck started to fly across the shark-infested canal, but halfway there, it was seized by the claws of a vulture. The duck dropped the egg, which went down toward the foamy waters. There it floated briefly on the waves before submerging and disappearing beneath the water's dark surface.

The Ladder

Flabbergasted, the friends looked at one another, unable to grasp what had just happened.

Ashley covered her face with her hands and said, "We'll never get out of here. We'll never see our homes again."

"Never say never, sis." Sean grabbed her by the shoulders. "You've escaped this place once. You'll do it again."

Ashley lowered her hands; her face was wet with tears.

"I don't believe you, Sean," she cried. "We're stuck here forever."

"Would you believe me if I say that I agree with Sean?" Eric asked. "I'm sure there's a way out of here, and I know we'll find it."

"Guys," Little Yaga called out. She was standing at the edge of the cliff, staring down at the water below. "I don't know if it's my imagination or there is a shark down there, holding an egg in its teeth?"

Everybody rushed over to join Little Yaga. Once again Eric quickly drew a pair of binoculars and wished it real. Peering through the binoculars, he announced, "I see the shark, and I see an egg in its jaws!"

"What's the shark doing?" Ashley asked.

"It's slapping the water with its tail."

Leesho took the binoculars from Eric.

"I think it wants us to go down there and take the egg," he said, staring at the fish.

Eric turned to Ashley and wiped away her tears.

"You see?" he said, cheering her. "You've been crying for nothing."

Ashley let out a sigh. "But how will we get there?" she asked.

"You won't, but I will," Eric replied. "I'll draw a backpack and a very long rope ladder. I'll wish them both real, climb down, take the egg out of the shark's jaws, put it into the backpack, and climb back up."

"How do you wish things real?" Ashley asked.

"No idea. It just happens."

While Eric was on his knees drawing, Little Yaga took the binoculars from Leesho.

"I think I've seen that fish before," she said. "Leesho, this is the shark that gave me Scraggard's ring back when it had fallen into the brook before I went to Ashley's birthday party, remember?"

"Are you sure?"

"Positive. And this is the shark that couldn't get to the food because of the big sharks."

"That is very interesting," Leesho said as he stared down, thinking.

Meanwhile, Eric and Sean were securing the ladder.

"I'll go with you," Sean volunteered.

"You better stay with the girls," Eric objected.

"Let him go," Leesho said. "I'll stay here with the girls."

"OK," Eric agreed. Gingerly, he and Sean began climbing down the ladder. The rungs strained and creaked under their feet, as though they would unravel or tear at any moment.

"I don't think you've drawn this ladder strong enough," Sean complained.

"Don't worry—it's strong. At least as strong as I could imagine it."

The powerful wind was tossing the ladder against the rocky wall of the cliff, and the boys scraped their fingers, knees, and foreheads.

"Next time, you'd better draw gloves, knee pads, and helmets," Sean shouted, but the wind muffled his words.

"What?" Eric hollered back.

"Never mind!"

The rough water was splashing up against the rocks so high that the boys were drenched through and through by the time they'd made it to the last rung.

The shark was patiently waiting for them. As soon as the boys reached the water, it jumped into the air, like a dolphin in a water park, and spat the egg out right toward them. Eric caught it with one hand but lost his balance. If Sean hadn't grabbed him by the collar of his T-shirt, he would've tumbled right into the jaws of the big sharks lurking below.

The trip up the ladder was even harder. The sun beat down mercilessly on the boys, burning their heads and necks. Their skinned knees and fingers were bleeding. When they finally reached the top, they were so exhausted that they had to use all their willpower to hurl themselves up onto the flat surface of the courtyard.

For some time, they couldn't move. Barely breathing, they lay flat on their stomachs, with their faces against the bricks and their eyes closed. When they finally staggered up to their feet, the first thing they heard was a greeting in a soft, quiet voice.

"Hello, Eric. Hi, Sean," the voice said. "At long last, we meet."

It's a Deal

Neither Eric nor Sean had ever seen anybody so gaunt. It seemed they were staring at a very tall skeleton wrapped in paper-thin skin and draped with black garments that flapped in the wind. Its mouth was stretched into a scary, lipless smile. Its eyes sat deep in their sockets, covered with half-shut eyelids without a single eyelash.

"Scraggard?" Eric asked.

"Your Scraggardness," Scraggard corrected with a smirk. "How did you guess, smart boy?"

Eric looked around. What he saw was horrifying. Ashley, Little Yaga, and Kikimra were tied to the trunk of the Oak Tree. Their mouths were gagged with crushed acorn shells. Leesho, ice-covered from head to toe and looking like a frozen statue, stood next to Scraggard, whose bony fingers were squeezing his frosty shoulders. There was someone else, whose face Eric couldn't see, lying on the ground at Scraggard's feet.

"I know what you've got in your rucksack," Scraggard said.

Eric unzipped his backpack and pulled out the egg. It was neither small nor big. He held it between his thumb and index finger, and everyone could see that it was pulsating like a human heart.

"You've got my life in your hands," Scraggard said, "and I've got his in mine." He removed his fingers from Leesho's shoulders and wrapped them around his stiff neck. "Let's trade."

"Don't," Leesho breathed out, moving his icy lips.

Eric looked at the girls. They were in shock. Little Yaga's eyes were filled with tears. Eric turned to Sean, who whispered, "If you don't kill him, he'll kill us. He's evil. I can see it in his eyes."

"If I kill him," Eric whispered back, "I'll be a murderer."

"No. You'll save everyone. You'll be a rescuer."

"So, Eric Rosebar," Scraggard said with a sneer, "do we have a deal?"

Eric didn't answer. Instead, he broke the egg's shell and took out the gold needle. It was gleaming in the sun. The tip of it was glowing black, and the eye was dark blue. Suddenly, the words from the inscription on Scraggard's ring ran through Eric's mind: "The eye's dark blue, and here's your clue: show your prowess without your powers."

Now those words made perfect sense, and at once, Eric knew exactly what he needed to do. "This needle is mine," he heard Scraggard saying. "Give it to me, and I'll let Leesho go."

"Never," Eric refused. "But if you free Leesho, I won't break the black tip off—I'll just get rid of the needle. I'll throw it into the waters of your canal."

Scraggard gritted his fangs, thinking.

"OK," he consented at last. "It's a deal. Ditch the needle, and I'll let Leesho go."

"Let him go first," Eric replied calmly.

Deliberately, one finger at a time, Scraggard removed his hands from Leesho's throat.

"You are free to go, you little traitor," he said. Rigidly, Leesho stepped forward, pieces of ice falling off his body with his every step.

"You see," Scraggard said, staring at Eric, "I did what you wanted me to. Now it's your turn to keep your word." His eyes were burning hot with agitation. "Dump the needle."

"Yes, you have," Eric agreed. "And I have no choice but to keep mine."

Looking straight at Scraggard, he raised his hand holding the needle. Scraggard gave him an encouraging smile. "Go ahead," he said quietly.

"I will," Eric assured the Immortal. "And as I promised, you won't die. But first I must make sure that you'll never harm anyone again."

With these words, Eric broke off the dark-blue eye of the needle and flung it over the edge of the cliff into the foaming waters below.

"Show your prowess without your powers," he shouted, and the rest of the needle followed the dark-blue eye. It slowly tumbled down, reflecting the setting sun. Just before it touched the water, a black raven swooped down, caught the needle in its beak, and whooshed back up into the sky, where it disappeared behind the idly moving clouds.

Leesho's Death

Smiling, Eric turned around. Scraggard was gone, and the girls were untied. They gathered around Leesho, who was sprawled on the ground, motionless. Little Yaga, knelt beside him, was crying. The smile left Eric's face.

"What's going on?"

"Forest girls don't cry," Kikimra growled, staring at Little Yaga.

"They do if they lose someone they love," Little Yaga said, sobbing.

"You don't love Leesho."

"Yes, I do."

"You've never said that before."

"I never realized that before. He was always around, and now that he's gone," Little Yaga wailed, "I know I can't live without him." The white smoke coming out of her mouth covered Leesho's body from head to toe.

"What happened?" Eric asked again.

"The second before you broke the needle, Scraggard snapped his fingers at Leesho, and he…he just dropped," Ashley stammered. She looked terrified. "Is there anything we can do to bring him back?"

"Nothing!" Kikimra howled, spitting clouds of black smoke. "Even Live Water won't revive a Forester killed by Scraggard."

"How about CPR?" a weak voice asked from behind.

Everybody turned around.

"Stanley?" Eric asked, incredulous. "What are you doing here?"

"He's Scraggard's spy," Ashley cried, outraged. "Don't trust him!"

"Ashley, I know I'm guilty," Stanley said, "but please don't be angry with me. I had no choice."

"Didn't you? Oh, you poor thing!" Ashley blinked her eyes in fake sympathy.

Ignoring her sarcasm, Stanley said, "I learned CPR from YouTube. I can revive your friend."

"You humans think too much of yourselves," Kikimra snarled angrily as wreaths of thick black smoke flew into Stanley's face. "You have no Live Water and no powers, so tell me, how can you possibly revive anyone?" She took a step closer to Stanley and snapped her teeth right under his nose. Unnerved, he shrank away from her. "Speaking of Live Water," Kikimra continued, "I'm off to fetch some to at least try to bring my friend back— because I do believe in miracles, OK?" She loudly snapped her fingers and disappeared.

"That's one smoky girl," Stanley said, waving the black fumes away from his face.

"Start the CPR," Eric said curtly, "and I'll draw a defibrillator."

"Do you know how to use one?" Ashley asked.

"Last week, during the Future Careers Night at school, an EMT guy showed me how."

"What's a defibrillator?" Little Yaga asked.

"A machine that restarts a heart when it stops beating."

"A Live Machine?"

"Sort of."

Stanley began forcefully pushing down on Leesho's chest.

"What are you doing, hurting him like that?" Little Yaga cried out, her moist eyes wide open. She raised her arm to snap Stanley off Leesho's body.

"Don't!" Eric hollered, interrupting her. "He's pumping Leesho's heart until the defibrillator's ready. Back off, and don't bother him!"

Bewildered, Little Yaga lowered her arm. "You humans are much more mysterious than anyone could've ever imagined," she said, staring at Leesho's chest, which was rising and falling as Stanley blew air into his mouth.

⊰⊱

When Kikimra returned, holding a vial of Live Water in her hand, Leesho stood up to greet her. Surprised, she dropped the vial and exclaimed, "Are you alive? How is it possible?"

"The humans brought me back." He smiled and touched his ribs. "I'm aching all over, but I'm alive."

"Stanley, I didn't know you were so good at CPR," Eric complimented his classmate.

"At what?" Kikimra asked, but nobody answered her.

Stanley was staring at Eric. "Man, I had no idea you were such a talented artist." As he said that, he realized he had no more hatred left inside him. He extended his hand and asked, "No hard feelings?"

Eric shook his hand.

"Well, guys," Leesho said, "thanks again."

"No problem," Stanley answered with a modest smile.

Kikimra looked at him and narrowed her eyes. "Show-off," she blurted, blowing a whole cloud of smoke into his face. Instead of getting angry, Stanley laughed, and suddenly, she did, too.

Away from the Palace

"Can we leave this terrible place already?" Ashley asked.

"Yes, we can," Eric answered, nodding.

"Do you mind taking me with you?" an unfamiliar voice questioned from behind.

Everybody turned to see who it was and saw a young man in wet clothes. There were fish scales clinging here and there to his pants and T-shirt.

"I used your ladder to climb up," he told Eric.

"Who are you?" Eric asked.

"My name is Daniel. I was a prisoner of Scraggard's for many years. He realized I was good with technology and forced me to make him a kind of a surveillance screen. When the screen was ready, he wanted to kill me, at first, to make sure I wouldn't make one for anybody else in the Forest, but then he changed his mind and turned me into a shark. Just now, when you stripped him of his powers, I got my human body back."

"Were you the shark that gave us the egg?" Sean asked.

"Yes, of course. When I saw it sinking, I dove down and grabbed it, right before the real sharks did." Daniel turned to Little Yaga. "And if you were wondering," he told her, "it was I who found Scraggard's ring when it had fallen into the brook a few days ago and gave it back to you."

"That's just what I said!" Little Yaga exclaimed.

Right then the rustling of wings was heard from above. Everybody looked up.

"Swan-Geese," Little Yaga whispered.

The birds, back in their feathery form, had left the roof of the palace and begun their slow descent to the courtyard.

"What do they want from us?" Kikimra asked, alarmed.

The birds touched down on the ground and, honking loudly, surrounded the teens and Daniel.

Leesho walked over to their leader and peered into its eyes. A moment later, he turned to his friends and said, "They are offering us a ride home." The teens and Daniel clapped their hands in gratitude.

Home, Sweet Home!

"Hello, Hut on a chicken leg,
"Turn to us your front,
"And to the Forest your back!"

Very slowly, as if unsure it had heard the chanting right, the Hut turned around. For a few moments, it stood still, appearing fixed to the ground by the foundation. Then, puffing streams of fireworks out of its chimney, it began jumping up and down on its chicken leg, like a young, newly built cabin.

"It's you!" the Hut exclaimed. Out of excitement, it turned 360 degrees to the left, then 360 degrees to the right. Then it threw its roof up into the sky. When the roof fell back onto its frame, it was a little lopsided, and the Hut had to make a few awkward moves to straighten it again.

Little Yaga ran over and hugged the chicken leg. Overwhelmed with emotion, the Hut began humming. The raucous screeching it produced hurt everyone's ears.

"Dear Hut," Little Yaga yelled, "I love you very much, but please, stop singing, or we'll all go deaf here."

"Sorry." The Hut stopped humming at once. "I am very happy to see you back home, safe and sound. I was afraid Scraggard would have you all killed. I never thought anyone could defeat him, but I know you have—the whole Forest is talking about it."

"We've deprived him of his destructive powers," Eric explained.

"So I've heard. I am so proud of you. I'm just beside myself!" And the Hut flung its door wide open.

"Welcome," it said and squatted down for Little Yaga and her friends' victorious entrance.

⇥⇤

"Cuckoo-one, cuckoo-two, cuckoo-three, cuckoo-four, cuckoo-five, cuckoo-six, cuckoo-seven, cuckoo-eight," the Cuckoo Bird counted, as loudly as she could, as the teens and Daniel walked in one by one.

"Is that it?" she asked when the door slammed shut behind Daniel, the last one in.

"Yes," the young man confirmed, "that's it."

"The heroes are here!" the bird exclaimed shrilly. "Cock-a-doodle-doo! Cock-a-doodle-doo!"

"Why on earth are you cock-a-doodle-doo-ing like a rooster?" Little Yaga asked.

"Because I want to wake up the whole neighborhood! I want everyone to know the heroes are back home!"

"You won't wake anyone."

"Why not?"

Little Yaga stared at the bird, amused. "Cuckoo Bird," she said, spreading her arms, "out of all of us here, you should be the one to know. Check with your clock. It's too early—nobody's asleep yet."

"I was," said a drowsy voice.

Everyone turned around to see a slender woman standing in the doorway between the kitchen and the bedroom, smiling. Eric's eyes almost popped out of his head.

"Mom?" he asked incredulously.

"Mrs. Rosebar?" Ashley, Sean, and Stanley cried out in unison.

"What are you doing here?" Eric was shocked to see his mother in Big Yaga's Hut.

"I came here to visit my mother, whom I haven't seen in thirteen years," Mrs. Rosebar said and gave her son a tender hug. "I was able to do so only because you had defeated Scraggard the Immortal, the Ruler of the Forest. And I am immensely proud of you."

"You've heard of Scraggard the Immortal?" Eric asked astounded. "And who's your mom? I didn't know you had one—I mean, I thought your mother was dead."

"Thank goodness she isn't. All these years, she's lived in this Forest, raising your sister."

Eric seemed lost. "My sister has always lived with us, Mom," he said.

"I'm talking about your twin sister."

Now Little Yaga was lost. She turned to Leesho and mouthed, "Do you follow?"

Leesho frowned and shook his head.

Suddenly, Little Yaga heard her grandmother's croaking voice.

"Stop it," she said. "You're confusing everybody now."

Big Yaga limped through the doorway, leaning on her stick and looking her usual self. Her gray hair was in disarray. Her crooked nose was almost touching her upper lip, and an ugly, hairy wart protruded from its usual place under her right eye. Still, there was something different about her. At first, Little Yaga couldn't pinpoint what it was, until suddenly, she realized her grandmother was glowing. Her beady eyes were sparkling, and her lips, ordinarily tightly pressed together, were stretched into something resembling a smile.

Little Yaga felt a wave of affection sweep through her body. Surprised at how much she had missed her grandmother, she rushed forward to give her a hug, but Big Yaga stuck out her stick.

"Back off," she grumbled. "I am not your comfort blanket."

"I wasn't going to hug you," Little Yaga lied, trying not to show that she was hurt. "I was going to bite off that ugly wart of yours."

Big Yaga gave her a pleased look.

"This trip has served you well," she said. "You sound less like a whiny human and more like a Forester. A few more challenges like this one, and I won't be ashamed of you bearing the Yaga name."

"Have you been ashamed of me, Grandma?" Little Yaga's voice quivered.

"When you ask stupid questions," Big Yaga griped, "you sound like a human again."

"Big Yaga," Mrs. Rosebar intervened, "there's nothing wrong with being a human."

"I know you believe that," Big Yaga said, sulking. "And since when do you call me by my first name?"

"Since now, until we tell the children the truth."

"And when are you planning on doing that?"

"After you've fed them, of course. They're too hungry now to digest anything but food."

Big Yaga looked at the kids, who'd been turning their heads back and forth from her to Mrs. Rosebar during their tetchy exchanges.

"Why should I feed them?" Big Yaga asked stubbornly. "You do it."

"This is your house. The laws of the Forest require you to feed a hungry guest."

"Don't teach me the laws of the Forest. I know them better than anyone else."

Big Yaga tightened her lips and snapped her fingers. At once a stained and tattered All-You-Can-Eat Tablecloth covered the kitchen table. The rusty-looking pots and pans that came with it were full of rotten food. The rancid smell filled the kitchen.

"Big Yaga," Mrs. Rosebar said, "you must feed your guests, not poison them."

Big Yaga's eyes glared crossly. She glided her hand over the table, and it was instantly empty. She snapped her fingers again. Another All-You-Can-Eat Tablecloth covered the table-top. This one had no stains or holes but was as crumpled as if someone had just chewed it up and spit it out. Its pots and pans seemed newer. The food in them wasn't rotten—it was burned.

"Big Yaga," Mrs. Rosebar insisted, "surely you can do better than that."

"I could if I wanted to, but I don't want to."

"Please," Mrs. Rosebar asked, "your guests have returned from a dangerous mission as the winners. They deserve a tasty, nutritious meal, served on the best tablecloth in the nicest dishes."

Big Yaga growled and gritted her teeth.

"Mind you, I am doing this under pressure and totally against my will," she grumbled and snapped her fingers for the third time.

At last, a sparkling-clean All-You-Can-Eat Tablecloth that smelled as fresh as the winter's first snow covered the table. Not a wrinkle or a tear marred its surface, and its dishware was made of the finest plants and flowers. The silverware was studded with precious stones, and the bowls, platters, pitchers, and decanters were overflowing with food and beverages that would suit anybody's palate.

"There you go," Mrs. Rosebar said with an approving smile. "That's the way to do it."

"Do I look like I care?" Big Yaga barked.

"I know you do."

From appetizers to desserts, there was so much food on the table that even after the hungry teenagers had devoured all they could, there was still plenty left.

"Now you can all go home and leave me alone," Big Yaga said, snapping the tablecloth gone and turning around to retreat into her bedroom.

"Wait a minute," Eric said, stopping her. "Didn't you and Mom want to tell us something after we ate? We are ready to listen."

Big Yaga groaned and looked at Mrs. Rosebar.

"Go ahead, Jane, or whatever your name is these days."

Mrs. Rosebar's Story

Before she started talking Mrs. Rosebar took a seat next to the children. "I haven't always lived in the human town," she began, looking specifically at Eric, "because I am a Forester, just like Leesho and Kikimra."

"No way," Eric said. He was so startled that he didn't know what else to say.

"Yes, sweetheart. I grew up right here, in this Hut, which has always belonged to my mother, Big Yaga."

"My grandmother is your mother?" Little Yaga asked, her eyes turning round like two saucers.

"Yes, Little Yaga, she is." Mrs. Rosebar gave her an intent look. "When I was only a few years older than you are now, I did the same thing that you did a short time ago. I helped a human, tricked into the Forest by Scraggard, escape."

"Go ahead," Big Yaga groused. "Keep bragging about it."

"That human was a young man," Mrs. Rosebar continued, ignoring Big Yaga's comment. "His name was Alan Rosebar."

"My father?" Eric asked.

"Yes. He was smart and handsome, and we fell in love at first sight. Of course, to be fair, I must admit that I hid my fangs and snapped the tufts of fur off my body. I helped him break out of the Forest and return to the human town, and there we secretly got married. Although we both longed to be together, for over a year we were bound to stay apart. He had to go back to the university in another human town to finish his studies, and while he was gone, I wanted to spend time with my mother because I knew I would be leaving soon and perhaps never see her again."

"Oh, sure," Big Yaga muttered.

"When I returned to the Forest, Scraggard itched to imprison me in one of his towers for the rest of my life. If it hadn't been for my aunt, Biggest Yaga, he would've done it. Nine months later, my twins, a boy and a girl, were born. We named the boy Eric because his father had told me once that he liked that name, and the girl..." Mrs. Rosebar trailed off and paused for a moment as if catching her breath. The teens were staring at her, speechless.

"We named the girl...Little Yaga."

Little Yaga jumped to her feet. Her nostrils flared, letting out streams of white fumes. Her heart pounded loudly against her chest.

"Are you talking about me?" she asked.

"Yes, sweetheart, about you."

"Does this mean you're my..." Little Yaga said, stammering. "You are my..." It seemed she was looking for the right word. "This means you're my mother?"

"Yes, that's what it means."

Little Yaga felt as if her flow of oxygen had been cut off. She started choking. Before her eyes, the room grew fuzzy at first, then went completely black. She clasped her throat with her hands and slowly went down to the floor. When she opened her eyes again, her face was wet from cold water it had been sprayed with.

"How come you left me here, in the Forest," she whispered hoarsely getting up to her feet, "and took Eric with you to the human town?"

"For a few months, we managed to keep your birth a secret from Scraggard, but one day, he learned the truth. He was insane with fury and caused a hurricane that ravaged half of the Forest. His goal was to destroy our Hut, but you know how smart our little dwelling is."

The proud Hut jumped up and down on its chicken leg in response, and everyone inside jumped up and down with it.

"Hey, stop it," Mrs. Rosebar said, stomping her foot against the floor. "You're too jerky today. You're making me dizzy." She looked back at the children and continued. "As soon as the Hut saw the wind coming, it fell through the surface of the earth, underground. It was stifling hot and pitch-black down there. You and Eric cried so wildly that I was afraid your wailing would cause an earthquake. The Hut stayed there until the hurricane had passed. When Scraggard learned we'd survived, he swore to come over here in person to kill me and capture you—half humans—for his perpetual source of energy. We couldn't afford to lose a second. We had to flee. While I was getting you kids ready, you, Little Yaga, broke out in a rash and a fever that spiked to a hundred and five degrees. Right before my eyes, your little body, hot as an oven, became covered in blisters. Your grandmother said you were too sick to make it to the human town.

"'I won't leave without my daughter,' I cried. 'I'd rather Scraggard torture me for the rest of my life than leave her here!'

"'If you want to lose her, take her,' your grandmother said, watching you, a vial of Live Water in her hand. She was afraid you would stop breathing at any moment. She shook the vial in front of my face and said, 'If she stays here, she'll survive. Scraggard won't use her energy for his benefit. You know how afraid he is of human diseases.'

"'But when she gets better, he will,' I insisted.

"'Oh no he won't,"' your grandmother promised. 'My sister, Biggest Yaga, will see to that.'

"Just then, Biggest Yaga's raven, Clair, flew in and croaked that Scraggard and his army were approaching. Hurriedly, I packed a few last things, kissed you good-bye, tried to hug my despondent mother, and left, never to see you again, until Ashley's birthday party."

Shivering as if she were cold, Little Yaga asked, "Why didn't you tell me you were my mother right then and there at the party?"

"Because right then and there, neither you nor Eric was ready for this information. Both of you would've thought I was insane."

"That's true," Eric agreed, trying not to show his emotions.

Little Yaga's Choice

"Sweetheart, now that we've finally been reunited," Mrs. Rosebar said as she took Little Yaga's hands and squeezed them lightly, "we can live together happily ever after."

"Who's *we*?" Little Yaga asked, cautiously.

"You; your father and I; your twin brother, Eric; and your little sister, Lisa."

"Where?" Little Yaga removed her hands from Mrs. Rosebar's gentle hold. "In the human town?"

"Yes, of course. You'll have a big room with a nice soft bed." Mrs. Rosebar sounded very excited. "And lots of new clothes."

"Not a bad idea." Eric patted Little Yaga on the back. "It'll be cool having a sister my age around. Besides, we're already good friends, aren't we?"

"Yes, we are," Little Yaga agreed, casting a look at her grandmother.

"Go, go," Big Yaga said and waved her stick in the direction of the door. "Let me have some peace and quiet for once. And who wants to live with a liar anyway?"

"What are you talking about?" Little Yaga was taken aback.

"You know I can read minds," Big Yaga growled. "When you said you wanted to bite my wart off, you lied. I knew you were thinking of giving me a hug."

"Yes, I was, because believe or not, Grandma, I love you." Little Yaga's eyes glistened and filled with suspicious moisture.

"Here you go, acting human again," Big Yaga mumbled with a disgusted expression on her face.

"You can despise me," Little Yaga told her, "but I've never wanted to leave you or the Hut or the Cuckoo Bird or Kikimra." She turned to Leesho. "Or you, of course." She gave him a sad smile. "I know you're in love with another girl, but when you died up there in Scraggard's courtyard, I realized how much you've always meant to me."

"Who told you I was in love with another girl?" Leesho asked, surprised.

"You did. Right before I left for Ashley's party."

"Oh yes," Leesho recalled with a chortle. "I did say I was in love with a girl, but I never said it was *another* girl."

Little Yaga gave him a bewildered look. "What do you mean?" she asked.

"I mean, I'm in love with you, Little Yaga," Leesho revealed. "I have always been."

"If I were a human," Kikimra said, sneering, "I'd cry." Eyes sparkling, she turned to Stanley. "Why aren't you crying, Stan?" she teased. "You're a human."

"I guess I'm not the crying type," he replied.

"You must have a little bit of a Forester in you, then."

"I must have," Stanley agreed, winking at Kikimra.

She blew a few smoke rings into his face, and they both laughed.

Kikimra's Idea

As Mrs. Rosebar, Eric, Ashley, Sean, Stanley, and Daniel stood by the gate, ready to leave, Mrs. Rosebar gently stroked Little Yaga's hair.

"I am very happy to have met you," she said. "I want you to know you've got a home with us. Anytime you feel like coming over or moving in, you are welcome. Our home is yours, too."

"Thank you, Mrs. Rosebar."

"Call me Mom."

"Thank you, Mom." Little Yaga felt funny using the word. "I would like to come over one day to meet my father." This last word sounded even stranger. "And my little sister." Then she thought, "Oh gosh, I also have a sister," but aloud she asked, "What is her name, Lisa?"

"Yes, Lisa," Mrs. Rosebar said. "Your dad and your sister will be delighted to meet you, too." She looked straight into Little Yaga's eyes. "And one more thing I want you to know. If you are ever in need of anything, just ask me. I'll do it for you. I am your mother."

"Mrs. Rosebar," Kikimra suddenly barged in, "can I talk to Little Yaga in private for a sec?"

"Sure."

"Make it quick," Sean said. "I want to go home."

"Don't worry." Kikimra grabbed Little Yaga by the sleeve, pulled her to the side, and whispered in her ear, "Ask her for her leg."

"What?" Little Yaga didn't understand.

"Remember when you told me you could get a bony leg if somebody agreed to trade with you?"

"You're right!" Little Yaga exclaimed, eyes sparkling. "I didn't think of that! Thanks, Kikimra, you're such a great friend. I love you."

"I hate to admit it," Kikimra said, her face turning sour, "but I love you, too."

"Are you sure she's got a bony leg, though?" Little Yaga asked, doubtful.

"If she's a true Forester, she must have. Ask her."

"Do you think she'll agree?"

"She just said she'd do anything for you, didn't she?"

Little Yaga and Kikimra returned to the gate.

"Mrs. Rosebar..." Little Yaga began.

"Mom," Mrs. Rosebar corrected her again.

"Mom, you said I could ask you for anything, right?"

"Absolutely," Mrs. Rosebar affirmed, "you are my daughter."

"Well..." Little Yaga paused, swallowed hard, and then blurted out, "Let's trade legs, then. My human leg for your bony one."

"Do you have a bony leg?" Eric looked down at his mother's feet.

"Why do you think I limp, son?"

"I've never thought about it. You've always limped. It's just how you are."

Mrs. Rosebar looked at Little Yaga pensively.

"I like that idea," she said at last. "I'm tired of always wearing slacks. I wouldn't mind putting on a skirt for a change. And my, how I'd like to get rid of this limp! Bony legs are made for hooves, not shoes. Human footwear has been killing my left foot for years." Turning to Big Yaga, Mrs. Rosebar asked, "What do you think, Mother?"

"Leave me out of it," Big Yaga barked.

"I think it's a great idea," the Hut screeched. "Don't hesitate—just do it. It'll be good for both of you."

"I've heard it can be done," Mrs. Rosebar contemplated aloud, "but I'm not sure how."

"Big Yaga, help the girls," the Hut asked. "I've no doubt that you know what to do."

"I don't." Big Yaga chewed on her lips, utterly irritated.

"How about my aunt?" Mrs. Rosebar asked.

"She does," Big Yaga admitted. "She can help."

"Biggest Yaga lives on Bold Mountain," Little Yaga said. "It's a long trip on foot."

"We can borrow your grandmother's barrel." Mrs. Rosebar motioned to the one parked under the spruce tree.

"I don't think so," Little Yaga objected, shaking her head. "I'm not allowed to fly barrels until I'm twenty-one."

"I am over twenty-one," Mrs. Rosebar said, laughing.

"But you don't know how to, right?"

"Of course, she doesn't." Eric grinned. "My mom knows how to drive cars, not fly barrels."

Mrs. Rosebar smiled. "Here you're wrong, son," she said. "I was flying barrels long before I learned how to drive cars."

"You haven't flown one in years," Big Yaga reluctantly reminded her. "I doubt you'll remember what to do."

"Mother," Mrs. Rosebar said, turning to Big Yaga, "flying a barrel is like riding a bike. Once you learn it, you never forget."

⚜

A few minutes later, Little Yaga and Mrs. Rosebar were up in the sky, heading toward Bold Mountain. The rest of the group had stayed at Big Yaga's, waiting for their return.

"Look, Mrs. Rosebar—I mean, Mom!" Little Yaga cried out. "I see a lot of Scraggard's soldiers down there!"

Mrs. Rosebar leaned over the edge of the barrel to see for herself.

"Yes—they look pretty battered!" She laughed and hugged her daughter. "A handful of you, green teenagers, defeated Scraggard's professional army—great job!"

"Oh, my goodness," Little Yaga said with a gasp. "I don't believe it. Mom, look who's there!"

"Where?"

"Right below us."

"I see three boys. Why are their clothes all torn and messy? Who are they?"

"They're my stupid classmates, Damon, Don-Key, and Canny. They were on Scraggard's side."

"I see." Mrs. Rosebar kept staring down until the Forest boys turned into three tiny dots and disappeared from view. "They look miserable, but it's their own fault."

"I wonder where Scraggard's now," Little Yaga mused.

"Hiding somewhere," Mrs. Rosebar said, chuckling. "He got what he deserves. Now that his evil powers are gone, nobody cares about his whereabouts."

"Mom," Little Yaga said, suddenly remembering something. "At Ashley's birthday party you gave her a bracelet that helped us find Scraggard's Oak Tree. Did you know she would be kidnapped?"

"Honestly, I knew she would have to use it one day. I just didn't know it would happen so soon."

At Biggest Yaga's

After a few more minutes, the barrel landed in front of Biggest Yaga's Hut.

"I know what you've come here for," Biggest Yaga said as she greeted her guests. She was sitting on her bench near the hearth. The black raven perched on her shoulder seemed to be sleeping, and so did the heap of a shaggy dog by her feet. "Let me see if I can help you." She stood up and slowly went toward her bedroom. The planks buckled and whined pitifully under her weight. When she returned, she held the thick, leather-bound book Little Yaga recognized from her previous visits. Biggest Yaga opened it and began reading, carefully moving her clawed finger under each line.

"Good news," she announced, closing the book and putting it down on her bench. "I can help you."

Little Yaga's heart soared. For a moment, she thought she was dreaming.

"Really?" she exclaimed.

"Very much so." Biggest Yaga stood up. "Go stand in front of your mother."

Little Yaga obeyed.

"Now, both of you put your left toes, knees, and hips together."

"How?" Mrs. Rosebar asked.

"Simple, Yaga. Toes to toes, knee to knee, hip to hip."

"Who's Yaga?" Little Yaga asked.

"Your mother," Biggest Yaga replied. "Who else?"

"Isn't your name Jane?" Little Yaga seemed confused.

"To humans, yes," Mrs. Rosebar said with a smile, "but back home in the Forest, I'm simply Yaga."

Incredulous, Little Yaga stared at her mother until Biggest Yaga asked, "Are you trading legs or not?"

"Yes," Little Yaga answered. She shifted her eyes to her great-aunt and said, "May I ask you one unrelated question first?"

"Yes, you may."

"When Ashley and I were running away from Scraggard the first time, there were two ravens that helped us get out of the Forest. I understand now that one of them was Clair—am I right?"

"Yes, Little Yaga, you are right."

"But who was the other one?"

"Clair's brother, Carl. He lives in a tree behind the Hut and always lends us a wing, so to speak, if we need help. He was the one, by the way, who caught Scraggard's needle right before it disappeared in the water."

"Wow!" Little Yaga exclaimed. "And where's the needle now?"

"Too many questions, young lady," Biggest Yaga said. "Watch your nose."

Little Yaga anxiously pinched the tip of her nose. It was still intact, and she decided to clarify one last thing, "Biggest Yaga," she said, "was it Borzy running after the rabbit when it had gotten out of the gold chest in Scraggard's courtyard?"

"Yes, it was," the old sorceress answered with a curt sigh and picked up her book again. "Now, if you have no more questions, let's do what you've come here for. I hate to rush you, but I am not supposed to keep this book out of my bedroom for too long."

Little Yaga and Mrs. Rosebar moved very close to each other and brought their toes, knees, and hips together.

"Now, close your eyes," Biggest Yaga ordered.

Little Yaga did as she was told, and instantly, excruciating pain like she'd never experienced before pierced her left leg from her hip down to her toes. Dark spots floated before her closed eyes. Her left knee buckled, and for the second time that day, she passed out.

The Wishes Come True!

Little Yaga opened her eyes to the smell of breakfast sneaking into her bedroom from the kitchen. She sat up abruptly on the wood block serving as her bed. She felt weird. There was something different about her, but she wasn't sure what. Was she sick? Little Yaga stood up and ambled over to her mirror on the wall. When she saw her reflection, she hollered, "Grandmother!"

She dashed out of her bedroom.

"It wasn't a dream! I've got my bony leg!" she shouted, her voice cracking from the excitement.

"That's yesterday's news," Big Yaga said grouchy.

Little Yaga raised her head and howled. A thunderous roar shook the Hut. Terrified, the Cuckoo Bird stuck its ruffled head out of its tiny door.

"What happened? Did I oversleep?"

"I've got my bony leg, and I can roar!" Little Yaga jumped up and down, and her new leg rattled, just like all her classmates' legs did. Little Yaga was beside herself with happiness. She wanted to give her grandmother a hug, but she knew better than to even try.

"Go ahead," Big Yaga suddenly said. "When nobody's around, you can do it, but never, ever embarrass me in front of others." She waved her crooked finger before her granddaughter's nose as a warning.

"Never," Little Yaga promised and gently hugged her grandmother. To her surprise, she felt a fleeting hug in return.

"What was that?" she asked gingerly.

"Don't you dare tell anyone." Big Yaga growled and let out a quiet moan. "I must be growing old."

All dressed up for school, wearing her new hooves—a farewell present from her mother, Mrs. Rosebar—Little Yaga was on her way to the door when she suddenly turned around.

"Grandma, because I passed out again, I never had a chance to say a proper good-bye to the humans. Are they ever coming back?"

"I don't see why not," Big Yaga replied. "Scraggard's definitely not a threat to them anymore."

"Am I allowed to go visit them?"

"Anytime you'd like."

"Not for a while. I just wanted to know."

Little Yaga was already by the door when she realized the military clock was no longer ticking on the wall.

"What happened to the new clock?" she asked rather curious than surprised.

"When I heard Scraggard had lost his powers," Big Yaga said, "I turned it back into soldiers and let them go."

⋈

Kikimra and Leesho were waiting by the gate.

"Let me see," Kikimra demanded when her friend came out. Little Yaga pulled up her skirt.

"Cool," Kikimra said approvingly. "How does it feel?"

"I love it." Little Yaga raised her new leg and admired the extendable mechanism at her knee. She felt her bony leg was the most beautiful thing in the whole Forest.

"It is," Leesho confirmed, nodding.

"I didn't know you could read minds," Little Yaga said, laughing.

"Only of those I care about."

"I bet it's also the fastest one around," Little Yaga boasted, dying to prove it.

Kikimra was up for a challenge.

"It's a race!" she yelled.

"A race it is," Leesho agreed, and the three friends extended their bony legs. Little Yaga's came out the longest. They took off and sprinted across the meadows and brooks, over the roots and rocks, all the way through the Forest toward their school. Never before had Little Yaga run so fast! The wind whistled happy songs in her ears. The trees and flowers cheered her on by waving their leaves and petals. Little Yaga felt like she was flying. Kikimra and Leesho were trailing far behind. By the time she reached the steps of their school, she was out of breath but elated. It was the first race she'd ever won, but she was sure there would be many, many more.

Acknowledgements

Thanks to my dear sister, Inna, for her tremendous support, devotion, and invaluable help every step of the way in making sure this book reaches its readers.

Thanks to my daughter, Olga, for her love, care, good taste, and constructive criticism.

Thanks to my son, Eric, for all the technical and moral support.

Thanks to my significant other, Volodya, for his patience during long nights and lonely weekends while I was working on this book.

Thanks to my parents, Lyubov and Boris, and my dear brother, Alik and his wife Alla for always believing in me.

Thanks to my talented editor, Dr. Krystyna Steiger, for her exceptional job!

Thanks to my friend, Julia, for her excellent comments and faith in my creative abilities.

Thanks to all my friends and family for all the feedback and encouragement.

In loving memory of my husband Boris, who would have been very proud of me today.

44039212R00245

Made in the USA
Middletown, DE
26 May 2017